THE MISSING
PIECE

BOARDING PASS
FIRST CLASS

FLIGHT: D 8637 S
GATE: D 07
FROM: ***

SEAT
C 01

NO. 0000000000000000

The Missing Piece

BOARDING
02-04 8:30AM

GATE NO.
D07

FIRST CLASS
TO : S CITY
FROM : H CITY   GATE : D07
FLIGHT :   D8637S   TIME : 8:30 AM
SEAT :   C01 C02

SHEN MO
JI MINGXUAN

AUTHOR   KUN YI WEI LOU

The Missing Piece

Author: Kun Yi Wei Lou
Translators: Lea Chung; K.
Proofreading: Mercury
Editors: Michaela M; Jack

978-1-77408-217-1

Published by Via Lactea Ltd.
twitter.com/ViaLactea_press

Via Lactea
Publishing Co.

CHECK-IN
CONTENT　　· · ·

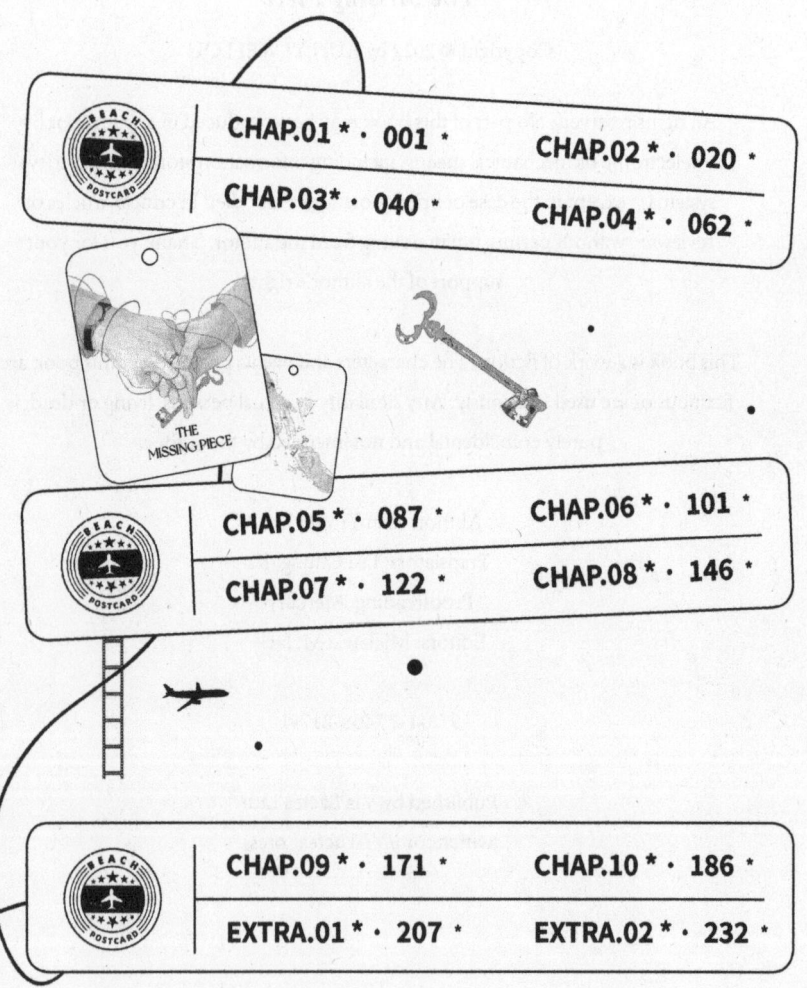

THE MISSING PIECE

CHECK-IN

· · · CONTENT

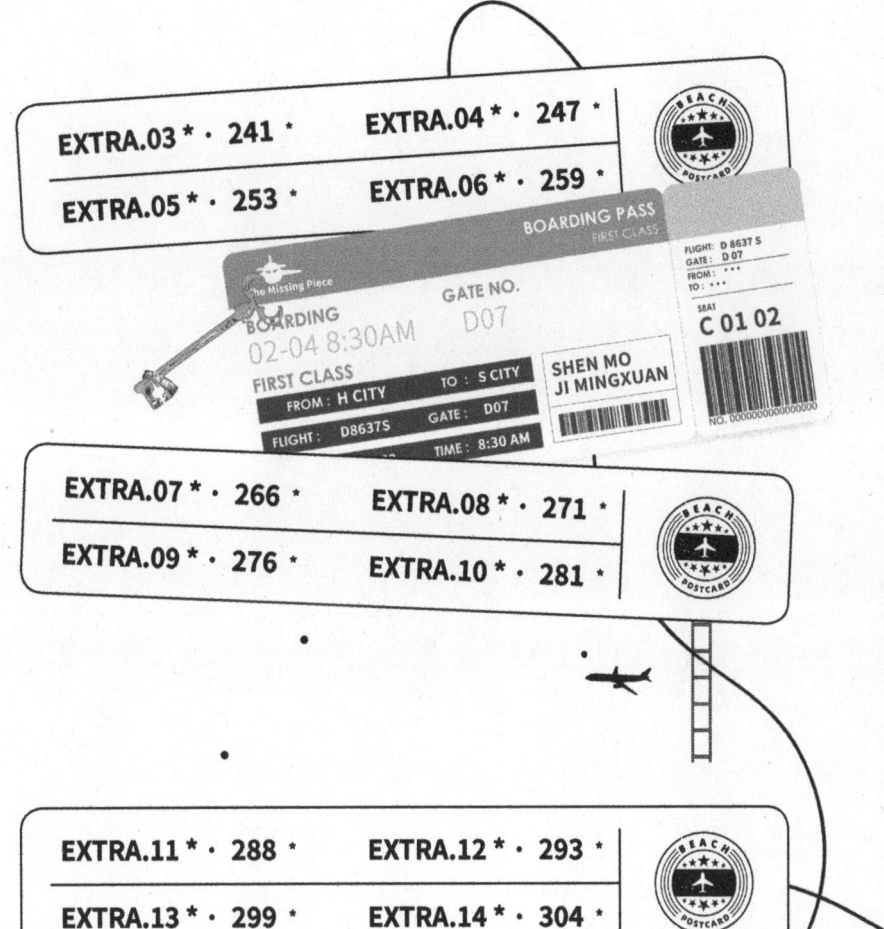

BOARDING PASS
FIRST CLASS

FLIGHT: D 8637 S
GATE: D 07
FROM: * * *
TO: * * *

SEAT
C 01 02

NO. 0000000000000000

The Missing Piece

BOARDING
02-04 8:30AM

GATE NO.
D07

FIRST CLASS

FROM: H CITY   TO: S CITY

FLIGHT: D8637S   GATE: D07

TIME: 8:30 AM

SHEN MO
JI MINGXUAN

THE MISSING PIECE

"Zhou Yang will be back from abroad tomorrow."

This sentence was heard by Shen Mo while he was kneeling on the ground, in the middle of sucking Ji Mingxuan off.

His knees were pressed harshly against the frigid marble floor even as his mouth was wrapped around the heat of Ji Mingxuan's erection, and the mix of cold and hot sensations was very unpleasant, but Zhou Yang's name was like a dull and rusted knife, stabbing abruptly into his heart and making his blood spurt everywhere. He felt as if he was having some sort of an out-of-body experience.

But then a sharp, physical pain pulled Shen Mo back to reality.

Ji Mingxuan had grabbed his hair. Pulling, he forced him to raise his head. Then he asked, "What? Just hearing your old lover's name is enough to make you lose your cool?"

Shen Mo still had Ji Mingxuan in his mouth, so he could only shake his head and make a muffled sound of disagreement. Then, to appease him, Shen Mo started to use more tongue.

Ji Mingxuan sighed, relaxing as his already sizeable erection stiffened in Shen Mo's mouth. He glanced carelessly over Shen Mo's body, seeming to see through everything. If he did, however, he didn't seem bothered enough to point it out. Instead, he merely looked down haughtily, saying, "Go deeper."

So Shen Mo busied himself again, sucking and swallowing as best he can.

He'd never been great at this, and, no matter how much porn he watched, he never made much improvement. Moreover, he was so distracted tonight that it seemed to affect Ji Mingxuan's mood as well. After using his mouth to bring his partner to climax just once, Shen Mo was dismissed.

When Shen Mo went to the bathroom to rinse out his mouth, he found his own reflection to be incredibly foreign. His hair had grown so long that his bangs almost covered his eyes. His lips were a little swollen, and there was still a trace of white fluid at the corner of his mouth.

He turned on the faucet, listening to the sound of water splashing into the sink.

Zhou Yang...

Him and Zhou Yang, it seemed as if their story had happened a lifetime ago.

Shen Mo wasn't even done swishing the water around his mouth when he heard the distant sound of a door shutting. Walking out of the bathroom, he found that Ji Mingxuan had already left. He must not have enjoyed himself enough and had surely left to look for more fun elsewhere.

Shen Mo reconsidered his earlier actions. He really shouldn't have been so absent-minded when entertaining Mr. Ji. Good thing Ji Mingxuan had never been in want of attractive partners who were both gentle and skilled in bed, so Shen Mo only felt guilty for a moment before he regained his peace of mind and settled in for the night.

He was usually a sound sleeper, typically able to sleep dreamlessly through the entire night. Tonight, however, he had a rare dream.

In his dream, he was back in his high school dormitory. The room was cramped, books and problem sets scattered all over both the top bunks and the bottom bunks. It was nearing dusk—the setting sun spreading its light over half the room while casting the other half in shadows.

Zhou Yang had him corralled against a corner of the room, bending down to reach his lips.

Haphazard footsteps sounded outside the dormitory.

They were both so young, and in their panic they both broke out in a cold sweat. Shen Mo raised his gaze slightly, eyes falling on the pubescent stubble on Zhou Yang's chin...

And then Shen Mo woke up.

In his dream, he had forgotten that he wasn't sleeping in his own home.

He'd slept so heavily that his face had gone numb, and it wasn't until he pinched his cheek a few times that feeling finally returned to it. He then cleaned himself up and went downstairs for breakfast, only to find that Ji Mingxuan was already neatly dressed for the day, sitting at the table and reading the newspaper.

Shen Mo took a look at the clock, then asked, "Won't you be going into the office today, Mr. Ji?"

Ji Mingxuan gave him a glance before his gaze fell back to the newspaper. "I'm going to the airport to pick someone up."

Shen Mo was momentarily dazed.

Who was he going to pick up? Zhou Yang?

Ji Mingxuan saw that he'd misunderstood and couldn't hold back a laugh in response. "An'an is also coming back today."

Now he was wide awake.

Ji An'an was both Ji Mingxuan's darling little sister and Zhou Yang's childhood friend. Their respective families had long since been trying to pair them up. They'd even sent them abroad to study together three years back.

Now that Zhou Yang was returning, Ji An'an would no doubt be coming with him.

Shen Mo got himself a glass of water, but then he heard Ji Mingxuan say, "You're coming with me."

Shen Mo almost spilt his water. "Mr. Ji..."

Ji Mingxuan didn't even look up, just slowly turned the silver band on his left ring finger. "Any objections?" he asked.

Shen Mo had the same ring on his finger. He looked down at his hand, then finally answered, "No."

Ji Mingxuan was satisfied, nodding. "Eat something."

Shen Mo ate without tasting the food.

They left for the airport at nine sharp. To make amends for his neglect last night, Shen Mo fetched Ji Mingxuan's coat and helped him put it on. Ji Mingxuan only looked more attractive in daylight than he did at night. After taking a few steps forward, he suddenly turned around and feld his hand out at Shen Mo, waving it a little.

Shen Mo didn't understand the gesture at first. "Mr. Ji..."

The corners of Ji Mingxuan's mouth rose a bit, and he said, "Shen Mo, is that what you're supposed to call me?" His voice was beyond gentle.

Shen Mo finally remembered who he was supposed to be. He walked up and clasped Ji Mingxuan's outstretched hand, correcting himself with, "Mingxuan."

Ji Mingxuan hummed in answer and leaned affectionately toward him, softly saying into his ear, "Don't forget who we are to each other."

"Lovers," Shen Mo answered fluidly with practiced ease.

Then, a beat later, he mentally amended, *fake lovers.*

Shen Mo had never been good at acting. It might have been better if he'd been one of those celebrities that Ji Mingxuan liked to sponsor. One of them might do a better job.

But instead he was Shen Mo.

The fact that Ji Mingxuan had to condescend to be with him instead was really something that Shen Mo felt quite guilty about.

It was still early when they got to the airport. Ji Mingxuan managed to make three phone calls and send two emails during their wait before that enormous metal bird finally landed.

Shen Mo had once longed to leave together with Zhou Yang. It was only later that he realized, all freedom had its price. So now, holding hands with Ji Mingxuan, he watched Zhou Yang and Ji An'an approach from afar. The two of them seemed made for each other.

Ji An'an was two years younger than Ji Mingxuan, which put her right at the peak of her youth. Wearing a pink cloak and a small beret, she flew into Ji Mingxuan's arms like a little bird.

"Brother!"

Ji Mingxuan patted her back, asking, "How was your time abroad?"

"Everything was great, except I didn't have you there."

At this, Ji Mingxuan chuckled. "I've been flying out to see you four or five times every year."

"There are three hundred and sixty-five days every year, how can four or five visits be enough?" answered Ji An'an.

Ji Mingxuan laughed.

Shen Mo stood to the side and watched them talk. Suddenly, someone tall blocked the sunlight in front of him.

Shen Mo turned around. What he saw first was Zhou Yang's chin.

He still remembered how their kisses had made him feel. The stubble that Zhou Yang had sported at the time seemed to always tickle his heart. After all these years, Zhou Yang was a little taller than Shen Mo remembered, although he looked as mature and reliable as ever with those rimless glasses on his face.

Their eyes met, though it wasn't as dramatic as what TV shows usually depicted. The words "long time no see" got stuck in Shen Mo's throat. As he hesitated to say them out loud, he heard Ji Mingxuan introducing him, "This is Shen Mo."

Then, Ji Mingxuan pointed at Zhou Yang and said, "This is Zhou Yang, my sister's boyfriend."

The word "boyfriend" was a sort of warning.

Shen Mo had to extend his hand. "Hello, Mr. Zhou."

Zhou Yang didn't shake hands with him. "What a coincidence." He looked at Shen Mo. "We were classmates in high school, Mr. Shen. Don't you remember?"

If this had happened several years ago, Shen Mo would've felt incredibly embarrassed. But in his years of being with Ji Mingxuan, he had, if nothing else, grown a thicker skin. He smiled and said, "I'm sorry. My memory's not so great."

They'd taken too long standing there greeting one another; Ji An'an began to complain about being hungry.

Ji Mingxuan immediately turned back to her and asked, "What do you want for lunch?"

"Seafood."

Ji Mingxuan had always been a good brother, giving her whatever she wanted. But this time, he refused, "Not today. We can have seafood on our own next time."

"Why not?"

Ji Mingxuan put a hand on Shen Mo's shoulder. It was neither too heavy nor too light, most suggestive of an ambiguously romantic sort of intimacy between them. He answered, "This guy is allergic to seafood."

Zhou Yang's expression shifted. He didn't say anything.

Although Ji An'an was a bit of a spoiled little princess, she wasn't very particular or hard to please. She waved her hand. "Then let's eat something else."

As she spoke, she studied Shen Mo quietly.

Ji Mingxuan didn't show anything on the surface. He held Shen Mo's hand the entire way to lunch.

They ended up eating at a European restaurant that Ji Mingxuan often went to. It wasn't big, but the atmosphere was good. Ji Mingxuan ordered a bottle of wine and flaunted the ring on his left hand when he picked up his wine glass. As expected of someone who hung out so often with actors, his performance was very natural and not at all pretentious.

Shen Mo was so utterly impressed that he almost wanted to applaud.

During their lunch, Ji An'an talked the most, babbling all the way about everything from the weather in England to her classmate from Korea. Zhou Yang was as quiet as usual. Ji Mingxuan was the busiest, paying attention to Ji An'an's chatter at the same time as taking care of Shen Mo, who wasn't used to European cuisine. Ji Mingxuan cut his steak for him, adding, "Next time we'll have Peking duck—I know you like it."

Seeing this, even Ji An'an had mixed feelings. "Brother, if you keep up on the PDA, I'm gonna get jealous."

Ji Mingxuan didn't reply. He only smiled and winked at Shen Mo.

At this, Shen Mo was flattered to the point of astonishment.

Luckily, he did have some amount of self-awareness.

Everyone knew of Mr. Ji's harsh temperament—he was only ever kind to his own family. That Shen Mo had been on the receiving end of such gentleness was only thanks to the presence of Ji An'an.

"You like Peking duck, Mr. Shen?" asked Zhou Yang, who had been silent this whole time.

Shen Mo answered, "That's right. I tend to prefer Chinese food."

Zhou Yang looked at him searchingly. "We were in the same homeroom for three years, but I never knew you were allergic to seafood."

"My allergy isn't very serious, so my reactions are mild. Maybe you didn't notice, Mr. Zhou."

Being a naturally guileless sort of person, Ji An'an didn't notice the vicious undercurrents of their conversation, and so she cut in, asking "You two were classmates, weren't you? Why are you so polite to each other?"

The corners of Zhou Yang's mouth twitched. "I'm not too familiar with Mr. Shen."

He then lowered his head and went back to his meal.

In the past, he'd always spoken little while Shen Mo talked a lot. Shen Mo could prattle on for ages about even the smallest of things. One time, they had been arguing with each other, and Zhou Yang had yelled, "Shen Mo, Shen Mo. Your name means silent, but why aren't you?"

After getting together with Ji Mingxuan, Shen Mo had indeed become quieter.

It was because he knew that no matter how much he spoke, nobody would listen.

Having been lost in his thoughts, Shen Mo's attention was suddenly pulled back to the conversation when Ji Mingxuan asked, "When are you getting married?"

Ji An'an's face immediately flushed. "Brother..."

"Or do you want to date him for your entire life? Even if I'm alright with it, the heads of the Zhou family would never let it happen."

"We just got back from abroad, and we have so many things to do. I've talked about this with Zhou Yang already—we'll think about everything else after his career is settled."

Ji Mingxuan teased her, "Not afraid that your boyfriend will run away with someone else?"

"There's no way. Zhou Yang isn't that kind of person," Ji An'an said with a sweet smile. She knocked her arm against Zhou Yang's and asked, "Are you?"

Zhou Yang didn't answer, instead just gazed at Shen Mo.

Shen Mo felt like he was sitting on pins and needles. He could only stand up. "Excuse me. I need to use the restroom."

Not many people were in the restaurant for lunch. Even fewer people were in the restroom. Shen Mo washed his face with cold water, thinking that he needed to get a hold of himself. He looked up only to find Ji Mingxuan reflected in the mirror as well.

"Mr. Ji."

Crossing his arms, Ji Mingxuan gave Shen Mo a significant smile. "Has your former love for Zhou Yang rekindled?"

Shen Mo denied it immediately. "I wasn't..."

"All you two have done this entire meal is flirt with your eyes."

"You're mistaken, Mr. Ji."

"Am I?"

Ji Mingxuan took a step forward, grabbed Shen Mo's chin, and asked, "Now that you've met An'an, what do you think of her?"

Shen Mo didn't dare to not answer. He replied honestly, "Miss Ji is sweet and innocent. She's very likable."

"The silly girl has been in love with Zhou Yang ever since she was young," said Ji Mingxuan, eyes showing a rare tenderness. He gently stroked a finger across Shen Mo's eyebrow. "I don't care if Zhou Yang loves men, if he loves women, or if he loves only comatose vegetables.

An'an likes him, so he can only be hers. Understood?"

Ji Mingxuan spoke in the lukewarm tone he usually used to nego-tiate business deals, but Shen Mo knew Ji Mingxuan well. If Shen Mo dared to say "no," he wouldn't even be able to find his own dead bones tomorrow. He squeezed the words through his teeth: "I know. I won't involve myself with him any further..."

"Good." After presenting him a stick, Ji Mingxuan offered a carrot, gently whispering, "Do as I say, and nothing will happen."

Meanwhile, his fingers slid along Shen Mo's neck and gradually into the collar of his shirt.

Afraid, Shen Mo paled. He reminded, "Mr. Ji, we're in public."

"Shh, do you want to get the whole restaurant in here?"

Ji Mingxuan always did what he said he'd do. Shen Mo had to bite his lip to stop himself from letting out his voice.

Ji Mingxuan knew his body well. With just a few light touches, Shen Mo's pale face flushed with color. Ji Mingxuan smiled. His fingers were devoted to teasing Shen Mo's chest before suddenly pressing heavily—

"Mm..." Shen Mo couldn't help but moan.

Ji Mingxuan had him pressed against the mirror above the sink. He kneed his legs apart, then reached in from the bottom hem of his coat.

All of Shen Mo fell into Ji Mingxuan's hand.

Shen Mo's legs trembled slightly. His capacity for reasoning was tak-en over by desire, and his mind was in a muddle. Ji Mingxuan was his only antidote. He held on to the man's shoulders and, in a small, plead-ing voice, he said, "Mr. Ji..."

Ji Mingxuan stroked Shen Mo's member relentlessly, asking, "What should you call me?"

"Mingxuan..." Shen Mo shivered, his voice sweet and tempting as he said, "Ji Mingxuan..."

"Good," Ji Mingxuan looked down and kissed the top of Shen Mo's head. His fingers sped up, finally bringing Shen Mo to a climax.

Blissed out in the aftermath of pleasure, Shen Mo grew boneless. With one arm around Shen Mo's waist, Ji Mingxuan brought his dirt-ied hand up to Shen Mo's mouth.

Shen Mo was about to lick those slender fingers when Ji Mingxuan started to chuckle. Then, raising his voice to be heard by someone outside the restroom, he said, "Have you seen enough, Zhou Yang?"

Hearing the name, Shen Mo suddenly woke to his senses. He wanted to turn back and look, but he was firmly trapped in Ji Mingxuan's embrace. After a while, Zhou Yang's voice came from the direction of the exit: "You were gone for too long. An'an was worried. She asked me to come and check on you."

"Oh, it's nothing. Shen Mo is feeling a bit unwell."

"Does he need to go to the hospital?"

"No. I'll just ask the driver to take him home."

Zhou Yang suddenly called out his full name, "Ji Mingxuan—"

Ji Mingxuan smiled. "Just call me 'Brother' as An'an does. We'll soon be family, anyway."

He spoke clearly and pointedly, emphasizing the word "family."

Zhou Yang stood silently for a moment. Then came the sound of his retreating footsteps.

Hearing the steps fade away, Shen Mo felt all of his strength leave him. Upon being released by Ji Mingxuan, he fell, sitting on the countertop beside the sink.

Ji Mingxuan let him be. He took off his ring, his movements neither fast nor slow, then turned on the tap to wash his hands.

Shen Mo couldn't help asking, "Did you do that on purpose, Mr. Ji?"

Ji Mingxuan was still washing his hands. He asked, "What do you think?"

Thus, Shen Mo knew the answer.

Ji Mingxuan had good-looking hands. When he finished washing them and put his ring back on, he glanced at Shen Mo, then said, "Would you believe me if I said that Zhou Yang and my sister will be engaged very soon?"

Shen Mo nodded. "I would." He looked at his left hand, then slowly added, "There's nothing you want to do that you can't do, Mr. Ji."

Ji Mingxuan narrowed his eyes, but it was unclear if it was in pleasure or anger. He turned around. "Let's go."

As he'd had some wine during lunch, Ji Mingxuan couldn't drive, so he called his driver to take Shen Mo back to the house. Shen Mo didn't feel sick, but, after entertaining Ji Mingxuan for so long, he did feel an undefinable sort of fatigue, and so he went straight for his bedroom and fell right asleep.

He slept so well that it was already ten at night when he woke up. He hadn't had any dinner, so he headed downstairs, intending to get something to eat. Only, the moment he entered the kitchen, he was met with Ji An'an.

They both paused in embarrassment, and in the end it was Ji An'an who spoke first: "Shen-ge[1]."

Shen Mo didn't know how Ji Mingxuan had explained their relationship to each other, so he replied with a mumbled acknowledgement and asked, "You didn't have dinner either?"

"I did, but I got hungry again. I came to see if I could find anything to eat."

"I wanted to make some noodles. Would you like some?"

Ji An'an might seem spoiled, but she wasn't a picky eater, so she readily agreed. Shen Mo got the noodles out of the cupboard, boiled some water, and added them to the pot. Ji An'an stood at the side to help him, occasionally chatting with him

"Shen-ge, do you feel better now?"

"Yeah, I was a little tired. I'm better now. I'm sorry I prevented you from eating seafood."

"It's okay. Brother said he'd make it up to me."

"You didn't have dinner together?"

Ji An'an seemed the slightest bit shy as she replied, "I went to the Zhou family for dinner. I haven't seen Mr. and Mrs. Zhou in a long time."

"Oh," Shen Mo said. "I heard the Zhou and Ji families have always gotten on. The Zhou family heads must like you a lot."

"The Zhou family has done some business with us, so I grew up with Zhou Yang. But he's quite a reticent person; I always had to be the one

[1] This is an honorific suffix or title that, while literally meaning "older brother," is used regardless of familial relation for any boy or man of the same nominal generation as the speaker.

to take initiative. Then we ended up abroad..." Ji An'an pursed her lips. As if talking to herself, she said, "I heard that a couple's relationship is stronger when it's the first relationship for both parties. I wonder if that's true."

The water had finished boiling. Hot air rose from the pot when Shen Mo lifted the lid. He blinked hard and softly replied, "...Of course."

In the end, Ji An'an was still a bit young and felt a bit uncomfortable discussing these things, so she changed the topic: "It's ten already. Why hasn't Brother come back yet?"

Shen Mo added two eggs to the pot and said, "He often has to attend social events in the evening."

"Shen-ge, you're really laid-back." Ji An'an was curious, asking, "How did you two meet each other? Was it love at first sight? Or did feelings develop with time?"

Not expecting Ji An'an to ask him such a question, Shen Mo accidentally scalded his hand a little. He retracted it at once.

For a long time, he didn't respond.

He stayed silent for so long that Ji An'an began to find it strange. Then, looking out the window at the dark sky above, he said calmly, "Mr. Ji... saved my life."

Without Ji Mingxuan, he might have been dead, or even worse than dead.

Shen Mo had nothing but his body for compensation. Unfortunately, using one's body as compensation also required certain technical skills. He wasn't exactly up to industry standard; Ji Mingxuan often said he behaved like a dead fish in bed.

That night also, Mr. Ji didn't return home.

Before Shen Mo went to bed, he did some serious self-reflection—he really needed to improve his technical skills.

Shen Mo rarely had nightmares, and even when he did, it was always the same scene. He was alone in the dark, trying to make a phone call. He knew the number so well that it seemed to be engraved in his heart.

But no one answered.

They had made countless phone calls in the heat of romance, exchanging such copious amounts of sweet nothings. But it had to be this one day that he couldn't even get through. No matter how many times he dialed, the other phone was always turned off.

Shen Mo was so scared that his fingers trembled as he dialed. Suddenly, a hand stretched out from the shadows and seized his ankle—

It was morning, and Shen Mo had been woken up by his alarm. He opened his eyes and looked at the time, realizing that it was Monday and that he needed to go to work. Ji Mingxuan was also the one who had given him a job, one at a small company that belonged to the Ji family. It was easy work; he had nothing to do except spend time sitting in the office every day.

All of his colleagues said he was easy-going and good-tempered. He did whatever they asked him to do, even when he was occasionally given random tasks. Today, the department manager came to him during lunch break and asked him to draw a poster.

Shen Mo shook his head and said, "I don't know how."

"Didn't you study art in university?"

He just replied, "I really don't know how."

The manager didn't push the matter. He nodded and left.

When afternoon came, Shen Mo heard people talking about him in the break room.

"I never knew Shen Mo was so full of himself."

"Don't you know? He's got connections here."

"Connections to who?"

"The one and only..."

"Mr. Ji? No way. Weren't there rumors about him and that one movie star?"

"Well, as rich as he is, of course he'd have multiple lovers."

Shen Mo let whatever they said go in one ear and out the other as if he never heard anything at all. Then he went back to the office, got a pen, and started drawing on a piece of paper. His right hand trembled very badly. It was like when he had been desperately dialing the number that day. The lines he drew were crooked and completely distorted.

He stared at that piece of paper for a long time. Then he balled it up and threw it in the trash.

He hadn't drawn in three years.

His family wasn't wealthy. In university, he'd worked part-time as a street artist, doing portraits for people. Sometimes, when he went a long while without any customers, Zhou Yang would come over and be his model. Those were the good times.

In the aftermath, he'd gone to several hospitals. All of the doctors had said that the injury to his right hand had already healed, that it wouldn't affect his daily life. It was likely due to psychological reasons that he couldn't pick up the paintbrush anymore.

So, Shen Mo didn't continue with treatment. Besides, ever since he'd taken up with Ji Mingxuan, he no longer needed to make a living through art. Everything that had happened had become no more than a memory. It was better to forget it all.

Shen Mo got ready to walk home after work, but his phone rang as soon as he stepped outside the front entrance to the company building. He was about to check the caller ID when he suddenly heard someone calling out to him: "Shen Mo!"

Shen Mo turned to look and saw a black car come to a slow stop at the side of the road. The window was half-open. Sitting in the driver's seat, Zhou Yang said, "Get in."

As always, he wasted no words, speaking directly and plainly. But Shen Mo was no longer the same Shen Mo of before. He stood still.

Zhou Yang said, "I just want to have dinner with you."

Shen Mo asked, "Where's Miss Ji?"

Zhou Yang frowned. "Does this have anything to do with her?"

"It might not be very appropriate for us to eat alone."

"Even if we did break up, we're still high school classmates. Why can't we have dinner together?" The sun was setting in the west, casting Zhou Yang's profile in fading sunlight and highlighting how handsome he was. His gaze fixed on Shen Mo, he said, "Get in, *xiao*-Mo[2]."

It reminded Shen Mo of the many times when he had sat in the

---

[2] *"Xiao-"* is a prefix for making diminutive nicknames, often used in affection. Literally, it means "little" or "young."

corner of the classroom at dusk, sketching Zhou Yang's face again and again. He closed his eyes for a while before finally opening the door and getting in the car.

Unexpectedly, Zhou Yang decided to treat him to seafood. Despite all the dishes on the table, Shen Mo didn't touch his chopsticks. Nor did Zhou Yang, who asked, "You're really allergic to seafood?"

"I get rashes on my body, but it's not too serious."

"Why didn't you tell me before?"

Shen Mo smiled.

He hadn't told him because he hadn't wanted to spoil his fun. People in love were always like that—even suffering felt sweet so long as it happened in the name of love.

Zhou Yang grabbed the menu to order some new dishes and said, self-mockingly, "Even Ji Mingxuan knows you better than I do."

Shen Mo thought that it was only natural—Mr. Ji must have investigated him before ever coming into contact with him. Ji Mingxuan was the typical perfectionist. Even when it came to putting on an act, he had to do it thoroughly.

The new dishes weren't ready yet, so Zhou Yang poured Shen Mo a cup of tea and asked, "How have you been doing these past few years?"

Three whole years. Countless days and nights. Shen Mo summed them all up in just two words: "Not bad."

"I thought you'd get a job related to art."

"My current one is better. The work is easy, and the salary is high."

"What about Ji Mingxuan? I hear he's pretty indiscriminate between men and women. People gossip about him and those young actors a lot."

A corner of Shen Mo's mouth twitched. "As high-profile as... as Ji Mingxuan is, it's no wonder that there are so many rumors about him. But rumors are just rumors. You saw how he treated me yesterday."

At the mention of yesterday, Zhou Yang's face darkened.

Shen Mo pretended not to see the change. He sipped his tea, then asked, "What about you? You look like you've lost weight while abroad."

"It was a foreign land, after all. It couldn't compare to here even in terms of just food. I fell sick one time, and all my friends and family were thousands of miles away. I felt truly helpless then. Good thing An'an was there to take care of me."

Shen Mo said sincerely, "You and Miss Ji are really a great match."

Zhou Yang didn't respond for a while. Then, all of a sudden, he grabbed Shen Mo's hand. "Shen Mo, you still owe me an explanation, don't you?"

"What?"

"Why did you break up with me?"

"Why?" Shen Mo repeated. He thought for a moment then answered, "I don't quite remember. Maybe it was because our personalities weren't compatible."

"We were together for so many years since high school. How could our personalities not match?"

"There are many aspects to personality. For example... you're the only heir of the Zhou family—will your parents accept our relationship?"

His words stabbed right into Zhou Yang's weak spot.

Zhou Yang's expression stiffened. Then he said, "My parents are old-fashioned people. It's true that they wouldn't let me have a relationship with a man. But I told you that I'd find a way to persuade them."

Shen Mo slowly pushed Zhou Yang's hands away from his own. "And the way you found was to go abroad together with Miss Ji?"

"...I knew it." Zhou Yang sighed, then said, "Yes, I accepted their arrangements; I went abroad for their sakes. But I wasn't in a relationship with An'an back then, and I booked return tickets the moment I got off the plane. But then? You refused to see me, and it was more than half a month before you called me. And even then, it was just to break up.

"I thought you were angry at me for going abroad. Looking back now..." Zhou Yang sneered and said, "Were you already in Ji Mingxuan's bed at that point?"

Shen Mo was momentarily stunned.

It felt as if a sudden earthquake had started just then. Mountains shook under his feet, and his ears could hear a roaring sound. But then, in the mere blink of an eye, everything went back to normal. He was still sitting in the restaurant amidst food and wine, and everything was fine.

But he'd already been wounded.

His innards twisted. His heart wrenched, and even his liver and his lungs hurt right along with it.

Shen Mo opened his mouth, but he didn't have the energy to say a single word.

Which was why he didn't tell Zhou Yang that, when Zhou Yang had come back looking for him, he'd been lying on a bed in the ICU. Nor did he tell him that, once, three years ago, he'd dialed Zhou Yang's number countless times, desperate and afraid, but that, at the time, Zhou Yang had been on a plane thousands of feet in the air, sitting beside Ji An'an.

They finished dinner in a bad mood.

Shen Mo didn't let Zhou Yang drive him home. Instead, he walked back by himself. It was almost eight by the time he arrived. The lights were off in several rooms; it seemed that Mr. Ji and Miss Ji hadn't yet returned. Shen Mo had been especially tired these past few days, so he went directly to his bedroom to sleep. He'd just gone in and was about to turn on the light when suddenly a cough sounded in the darkness.

Shen Mo was startled, but he immediately recognized whose voice it was and said, "Mr. Ji? You're back already?"

Then he asked, "Why didn't you turn on the light?"

As he said that, he moved towards the light switch, but Ji Mingxuan said, "Don't bother with the light. Come over here first."

Shen Mo's eyes gradually adapted to the darkness. He could vaguely make out Ji Mingxuan sitting alone by the window. Outside the window was the breathtaking nightscape of the city. He felt his way over to Ji Mingxuan, but, halfway through, he tripped and almost fell.

Just in time, Ji Mingxuan reached out to help him.

Shen Mo was going to thank him when Ji Mingxuan dragged him into his arms. The night was too quiet. His head bumped against Ji Mingxuan's chest, and he caught the faint scent of tobacco.

Shen Mo looked up and asked, "Have you had dinner yet, Mr. Ji?"

"I did," Ji Mingxuan replied. "I wanted to have dinner with you, but you seem quite busy these days."

Shen Mo then remembered that he'd gotten a call after work. Zhou Yang had stopped him, so he hadn't had the chance to see the caller ID.

"I'm sorry. I..." He was so bad at lying that he could find no excuse.

Ji Mingxuan knew everything already. He let go of Shen Mo. "A wise man learns from his mistakes, while a fool will fall into the same pit twice. Shen Mo, don't you think that you're being foolish beyond help?"

Shen Mo answered carefully. "It's okay that I'm foolish, Mr. Ji, as long as you're a wise man."

Perhaps his words satisfied Ji Mingxuan—Shen Mo heard him let out a low laugh.

"You had dinner with Zhou Yang tonight?"

"I did," Shen Mo admitted, then followed it immediately with a resolution, "but I won't meet with him alone anymore. He and Miss Ji are meant to be together."

"I'm glad that you understand."

Ji Mingxuan chuckled again, but it was dark, and Shen Mo couldn't work out the expression on his face. Ji Mingxuan's fingers brushed against Shen Mo's hair as he said, "Take off your clothes."

Shen Mo let out a breath of relief. He hurried to unbutton his shirt.

When he was almost finished, Ji Mingxuan gestured for him to approach. Shen Mo immediately understood and took initiative, straddling across Ji Mingxuan's lap.

Ji Mingxuan put two fingers into Shen Mo's mouth. Earnestly, Shen Mo began to lick them. He wasn't good at sex, but he had always believed that he could make up for it with diligence. He worked hard every time.

Seeing Shen Mo's effort, Ji Mingxuan didn't criticize his lack of technique too much this time. After his fingers were wet, Ji Mingxuan pushed them inside Shen Mo.

Shem Mo let out a moan. His body shivered.

Ji Mingxuan began to arouse as well. Whispering into Shen Mo's ear, he said, "Relax."

Shen Mo wrapped his arms around Ji Mingxuan's neck and tried to raise his hips so that Ji Mingxuan's fingers could enter more easily.

Soon, his entrance softened, slick with moisture. It pulsed in anticipation for something to enter, something larger than just fingers.

Ji Mingxuan was very patient, in no hurry to claim him. Instead, he continued to play with him, using just his fingers. At times, he rubbed against Shen Mo's soft inner walls, and at other times, he pressed firmly against Shen Mo's most sensitive spot. Pleasure accumulated, yet climax eluded Shen Mo. He flexed his hips impatiently, aligning his own erection between Ji Mingxuan's legs.

"Mr. Ji..." Shen Mo begged, flushed scarlet from head to toe.

Ji Mingxuan's eyes darkened. Removing his fingers, he said, "Do it yourself."

Shen Mo looked down, unzipped Ji Mingxuan's pants, and rubbed himself against what he found inside. Then, he held open his already slick entrance and lowered himself, inch by inch, onto that enormous length.

Ji Mingxuan grabbed his waist with both hands, then thrust fiercely upwards.

"Ah..." Shen Mo's heart thumped, and he senselessly called, "Mr. Ji..."

Ji Mingxuan only held him tighter, sliding in and out of his body. Shen Mo felt as if he was struggling amid ocean waves. Every time he thought he would be rescued, a higher tide would overcome him.

Ji Mingxuan's mood was particularly good tonight, and Shen Mo ran out of strength by the end. Hoarsely, he said, "Mr. Ji, I can't anymore..."

At this, Ji Mingxuan finally let him off the hook. He moved them to the bed and, lifting Shen Mo's legs, started moving again. At last, he thrust relentlessly forward, plunging firmly into Shen Mo's depths.

Shen Mo felt electrified, and he began to tremble in response.

Ji Mingxuan gazed at him in the dim light. Then, he suddenly lowered his head to kiss him.

Although they'd had sex countless times, they rarely behaved so intimately. Shen Mo froze, then, on reflex, turned his head away. "Shen Mo," Ji Mingxuan said before he closed in again, catching his lips in a kiss.

He was good at kissing. Shen Mo almost drowned in the tenderness of it. However, right then, Ji Mingxuan smiled and bit down viciously on Shen Mo's lip.

When Shen Mo got up and went to the mirror the next morning, he wasn't surprised to find a wound at the corner of his mouth. Ji Mingxuan's bite mark was clear and distinct, impossible to hide.

If he went to the office with it, there would be a storm of gossip. But... that must be exactly what Mr. Ji wanted.

Shen Mo sighed, cleaned himself up, and went downstairs with the wound visible at his lips.

Even from afar, he could hear Ji An'an's laughter. The Ji siblings were chatting happily. As Shen Mo went over to greet them, Ji An'an looked up and said, "Shen-ge..."

She trailed off as her gaze fell on his lips.

"Wait. Shen-ge, what happened to your mouth?"

Shen Mo sat down and replied, "It's nothing. I accidentally bumped it yesterday."

"You bumped it? How? It looks more like..."

"An'an," Ji Mingxuan said, tapping a finger against the table, "finish your meal."

Ji An'an looked at Ji Mingxuan first, then at Shen Mo. Suddenly, she understood, and realization dawned on her face. She laughed a little and said, "Of course, of course. I'll just eat. You two can talk."

But Ji Mingxuan ignored Shen Mo, and Shen Mo didn't have much to say either. They both just enjoyed their food. It was Ji An'an who livened up the atmosphere at last, saying that she was going to attend a job interview today.

Ji Mingxuan suggested, "Why go out and find a job by yourself? Isn't it better to come help me at my company?"

"I'm not Shen-ge. I don't want to see you every day."

As they chatted, Ji An'an's phone rang. She turned aside to answer the call. Even the tone of her voice exuded sweetness as she said, "Yeah, I already had breakfast. Yeah, I'm coming."

Ji Mingxuan said, "Looks like the person you do want to see every day is here to pick you up."

Ji An'an didn't deny it. She only said, "Enjoy your breakfast," and rushed out the door.

Shen Mo seemed to hear the sound of the car moving. He remembered how he had also been so eager to meet up with Zhou Yang back when they'd been dating. When his attention returned, he found Ji Mingxuan staring at him with half a smile on his face.

"Mr. Ji..." Shen Mo felt a little guilty.

"Yes." Ji Mingxuan grabbed Shen Mo's chin and carefully looked at his face before asking, "Does your lip still hurt?"

Shen Mo immediately replied, "Not really."

Ji Mingxuan then smiled, lowering his head to kiss Shen Mo on the lips. He licked a little at the wound, purposefully so.

Feeling a prick of pain, Shen Mo complained, "Mr. Ji..."

Ji Mingxuan didn't let go of Shen Mo until he felt satisfied. "To sterilize the wound," he explained, smugly self-righteous.

Shen Mo paused for a moment. Then, having no other choice, he said, "Thank you."

With a smile as warm as a spring breeze, Ji Mingxuan stood up and said, "It's time for work. I'll drive you there."

Shen Mo had been with Ji Mingxuan for three years, yet he still didn't understand Ji Mingxuan's temperament; he could be laughing one second and heartless the next, mysterious and mercurial. Obedience was the best way to deal with it.

So Shen Mo took Ji Mingxuan's car to the office.

The wound on his mouth caught the attention of many, but his colleagues were at least civil enough to not gossip to his face.

A few days later, Shen Mo's wound was healed, and Ji An'an had gotten a new job too. It was the end of the week, and Ji Mingxuan was as busy as usual. Ji An'an knocked on Shen Mo's bedroom door and asked, "Shen-ge, are you free this afternoon?"

"Yes. What is it?"

"Zhou Yang's birthday is coming up in a few days. I want to buy him a present. Can you come shopping with me?"

Shen Mo then remembered that Zhou Yang's birthday was in the winter. He had been trying not to think of the past, but it was still a surprise that he had forgotten so much.

He was still thinking about how to politely turn her down when Ji An'an continued, trying to persuade him, "Every year, I have trouble deciding on a present. You were classmates with Zhou Yang, so you should be able to help me brainstorm."

Shen Mo forced a smile. "I'm not too familiar with Zhou Yang."

"That's okay. You can help me carry things."

Shen Mo didn't know how to reject people, so, in face of Ji An'an's persistent nagging, he finally agreed.

Ji An'an went directly to the department store. Shen Mo did her the favor of carrying the things she bought. For the first time, he realized how troublesome shopping with a woman could be. They spent hours just in the men's department—Shen Mo tried on so many clothes that even his hands grew sore. Later, Ji An'an found a pair of cufflinks, but she hesitated between two styles. Shen Mo suggested that she buy them both.

Ji An'an thought for a moment and agreed, "Sounds good. We can give the other one to my brother."

She was satisfied with the presents she had bought. Noticing that it was late already, she suggested that they have dinner at a restaurant nearby, "Brother recommended it to me. I heard the signature dishes there are quite good."

Shen Mo was extremely tired. All he wanted was to sit down and rest for a bit, so he naturally acquiesced.

The restaurant wasn't too far away, so they went there on foot. But when they arrived, they were told that they had to make a reservation. Ji An'an could only bring up Ji Mingxuan's name. And what serendipity—just then, a couple of new customers came in, and Shen Mo looked up, immediately seeing that one of them was Ji Mingxuan.

Ji An'an was astonished. "Brother, you're also having dinner here?"

Ji Mingxuan is momentarily taken aback. "Why are you here?" he asked.

Ji An'an grabbed Shen Mo's arm. "You're always so busy with work. I had to ask Shen-ge to come with me."

Then she added, "We didn't make any reservations."

Ji Mingxuan stroked her hair and smiled. "Don't worry. I won't let you leave hungry."

Then he turned back and asked the person next to him, "You don't mind eating together, do you?"

The man next to him was an attractive actor called Zhao Yi. He seemed to be quite popular these days, frequently appearing at various events. Having watched several shows he'd starred in, Shen Mo thought he looked even more charming in real life than he did on television.

Zhao Yi smiled with impeccable graciousness. "Of course not."

Ji Mingxuan had already made a reservation. The private room he'd booked was more than large enough for four people.

After taking a seat, Zhao Yi looked at Ji An'an and Shen Mo. "Mr. Ji, won't you introduce us?"

Ji Mingxuan pointed at Ji An'an. "My sister."

But he didn't introduce Shen Mo.

"Oh, so it's Miss Ji." Zhao Yi waited, but no further introductions came, so he could only guess on his own, "Is this Miss Ji's boyfriend?"

Ji An'an chuckled aloud at this.

"Wrong." Ji Mingxuan turned to the menu and answered, slowly and casually, "This is the future Mrs. Ji."

Zhao Yi's smile froze on his face.

Even Ji An'an almost choked on her tea.

But Zhao Yi was jaded enough from his many years in the entertainment industry that he got over it in no time and said, "Mr. Ji, you have a great sense of humor."

Ji Mingxuan didn't deny it, instead, he tossed the menu on the table. "Order something."

It was the first time that Ji An'an and Shen Mo had been to this restaurant. Zhao Yi ordered several dishes before asking about their preferences, "Their signature dish is a must-have... Miss Ji, how is your spice tolerance?"

He was truly very charming.

Feeling quite inadequate in comparison, Shen Mo just sipped at his tea.

Though Ji Mingxuan's joke had startled the others just now, Shen Mo had actually remained quite calm. He'd once signed a contract with Ji Mingxuan three years ago after he'd recovered enough to leave the hospital. Everything had been quite perfunctory, of course. Even the rings on their fingers had been bought by Ji Mingxuan's secretary on short notice.

At the time, Shen Mo had been in a sort of trance. Everything had seemed dream-like; nothing had felt real. He'd even thought that it was a good thing Zhou Yang hadn't been some kind of playboy. Otherwise, for the sake of his sister alone, how many times would Ji Mingxuan have had to marry?

The restaurant they were at was quite speedy with their service, and the food was also pretty tasty, especially their signature dish—a suckling pig, roasted and golden, crispy on the outside and tender within, rich but not overly greasy. Ji An'an kept praising it.

Then she heard that Zhao Yi was an actor, and she couldn't help but ask curiously for insider gossip on the entertainment industry.

Zhao Yi was also talkative—even when it came to boring trivialities, he could describe them in vivid and exciting ways, making Ji An'an laugh.

Ji Mingxuan could only ask her during a break in their conversation, "An'an, how did shopping go today?"

Ji An'an said, "Thanks to Shen-ge's help, I've already bought Zhou Yang a present."

Ji Mingxuan glanced at Shen Mo and said, "I see. A present for Zhou Yang."

Ji An'an immediately took out the pair of cuff-links she bought. "And here's one for you."

And then she specifically added, "Shen-ge picked it out."

Shen Mo wanted to explain, but Ji Mingxuan had already unwrapped the cufflinks without a word, immediately putting them on.

Zhao Yi praised, "Mr. Shen has good taste."

Ji Mingxuan smiled. "Not bad."

The meal was quite enjoyable.

At last, Ji An'an excused herself to the restroom while Ji Mingxuan stepped out to answer a call, leaving Shen Mo in the room with Zhao Yi.

Zhao Yi asked, "Was the food today not to your taste? You didn't eat much, Mr. Shen."

"Not at all. I just don't eat a lot."

Zhao Yi looked at Shen Mo's left hand and said, "It looks like the one on Mr. Ji's finger."

Not knowing whether he should deny it or not, Shen Mo just gave a noncommittal hum.

The atmosphere suddenly became leaden, almost suffocating.

Zhao Yi poured some water into his own cup before suddenly asking, "Do you live in Jinxiu Villa, Mr. Shen?"

Jinxiu Villa was a prime location in H City. The properties there were shockingly expensive. Shen Mo didn't have a lot of savings, so of course he couldn't afford to live there. Furthermore, he had been living in Ji Mingxuan's house for the past three years. There was nothing to hide, so Shen Mo answered honestly, "No."

Zhao Yi smiled immediately. He was born with good looks, and with a smile like this, he looked even more charming. The whole room seemed to light up.

Shen Mo was curious. "Why do you ask, Mr. Zhao?"

"It's nothing." Zhao Yi blinked once. "I mistook you for someone else."

Zhao Yi stopped and didn't continue the subject.

It took a while for Shen Mo to realize that Ji Mingxuan also had a property in Jinxiu Villa and that the person who lived there must be Zhao Yi's actual rival in love. As for Shen Mo... after seeing him, Zhao Yi probably thought that he wasn't qualified enough.

The temperature set in the room was a little high. Shen Mo felt that it was a little stuffy.

Soon, Ji An'an came back from the restroom and Ji Mingxuan also finished his call. Paying the bill, he said, "It's late. Let's go home."

The parking lot was rather far from here.

It was cold and windy at night. As Shen Mo stood by the road, waiting for the driver to come, the wind reddened his ears. Ji Mingxuan happened to be standing right next to him. Naturally, he took one of Shen Mo's hands and put it into his coat pocket along with his own hand.

Shen Mo felt a little awkward. "Mr. Ji."

Ji Mingxuan replied as if nothing had happened, "Yes?"

"...Nothing."

Shen Mo glanced at Zhao Yi, who was standing at a distance from them. He wondered what Ji Mingxuan was thinking about. Was he so bored that he wanted to watch his lovers fight each other? Shen Mo began to evaluate himself. He knew he had terrible skills in bed, but he thought he might still win in a physical fight.

He was in the middle of considering what to do if he and Zhao Yi really did start fighting when he felt Ji Mingxuan squeeze his hand.

Ji Mingxuan asked, "When is Zhou Yang's birthday?"

Shen Mo's heart thumped. He replied almost reflexively, "I don't remember."

Ji Mingxuan nodded and asked, "When is yours?"

Of course, Shen Mo knew this one. But after he replied, he didn't expect Ji Mingxuan to ask him again, "What about mine?"

Shen Mo was speechless.

He could never have imagined that Ji Mingxuan would quiz him like this. Mr. Ji could say what Shen Mo's birthday was without hesitation, but Shen Mo didn't have such a good memory.

The night was blurry. Ji Mingxuan turned to look at him. The most beautiful evening of this city was reflected in his black pupils.

Shen Mo's hands were almost sweating.

Ji Mingxuan suddenly smiled and let go of his hand. "I knew you wouldn't remember."

The driver had already driven the car over. Ji Mingxuan opened the door for Ji An'an and said, "Take care on the road."

"Brother, aren't you coming home with us?"

"I'll give Zhao Yi a lift."

When Shen Mo got into the car, Ji Mingxuan shut the door and gestured to the driver. The car gradually started moving forward. Shen Mo sat in the back seat, watching Ji Mingxuan's reflection grow smaller and smaller in the rearview mirror.

On their way home, he immediately began prodding Ji An'an about Ji Mingxuan's birthday.

Ji An'an said, "Brother's birthday is easy to remember. It's the first day of spring by the traditional calendar. What's the matter? Shen-ge, are you already thinking about presents?"

Shen Mo smiled. Everything that Shen Mo had, Ji Mingxuan had as well, and also everything he didn't have. What could Shen Mo possibly give to Ji Mingxuan?

Mulling over the question, he fell asleep that night. But even when the second evening came, Ji Mingxuan still hadn't come home. What surprised Shen Mo was Zhao Yi hitting the headlines—a reporter had hidden in the building where Zhao Yi lived and had taken a blurry photo.

The title was quite eye-catching, but no actual evidence was reported. It only caused a battle between his fans and his antis.

Ji An'an looked carefully at the photo before letting out a sigh of relief. "It's not Brother."

The photo only captured two people from the back. At night and with little light, it was impossible to tell whether it was Ji Mingxuan or not. Ji An'an still comforted Shen Mo, though, "Brother must be busy at work. He's obviously just friends with Zhao Yi."

Shen Mo kept a smile on his face and said, "Of course."

He was so tired of acting.

It'd been like this since his childhood. He worked much harder than others, yet he never got first place. Whether in academics, art, or love—even now that he was Ji Mingxuan's lover, he was still no match for other people.

Although Shen Mo was discouraged, he didn't give up. He wasn't as talented as Zhao Yi, so he had to work twice as hard. He sacrificed sleep to download gay porn, saving them to a new folder he named "Study Materials" and taking notes while watching them.

He was still focused on this task when his phone suddenly rang.

Shen Mo picked it up only to hear a familiar voice. "Shen Mo, it's me."

Shen Mo recognized Zhou Yang's voice at once and he scrambled to close the video. Then, he held the phone in his hand for a long while before finally asking, "How did you get my number?"

"An'an told me."

"Oh..." Shen Mo had nearly forgotten about Ji An'an. "Why are you calling me so late?"

Zhou Yang hesitated for a while and said, "I heard some rumors... about Ji Mingxuan..."

"Is it about Mingxuan and Zhao Yi? I've also heard about them. It was just a misunderstanding, though."

"I might know a little more than you do."

"Congratulations. You can sell it to the newspaper."

Zhou Yang was silent for a while before he said, "Shen Mo, can we meet?"

"I told you I won't meet you alone."

"If you were happy with Ji Mingxuan, I wouldn't bother you. But you aren't. I heard from An'an that you chose to be with him because you wanted to repay him."

Shen Mo was starting to regret telling Ji An'an so much. However, he was an experienced actor, so he replied without hesitation, "Mingxuan did save me once. That was how we met. And after that... of course it was love that made us start dating. Otherwise, if we didn't feel anything towards each other, how could we have lived together for these past three years?"

Toward the end, even Shen Mo almost believed himself.

But Zhou Yang insisted, "I want to meet you."

"Would anything change even if we did meet?"

"I..." Zhou Yang's voice came through the phone, so deep that it sounded somewhat muffled. "I can take you away."

Shen Mo suddenly gripped his phone.

Three years ago, he had longed day and night to hear those words. If only Zhou Yang had been able to say them out loud, Shen Mo would have gone to the ends of the earth for him.

Yet it never happened.

Things had changed. Zhou Yang had too many responsibilities and worries. So did he.

"You're the only son of the Zhou family. Your parents won't let you."

"It doesn't matter even if they don't. I didn't join my father's company. I want to start my own business."

"What about Miss Ji?"

"An'an... I'll talk to her."

Shen Mo stayed silent.

"Xiao-Mo," Zhou Yang used his old nickname for Shen Mo, "do you still remember where we had our first date? It was Tianhe Park. We were still in high school then. We were so silly, going to see plum blossoms while it was snowing, and then we ended up missing our bus stop..."

Of course Shen Mo remembered.

He remembered how happy he had been, babbling the whole way. It was unbelievable that Zhou Yang, whom he'd had a crush on for so long, also liked him back.

And now Zhou Yang was speaking right by his ears, "Xiao-Mo, I'll wait for you at the same place tomorrow. Let's... start over again."

Shen Mo suddenly came back to himself. "I have work tomorrow."

He hung up as soon as he finished.

Later, his phone rang again. Seeing Zhou Yang's name on the screen, Shen Mo only turned off his phone and went to sleep.

That night, Ji Mingxuan still didn't come return home.

The next day, Shen Mo asked for a leave of absence and didn't go to work. He didn't go to meet Zhou Yang either. He stayed at home and did some cleaning. The cleaning service came once a week, which meant Shen Mo didn't usually need to do housework. He only did it when he was in a bad mood.

It was easy to forget one's worries while focused on something else.

The weather was getting colder, and the sky looked dim, as if it would snow. Shen Mo looked at his phone, which he'd turned off, and continued cleaning, wiping down the windows in every room. He remembered the weather on the day he'd had his first date with Zhou Yang. It'd been almost the same as the weather was today. He'd stood in the cold wind, waiting for Zhou Yang. It'd been so cold that he'd needed to stomp his feet to keep his blood flowing to his toes, but he'd still felt sweet inside.

But the past could only remain in the past.

There were many people out there who could mend a broken relationship.

But he and Zhou Yang weren't among those people.

The day seemed extremely long. The sky finally darkened, and it was when Shen Mo was wiping a dirty spot on the ground that the doorbell rang. He tossed the rag aside and hurried to open the door. To his surprise, he saw Ji Mingxuan standing outside.

"Mr. Ji? Did you not take your keys?"

Ji Mingxuan didn't say anything. Propping one hand against the door, he looked at Shen Mo with narrowed eyes.

As Shen Mo took a step forward, the pungent smell of alcohol came to his nose.

"Mr. Ji, did you drink today?"

Ji Mingxuan replied, "A little."

Ji Mingxuan had a high tolerance for alcohol. Sometimes, when he went out for business dinners, he'd remain in high spirits well after his clients were already passed out drunk on the table, and he'd even be able to continue working on documents when he came back home. Shen Mo had been living with him for three years and he still hadn't seen him drunk, so Shen Mo didn't let it bother himself too much and went back to cleaning the floor.

But unexpectedly, after Ji Mingxuan entered the living room, he slowly slid down the wall until he eventually sat down on the ground.

Surprised, Shen Mo hurried over to help him up. Only then did he notice that one of Ji Mingxuan's gloves was missing. Even Ji Mingxuan's left foot was drenched, possibly after having stepped into a puddle. He'd known Ji Mingxuan for so long, yet he had never seen Ji Mingxuan in such a terrible state.

Shen Mo helped him to the sofa and asked, "Mr. Ji, are you drunk?"

Ji Mingxuan tilted his head and kept staring at Shen Mo, as if he was trying to recognize Shen Mo's face.

Shen Mo realized that he was really quite drunk.

"I'll get you a cup of honey water."

Drunk Ji Mingxuan had a better temperament than he normally did. He made no fuss, just sat quietly on the sofa. Later, when Shen Mo came back with the honey water, he took a sip from the cup in Shen Mo's hand. He then touched Shen Mo's face, asking in a low voice, "... Shen Mo, is that you?"

He was too drunk even to recognize the face of a lover.

Shen Mo was speechless, but he still answered patiently, "Yes, Mr. Ji, it's me."

Ji Mingxuan asked again, "Why are you here?"

The question made Shen Mo feel somewhat awkward. "Mr. Ji, did you forget? I've always lived here."

Ji Mingxuan replied, "Right." For some reason, he suddenly began to laugh. He had a handsome face in the first place, and his eyes were even more alluring when he smiled. He said gently, "Shen Mo, come closer."

Shen Mo had never seen Ji Mingxuan be so gentle before. He couldn't help but lean forward.

Ji Mingxuan gave him another smile.

As Shen Mo let down his guard, Ji Mingxuan suddenly grabbed his arms and pulled hard.

Shen Mo slammed into Ji Mingxuan. He couldn't see the expression on Ji Mingxuan's face, but he felt Ji Mingxuan's warm breaths beside his ear. In a low and hoarse voice, the man spoke, one word at a time, "I caught you."

As if he were a hunter who had finally caught the prey he'd long since been waiting for.

Shen Mo's heart shuddered.

The whole world spun the next second. Ji Mingxuan turned him over and pinned him down on the sofa.

"Mr. Ji?"

Ji Mingxuan bit the nape of his neck and panted. "Don't move."

Shen Mo was afraid. He tried to struggle out of Ji Mingxuan's hold, but Ji Mingxuan pulled him back with ease; even his arms and legs were firmly pinned down. Unzipping Shen Mo's pants, Ji Mingxuan pressed his erection against Shen Mo's cleft. Their position was reminiscent of bestial copulation.

But Shen Mo was too nervous. Ji Mingxuan tried several times, but he still couldn't find a way in. He had to slow down. Reaching for the cup of honey water on the table, he poured some in his hands as lubricant.

The lukewarm water spread over Shen Mo's lower half, soaking him. Ji Mingxuan's hand circled to the front, gently stroking Shen Mo's sensitive member.

A primal lust rose from the depths of Shen Mo's body. He ground his hips impatiently, quietly whimpering.

Ji Mingxuan turned Shen Mo's head around and kissed him.

He licked across Shen Mo's teeth, causing a sensation that was strangely pleasurable. He then nipped at Shen Mo's lips, coaxing, "Shen Mo."

"Mm... Mr. Ji..."

"Spread your legs wider."

Shen Mo's body felt too limp. He couldn't exert any strength.

So Ji Mingxuan tightened his grip, firmly clasping down on the source of of Shen Mo's pleasure.

"Ah..." Shen Mo cried. Waves of tingling pleasure crawled up his spine, yet no matter what he did he couldn't find any release. He could only obey, trying his best to spread his legs wider.

"Good boy."

As a reward, Ji Mingxuan planted a kiss on Shen Mo's eyelid before he plunged right in, burying his entire length in Shen Mo's fair body, completely conquering his prey.

"Ah..."

Shen Mo let out a low cry of pain. He trembled despite himself, as if he were a wild creature on the verge of being tamed.

At this thought, Ji Mingxuan felt himself grow even bigger inside of Shen Mo. He took off Shen Mo's clothes. Then he continued to thrust again and again into that tender heat as he kissed his way down Shen Mo's smooth, bare back.

When Ji Mingxuan hit a certain spot, Shen Mo couldn't help but arch his back, crying, "Mr. Ji, don't..."

Ignoring him, Ji Mingxuan seized his waist with both hands and kept on aiming for that same spot. Shen Mo still felt a bit of pain, but amid the pain also came an indescribable pleasure. Before long, he peaked, his emission sticky as it shot out of his length.

After driving into Shen Mo's body a few more times, Ji Mingxuan thrust forward hard and came as well.

When they finished, Shen Mo made to get up and go to the bathroom, but Ji Mingxuan pulled him back. They lay on the sofa together.

Shen Mo looked at the clock and said, "Mr. Ji, Miss Ji will be coming back soon."

"It's okay." Ji Mingxuan kissed the patch of skin behind his ear. "An'an won't be coming back tonight."

Wrapping one arm around Shen Mo's waist, Ji Mingxuan stroked down the curve of Shen Mo's back until he reached the entrance that had just been pummeled by him. He tentatively put in a finger.

Shen Mo shuddered once, crying in a low voice, "Mr. Ji."

It sounded like he was begging.

But Ji Mingxuan swiftly added in another finger, coaxing, "I was too impatient just now. Let me see if you got hurt."

Shen Mo's entrance looked somewhat swollen, but luckily it wasn't bleeding. It was filled with Ji Mingxuan's come, squelching as he stirred his fingers inside.

The noise sounded extremely erotic in the empty living room. Ji Mingxuan parted the hole slightly, biting Shen Mo's ear. "Seems like you didn't get hurt. It's all soft and wet here now..."

Shen Mo felt his body flush hot. With just a slight twitch, the white fluid trickled down between his thighs. Ji Mingxuan took some of it and smeared it across Shen Mo's chest.

Shen Mo hadn't recovered from his climax yet; his body was still quite oversensitive. Ji Mingxuan's touch aroused him, and he shrank back. "Mr. Ji, I can't anymore..."

"Yes, you can," Ji Mingxuan replied as he rubbed and teased at Shen Mo's nipples.

"Mm..."

Shen Mo let out a groan. He was already at his limit, yet his nipples still stiffened. Ji Mingxuan had successfully gotten his body interested again.

Soon, Ji Mingxuan was also erect once more. He bent one of Shen Mo's legs and entered Shen Mo's body from the side. Shen Mo was still slick from earlier, so the entry was smoother than usual. Ji Mingxuan wasn't as impatient as before, either. Holding Shen Mo in his arms, he thrust slowly, at times stroking Shen Mo's erection with both hands.

"Ah... Mr. Ji..."

It was a different kind of torment. With stimulation from both sides, Shen Mo soon climaxed again.

Yet Ji Mingxuan was still far from being satisfied. He kept going, changing positions a few more times. It wasn't until Shen Mo was about to lose his voice that Ji Mingxuan finally came inside his body.

They slept on the sofa that night. Before dawn, Ji Mingxuan picked him up and brought him to the shower, fucking him there one last time. Shen Mo's body was completely sore. He had to hang onto Ji Mingxuan's shoulders with both hands—he almost couldn't put his legs together.

When they woke up the following day, the sky outside the window was surprisingly bright.

Shen Mo opened his eyes. He felt sore, as if his bones had been scattered and then pieced back together. Ji Mingxuan was still asleep, one hand resting on Shen Mo's waist.

The curtains in the bedroom hadn't been closed. Shen Mo sat up and looked out the window to be greeted by a vast expanse of white.

So it had snowed last night.

The floor was a mess. Not knowing when Ji An'an would be back, Shen Mo made to get up, wanting to pick up the clothes strewn across the floor, but then he heard Ji Mingxuan say from beside him, "Sleep a little longer."

Shen Mo turned around and saw the sunlight on Ji Mingxuan's face. "You're awake, Mr. Ji?"

His eyes half-closed, Ji Mingxuan hummed in confirmation.

"Mr. Ji, you were drunk yesterday."

Ji Mingxuan said nothing. Instead, he drew Shen Mo back into his arms. Shen Mo knew that some people, upon sobering up, tended to forget what had happened while they'd been drunk. He wasn't sure if Ji Mingxuan was the same, but it was already getting late.

"Mr. Ji, I'm going to be late for work."

Ji Mingxuan replied in a lazy tone, "Then take another day off."

Shen Mo was surprised, asking, "How did you know that I took a day off yesterday, Mr. Ji?"

Ji Mingxuan opened his eyes and glanced at him. "Don't you remember whose company you're working for?"

Of course Shen Mo knew that the company he worked for belonged to the Ji family. But did they report to the CEO whenever a mere employee took a day off?

Ji Mingxuan reached out. "Give me your phone. I'll help you ask for a leave."

Shen Mo's phone was on the tea table in the living room. Immediately, he went to get it and handed it to Ji Mingxuan. Ji Mingxuan looked at his phone. "It's powered off."

Only then did Shen Mo notice that he'd forgotten to turn his phone back on this whole time. He couldn't say it had been because of Zhou Yang, so his only excuse was, "Maybe I'm too busy these days."

Ji Mingxuan didn't press him for more. He simply turned on the phone.

The moment the phone powered on, a series of text notifications sounded.

Ji Mingxuan smiled, glancing at him, "You have many new messages."

Shen Mo knew who had sent them, but he still replied, "It must be spam."

"Do you want to take a look?"

Shen Mo felt his heart jolt. He heard himself saying, "...Just delete them all."

"Are you sure?"

"Yeah."

Ji Mingxuan smiled enigmatically. "Don't regret this in the future."

Shen Mo said, "I won't."

Thus Ji Mingxuan deleted those messages right there in front of him.

Shen Mo sat next to Ji Mingxuan quietly. He felt as if he could see many of his memories pass by before his eyes. Maybe what he missed wasn't actually Zhou Yang, but rather the carefree days of his youth.

But it had been three years already. Anyone else would have moved on by now.

Ji Mingxuan called Shen Mo's supervisor to ask for a leave before calling his own assistant, saying that he wouldn't be going to the company this morning. Then, he tossed the phone to the side, giving Shen Mo a wave of his hand. "Let's sleep a little longer."

Nothing was better than sleeping in on such a snowy day.

Now that Mr. Ji had given his word, Shen Mo had the rare chance to be a bit lazy. He lay back down on the sofa.

The heating in the living room was set at a pleasant temperature. Ji Mingxuan had his arm around Shen Mo's waist, and his chin rested on Shen Mo's shoulder. Shen Mo soon fell asleep. He should have many things on his mind right now, but for some reason, they didn't trouble him as he slowly lost consciousness.

It was almost noon when Shen Mo woke again.

He got up to tidy up the living room, but when he finished dressing and looked back, he found that Ji Mingxuan was still sleeping.

"Mr. Ji, it's time for lunch."

"Mr. Ji?"

Shen Mo called his name a few more times, but Ji Mingxuan didn't respond. He reached out and gently nudged him, only to find that Ji Mingxuan's wrist was alarmingly hot.

Surprised, Shen Mo immediately put his hand to Ji Mingxuan's forehead. As expected, it was also burning.

He knew now that Ji Mingxuan was sick. As it was undoubtedly bad for a sick person to sleep on the sofa, Shen Mo laboriously coaxed Ji Mingxuan into the bedroom. Only half awake, Ji Mingxuan managed to get in bed before falling asleep once more.

Thinking that Ji Mingxuan might be hungry soon, Shen Mo went to the kitchen and made some congee. He brought it to the bedroom, woke Ji Mingxuan up, and told him to have some.

Ji Mingxuan didn't look well, but he still ate the congee.

Shen Mo quietly observed Ji Mingxuan's expression. "Mr. Ji, I think you're sick."

Ji Mingxuan gave an indifferent reply, "I'm just a little tired."

"You have a fever." Shen Mo asked, "Should we go to the hospital?"

Ji Mingxuan frowned the moment he heard the word "hospital." He refused without thinking, "No."

"Should I get the doctor, then?"

"It's just a fever. Don't bother."

"But..."

"Don't be so loud." Ji Mingxuan lay back on the bed and even pulled the blanket over his face. "I'll be fine after I sleep for a bit."

Shen Mo didn't know how to respond.

He didn't expect that a man like Mr. Ji would refuse to see a doctor when sick.

Thinking back to the sex they'd had last night, Shen Mo felt a little guilty, wondering if Ji Mingxuan was sick because it had been too much. He rummaged around and found some fever medication to give to Ji Mingxuan. Afterwards, he stayed at the bedside to take care of him.

Because of the high fever, Ji Mingxuan didn't sleep too well. Still asleep, he suddenly called out, "Shen Mo."

At once, Shen Mo grabbed his hand. "Mr. Ji, I'm here."

Ji Mingxuan didn't say anything else. His knitted brows relaxed a little, but his palms were still hot. Just as Shen Mo was about to let go, Ji Mingxuan caught his hand.

Shen Mo struggled a little with no use. He could only let Ji Mingxuan keep hold.

Time flew by.

It wasn't until the sunset was flooding through the window that he noticed he'd been sitting there for the entire afternoon.

Ji Mingxuan's fever was relatively stable, but they'd run out of fever medication at home. Shen Mo changed his clothes so that he could buy some more before the sky darkened. The snow on the roads had mostly melted, but it was still inconvenient to walk. Fortunately, Ji Mingxuan's driver hadn't gotten off work yet, so Shen Mo went by car.

On their way there, the driver, *lao*-Zhang[1], mentioned how Ji Mingxuan had gotten drunk: "Mr. Ji met up with someone the night before. He was in a bad mood all day yesterday. Later, he got so drunk that he couldn't even walk properly."

"Mr. Ji's shoes were wet. Did he fall?"

Lao-Zhang never dared to say anything bad about Ji Mingxuan. He laughed instead. "Mr. Ji was going to go to Jinxiu Villa, but it was snowing so bad last night, and he was so drunk. I was afraid an accident might happen on our way there, so I drove him home instead. Was he mad?"

Hearing him mention Jinxiu Villa, Shen Mo was momentarily surprised.

Lao-Zhang asked again, "Mr. Shen, did Mr. Ji get angry?"

"No," Shen Mo replied, "he didn't."

He remembered that last night, it had taken Ji Mingxuan quite a while to recognize his face.

He fiddled unwittingly with the silver ring on his left hand. *No wonder*, he thought.

---

[1] *"Lao-"* is a prefix used for making nicknames, often for men who are middle aged or older. This method of address conveys a certain sense of familiarity. Literally, it means "old."

Lao-Zhang was a good driver; they soon reached the pharmacy. Shen Mo got out of the car and bought the medication. When he got back in the car, he felt a pain in his stomach. Only then did he realize that, while focused on taking care of Ji Mingxuan, he had forgotten to eat lunch.

The sky was already dark when Shen Mo got home. He got himself something to eat and made some more congee for Ji Mingxuan. He then persuaded Ji Mingxuan to eat the congee along with the medication he'd just bought.

They didn't call for any doctors. Worried, Shen Mo stayed by the bed and took Ji Mingxuan's temperature every half-hour.

Luckily, Ji Mingxuan's temperature went down.

Past midnight, Shen Mo was too tired to stay awake and fell asleep beside the bed.

He began to dream. In the dream, snow had fallen. All he saw was a vast whiteness. Everyone was walking fast on the streets, their heads hanging low. The snow hadn't melted yet. It had even frozen in some places, making it difficult for people to walk on.

But someone was holding his hand the entire way.

Shen Mo didn't find the walk difficult. He felt happy instead, talking to the person as he walked.

"Today, my coworkers shunned me at work again."

"In truth, I still prefer painting."

These were all honest words he usually never told anyone. However, it was strange that the person next to him didn't say anything.

Shen Mo turned around and asked, "Zhou Yang, why aren't you saying anything?"

The man stopped and said, "I'm not Zhou Yang."

Shen Mo looked up only to find that the man, tall and handsome, was actually Ji Mingxuan.

"Mr. Ji..."

Ji Mingxuan laughed coldly and let go of his hand. The force of the removal made Shen Mo fall on the icy snow on the ground, as if he had suddenly lost his ability to walk.

He was instantly woken up, only to hear Ji Mingxuan's voice: "How are you able to fall on the ground even as you sleep?"

As he said this, Ji Mingxuan turned on the wall lamp.

Confused, Shen Mo looked at Ji Mingxuan for a while, as if he still dreamt. Then he realized that he'd fallen from the bed. He slowly got up from the floor, his expression still a little confused.

Ji Mingxuan lifted the blanket. "Come here."

His body cold, Shen Mo got under the blanket. It was warm in Ji Mingxuan's arms. The heat even felt a little uncomfortable to Shen Mo, so he shifted to the side.

But right away, Ji Mingxuan pulled him back.

With one arm wrapped around him, Ji Mingxuan said, "Don't move. Do you want to fall again?"

Shen Mo didn't dare to move. After the fall, he was finding it hard to go back to sleep. "Mr. Ji, did I wake you up?"

"I slept for a whole day. I've had enough sleep."

"Are you feeling better now, Mr. Ji?"

Ji Mingxuan lowered his head, touching his forehead against Shen

Mo's, and replied, "I'm okay now."

Shen Mo only felt that it was warm. He couldn't figure out if Ji Mingxuan's temperature had gone down or not. Thinking for a moment, he said, "You should go to the hospital."

Aversion immediately appeared on Ji Mingxuan's face. "No."

Shen Mo hadn't expected Ji Mingxuan to hate going to the hospital so much. He recalled that three years ago, when he had been hospitalized, Ji Mingxuan had visited him.

Later, he'd recovered and left the hospital. For about half a year, his life had been a complete mess. Sometimes he would just sit at the window, watching cars drive by, and the day would be gone. He had few memories from those times. He only remembered that he'd been kicked out by the landlord because he couldn't afford the rent. It had been Ji Mingxuan who had taken him to his house, who had later given him a job. And then his life had finally gotten back on track.

What exactly had happened in those six months? Why didn't he remember anything about them?

Shen Mo couldn't recall anything no matter how hard he tried. Soon, he drifted off to sleep.

Ji Mingxuan's fever left as quickly as it had come. The next day, the heat went down, and Ji Mingxuan was able to sit upright in bed and deal with business matters. Ji An'an hadn't come home yet, so Shen Mo took another day off to take care of Ji Mingxuan.

Ji Mingxuan didn't hesitate to order Shen Mo around as he pleased. Before lunch, he even listed a couple of dishes he wanted to eat. Luckily, Shen Mo wasn't a bad cook. He tried to make a few of the dishes and was just passable enough to satisfy Mr. Ji.

In the afternoon, Shen Mo went out for groceries. When he returned, he found that some of his clothes and toiletries had been taken to Ji Mingxuan's room.

Ji Mingxuan was sending an email on his laptop when Shen Mo mentioned it to him. He didn't even look at Shen Mo as he replied, "Aren't you taking care of me these days? It'll be more convenient for you this way."

"Mr. Ji, I thought you already gotten better."

Conveniently, Ji Mingxuan coughed just then. "Not completely."

Shen Mo could only ask, "When will Miss Ji be back?"

"An'an went traveling. She'll be back next week."

"Did Miss Ji go on her own?"

A corner of Ji Mingxuan's lips pulled. He tilted his head and glanced at Shen Mo. "What do you think?"

Shen Mo instantly realized. "She went with Zhou Yang?"

Ji Mingxuan nodded, adding, "She left on the twelfth."

The day that it had snowed.

Zhou Yang had wanted to meet him. He had said he'd wait for him at the location of their first date, but Shen Mo hadn't gone. Zhou Yang hadn't seen him, so he'd left with Ji An'an instead.

What if Shen Mo had gone?

Shen Mo looked at the bright sunlight outside the window and stopped thinking about it.

After he spent another two days resting at home, Ji Mingxuan went back to work. Shen Mo also went back to work and continued idling. His colleagues were still unfriendly to him. Days went by. Nothing changed.

Except for Ji Mingxuan.

Previously, he would often be busy at work all day. He would also have many business appointments, and he'd often come home very late at night—it was even normal for him to spend the whole night outside. But he changed a lot these next few days. He went to work on time, came home early, and also ate dinner at home. He even sent a list of the dishes he wanted to eat to Shen Mo's phone every afternoon.

Even lao-Zhang said, "Mr. Ji is finally settling down. Work is so much easier now that I don't have to drive at night."

Shen Mo said, "But you get less overtime pay, don't you?"

Lao-Zhang didn't mind it all that much. "I'd rather spend more time with my wife and kids."

Shen Mo didn't know why Ji Mingxuan had changed so much.

Ji Mingxuan had a capricious nature, so Shen Mo didn't dare to guess. It'd be quite embarrassing if Shen Mo's guess turned out to be wrong.

At the end of the week, Ji An'an finally returned.

She had gone to a well-known resort—an island somewhere in the Pacific. Upon her return, it seemed that she'd been somewhat reddened by the sun, wearing quite a fashionable outfit. Her gaze was as gentle as seawater.

Ji An'an took out the gifts she had bought for Shen Mo the moment she entered the house, saying with a smile, "It's such a pity that Zhou Yang had a bit of a family emergency and had to come home as soon as possible, or I would've gotten you more."

"This is more than enough." Shen Mo asked, "Did you have a good time?"

"Of course. The water was so blue. We went out to sea by boat in the morning and didn't come back until the evening. We held hands as we walked along the beach at night. And under the moonlight, the beach looked even more beautiful than it had during the day... I wish I could have stayed there forever."

Ji Mingxuan said, "You were only there for a visit, but you've gone and caught a case of wanderlust."

Ji An'an turned around and hugged his arm. "Brother, thank you so much for giving me the plane tickets. Next time, you should go there with Shen-ge."

Shen Mo looked up at Ji Mingxuan, asking, "Mr. Ji arranged the trip for you?"

Their eyes met. Ji Mingxuan replied calmly, "That's right."

Ji An'an said, "When he gave me the tickets that day, I was so surprised. It was so soon—I didn't even have time to pack."

"It was supposed to be a surprise."

"But we did have a great time, and Zhou Yang..." Ji An'an's face suddenly flushed. She stopped and looked at Ji Mingxuan. "Brother, I have something to tell you."

Shen Mo knew what he was supposed to do. He immediately said, "I'm going to go make dinner."

He then went to the kitchen, leaving the siblings to talk in the living room.

It was dinner time already—the aroma of outside food wafted in through the window. The ingredients were all present. Shen Mo took some vegetables out of the fridge and washed them.

He remembered that on the twelfth of this month, Zhou Yang had asked him to meet at the location of their first date. And on the same day, Ji Mingxuan had given the plane tickets to Ji An'an.

Was it a coincidence?

What if he had gone there that day?

Maybe he would've stood waiting amid the heavy snow again, all the way until the sky grew completely dark.

The water was so cold that it seemed to pierce his bones. Shen Mo's hands trembled slightly as he hurried to turn off the tap. He heard Ji Mingxuan come in from outside, asking, "Do you need help?"

Shen Mo said, "No, I'm fine. I'll get everything ready soon. Is Miss Ji hungry already?"

"No. She was tired and went to her bedroom to rest for a bit."

Ji Mingxuan stayed silent after that, but he didn't leave either. Leaning on the door, he watched Shen Mo cook. After washing the vegetables, Shen Mo peeled some potatoes. Debating whether to braise the potatoes or to curry them, he began to chop.

He was about to ask Ji Mingxuan for his opinion when he heard Ji Mingxuan say, "An'an just told me that Zhou Yang proposed to her."

Shen Mo placed a cut. His cut was wonky, and the potato chunk came out a bit too big.

Oh, he thought, *now I can only make curried potatoes.*

Looking down, he continued to cut the potatoes, piece by piece.

Ji Mingxuan gazed at him and said, "An'an has already accepted the proposal."

"That's great." Mind busy thinking about how to make curried potatoes, Shen Mo mechanically said, "They've been dating for so long. It was only a matter of time before they got married."

Standing at the door, Ji Mingxuan looked at him for a moment. He then turned around and left.

At dinner, Shen Mo toasted Ji An'an and asked her when the wedding would be.

Ji An'an had only drunk a little, but her face was very red. "We won't be getting married so soon, but Brother said we should get engaged first."

"I'll discuss it with the elders of the Zhou family." Ji Mingxuan patted Shen Mo's hand and said, "Zhou Yang will be part of our family soon."

Shen Mo didn't know how he got here, that he too would count as a part of this family.

Ji An'an took a bite of the potatoes and teased, "Shen-ge, you messed up today. The potatoes are too salty."

Shen Mo tried some as well.

They really were salty—salty to the point of bitterness. Still, he swallowed it and said calmly, "I'll braise them next time."

In the evening, Shen Mo forgot to move back to his own room, and he still slept in the same bed as Ji Mingxuan. He thought that he might not be able to fall asleep easily, but he slept through the whole night. He even overslept the next day. When he woke up, Ji Mingxuan had already gone to work.

He cleaned himself up and went to work in a hurry, although he was still a little late. No one cared about him, anyway. His colleagues only glanced at him before they continued to gossip.

"Rich people these days sure like to play around, huh. They keep so many lovers around."

"Shh, aren't you afraid someone might hear you?"

"Lovers aren't that big of a deal. The most laughable is when illegitimate children start cropping up. I heard that the Zhou family..."

"Which one?"

"The famous one..."

"Oh, I thought they only have one son."

"Not anymore. They recently brought back an illegitimate son who's in his twenties already. And now everyone is calling him *ershao*[1]."

"An adult son? They're definitely gonna be fighting over inheritance soon."

"Not necessarily. If the Zhou family and the Ji family do an arranged marriage..."

The voices behind Shen Mo gradually faded away. He could no longer hear them, but what he'd already heard was enough to surprise him. When people talked about the famous Zhou family of H city, they always meant Zhou Yang's family. But what illegitimate son? Did Zhou Yang really have a younger brother?

This was indeed no secret. Shen Mo didn't even have to poke around. He only casually asked Ji An'an a few questions, and she told him everything.

"It's true. There *is* such a person. His mother was Mr. Zhou's old lover; he's only two years younger than Zhou Yang. The Zhou family acknowledged him not too long ago.

"I saw him when I came back yesterday. He looked a bit frivolous, but he's very glib with his words. Mr. Zhou seems to really like him, though. He even arranged for him to work at the company. That was also the reason why Mrs. Zhou wanted Zhou Yang to come back as soon as possible.

"Mr. and Mrs. Zhou are always so respectful and loving toward each other. Many people admired their relationship. Who could've known something like this would happen?" Ji An'an sighed, but she soon smiled. "But Zhou Yang and I are different from them. We've known each other since we were young and we've had feelings for each other for so long. Nobody could compare to us."

Shen Mo felt a tightness in his chest. He chatted with Ji An'an a little longer before he turned in for the night. Later, Ji Mingxuan finished working and got in bed as well.

---

[1] This honorific title is used for second sons, typically only ones that come from families of a certain station. Its meaning is more or less equivalent to "second young [master]."

After the lights were turned off, Shen Mo said in the dark, "It's unfair to Miss Ji."

"What?"

"She thinks she and Zhou Yang are really in love."

Ji Mingxuan replied, "Are they not?"

Shen Mo was quiet for a moment. "On the twelfth, Zhou Yang asked to see me first."

Ji Mingxuan didn't seem surprised at all.

Shen Mo's heart raced. He'd long since been suspicious that Ji Mingxuan had known from the beginning, but only now was he absolutely sure.

The two tickets... Had he booked them on purpose?

"So what if he called you out? He still chose An'an in the end."

"Because you interfered, Mr. Ji."

Ji Mingxuan gave a light snort. "You think I threatened Zhou Yang? You're wrong. There was no way for me to do something like that. I only told him about his father's illegitimate son ahead of time. He wasn't the only heir of the Zhou family, so whatever he did would affect his status in his family. I showed him the stakes, and..."

Ji Mingxuan smiled and continued, "He made the choice by himself."

Shen Mo had known since three years ago what kind of choice Zhou Yang would make. What had happened this time was just a kind of repetition. His own heart was numb already. He was only worried about Ji An'an.

"What comes out of this will be nothing more than fake love."

"Only high-schoolers care about love nowadays. Adults care about profit. Do you know how many benefits an arranged marriage between the Zhou and Ji families could bring? As for love..." Although they were in the dark, Shen Mo could imagine the dismissive expression on Ji Mingxuan's face. "It doesn't matter whether or not he likes her. As long as they're tied together for now, feelings will eventually form."

"What if no feelings form between them?"

"If so," it seemed as if Ji Mingxuan smiled, replying in a low voice, "they will have already spent their entire lives together, anyway."

It was nothing more than self-deception.

Of course, Shen Mo, too, knew that it was true of most arranged marriages.

"Wouldn't they be just like Zhou Yang's parents, then?"

Ji Mingxuan replied coldly, "Or else what? Should they elope like you and Zhou Yang wanted to?"

Shen Mo was stunned for a moment.

Ji Mingxuan also seemed to notice that he had lost his cool. He ended the conversation there and went to sleep, turning his back to Shen Mo.

Yet, for a while, Shen Mo wasn't able to fall asleep. Thinking about what they had just talked about, he felt his face burn.

Ji Mingxuan had used the word "elope," and he'd been right. Wasn't eloping exactly what Shen Mo had dreamt of when he'd still been young and naïve? However, this dream of his had been shattered by reality.

He didn't know how he had found the courage to talk to Mr. Ji that way. Did it really matter that Ji Mingxuan's view of love was completely different from his own? Did he have to argue like that with Ji Mingxuan?

He didn't.

And he didn't have the right to.

It was normal that he was in a bad mood, feeling abandoned now that his ex was getting married—this is how Shen Mo convinced himself enough to finally fall asleep.

He woke up late again the next morning. He only got to work on time after hurrying as much as he could. His colleagues were still gossiping in the office. The illegitimate son was causing quite the disturbance in the Zhou family, but it was just gossip to other people, so, overnight, the subject had changed, and they'd switched to discussing celebrity rumors.

"That Zhao Yi, the one who's been popular recently—everyone's saying he has some special connections."

"Who doesn't have connections in the entertainment industry?"

"But he's incredibly handsome, and he knows how to get along with people. He used to be a nobody, but his luck has gotten better recently. He has major roles in almost every show."

"It's because he has sharp eyes and played up to the right connections."

Everyone laughed when they heard it.

Shen Mo felt a little hot, so he stood up and opened a window to let some air in.

When he got home in the evening, he found that Ji An'an was sulking. He asked why and was told that Ji Mingxuan had promised to have dinner with her, but a social event came up at the last minute.

"He's always attending these events. I don't even know how many times we can eat together in a whole year. Shen-ge, how can you stand him?"

How could Shen Mo reply? He could only say, "I'm used to it."

Then he asked, "Why don't you ask Zhou Yang to have dinner with you?"

"Zhou Yang is busy dealing with family business." Ji An'an sighed, adding, "But it's okay. Brother said it'll be over soon."

She trusted Ji Mingxuan with all her heart.

Shen Mo opened his mouth, but he still didn't say anything. Perhaps Ji Mingxuan was right. Zhou Yang and Ji An'an would take what they needed from each other—this way, they could still live together for their entire lives.

Shen Mo thought that Ji Mingxuan would spend the night outside after the event, just as usual. To Shen Mo's surprise, Ji Mingxuan came home at night, even though it was already past ten. There was the scent of tobacco on Ji Mingxuan's clothes, but his eyes looked clear. He didn't seem drunk.

It was as Shen Mo had expected; it was rare to see Mr. Ji drunk.

"Mr. Ji, you're back."

He hummed in acknowledgement.

"Miss Ji was complaining about you not having dinner with her."

"I know."

Ji Mingxuan went to shower before he got in bed. During this time, he only said two sentences to Shen Mo. The next day, Ji Mingxuan made up for the meal he owed Ji An'an. He spent all his time attending to her, not giving Shen Mo a single glance.

A few days passed, and Shen Mo gradually realized that Ji Mingxuan was being passive-aggressive toward him.

Shen Mo didn't remember any instance of this happening in the past. Before, when Ji Mingxuan had wanted to ignore him, Ji Mingxuan would leave home for anywhere between a few days up to a fortnight. It was different this time, though. No matter how late Ji Mingxuan came back, he'd sleep at home and turn his back to Shen Mo on purpose.

Without thinking, Shen Mo knew that what he'd said that night had offended Mr. Ji. He wasn't afraid of the cold shoulder—he was used to being completely ignored at work anyway. Like he'd told Ji An'an, he had gradually gotten used to many things.

Perhaps it was time to move back to his own bedroom.

Those who wore matching rings weren't necessarily lovers.

Those who lay in the same bed didn't necessarily know each other's hearts.

They slept together yet dreamed of different things.

Shen Mo moved back to his bedroom quietly. At night, he fell asleep the moment his head hit the pillow. The next morning, he woke up only to find that Ji Mingxuan was still sleeping next to him. For a moment, he was stunned—he even thought that he might have sleepwalked. Only when he was a little more awake did he realize that he was indeed in his own bedroom.

Ji Mingxuan was sleeping soundly.

The sky had almost brightened.

The morning light shone on Ji Mingxuan's face. His eyes were closed and his hair was a little messy, making him look less domineering and much younger than usual.

As Shen Mo got closer, he could see the shadows cast by Ji Mingxuan's long eyelashes.

Right then, Ji Mingxuan opened his eyes. His dark eyes looked straight into Shen Mo's.

Somehow, Shen Mo felt a little flustered. He turned to the side and asked, "Mr. Ji, you're awake?"

It was as though Ji Mingxuan hadn't fully woken up yet. He gazed at Shen Mo for a while longer before he nodded, then he hummed in affirmation.

"Mr. Ji, why did you sleep here last night?"

Ji Mingxuan slowly sat up, replying calmly, "If we slept in two rooms, wouldn't we make An'an suspicious?"

Ji Mingxuan didn't mention how he himself had used to stay out late in the past.

With his awkward personality, Shen Mo couldn't come up with a retort in time. Ji Mingxuan had made the decision already. "Let's sleep here these next few days."

As he spoke, he lifted the covers and got out of bed.

When Ji Mingxuan was putting on his shirt, Shen Mo inadvertently noticed that Ji Mingxuan still wore the cufflinks Ji An'an had bought him. Shen Mo could tell that Ji Mingxuan really loved his only sister. Shen Mo could only help him finish the act.

Today was the weekend again.

Ji Mingxuan went to work after breakfast. Ji An'an didn't have to go to work, so she moved to the seat beside Shen Mo and asked, "Shen-ge, did something happen between you and my brother?"

Shen Mo hadn't expected her to notice it. He denied, "No, Mingxuan and I... We're fine."

Ji An'an didn't believe him. "I don't know anything else, but I can tell when Brother is in a bad mood. He's clearly been sulking these days."

Shen Mo couldn't admit it. He remained silent instead.

Ji An'an said, "Our mother passed away when I was young, and our father was always busy with the business. I was basically brought up by my brother alone. He has a bad temper, but he spoils his family a lot. If you two are really fighting, you just need to coax him."

Coax Ji Mingxuan?

Mr. Ji wasn't an elementary school kid. How could he coax Mr. Ji?

Just the idea of it amused Shen Mo. But before the passive-aggression between him and Ji Mingxuan ended, the day of An'an and Zhou Yang's engagement was already set.

The Zhou family's situation was complicated, so maybe they would need to conduct the marriage very soon. That might have been why the engagement date was also chosen to be so early. The engagement banquet was to be held in Dynasty Hotel, the most famous hotel in H city.

Shen Mo had wanted to find an excuse, but he han't been able to turn down Ji An'an's relentless invitations. In the end, he decided to attend.

On the day of the engagement, the weather was excellent. Most of the people present were business partners of the Zhou and Ji families. Shen Mo didn't see anyone he knew, so he wandered around by himself. The hotel's lobby was splendid—the crystal lights hanging above looked especially beautiful, reflecting a myriad of colors.

Lost in thought, Shen Mo suddenly heard someone call his name, "Mr. Shen."

Shen Mo turned around and saw Zhao Yi in a white suit. Zhao Yi was good-looking to begin with, but he looked even more charming in white. He almost seemed to shine among the crowd, his every move attracting the other people's attentions.

Shen Mo didn't expect to meet Zhao Yi here. He was surprised for a moment before he greeted, "Mr. Zhao, you also came?"

"The marriage between the Zhou and Ji families is quite a story in this city. Of course I wanted to come and take a look. Besides, I received my invitation..." Zhao Yi smiled at Shen Mo as he continued, "from Mr. Ji himself."

Hearing Zhao Yi says this, Shen Mo realized that it had already been a few days since the last time he'd seen Ji Mingxuan. He slept heavily at night while Ji Mingxuan had been busy preparing for the engagement. He didn't even know whether Ji Mingxuan had been sleeping at home or not.

Zhao Yi looked around, asking, "Where's Mr. Ji?"

Shen Mo replied, "Mingxuan has a lot of friends. He's busy greeting the guests."

"What a busy guy."

"Yes, he's always been this way."

Somehow, greeting Zhao Yi made Shen Mo feel a little embarrassed. Shen Mo wanted to finish the conversation and leave, but unexpectedly, the lights within the hall dimmed.

As the music started, Zhou Yang and Ji An'an came out hand in hand. They were both in formal clothes. Zhou Yang's black suit and Ji An'an's white dress made them quite a matching pair. A single beam of light illuminated the two, and they were rather dazzling.

Shen Mo looked at them from afar. Nothing felt natural to him. The Zhou Yang of his memories was from three years ago—the man before him who was about to become Ji An'an's husband seemed so unfamiliar to him.

Shen Mo didn't notice until a while later that Ji Mingxuan was also standing nearby.

Ji Mingxuan cast his gaze over. It seemed to land on Shen Mo for an instant before it left.

Shen Mo wasn't sure if it had been his imagination.

He heard someone at the side whisper, "The Ji family is full of good-looking people."

"The sister is getting married soon, but the brother is still single."

"There's a lot of gossip around Mr. Ji. If he wants to get married, he can have his pick among so many wealthy ladies."

Also hearing these words, Zhao Yi glanced at Shen Mo and raised his eyebrows slightly.

Shen Mo felt even more uncomfortable.

Fortunately, the engagement banquet was nothing more than a necessary part of the procedure. Everything was finished after Zhou Yang and Ji An'an cut the cake and poured the champagne. Everyone applauded when the two kissed. Shen Mo's hands even started to hurt from clapping with the crowd.

Later, the lights came on again. Considering Shen Mo to be family, Ji An'an directly came to talk to him. She'd had some champagne on the stage just now. Her cheeks were flushed, adding a touch of color to her face. She was already wearing the engagement ring on her left hand; it refracted a dazzling light under the chandelier.

Ji An'an patted her chest and said, "I was so nervous just now."

"Anyone would feel that way." Shen Mo said sincerely, "Congratulations."

Ji An'an smiled as she sipped her champagne, asking, "I can tell that Brother's in a good mood today. Have you two made up already?"

Shen Mo replied without thinking, "Of course."

Ji An'an was envious. "Zhou Yang and I... I hope we can be like you and Brother."

Shen Mo said, "You two will definitely be better than us."

As they chatted, they saw Zhao Yi approach Ji Mingxuan with a glass of champagne in his hand.

Ji An'an had also heard of the rumors. She looked a little annoyed, muttering, "Why did he come too?"

As she spoke, she grabbed Shen Mo's hand. "Come, let's go to find Brother."

Shen Mo couldn't get his hand out of her grip, so he could only follow her toward Ji Mingxuan.

Halfway through, Shen Mo passed a tall man. The man looked fine at first, but a deep scar on his brow made him quite conspicuous.

With only a glance at the man, Shen Mo's face turned pale. Feeling his legs weigh him down, he froze where he stood, unable to take another step.

Ji An'an turned around and asked, "Shen-ge, what's the matter?"

Shen Mo's hand, held by hers, also grew cold. He said, "The person just now..."

"Who?" Ji An'an turned, looking around as she said, "Oh, you mean the guy with a scar on his face? Mrs. Zhou hired him as a bodyguard. He's responsible for the security of the engagement banquet. I think he's a distant cousin of Zhou Yang's too.

"He looks so aggressive and scary," Ji An'an whispered. "I heard he's involved with gangs. He's been in jail before. He got out not too long ago."

There was not a trace of blood on Shen Mo's face. It took him quite some time to regain his voice. He murmured, "...I know."

Ji An'an couldn't catch what Shen Mo had said, adding, "I don't like this cousin of Zhou Yang's either, but I have no choice. Mrs. Zhou favors her relatives. Whoever he is, it'll be fine as long as we don't bother him."

Shen Mo said, "Okay."

A tremble had crept into his voice. He knew exactly what would happen if he bothered the man.

That was when Ji An'an noticed that there was really something wrong with Shen Mo. "Shen-ge?"

Like a bird at the sight of a bow, Shen Mo flinched when he heard her voice.

Standing in the crowded hall of the hotel, Shen Mo felt as if he had returned to that day three years ago. It had been a day like any other. Zhou Yang had gone back to the Zhou family for a few days, so Shen Mo had gone out alone to do some shopping. He would never have guessed that he'd be abducted.

"Shen-ge, are you okay?" Ji An'an called him again.

As his attention returned to the present, Shen Mo tried to calm down. He said, "I don't feel too well. I'm going to the restroom."

Ji An'an saw that his face did look pale, so she let go of his hand, asking, "Do you need Brother to go with you?"

Shen Mo looked at where Ji Mingxuan was standing.

Ji Mingxuan was talking to Zhao Yi. Whatever they were talking about, Zhao Yi laughed quite happily, his eyes fixed on Ji Mingxuan.

Shen Mo shook his head. "No. I'll be fine after some rest."

He left the crowd and headed for the restroom.

The lighting of the hall was a little too bright, shedding a whiteness over people's faces. Everyone—no matter man or woman, old or young—seemed to have a gruesome scar on their brow bone. The way to the restroom was short, but Shen Mo's pace was jolting and slow. When he entered the restroom, sweat had covered his forehead. Even the hair on his temples was wet.

In the mirror, his face looked frighteningly pale. After taking a look at it, Shen Mo looked down and washed his hands.

Cold water ran along his skin.

The injury on his right hand had healed long ago, leaving behind not even the trace of a scar. But he would never forget how someone had stepped on his hand and broken his fingers, one by one.

When he had been abducted, he'd originally had the chance to escape. He had hidden in the grass and dialed Zhou Yang's number over and over, but he hadn't been able to get through to him no matter what, even though the string of numbers had been engraved in his heart.

Later, he had been caught and taken back again, only to find out from his abductors that Zhou Yang had already gone abroad with Ji An'an. Ridiculous—he, the one who had been left behind, had been the last to know the truth.

At the time, he lay on the ground, his body covered in injuries. His fingers were being crushed, and as he listened to his bones crack, he couldn't even cry out in pain.

The pain had left an indelible scar in him.

Tap. Tap. Tap.

Suddenly, from outside the restroom came a series of footsteps.

Shen Mo's hands trembled, as if he'd returned to that time when he had been desperately trying to escape. In a hurry, he hid in one of the stalls and locked the door firmly.

The footsteps were getting closer. Finally, the person entered the restroom. The person stopped for a few moments in front of every stall, as if he was looking for someone.

Shen Mo was scared. He took his phone out of his pocket and rapidly dialed a number he'd long since memorized.

The name "Ji Mingxuan" popped up on the phone screen.

Staring at the name, Shen Mo was stunned.

He had almost forgotten where he was, but he still remembered that he was being ignored by Ji Mingxuan.

If he dialed the number, would Mr. Ji answer the phone?

He was scared of the man with a scar on his face. He was scared of the nightmarish memories. But what scared him the most... was the possibility that nobody would answer, even if he dialed the number.

Perhaps Ji Mingxuan would still be talking to Zhao Yi. He wouldn't even hear his phone ring.

Shen Mo stared at the name on the screen. Only when his eyes began to feel sore did he press delete, his fingers cold.

That day, three years ago, he had called Zhou Yang's name countless times.

He didn't learn the lesson until after he woke up in the hospital room. Nobody could save him except for himself.

The footsteps were getting closer and closer.

Shen Mo took a deep breath. He gripped his phone in one hand and clenched his other into a fist.

The footsteps stopped in front of the stall in which Shen Mo was hiding. Next, a few knocks sounded from beyond the door.

Shen Mo couldn't stop shaking. Afraid that he might make a noise, he bit his fingers hard. Just then, he heard the person outside call his name, "Shen Mo."

The voice sounded too familiar to him.

Shen Mo jolted, as if he'd suddenly fallen into a dream. The last shred of strength disappeared from his body. Putting his hands against the door, he whispered, "Mr. Ji?"

He was afraid that his own voice would wake him from the dream.

Ji Mingxuan replied, "It's me."

Shen Mo was quiet for a little longer before he slowly opened the stall door.

Standing outside the stall was Ji Mingxuan, of course. For the sake of Ji An'an's engagement, he was particularly well-dressed. He looked quite handsome in his tailored suit.

He studied Shen Mo and asked, "I heard from An'an that you're not feeling well?"

Shen Mo didn't reply. Stunned, he gazed at Ji Mingxuan for a while before he looked down and fumbled for his phone. After he typed string of numbers, the name "Ji Mingxuan" showed on the screen again. This time, he didn't hesitate and pressed down on the call button.

A ringtone sounded at once.

Ji Mingxuan looked a little surprised, but he still took out his phone.

Shen Mo held the phone and looked straight into Ji Mingxuan's eyes. As he listened to the phone beep beside his ear, Shen Mo was so nervous that sweat started seeping from his palms. He didn't know how long had passed when Ji Mingxuan's low voice came through the phone: "Shen Mo?"

After so many tries... someone had finally picked up the call.

Shen Mo's legs gave out. He almost fell to the ground.

Ji Mingxuan grabbed his arm just in time. "What's wrong? Are you feeling sick?"

"Mr. Ji..." Shen Mo held onto Ji Mingxuan's clothes and said, "I saw him..."

"Who?"

Not knowing how to describe the man, Shen Mo only pointed at his own brow bone and said, "He... has a scar here."

His words were quite jumbled. Even he himself thought that he'd been too incoherent. But Ji Mingxuan understood.

Ji Mingxuan nodded and said, "So it was him."

He added, "Who would've thought that he'd be out of jail so soon?"

Shen Mo found it a little strange. "You still remember him, Mr. Ji?"

Ji Mingxuan didn't reply. He reached for Shen Mo's chin, looked into Shen Mo's eyes, and asked, "Are you scared?"

Shen Mo opened his mouth, but he couldn't say anything.

He, too, knew that he was being a little delusional. That year, he had been abducted only because of Zhou Yang. He had nothing to do with Zhou Yang now. Would anyone even give him a second glance?

And yet, his body still remembered the fear from back then. He really couldn't control it.

Shen Mo didn't say anything, so Ji Mingxuan didn't press on. He squeezed Shen Mo's hand and asked, "Why are you so cold?"

As he spoke, he took off his suit jacket and tossed it to Shen Mo.

Startled, Shen Mo clumsily caught the jacket.

Ji Mingxuan rolled up the sleeves of his shirt as he told Shen Mo, "Wait for me here."

"Mr. Ji?" Shen Mo was puzzled.

Ji Mingxuan didn't respond and went straight toward the door. When he was almost at the door, he turned around and said with a faint smile, "Just wait."

Shen Mo was so used to listening to Ji Mingxuan that he didn't even think of doing anything else. He simply held the jacket and waited for Ji Mingxuan in the stall.

He could still feel Ji Mingxuan's warmth on the jacket.

It was strange that Shen Mo could calm down after exchanging just a few words with Ji Mingxuan. The fear that he had felt faded away like a receding tide.

Shen Mo didn't know how long had passed when strange sounds suddenly came from outside.

He didn't know what had happened, so he went out and ran toward the noise. Soon, he saw a crowd gathered in the hallway leading to the main hall. He could hear the people's chatter even from afar.

"What a surprise. That Mr. Ji really..."

"Is he drunk?"

"Who knows? Strange things happen every year. There have been quite a lot this year."

When he heard that it was related to Ji Mingxuan, Shen Mo grew even more nervous. He held the jacket tightly and squeezed his way through the crowd. When he finally got in, he saw Ji Mingxuan standing there wearing a single layer, the sleeves of his shirt rolled up to his elbows. For some reason, his right hand was injured, bleeding slightly.

Not far from Ji Mingxuan, a man lay on the ground. He had a hideous scar on his brow bone, but his face was black and blue. It was quite an embarrassing look.

Seeing such a scene, even if he'd been an idiot, Shen Mo would have understood what had happened.

He stood still.

Ji Mingxuan glanced around and soon saw Shen Mo. He waved at Shen Mo as though nothing had happened. "I told you to wait for me, didn't I?"

Shen Mo felt his heart beat faster than ever.

Step by step, he walked toward Ji Mingxuan.

He had long since learned that, apart from himself, no one would come to his rescue.

But what if he couldn't rescue himself?

In that case...

In that case he would still have Mr. Ji.

Shen Mo didn't know how he had walked to Ji Mingxuan. When his attention returned, Ji Mingxuan was already holding his hand tightly.

A while later, Zhou Yang hurried over. When he saw Ji Mingxuan holding hands with Shen Mo, he looked surprised for a moment, but he quickly concealed it, asking, "What happened?"

"Nothing," Ji Mingxuan unrolled the sleeves of his shirt and replied. "I drank too much and accidentally knocked into him."

Seeing the current situation, Zhou Yang knew that what Ji Mingxuan had said was not true. Although the people around them were whispering, no one refuted Ji Mingxuan.

And so, Zhou Yang said, "I see."

Ji Mingxuan patted Zhou Yang's shoulder and spoke naturally, "Help me handle it, Brother-in-law."

"Of course," Zhou Yang swallowed before he said, "Brother."

After his reply, Zhou Yang looked to Shen Mo. But before Shen Mo could meet his eyes, Ji Mingxuan had already pulled Shen Mo away.

Shen Mo followed Ji Mingxuan without thinking. He caught a glimpse of Zhao Yi standing in the crowd, but Ji Mingxuan went straight out of the hotel's hall, not even giving Zhao Yi a single glance.

There was a small garden outside the hall. The hotel had spent a great deal of money crafting the beautiful scenery. A variety of unknown plants surrounded the garden, and in the middle of the garden flowed a small stream. That night it was the fifteenth of the month according to the lunar calendar, so the moon looked big and round, and the moonlight shone quietly down on the ground, creating a quiet, pleasant atmosphere.

Ji Mingxuan slowed down and said, "I wanted to get some fresh air and sober up a little."

Shen Mo had seen Ji Mingxuan drunk. He knew that Ji Mingxuan was more than sober now, but he didn't point it out. He looked at Ji Mingxuan's hand and said, "You got hurt, Mr. Ji."

Only now did Ji Mingxuan remember. He said, nonchalant, "It's just a scratch."

Shen Mo grabbed Ji Mingxuan's hand and examined it in the moonlight. The injury was just a scratch indeed, but it also meant that Ji Mingxuan had really meant to do harm during that fight.

Shen Mo's heart beat faster than usual. He felt as if he was still in a dream.

Only, not even in his dreams would Shen Mo ever have expected Mr. Ji to fight someone in public.

Gripping Ji Mingxuan's hand, Shen Mo asked, "Do you want to go to the hospital?"

Then Shen Mo said to himself, "So many people saw you hit that guy. How will they write about it in the newspapers tomorrow?"

Ji Mingxuan laughed. "What do you think? They'll probably write about the marriage between the Ji and Zhou families and what a good match the couple is. Nothing else will be mentioned."

With Ji Mingxuan's abilities, it'd be extremely easy to cover up this incident. But people like him usually held their social statuses in high regard; they'd never lose their grace in public like he had.

And that was why so many people had been shocked by Ji Mingxuan's behavior today.

"Mr. Ji."

"Yes?"

"Why did you... hit him?"

Shen Mo thought he might know the answer, but he wasn't sure. He wanted to hear it from Ji Mingxuan directly.

Yet, Ji Mingxuan didn't answer the question. Instead, he clasped Shen Mo's hand and said, "Walk with me."

The garden wasn't big; they reached its end after just a while. As if he wasn't satisfied, Ji Mingxuan held Shen Mo's hand and walked around the garden over and over again.

When Shen Mo saw that Ji Mingxuan wasn't saying anything, his mind began to wander. He didn't know what he'd been thinking about when he suddenly heard Ji Mingxuan call his name: "Shen Mo."

Shen Mo absently turned around, only to find that Ji Mingxuan had already stopped and was now looking down at him.

Ji Mingxuan's features looked quite beautiful in the hazy moonlight.

Ji Mingxuan gazed at Shen Mo quietly, as if he had been looking at Shen Mo for a long time. His eyes were as tender as water, gently sweeping over Shen Mo's face.

Shen Mo's heartbeat quickened again. He could only say, "Mr. Ji..."

All was silent in the moonlight.

Ji Mingxuan said nothing. He lowered his head, and then tenderly kissed Shen Mo on his lips.

Shen Mo didn't sleep well that night. He woke up drowsily the next morning. He clearly hadn't had any alcohol, but he still felt like he had been drunk. Many of his memories were hazy—like that of Zhou Yang and Ji An'an's impressive engagement banquet or the scar-faced man who had scared him so much that he'd started shaking. The only thing that he could remember clearly was how Ji Mingxuan had rolled up his sleeves before the fight, and... the kiss beneath the moonlight.

Shen Mo touched his lips. Even after an entire night, he still felt a slight tingle there.

He had woken up late this morning. When he got downstairs, the Ji siblings were already in the dining room. Ji An'an was asking Ji Mingxuan what had happened last night.

"I heard Zhou Yang's cousin used to be involved with gangs. Brother, how could you fight him? Weren't you worried that he'd knock you over in a single punch? What if something happened to you?"

Due to her nagging, Ji Mingxuan could only answer, "I knew that. I wasn't worried. That could never happen."

Ji An'an's curiosity wasn't satisfied yet. Cupping her chin in her hands, she added, "They said you were drunk. But from what I know, your tolerance shouldn't be that bad."

Ji Mingxuan replied casually, "They can say whatever they want."

Obviously, Ji An'an wasn't content with such an answer. When she saw Shen Mo come over, she asked, "Shen-ge, you were with my brother yesterday. Do you think he was actually drunk?"

Although Shen Mo knew the truth, he couldn't explain it to Ji An'an. Fortunately, Ji Mingxuan helped him out and changed the subject. "An'an, do you have today off?"

"Yeah, it's the weekend today."

"There's an auto show in the afternoon. Pick a car there. Think of it as my engagement present for you."

"There are so many cars in the garage already. We can drive any one of them. Why buy a new one?"

"But this is different." Ji Mingxuan smiled as he turned to Shen Mo. "I'm busy today. You can go with An'an, and also see if there's any car that you like. You have a driving license, don't you? There's no need to walk to work every day."

Shen Mo didn't expect that he'd also be asked to go. He was about to turn down the offer, but Ji An'an spoke before him, "Alright, alright. If I go with Shen-ge, I'll definitely find a car I like. Don't worry, Brother."

As she spoke, she winked at Ji Mingxuan.

Ji Mingxuan let out a laugh and didn't say anything else. After breakfast, he went to work.

Ji An'an returned to her bedroom, got changed, and put on makeup. Then she begged Shen Mo to go with her. Shen Mo had no choice but to accompany her to the auto show.

They had lunch outside. Ji An'an talked about cars the entire way, asking Shen Mo for his favorite brand, type, and output volume of a car. Shen Mo never paid too much attention to cars, so he didn't really know what he liked. He could only reply, "Pick whatever you like. I just came to take a look. I don't actually have to buy a car."

Ji An'an gave him one glance and couldn't help laughing. "Did you think Brother really wanted to give me an engagement present? He wanted to buy you a car, but he was too embarrassed to mention it, so he used me as an excuse. Believe it or not, if you don't buy a car today, he'll give you one tomorrow—an extremely expensive one, too."

In the past, Shen Mo would never have believed this. But after what had happened last night, he wasn't so sure anymore. He had a straight-forward personality, unlike Ji Mingxuan, who would go in such a roundabout way just to buy him a car, so he'd always found it hard to fathom Mr. Ji's thoughts.

Ji Mingxuan was the only thing on Shen Mo's mind. At the auto show, however, he just so happened to run into Zhou Yang.

Ji An'an was also surprised. She whispered, "I just sent him a mes-sage. I didn't ask him to come."

But after all, Ji An'an was in love with Zhou Yang. She was naturally glad to see him, asking with a grin, "Why are you here?"

"My fiancée wants to buy a car. Of course I have to come and see."

"Didn't you say you had some family business to deal with? That cousin of yours..."

"I've dealt with it already." Zhou Yang's face looked unpleasant for a moment. Whether intentionally or not, his eyes swept over Shen Mo's face as he added, "He offended someone he shouldn't have offended. Looks like it'll be tough on him."

Ji An'an immediately spoke up for her brother, "My brother isn't the kind of person to abuse his power either. There was definitely a reason why he lashed out at the engagement banquet last night."

Zhou Yang nodded. "I think so too."

He seemed like he didn't want to talk about the matter any longer, suggesting, "Let's check out the cars first."

Yet, Ji An'an pointed to the distance and exclaimed, "Isn't that your new brother?"

At the engagement banquet yesterday, Shen Mo had also noticed Zhou Yang's half-brother from afar. Now that he was closer, he found that the guy did look a little like Zhou Yang. But the two really had different temperaments. Zhou Yang didn't talk much, while his younger brother, Zhou Chu, was quite talkative and charming.

Zhou Yang didn't like this younger brother of his who had just been accepted into the family. He said with indifference, "He just joined the Zhou family and he doesn't have a car yet, so he came with me to take a look."

"Should we go say hi to him?"

"No. Just ignore him."

Ji An'an didn't like Zhou Chu very much, so she grabbed Zhou Yang's hand and walked on. It was unavoidable that Shen Mo felt awkward beside the couple, so he suggested looking around on his own.

Ji An'an still remembered the "task" that Ji Mingxuan had assigned her. However, Zhou Yang was the one to say, "Men and women have different tastes. Shen Mo can look around on his own."

Ji An'an then agreed and left with Zhou Yang.

Shen Mo remembered that Ji Mingxuan had suggested buying him a car before, but he'd always turned down the offers. This time, he really considered the idea. He thought that a car would prove to be quite convenient. Of course, he didn't need to use Ji Mingxuan's money. He'd been working for a few years now, so he could at least afford a car that was practical and not too expensive.

Now that the idea had formed in his mind, Shen Mo began taking a closer look at the cars. Sometime later, he really found a car that satisfied his needs. When he was about to get in and try it out, someone patted him on the shoulder.

Shen Mo turned around. Surprisingly, it was Zhou Yang.

Shen Mo looked around but couldn't find Ji An'an. "Where's Miss Ji?"

"She went to the restroom." Zhou Yang grabbed Shen Mo's arm and said, "I want to talk to you."

Shen Mo refused instantly, "We have nothing to say to each other."

"Shen Mo..." As there were so many people around them, Zhou Yang tried to lower his voice. "At first, I wasn't going to come, but I heard An'an say you were here and I came to find you."

"Don't forget that you got engaged to Miss Ji yesterday."

Zhou Yang's face immediately darkened.

But he didn't let go of Shen Mo. He said, "Let's talk somewhere else."

Shen Mo didn't want to argue with Zhou Yang in public, so he followed Zhou Yang to the emergency exit. After they got to the stairway, he didn't want to go any farther, so he threw off Zhou Yang's hand and asked, "So what do you want to tell me?"

But Zhou Yang kept silent. With a complicated expression, he gazed at Shen Mo for a long time before he finally said, "Three years ago, when I was abroad... did something happen?"

Shen Mo froze a little. A while later, he replied, "It's been too long. I don't remember."

"I found it strange when Ji Mingxuan attacked that guy last night. How could a man as proud as him get so hung up on a bodyguard? Afterward, I spent a long time trying to get that cousin of mine to talk. He said he'd caused you trouble before."

Unconsciously, Shen Mo gripped his own right hand.

Zhou Yang had been standing close to Shen Mo. Now, he took a step closer and asked, "What happened while I was abroad? I couldn't get in touch with you after I got back. Where were you then?"

"What's the point of talking about this now?"

"Of course there's a point! I'd always thought you broke up with me because you no longer loved me. But if..."

"If that wasn't the reason, what would you do? Cancel your engagement with Miss Ji? Have you considered why your cousin abducted me even though I never did anything to him?"

Zhou Yang didn't know how to respond.

Seeing how Zhou Yang looked, Shen Mo suddenly wanted to laugh.

And he did smile a little. He reached out to fix Zhou Yang's collar. This was one of the things he'd often done when they'd been together.

"You know the reason. You just don't have the courage to admit it. Your parents—at least your mother—had known about our relationship for a long time. She went out of her way to hire someone to warn me. It was her way of telling me to never show up in your life again."

Zhou Yang's face paled. "Back then, you..."

"The past is in the past." After fixing Zhou Yang's collar, Shen Mo gently smoothed out the creases on his shirt, adding, "You should cherish the present instead. Miss Ji loves you with all her heart. Don't disappoint her."

Right after the accident three years ago, Shen Mo had indeed felt some kind of resentment. But he'd already gotten over it. Countless relationships in this world ended in regret. There was no need to seek death over them.

Shen Mo finished what he thought he had to say. He didn't care what Zhou Yang thought, and so he left the stairway.

When Shen Mo reached the exit, he suddenly heard a light clink.

Shen Mo took a casual glance. It turned out that somebody was smoking, leaning against the wall. He also happened to look up at Shen Mo. Shen Mo found his features somewhat familiar—they belonged to Zhou Yang's younger brother, Zhou Chu.

Shen Mo was surprised. He didn't know when Zhou Chu had come here. Did Zhou Chu hear what he said to Zhou Yang?

Zhou Chu was quite the natural socializer. His slender eyes narrowed as he smiled at Shen Mo.

Considering how there'd been nothing wrong with the conversation between him and Zhou Yang, Shen Mo didn't really mind this incident. He nodded at Zhou Chu and left.

After the interruption, Shen Mo's interest in buying a car also faded a little. His eyes swept past the cars; he didn't find any he liked. On the other hand, Ji An'an picked a car, and Zhou Yang paid the bill.

Although Zhou Yang had to go back home and couldn't have dinner with his fiancée, the latter was still in a good mood, laughing and chattering alongside Shen Mo the whole way back. When Ji Mingxuan came home at night, she immediately told him all about it.

Listening, Ji Mingxuan said with a wistful smile, "I was the one who wanted to buy you a present. Who would've thought my brother-in-law beat me to it?"

Ji An'an immediately mentioned Shen Mo, "Brother, you can give one to Shen-ge."

Ji Mingxuan then turned to Shen Mo and asked, "How was it? Did you find a car you like?"

"No. There weren't any suitable ones."

"Don't mind it, then."

Ji Mingxuan's tone was indifferent, showing no emotion at all.

Shen Mo had previously been extremely afraid of seeing Ji Mingxuan like this. He'd often been worried that he might have offended Mr. Ji. But now, he was no longer afraid. He only turned his gaze to Ji Mingxuan's right hand.

Ji Mingxuan had injured his hand in the fight yesterday. When they got home, Shen Mo had helped him apply ointment. Shen Mo had then rummaged around for a band-aid and stuck it to his hand. The band-aid, perhaps one of Ji An'an's purchases, had a cartoon figure on it. Ji Mingxuan had worn it to work the next morning, but it was a surprise that Ji Mingxuan still had it on his hand when he came back home from work.

Had Mr. Ji attended his meetings with this sort of band-aid on his hand?

Ji Mingxuan also noticed Shen Mo looking at him. He cleared his throat and hid his hand behind his back. "Let's have dinner."

After dinner, Ji Mingxuan went to shower first. He'd already taken off the band-aid when he went out of the washroom. Shen Mo thought that Ji Mingxuan might have thrown it away. But, after showering, Shen Mo was about to brush his teeth when he found that Ji Mingxuan's cup didn't look quite the same as usual.

There was something colorful on the plain cup. Shen Mo picked it up, only to find that there was a cartoon figure on it. Wasn't this the band-aid that had been stuck on Ji Mingxuan's hand for the entire day?

He couldn't help but feel a little touched. Holding the cup, he looked at it over and over again before he quietly put it back.

That night, Ji Mingxuan didn't sleep too well.

Even after the lamp was turned off, Ji Mingxuan tossed and turned in bed—it was as if there was a pea underneath the mattress that bruised Princess Ji's skin, preventing him from falling asleep.

Shen Mo was the kind of person who slept extremely well, able to fall asleep the moment he laid his head on the pillow. This time, however, he couldn't sleep either, since Ji Mingxuan kept on moving. Just as he considered counting sheep, he heard Ji Mingxuan call in a low voice, "Shen Mo..."

Shen Mo thought it wouldn't be a good idea to pretend that he was asleep, so he replied, "Yes?"

"You're still awake?"

"Yeah."

Ji Mingxuan stayed quiet for a while before he suddenly sat up and turned on the bedside lamp.

The light was a little too bright. Shen Mo had to raise his hand to keep it from his eyes. He vaguely saw Ji Mingxuan reach for something under his pillow.

Was there really a pea?

As he was thinking, he saw Ji Mingxuan toss a small "weapon" toward him. Ji Mingxuan added casually, "It was collecting dust in the garage anyways. You can take it."

Surprised, Shen Mo sat up and saw that what Ji Mingxuan had tossed to him was actually a car key.

As Shen Mo had been at the auto show for almost the whole day, he knew the price of the car the moment he saw the logo on the key. He could never fall asleep now. Clutching the car key in his hand, he didn't know whether or not he should take it.

"Mr. Ji..."

But Ji Mingxuan didn't let Shen Mo finish speaking. He turned off the light. "All right. Go to sleep."

Ji Mingxuan fell asleep soon, and it was Shen Mo's turn to have trouble sleeping. Even when he finally fell asleep, he dreamed that someone was chasing after him to kill him. After trying all he could to dodge the hidden weapons being thrown at him, he took a closer look and realized—hidden weapons? The ground was covered in car keys instead.

The next day, when Ji An'an heard about the gifted car, she quietly laughed to herself for most of the morning.

Shen Mo hesitated for quite some time. But, on Monday, he still ended up driving the car Ji Mingxuan had given him to the company. He was worried that if he didn't, a certain princess would get mad at him again. Only in the past few days had he realized that it wasn't actually so difficult to get along with Ji Mingxuan. The important thing was to do what Ji Mingxuan wanted.

Ji Mingxuan knew what was appropriate—the car he had given Shen Mo wasn't overly luxurious. It was still rather expensive, though. Having driven to work out of the blue, Shen Mo did receive quite some attention.

Fortunately, Shen Mo was used to being mocked by his colleagues. He was focused only on work, ignoring everyone else.

Time flew by. The new year passed just like that.

During this time, Zhou Yang made several phone calls to Shen Mo, but Shen Mo never answered. Shen Mo had originally been receiving the cold shoulder from Ji Mingxuan, but after the night of the engagement banquet, it seemed that the fight was over. Unless Ji Mingxuan was really too busy with work, he went back home for dinner every day and slept beside Shen Mo, almost as if they were an old married couple.

But what did Ji Mingxuan really think of their relationship? Was it a contractual relationship or something else? Ji Mingxuan had never made it clear to Shen Mo.

Shen Mo didn't really notice the passage of time. Only when January was almost over did he realize that spring was approaching.

Ji Mingxuan's birthday was the first day of spring.

It'd been fine before since he hadn't known, but now that he did know and had even received a car from Ji Mingxuan, he knew he was supposed to give Ji Mingxuan a present too.

Shen Mo found it hard to decide on a present. Luckily, he had Ji An'an to help him with it.

"Do you think there's anything my brother can't buy? A normal present would be so boring. How about..." Ji An'an thought for a bit before continuing, "you book two plane tickets and go on an overseas trip with him?"

"A trip?"

"Yeah, the island Zhou Yang and I went to last time was really nice. The beach, the moonlight, the bay... It was so romantic. One day we were planning to go out to sea. But when I got on the yacht and looked—the deck was covered in roses."

Ji An'an must be talking about what had happened when Zhou Yang proposed to her. When she mentioned the memory, her expression was incredibly tender.

But for Shen Mo and Ji Mingxuan to go to the island? It wouldn't be romantic. Instead, it might become some kind of torment.

Shen Mo couldn't directly turn down her suggestion. He found an excuse instead, "That sounds good, but work will be busy around then. Mr. Ji. might not have the time."

"That's easy. Can't we just ask him?"

Ji An'an did exactly what she said. During dinner that evening, she tried to ask the question tactfully.

But it was so obvious that Ji Mingxuan realized her purpose immediately. "Am I free the first few days of February? Why? Do you need me for something?"

"Brother, just let me know if you're free. If you are, then you and Shen-ge can..."

"An'an!"

Shen Mo immediately stopped her.

Ji An'an winked and didn't finish her words.

Ji Mingxuan eyed the two. He frowned a little, as though he was thinking about it, before he answered, "I'll have to check my schedule for next month."

"Then hurry up and ask your secretary."

"What's the rush?" Ji Mingxuan glanced at her and slowly replied, "Let's have dinner first."

After dinner, Ji Mingxuan went into his study.

Shen Mo wanted to watch television in the living room for a bit, yet Ji An'an urged him to ask Ji Mingxuan about the schedule.

"Hurry, hurry. My brother probably didn't think it was such an important thing. He'll end up forgetting it in a second."

Shen Mo had always been unable to dissuade her, and so he went.

Shen Mo didn't want to go to the island at all, so he planned to stop at the door of the study and pretend he'd already asked Ji Mingxuan. To his surprise, the door wasn't completely closed. When he got to the door, he heard Ji Mingxuan calling someone.

"That's right, the first few days of February... What meeting? That's right, it doesn't matter... I don't care how you do it, move it ahead or delay it. Just free up those few days by any means necessary..."

Hearing these words, Shen Mo was stunned. His hands were already on the door knob, but he retracted them after some hesitation. He stood quietly outside the study for a while before he walked back to the living room.

Ji An'an was watching television on the sofa. When she saw that Shen Mo was back, she asked, "How was it? Is my brother free or not?"

Shen Mo was a little absent-minded. He thought for a while and said, "He's probably free."

"Free is free; not free is not free. What does 'probably' mean? Is his schedule not finalized yet?"

Shen Mo's thoughts had long since flown to some unknown place. He didn't explain it to her.

Ji An'an was about to ask him again when her phone suddenly rang. Seeing Zhou Yang's name on the screen, she went to her bedroom to answer the phone.

Shen Mo sat alone in the empty living room. Like during the night of the engagement banquet, when Ji Mingxuan had kissed him under the moonlight, Shen Mo couldn't slow down his heartbeat no matter what he tried.

He thought he should find something to do, so he turned on his laptop and opened his browser. But before he realized it, he found himself checking out plane tickets.

Did he really plan on going to the island with Ji Mingxuan? No, no, no—that was where Zhou Yang had proposed to Ji An'an.

But what if Ji Mingxuan made time for the trip?

Shen Mo considered this problem seriously.

Before they went to bed, Ji Mingxuan came out of the bathroom. He dried his hair as he asked, "Tell me. What are you and An'an planning to do? Early February... is when my birthday is, right?"

Shen Mo was an honest person. He knew he couldn't hide it, so he told Ji Mingxuan everything.

After Ji Mingxuan listened to what Shen Mo said, he looked at Shen Mo and asked, "An'an made the suggestion, and you agreed to it?"

In the beginning, Shen Mo didn't want to go to the island at all. But now that Ji Mingxuan was asking him, for some reason, he replied, "If you want to go, Mr. Ji, of course I'll be down for it."

Ji Mingxuan nodded. He thought for a while before he said, "I don't like that island. Let's go somewhere else. I'll tell my secretary to book the tickets. Just spend these few days packing up your things."

Shen Mo didn't expect Ji Mingxuan to make the decision so soon. He couldn't help but ask, "Will you be free then, Mr. Ji?"

Ji Mingxuan paused for two seconds. Without even blinking his eyes, he replied, "I've asked my secretary to check my schedule. It's quite a coincidence, but I happen to be rather free on those days."

Shen Mo replied with an "oh." It was the first time he realized how good Ji Mingxuan was at lying.

Had Ji Mingxuan concealed himself too well, or was it just that Shen Mo had hidden in his own shell too much to pay attention to him?

Now that the trip was settled, their conversation was finished. After Ji Mingxuan dried his hair, he turned off the lights and went to bed.

Yet, he soon remembered something and turned to Shen Mo. "I'm a bit busy the next few days. I'll be coming home later."

Shen Mo knew that Ji Mingxuan must have moved his work earlier.

Right now was the end of the lunar year, so everyone at the company was probably busy with work. It would definitely take Ji Mingxuan quite a lot of energy after those rushed arrangements he'd made. But when Ji Mingxuan had mentioned it, it was no more than "I happen to be quite free."

Thinking of this, Shen Mo suddenly couldn't wait any longer.

He could keep up the pretense for now, but he couldn't keep it up for his whole life. If there was something Ji Mingxuan didn't want to say out loud, Shen Mo could only say it instead.

He knew Ji Mingxuan hadn't fallen asleep yet, so he called, "Mr. Ji."

"What is it?"

"On the day of Miss Ji's engagement banquet, why did you lash out at that guy?"

Ji Mingxuan hadn't answered him before, and this time he still kept quiet.

But Shen Mo refused to take silence as an answer, asking again, "Mr. Ji?"

Ji Mingxuan sighed. He reached for Shen Mo's hand underneath the blanket, asking Shen Mo instead, "What do you think? Why do you think I did it?"

With his hand being held by Ji Mingxuan, Shen Mo felt his face heat up as well. He was glad that the lights in the room were all off, which gave him the courage to finish his words. He heard himself say in the dark, "Mr. Ji... you must like me a bit, don't you?"

The room was frighteningly quiet.

When Shen Mo said those words, he got so nervous that his palms sweat slightly.

Ji Mingxuan didn't say anything.

So long had passed that Shen Mo thought Ji Mingxuan had already fallen asleep. Yet, suddenly, Ji Mingxuan threw off the blanket and pushed Shen Mo down.

Shen Mo was surprised. "Mr. Ji, you..."

The rest of Shen Mo's sentence was smothered by Ji Mingxuan's kiss.

Ji Mingxuan kissed aggressively. He reached into Shen Mo's pajamas, rubbing Shen Mo's chest somewhat impatiently.

Shivers crawled down Shen Mo's spine. He was erect almost immediately. He remembered that they hadn't had sex in quite a long time. It wasn't the time to succumb to desire, though. Blink once and he'd be fooled by Ji Mingxuan's charms again.

He tried to struggle, but Ji Mingxuan was stronger than him, quickly managing to hold him down. Ji Mingxuan pinned his hands above his head and said in a hoarse voice, "Don't move."

Ji Mingxuan's breaths were a little hurried, just like when he was drunk.

Shen Mo obeyed and stopped moving.

Ji Mingxuan didn't continue the kiss. Instead, he tenderly stroked Shen Mo's face in the dark, all the way from his eyebrows to his eyes, and gradually to his nose. He touched every part of Shen Mo's face before finally stopping at his lips. He asked quietly, "Shen Mo?"

His tone was indescribably gentle.

Shen Mo's heart throbbed. He couldn't help replying, "Yes, Mr. Ji."

Just as he finished, he felt Ji Mingxuan's kiss fall aggressively on him.

The kiss took Shen Mo's breath away. He'd long since forgotten the question he'd been asking before.

As Ji Mingxuan kissed Shen Mo, he played with Shen Mo's nipples, which were very sensitive. It didn't take long for him to cry out, begging, "Mr. Ji..."

Ji Mingxuan kissed Shen Mo for a while before he got up and took off his clothes. He then got on top of Shen Mo again. He had been erect for a while. Slowly and deliberately, he rubbed his erection against Shen Mo's groin.

The motion brought both pleasure and torment to Shen Mo. He grew even harder—wetness gathered between his legs.

Finally, Ji Mingxuan parted Shen Mo's legs and entered Shen Mo's body.

It was a little uncomfortable for Shen Mo, so he instinctively shrunk back. Ji Mingxuan gripped his waist and thrust twice. Heart pounding, Shen Mo couldn't help but cry aloud.

Only when Ji Mingxuan saw that Shen Mo really couldn't withstand it did he slow down, sliding in and out of Shen Mo. Just a few thrusts later, and he felt Shen Mo's insides yield to him, clinging to his erection.

Ji Mingxuan bent one of Shen Mo's legs so that he could go deeper. He drove into Shen Mo's sensitive spot every time he plunged in.

Shen Mo arched his back, exclaiming unconsciously, "Mr. Ji..."

Ji Mingxuan kissed and sucked Shen Mo's earlobe as he said, "Say my name."

Shen Mo wrapped his arms around Ji Mingxuan's shoulders, finally calling, "Mingxuan... Ji Mingxuan..."

Ji Mingxuan's eyes darkened. He slowly drew out of Shen Mo's body before sinking in again. This time, he went even deeper than before. Both of them couldn't help but gasp.

Shen Mo quivered uncontrollably.

Ji Mingxuan kissed downward, in the end landing on Shen Mo's fair neck. He gently nipped at Shen Mo's skin.

"Shen Mo."

Ji Mingxuan still called Shen Mo's name using that tender tone. In the dark, there was an indescribable sense of danger to it.

But this kind of danger was irresistible.

A bit out of his mind, Shen Mo gave an answering hum.

Ji Mingxuan took Shen Mo's hand toward where they were connected. It was wet and sticky there, creating quite an obscene sight. Shen Mo felt as though his heart was going to jump out of his chest.

Ji Mingxuan licked Shen Mo's neck as if he would bite down at any moment He said in a muffled voice, "If I didn't like you, how could you turn me on so much?"

When Shen Mo got up the next morning, he saw a red hickey on his neck in the mirror. Ji Mingxuan had left it last night.

Last night... had really been too much...

Toward the end, he'd been in quite the daze. He wasn't even sure how many times they'd done it. When they had gone to the washroom to shower, fluid had trickled down his thighs as he'd walked.

But what Ji Mingxuan had said last night still felt unreal to him.

Mr. Ji... really liked him?

When had that started?

Unfortunately, Ji Mingxuan kept avoiding the question. Every time Shen Mo had asked him, he'd used his charms to change the topic and his body to show Shen Mo how much he loved him.

In the end, Shen Mo had to use a turtleneck to cover the hickey before he went to work.

From that day on, Ji Mingxuan did get busier at work. But no matter how late he finished, he still slept at home. Now that the two of them had been together for so long, it seemed that they didn't need to say sweet words to each other. It was just that every morning when Shen Mo woke up, he always found himself lying in Ji Mingxuan's arms.

A highly efficient person, Ji Mingxuan's secretary didn't take long to book the plane tickets for the trip. Shen Mo took a glance. It was still a romantic island, a well-known honeymoon destination. Things like the hotel and whatnot had also already been arranged. Shen Mo just needed to take some time to pack his belongings.

But after just a few days of lounging around, Shen Mo was caught by Ji An'an. The date of Ji An'an's wedding had already been determined, and she had to start making preparations for it. Ji Mingxuan was only responsible for paying the bill, and Ji An'an didn't have many close friends in China either. In the end, she could only go to Shen Mo for help.

Conveniently, Shen Mo had a car now, so he could act as a driver for her.

It was still early after they finished shopping, so they went to the nearby Dynasty Hotel for afternoon tea. Ji An'an loved one of the desserts there. Shen Mo found it too sweet, so he only ordered a cup of coffee.

It would be February in a few days. The two were talking about the trip when Shen Mo looked up and saw a familiar figure.

It was quite an attractive lady. Although she was no longer young, time seemed to have treated her well, leaving few traces on her face. She was wearing an ash-gray dress and a set of pearl jewelry in the same color. The outfit was befitting and elegant. On the other hand, Zhou Yang's younger brother, Zhou Chu, was grinning by her side.

Still holding the coffee cup, Shen Mo's hand froze.

Seeing Shen Mo's expression, Ji An'an also turned to look. She was immediately surprised. "Hey, it's Mrs. Zhou. Why is Zhou Chu also beside her?"

Shen Mo didn't say a word.

He'd also seen Mrs. Zhou back at the engagement banquet. He knew that she had been born to a wealthy family and that she had quite a calculating personality. Even Zhou Yang's father probably wasn't her match. Back then, she had been the one... who had broken up him and Zhou Yang.

Ji An'an didn't know about this. She stood up and suggested, "Let's go and say hi to Mrs. Zhou."

Shen Mo, of course, didn't want to greet her. He had long since broken up with Zhou Yang, but he still didn't want anything unnecessary to happen at this point. So he leaned to one side and said, "I'm not that familiar with Mrs. Zhou. I'll just stay here."

Ji An'an complained, "Won't we be family soon anyways?"

But since Shen Mo didn't want to go, she didn't force him. She walked over on her own.

Mrs. Zhou was clearly quite satisfied with Ji An'an as her future daughter-in-law. She grabbed Ji An'an's arm intimately when she saw her. After they talk for a while, Mrs. Zhou decided to straight up drag Ji An'an along with her.

Ji An'an immediately turned around and gave Shen Mo a look. Shen Mo nodded and gestured that he'd wait for her at the same spot.

Even when it came to afternoon tea, someone of Mrs. Zhou's social status couldn't be too casual about it. Soon, someone led them to the

VIP private room.

Shen Mo continued to drink coffee outside.

The afternoon sunshine was quite pleasant, making him feel drowsy. Shen Mo casually flipped through several magazines, in which he happened to see a lot of content related to travel.

He hadn't been interested in these things before. But this time, for some reason, he really began searching for travel guides.

Was it because he was going with Mr. Ji?

Ji Mingxuan had already confessed, but it was still a little vague on Shen Mo's side. Did he like Ji Mingxuan too? Or was he just used to this kind of relationship?

The strange thing was that Ji Mingxuan didn't even ask him about it.

Shen Mo found it quite funny. He was no longer a high school student, but he still felt the butterflies of puppy love.

He did look forward to the moonlit beach, though. He even considered imitating Zhou Yang and covering the bed in roses.

As he thought about this, his phone suddenly vibrated.

It was a new message.

Shen Mo looked down. To his surprise, it was from Ji An'an: "Shenge, I don't really feel well. I'm resting in Room 6018. Could you come over?"

Surprised, Shen Mo immediately stood up from his seat.

He remembered that Ji Mingxuan had mentioned it several times. Ji An'an's health had been bad ever since she was young. If she felt unwell, she should go to the hospital as soon as she could. Ji An'an was outgoing and never looked like a sickly person, but her face was indeed a little paler than the ordinary person's.

Worried about her, Shen Mo walked towards the elevator as he called her on his phone.

Yet no one answered.

Shen Mo pressed the elevator button. Looking at the number flashing red on the screen, he suddenly felt that something was wrong. Ji An'an was in the VIP room with Mrs. Zhou. If she felt ill, she'd be taken under the care of the Zhou family. Why did she ask for him to come over instead? Even if she considered him family and wouldn't feel safe unless she saw him, she could have simply called him. Why did she text him instead?

Shen Mo's eyelid twitched. He felt that this whole matter was odd in every way. But when the elevator arrived, he still walked in. He then called Ji Mingxuan.

Ji Mingxuan really cared about his younger sister. When he heard about it, he replied immediately, "I'll head over at once."

It took at least thirty minutes to get from the company to the hotel. Ji Mingxuan thought about it some more before saying, "An'an is with the Zhou family, so I don't think anything will go wrong. I'm only worried about her health... If the situation is really bad, just call an ambulance."

His words stunned Shen Mo. Was Ji An'an really in such terrible health? Or was Ji Mingxuan just over-worried?

But Shen Mo still answered, "Okay. I'll try to get through to Miss Ji first."

When he hung up, the elevator stopped right at the sixth floor.

No matter if Ji An'an had been the one who had sent the message, something must have happened to her. So Shen Mo didn't think too much about it, walking straight toward Room 6018. Knowing that Ji Mingxuan would arrive later, Shen Mo felt quite confident as well. Whatever was waiting for him, he would just go and see.

When he reached Room 6018, he found that the door wasn't fully closed. Faint sounds came from within.

"An'an?"

Shen Mo called before pushing through the door and walking inside.

It was a two-room suite. It seemed like no one was in the living room in the front. However, a man walked out of the bedroom in the back, his upper body naked. The man asked, "Why did it take you so long to get a shirt?"

When the two made eye contact, both of them were surprised.

"Shen Mo?" Zhou Yang was the first to recover, asking, "Why are you here?"

Shen Mo didn't answer. He only asked, "Where's Miss Ji?"

"An'an? She's having tea with my mom downstairs."

Shen Mo felt relieved. Knowing that he shouldn't stay here for too long, he turned around to leave.

It was at this time that he heard a sudden slam. Someone had shut the door.

Shen Mo rushed over to open the door, but for some reason, he couldn't open it no matter what.

"What's wrong?"

Zhou Yang also came over and made a few attempts, but he couldn't do it either. He understood what was going on after thinking for just a few moments. His face turned dark. "Zhou Chu, that bastard!"

Shen Mo asked, "Your brother set this up?"

"He spilled coffee on me on purpose and then booked a room for me to change my clothes." Zhou Yang glanced at Shen Mo and asked, "What about you?"

"He texted me on Miss Ji's phone."

"What a coincidence. You were in this hotel with Ji An'an too?"

"Miss Ji likes one of the desserts here. We've been coming here often."

Zhou Yang frowned as he said, "Zhou Chu was the one who suggested that we have tea here, today."

It wasn't a coincidence. Someone had planned this on purpose.

Shen Mo immediately remembered the way Zhou Chu had leaned against the wall while smoking at the auto show that day. "Your brother probably already knows about how we used to be."

Zhou Yang's expression changed slightly.

Shen Mo found it a little funny. He said, "What are you afraid of? Do you think he's going to help us come out? Besides, we no longer have anything to do with each other."

Shen Mo's words rendered Zhou Yang speechless.

But Zhou Chu had tried so hard to set up the trap. His goal was clearly not so simple. Shen Mo didn't dare to waste any time. He called the hotel's front desk, asking them to send someone up to open the door. Next, when he remembered that Ji Mingxuan was still on his way here, he called again.

"Hello, Mr. Ji..."

Shen Mo had spoken just a few words when he felt the weight lift in his hand. Zhou Yang had grabbed his phone. When Zhou Yang saw the contact's name on the screen, he threw the phone far away.

Shen Mo's phone wasn't too sturdy. After the drop, it shut down automatically. He couldn't help exclaiming in surprise, "What's wrong with you?"

He went to pick up the phone as he spoke, but Zhou Yang immediately pulled him back.

"Do you really think Ji Mingxuan is such a good person?" Zhou Yang grabbed Shen Mo's arm. "He's the same as Zhou Chu. He'll do anything to get what he wants."

Shen Mo felt chills creep down his back. He asked, "What are you talking about?"

"I looked into what happened back then. It was my fault. I shouldn't have gone abroad without letting you know. But guess what Ji Mingxuan did?" Zhou Yang sneered. He spoke one word at a time, "He was the one... who revealed your identity to my parents."

Zhou Yang didn't speak in a loud voice, but Shen Mo felt as if something had exploded in his ears. He stood stunned for a long time.

There had been a time during which Shen Mo's memory was quite blurry. Between the accident and his recovery, about half a year had passed. Every day had felt hazy to him. He could hardly remember anything except for a few trivialities.

For example—on the day of his abduction, halfway through, he'd found the chance to escape. He called the police first, and then he desperately tried to call Zhou Yang. But in the end, it'd been Ji Mingxuan who'd saved him.

How had Mr. Ji reached him before the police?

Or had the police saved him first whereas Mr. Ji showed up later?

Shen Mo couldn't recall the truth no matter what.

It was also because he had tried as hard as he could to avoid thinking about the accident at all that he'd missed such a detail. But in any case, Ji Mingxuan must have known about his relationship with Zhou Yang since a long time ago.

With what Zhou Yang had just said, Shen Mo felt as if the memories were overcoming him like tidewater. He froze, unable to move.

Everything seemed to have followed somebody's plan—right after Zhou Yang had gone abroad, Shen Mo was abducted. Was it because Zhou Yang's parents knew about their relationship? Or was it because Ji Mingxuan had to get rid of him for the sake of his sister's happiness?

Thinking of Ji Mingxuan's confession to him that night, Shen Mo felt a coldness ripple in his chest.

Was Ji Mingxuan's "love" a lie as well?

"Ji Mingxuan is someone who puts his own interests first," Zhou Yang continued. "He spent so much effort breaking us up only to set the stage for the marriage between the Zhou and Ji families."

Instinctively, Shen Mo protested for Ji Mingxuan, "He did it for his sister..."

"Do you really believe his lies? He knows I don't love Ji An'an at all, but he still forced us together. Does he really have his sister's best interests at heart?"

It was also what Shen Mo could never understand.

Ji Mingxuan seemed to spoil Ji An'an too much. Ji An'an could want anything, and he'd fulfill her wishes no matter right or wrong, by any and all means.

"Mr. Ji meddled with things, but you did all this out of your own will, didn't you? You willingly went abroad with Miss Ji and you willingly got engaged with her. You don't love her, but you've always been lying to her that you do. Mr. Ji set up the trap, but you were the one who step by step walked into it." Shen Mo took a deep breath. "As you said, Mr. Ji might really have been the one who told them about our relationship. But so what? If he didn't, would you have kept it a secret for the rest of your life? And then marry a woman and have children, and keep me as your secret lover?"

Zhou Yang was speechless.

Shen Mo could imagine it. Zhou Yang had indeed thought about this before.

Shen Mo's arm was still in Zhou Yang's grip. They were standing impossibly close. The man Shen Mo had used to love still looked so gentle and handsome.

Shen Mo stared at Zhou Yang for a few moments. He couldn't help but soften his tone. "If two people truly loved each other, no trick could drive them apart."

If two people broke up, it must be because they didn't love each other deeply enough.

Zhou Yang spoke dejectedly. "Can we... really not start over again?"

Shen Mo answered without thinking, "Of course not."

Zhou Yang nodded. Suddenly, he wrapped his arms around Shen Mo and lowered his head to kiss him.

Surprised, Shen Mo instantly raised his knee to kick Zhou Yang. As the kick landed, Zhou Yang groaned in pain, yet he still didn't let go of Shen Mo. As they struggled, they heard someone open the door.

They were both surprised and turned around. The door, which had been firmly closed, was already open. And standing outside the door—was Ji An'an.

The smile that she usually wore on her face had long since disappeared, replaced by an expression so empty that it almost looked numb. She stared straight at Zhou Yang.

Zhou Yang didn't dare to look into her eyes. He cried out, "An'an..."

Shen Mo pushed Zhou Yang aside and said, "An'an, you misunderstood. I actually... received a text message..."

Shen Mo's thoughts were in a mess. He felt like he was the main character of a shoddy romance drama, who could only use the most unconvincing words to speak for himself.

Obviously, Ji An'an didn't believe him.

"You don't have to say anything." She took off something that looked like an earbud from beside her ear. "I heard everything."

Shen Mo processed this for a moment before realizing that someone had probably bugged the room. There might even be a pinhole camera.

And all this must have been Zhou Chu's doing.

Zhou Chu had racked his brains trying to get Zhou Yang and Shen Mo to meet each other so that he could reveal the truth to Ji An'an. He was an illegitimate son who had just been accepted into the Zhou family, so he was probably having quite a tough time. But if he could destroy the marriage between the Zhou and Ji families, Zhou Yang would lose the support of the Ji family, and the situation would be vastly different.

Sure enough, Shen Mo heard Ji An'an say, "I didn't believe what your brother said at first, but who would've known... Zhou Yang, was everything you just said true?"

Ji An'an took a step forward, standing face to face with Zhou Yang, and asked, "You've been lying to me all this time?"

For a long time, Zhou Yang didn't answer.

Only when Ji An'an asked again did Zhou Yang let out a long sigh. He took off his glasses and massaged the bridge of his nose. He'd always cared about his image; even now, he was no different. He put the glasses back on his face and then looked right into Ji An'an's eyes, parting his lips to utter, "That's right."

Ji An'an's body shuddered. Blood drained from her face in an instant.

Zhou Yang saw how she looked, but he continued nonetheless, "I, Zhou Yang, have never loved Ji An'an."

Right as he finished, he received a punch in the face.

It was Shen Mo who had punched him. Shen Mo shook his right hand, realizing for the first time how good it felt to hit someone. Perhaps he should have hit Zhou Yang a long time ago.

Ignoring Zhou Yang's pained groan, Shen Mo turned to Ji An'an and took her hand. "An'an, it's really complicated. Let's talk somewhere else."

Ji An'an shook her head. She was still staring at Zhou Yang, one of whose eyes was swollen. She asked, "Why did you lie to me?"

Zhou Yang chuckled as he covered his right eye. "You should ask your dear brother instead. If he didn't try everything he could to set us up, how could I have ever gotten together with you? How could I have ever... broken up with Shen Mo?"

Ji An'an trembled. It wasn't until then that she finally looked at Shen Mo, asking, "Shen-ge, are you and my brother... also just an act?"

Shen Mo didn't know how to answer the question. "Mr. Ji is already on his way. He can explain everything to you when he gets here."

Ji An'an refused to let go of him, asking stubbornly, "You were together with Zhou Yang in the beginning, weren't you?"

Under such circumstances, Shen Mo could no longer lie to her. He stayed silent for a long while before he said, "It's all in the past."

As Ji An'an blinked, a tear dropped from her right eye, rolling down her cheek. Then she forced her lips into a pale smile. She whispered, "I understand."

Shen Mo hurried to say, "An'an..."

Ji An'an shook off his hand and looked straight ahead with dark, vacuous eyes. She murmured, "So it was all a lie..."

As she spoke, she turned around and stumbled out of the room.

Seeing how she looked, Shen Mo was about to go after her when Zhou Yang caught his wrist.

Shen Mo looked back at Zhou Yang, enraged. "Why did you talk to An'an like that?"

Zhou Yang's glasses were askew from the punch. He looked quite miserable, smiling bitterly. "With what happened, could I keep on lying to her? She'd know the truth sooner or later. Finding out is better than being lied to for the rest of her life."

Shen Mo was so angry that he wanted to punch Zhou Yang again. But he was worried about Ji An'an, so he didn't waste time here. He struggled out of Zhou Yang's grip and went out of the room.

Yet, he was in such a hurry that he ran into the man who'd just rushed in.

Shen Mo looked up. The man in front of him was no other than Ji Mingxuan. Although Shen Mo had known Ji Mingxuan would come over, a mixture of feelings arose when he saw his face. For a moment, Shen Mo couldn't say anything.

Ji Mingxuan was a little out of breath, perhaps from running up to the sixth floor. He first looked at Shen Mo before turning to Zhou Yang, who was still in the room. He was somewhat surprised, but he didn't show any emotion on his face, only asking, "Where's An'an?"

Shen Mo didn't dare to conceal anything. He spoke directly, "Miss Ji found out about everything."

"About what?"

"What happened between Zhou Yang and me."

Ji Mingxuan's face paled. He asked at once, "Where is she?"

"She just ran out."

Ji Mingxuan turned around to run after her.

Shen Mo couldn't help asking, "Mr. Ji, were you... the one who told the Zhou family about my relationship with Zhou Yang?"

Ji Mingxuan stopped for a moment, but he didn't answer the question. He only rushed out of the room.

Shen Mo wanted to follow him, but suddenly he felt as if he no longer had the strength to take even a single step.

Was he afraid of finding out the answer?

Now that all this had happened, what would his relationship with Ji Mingxuan become?

Shen Mo leaned against the door, at a loss as to what to do. Just then, he heard Ji Mingxuan shouting outside, "An'an!"

Shen Mo felt as though something had stung him. His heart raced. An indescribable fear occupied him.

He couldn't help but look back at Zhou Yang.

Zhou Yang was also looking at him.

They both saw terror in each other's eyes.

Zhou Yang straightened his glasses, murmuring, "It'll be okay. I know An'an's personality. She wouldn't do something like that."

One couldn't tell if he was trying to comfort Shen Mo or himself.

Shen Mo rushed out to search for Ji An'an, but his legs gave out and he almost fell to the ground. It was Zhou Yang who helped steady him.

Because of this, they were just a second too late. Following the noise, they caught up right when the elevator was slowly closing. Shen Mo took a quick glance and saw Ji Mingxuan standing inside, his face cold. Ji An'an was lying in his arms with closed eyes. Her face looked bloodless.

Then the elevator closed.

Shen Mo ran so fast that he almost collided with the door. Trying to calm down, he quickly pressed the down button. A few spectators happened to be standing around, so Zhou Yang asked them what had happened.

"What happened? Oh, somebody passed out. But that tall guy looked like he was her family. He probably took her to the hospital."

Hearing that Ji An'an just wasn't feeling well and that nothing had happened to her, Shen Mo felt somewhat relieved. The more anxious he grew, the slower he thought the elevator was. By the time he and Zhou Yang arrived at the first floor, Ji Mingxuan was already driving Ji An'an to the hospital.

Shen Mo gotten here by car too, but he had no idea which hospital Ji Mingxuan had gone to, making it impossible for him to follow them.

On the other hand, after borrowing some clothes from the hotel, Zhou Yang regained his gentlemanly appearance. He took out his phone and made a call. "Yes, Ji An'an... Find out which hospital it is..."

The incident had caused quite some chaos, so of course, Mrs. Zhou had heard about it as well. She hurried out of the VIP room. When she saw Zhou Yang standing next to Shen Mo, she was undoubtedly stunned for an instant. She didn't show anything on the surface, however, and only waved at Zhou Yang.

Shen Mo watched from afar as Zhou Yang walked to her and told her a few things. Then, Mrs. Zhou fumed and slapped Zhou Yang.

With this on top of the punch from before, Zhou Yang's face was even more bruised now. He was in quite a sorry state.

After the slap, Mrs. Zhou pressed her lips tightly together and turned to Shen Mo. Compared to her elegant appearance, her eyes looked so harsh that they could almost devour someone whole.

Shen Mo might have been somewhat scared of her once, but now he didn't mind her all that much. He waited for over half an hour in the hotel's lobby before he finally found out which hospital Ji An'an had been sent to. He didn't want to go there with Zhou Yang, so he drove there by himself.

On his way to the hospital, Shen Mo felt a little apprehensive.

He couldn't forget Ji Mingxuan's shout no matter what. In his memory, seldom had Mr. Ji lost his composure in such a way. When Ji Mingxuan had said that Ji An'an was in poor health, what exactly did he mean? Was it that she was prone to fainting when under stress?

Shen Mo ran two red lights before he reached the hospital. Looking around, he finally found Ji Mingxuan outside the emergency room. Ji Mingxuan sat alone on the bench. His suit had been ironed well, yet it was crumpled now. There was a deep sense of fatigue to him.

Shen Mo couldn't help but slow down, approaching step by step. As if noticing his presence, Ji Mingxuan suddenly turned around to look at him.

His gaze felt lonely beyond words.

Shen Mo paused.

But Ji Mingxuan's frown relaxed. He said, "You came?"

Shen Mo walked over and asked, "How's Miss Ji?"

"She's still in the emergency room."

"Just... what happened to her?"

Ji Mingxuan pointed at the empty spot beside him. "Have a seat."

Shen Mo sat down next to him.

Ji Mingxuan adjusted his posture, folding his hands together as though he was immersed in long-gone memories. A while later, he finally began, "An'an is eight years younger than me. I remember she was born in spring. The wind had felt quite warm that day. It even carried the vague scent of flowers. An'an has always had a good temper. She never cried or threw tantrums and she smiled at everyone she saw."

As Ji Mingxuan spoke, a flicker of a smile bloomed on his face.

"An'an looks a lot like my mother. It's a pity that she passed away not long after she gave birth to An'an." Ji Mingxuan sighed as he continued, "She had a congenital heart disease."

Ji Mingxuan paused, the smile on his face fading away. He said, "An'an inherited the disease."

Shen Mo had noticed a few hints of this before. Only when he heard this now did he come to understand why Ji Mingxuan always spoiled Ji An'an so much. Ji Mingxuan had lost his mother at an early age, and his only sister had been born with poor health. He naturally devoted all his tenderness to this sister of his.

Shen Mo wasn't too good at comforting others. He thought for a while and said, "Medicine is so advanced nowadays. Heart diseases aren't necessarily incurable, either."

"Yes. An'an underwent surgery at a very young age. But the results weren't ideal. Nobody knows when she'll leave this world." Ji Mingxuan closed his eyes for a moment. "I've always thought, no matter what An'an wants, I'll do everything I can to fulfill her wishes. I want her to live happily every day, every minute, every second of her life."

He could sacrifice everything he had so as to offer his sister the entire world.

But...

"But what she wanted was Zhou Yang." Ji Mingxuan sneered. "Hah, Zhou Yang. I never liked Zhou Yang, but it didn't matter as long as An'an loved him. Everyone wanted to see a marriage between the Zhou and Ji families, but who could've known..."

He glanced at Shen Mo and didn't continue.

Shen Mo added silently, *Who could've known that I'd be there as a roadblock?*

"There were unforeseen circumstances, but Zhou Yang still knew what his best choice was. He was willing to cooperate, so I didn't mind presenting an illusion to An'an either..." Ji Mingxuan's voice trembled a little. "An illusion that would make An'an happy."

However, the moment such an illusion fell through, the aftermath would be unimaginable.

Shen Mo remembered that he hadn't yet explained what had happened today, so he briefly told Ji Mingxuan about it.

Ji Mingxuan listened quietly. He only frowned when he heard the name Zhou Chu. In the end, he said, "I understand."

Right now, he was only concerned about Ji An'an's health. He didn't want to waste time on anything unrelated; he could only wait to deal with this matter once she got better.

It didn't take long for Zhou Yang to get there. He had changed his outfit again and treated the wounds on his face somewhat. Whether out of guilt or genuine worry, he asked right as he arrived, "Where's An'an?"

His face cold, Ji Mingxuan didn't even look at Zhou Yang. Shen Mo didn't really want to talk to Zhou Yang either. It was quite awkward for Zhou Yang. Feeling too embarrassed to sit down, he only stood against the wall as he waited.

The atmosphere was solemn. Every instant felt like torture.

Finally, Ji An'an was brought out of the emergency room. Although she was still unconscious, the doctor said her condition had already stabilized and she was no longer in danger.

Ji Mingxuan went to the doctor's office. When he came out, his face was frightfully grim. No matter how Zhou Yang persisted, he answered no questions at all. Eyeing Zhou Yang coldly, he only said, "Get out."

Zhou Yang refused to leave of course, but in fear of causing Ji An'an more distress, he didn't enter the sickroom and instead waited outside.

Shen Mo remembered that Ji An'an had been brought over in a hurry and without any chance to prepare, so he went out to buy some toiletries.

Late into the night, Ji An'an finally woke up.

Shen Mo didn't dare go in. He only watched from behind the glass as Ji Mingxuan leaned down to say a few words to her. He then stroked her hair with tenderness.

Ji An'an nodded, slowly closed her eyes, and fell asleep again.

In the same posture, Ji Mingxuan continued to gaze at her. It wasn't until a long, long time had passed that he gently tucked her in.

For a moment, Shen Mo really felt that Ji An'an was the person Ji Mingxuan loved the most in this world.

Later, Ji Mingxuan left the room.

Zhou Yang and Shen Mo immediately approached him.

Ji Mingxuan spoke only one sentence to Zhou Yang, "An'an said she doesn't want to see you again."

Then he turned to Shen Mo.

Shen Mo clenched his fists, feeling almost as if he was awaiting his sentence.

Ji Mingxuan gazed at Shen Mo for a while before he said, "Let me tell you a few things."

Nowhere in the hospital was suitable for talking, so they ended up choosing to stand in a corner beside the window. It would be the first day of spring in just a few days. The faint scent of flowers seemed to drift along with the breeze.

Shen Mo had been feeling tense the entire day, and he hadn't had much rest. Surprisingly, he was somewhat absent-minded right now. He thought that if Ji An'an hadn't encountered such an incident, he and Ji Mingxuan would be flying to that island in just a few days. He could almost hear the swishing tides...

"Shen Mo."

Ji Mingxuan's voice drew Shen Mo back to reality.

Shen Mo recovered and asked, "What did Miss Ji say? Does she... not want to see me, either?"

Shen Mo had long since mentally prepared himself, but Ji Mingxuan didn't answer directly. Instead, Ji Mingxuan said, "When we were in the hotel, you asked me if I had been the one who told the Zhou family about your relationship with Zhou Yang. I'll give you the answer now."

Shen Mo's heart sped up. A sense of foreboding suddenly overcame him. He hurried to grab Ji Mingxuan's hand. "Mr. Ji, it's fine. I don't want to know anymore..."

Ji Mingxuan turned his wrist so that he also held Shen Mo's hand. He patted it gently, just once.

The gesture was more than usual, but Shen Mo thought that Ji Mingxuan had never been as gentle as he was at this moment. Then, he heard Ji Mingxuan say, "Yes, it was me."

Two weeks later, Shen Mo had a meeting with Ji Mingxuan's lawyer.

When Ji Mingxuan had told him those words back in the hospital, Shen Mo already known that this day would come. No matter if what Ji Mingxuan said was true or not, the fact that he said it meant that the two of them could no longer carry on like they had before.

But Shen Mo hadn't expected that, even when breaking up, Ji Mingxuan refused to come in person. Ji Mingxuan had gotten a lawyer to discuss things with Shen Mo instead.

Was Ji Mingxuan too rational or too cold-blooded?

Or, perhaps, it had all been no more than a contract to Ji Mingxuan, from the beginning to end. Now that the contract was invalid, of course he'd found the most appropriate way to solve the problem.

Ji Mingxuan's lawyer, whose last name was Chen, was a handsome young man. He looked quite professional as he introduced himself, shaking Shen Mo's hand.

After the greeting, Shen Mo immediately asked, "Where's Mr. Ji?"

"He went abroad." Mr. Chen said as he took the documents out of his briefcase, "As soon as Miss Ji's situation stabilized, she was transferred abroad for further treatment."

Shen Mo hadn't seen Ji An'an again after what had happened. Hearing about her now, he felt somewhat relieved.

One by one, Mr. Chen handed Shen Mo the documents he'd brought. "Mr. Shen, according to the contract you signed with Mr. Ji, these are what would be yours."

Shen Mo took a casual glance. They were mostly stocks and properties. Although he didn't really have an idea as to specifically what they were, he knew they must be valuable.

Ji Mingxuan was a businessman for sure. He put price tags on even his affection.

After Shen Mo flipped through the documents with indifference, he said, "Mr. Ji is quite generous."

Mr. Chen smiled and agreed, "He has always been this way."

With how experienced Mr. Chen seemed, it was probably not his first time handling break-ups for Ji Mingxuan. Shen Mo didn't think about this any further. He picked up the pen and asked, "I just need to sign my name, right?"

"Yes. Also, Mr. Ji also said you should feel free to ask for any other assests. However," Mr. Chen looked around before he continued, "this is the house where Miss Ji grew up..."

Shen Mo immediately knew what Mr. Chen was implying. "I understand. I'll pack up my things and move out in a few days."

Seeing how understanding Shen Mo was, Mr. Chen also relaxed. Mr. Chen pointed at the documents on the table, adding, "Mr. Ji is really quite generous. Some of these properties have excellent structures and layouts. After the formalities, you can move in anytime, Mr. Shen."

Shen Mo nodded and lowered his head to sign his name.

As somebody who had recently broken up with his lover, Shen Mo thought he had truly been exceedingly calm

Perhaps it was because he'd never really had a relationship with Ji Mingxuan in the first place.

There had been only a sort of ambiguous affection between them. Before the embers could even ignite, they'd already turned to ash.

Fair enough.

Half way through the documents, Shen Mo heard Mr. Chen ask, "Oh, right. Mr. Ji said you can, of course, keep everything he gave you. There's only one thing he's hoping you can return to him."

Shen Mo looked up and asked, "What is it?"

The car?

Or the ring?

Whatever it was, Shen Mo had no objections. Yet, Mr. Chen said, "It's the property in Jinxiu Villa."

Shen Mo's hand trembled, his pen dragging out a long mark on the paper. He didn't notice it. Eyes widened, he asked, "What did you say? What property?"

"You don't know, Mr. Shen?" Mr. Chen was even more surprised than Shen Mo. He looked through his materials before affirming, "About three years ago, Mr. Ji transferred a property in Jinxiu Villa to your name."

Shen Mo had heard people mention the name "Jinxiu Villa" several times.

The first time was with Zhao Yi, the one who mistook him for the person living in Jinxiu Villa. The second time was the driver, lao-Zhang, who said Ji Mingxuan had insisted on going to Jinxiu Villa when he was drunk.

Obviously, the property in Jinxiu Villa was where Ji Mingxuan spent time with his lovers. But how come it was in Shen Mo's name now?

Did Ji Mingxuan buy the entire property block for the sake of convenience so that all his lovers could be neighbors with one another?

Anyways, there was definitely something strange about Jinxiu Villa.

Shen Mo spun the pen in his hand before he asked Mr. Chen, "I want to go there and take a look. Could you give me the keys?"

Mr. Chen was surprised, but he still maintained a professional smile on his face. "Aren't the keys with you, Mr. Shen?"

Shen Mo finally realized.

That was right. If Ji Mingxuan had given him a property, of course he'd be given a key as well. But how come he didn't remember a thing about it?

Three years ago...

It was during the time when his memory was the blurriest. It wasn't because he had a bad memory. He'd just been depressed then, and he hadn't paid much attention to things. Every day, he would watch the sun rise, and in the blink of an eye, the sky would darken again. He had no idea how he'd passed his days.

Was that when Ji Mingxuan had given him the property?

Shen Mo wasn't sure either. But he'd been living in this house for several years now. If he really had the key, it couldn't be anywhere else. After their exchange was finished, Shen Mo saw Mr. Chen off and began to rummage around for the key.

Shen Mo was a nostalgic person who didn't like throwing things away. As he searched, he happened to find some interesting items—a phone he'd used several years ago, a yellowing diary, and some random doodles. Finally, he found a gift box with dust on its surface in a corner of the drawer.

It was an ordinary gift box. On its lid rested a silly bowtie.

When he saw it, he was surprised for a second.

He remembered the box. It had been his birthday once. Ji Mingxuan had gone to see him in his rental apartment and had given it to him.

It had only been a casual present from Ji Mingxuan, so he had also received it casually. He couldn't even remember if he had opened it or not.

Maybe he had just stuffed it into the drawer without much thought. Or perhaps he had seen what was inside but hadn't thought it was of any importance. He only remembered that, soon after, he had been kicked out because his rent had been due. When he had become homeless, Ji Mingxuan had brought him back, and then they'd signed the contract.

Now that Shen Mo thought about it, he felt that the timeline seemed somewhat contradictory.

This meant Ji Mingxuan had already given him a property before they'd signed the contract. What was this supposed to have been? A deposit or something?

He opened the box and, unsurprisingly, saw a key inside. On the note that came along with the key was the address of the property in Jinxiu Villa. He was quite familiar with the handwriting. The note had indeed been written by Ji Mingxuan.

Gripping the key, Shen Mo decided to go right away and take a look.

The community of Jinxiu Villa was situated in a prime location. Although it was in the city center, it was quiet amid its bustling surroundings, separated from the busy downtown by a tree-lined boulevard. There was a tranquil seclusion to it.

Shen Mo drove there and followed the address to Ji Mingxuan's property.

It'd already been three years, but the lock hadn't been changed. Shen Mo opened the door and walked in. It was a four-room apartment, decorated elegantly. It looked so spotless that it was ovbious someone must have cleaned it often.

The kitchen and living room were all fully furnished. So were the master bedroom and the guest room. Inside the wardrobe hung a few suits of Ji Mingxuan's size. He probably spent his nights here at times. However, there was no sign that anyone else had lived here.

Everything seemed normal.

Shen Mo felt somewhat disappointed.

Like a person who had been waiting to uncover a dust-laden secret, only to find that nothing had ever been there.

The study was the only room Shen Mo hadn't gone inside yet. With no expectations, he pushed the door open—he froze at first sight.

The study had been transformed into a studio. It had the best natural lighting among all the rooms in the entire place. On the ground lay all kinds of paint tools, while on the wall hung various paintings.

The paintings ranged from landscapes to figures, scribbled drafts to carefully framed pieces. Yet, all of the paintings were of the same style, and all of the signatures were the same as well.

—Shen Mo.

Shen Mo felt an excruciating pain in his fingers.

Unable to bear the pain, he awoke from his coma, opening his eyes in a panic. What he saw were miserable shades of white—white walls, white sheets, white gauze... He was confused for a while before he realized that he was in a hospital. Recalling what had happened before he fell unconscious, he curled up out of instinct.

He had been kidnapped on his way home. The abandoned warehouse had reeked of mold. The endless beatings and torture had made the passing of time feel especially slow. With his head pressed against the ground, Shen Mo had watched the sky darken little by little through the cobwebbed window. And then, a glimmer of light had seeped through the boundless dark.

Although he had been unconscious, he had still called out Zhou Yang's name over and over again, ceaselessly.

But the man had never come to save him.

"Zhou Yang..."

Shen Mo trembled underneath the blanket, subconsciously repeating the name again. Wrapped in a thick gauze, his right hand hurt so much that he almost couldn't feel it. He remembered how the scar-faced man had stepped on his fingers one by one, sneering while telling him that Zhou Yang would never show up.

Zhou Yang was abroad with his childhood sweetheart. No matter how many phone calls Shen Mo had made, no one had answered.

The sound of his fingers being crushed still echoed in Shen Mo's ears. He closed his eyes. That sound then changed to the creak of a door.

The door to the hospital room opened. A tall man came in.

Shen Mo thought it would be Zhou Yang. But when he looked up, he saw an unfamiliar face. An emptiness filled his heart. He didn't know what he felt, but suddenly he was no longer afraid.

Was there anything scarier than what he had just experienced?

The man looked quite young, and he had a handsome face. His eyes were as cold as winter nights. He examined Shen Mo as he said, "You're awake."

Shen Mo did not reply.

The man continued, "The doctor said you're no longer in danger, but the injury on your right hand is the most serious. There might be long-term effects."

Shen Mo finally responded. His lips twitched, but he didn't ask about his hand. He only uttered two syllables instead, "Zhou Yang..."

The man's gaze seemed to grow even colder. "Zhou Yang is abroad. He's with my sister."

The man paused before adding, "My sister is Ji An'an."

Shen Mo immediately understood that he was talking about—Miss Ji, Zhou Yang's childhood sweetheart. So this man... was Miss Ji's brother? Shen Mo couldn't help but look at him.

The man was also quietly gazing at Shen Mo.

"I forgot to introduce myself." The man raised his hand to smooth out his tie and said, "My name is Ji Mingxuan."

After hearing about Zhou Yang that day, Shen Mo didn't say anything at all for three entire days. When Ji Mingxuan visited him on the fourth day, he suddenly said, "I want to call Zhou Yang."

Ji Mingxuan frowned minutely, but he still nodded and said, "Of course."

Shen Mo could sit up on the bed already. But with one hand wrapped in gauze and the other attached to a drip, he couldn't even dial the number. Ji Mingxuan dialed Zhou Yang's number for him.

Shen Mo remained extremely calm. From the beginning until the end, he only spoke three sentences to Zhou Yang.

"It's me."

"Let's break up."

"No reason. I'm just tired of it."

And then, disregarding Zhou Yang's interrogation from the other end of the call, Shen Mo looked at Ji Mingxuan calmly.

Ji Mingxuan understood and hung up. He eyed Shen Mo for a while before he asked, "Just like this, you're breaking up with Zhou Yang?"

Shen Mo looked at his right hand, speaking as though the matter didn't concern himself, "When they tortured me, they said that if I didn't break up with Zhou Yang, my family would be in trouble next."

Ji Mingxuan rubbed the center of his brows and sat down on a chair by the bed. He said, "The abductors have already been arrested. When you feel better, the police will ask you for a statement."

Shen Mo nodded and said, "Okay." He then asked, "That day... were you the one who saved me, Mr. Ji?"

Ji Mingxuan paused for a few seconds before replying, "No. It was all because you called the police ahead of time that they made it in time."

Shen Mo asked, "Mr. Ji, why did you pay all those expensive medical bills for me?"

"Zhou Yang left with An'an. Take it as a kind of compensation."

Shen Mo and Ji Mingxuan were strangers, so they had nothing else to talk about. Ji Mingxuan sat for a while before he left. Afterwards, he sent his assistant to check up on Shen Mo several times, but he never showed up personally again.

A month later, Shen Mo recovered and left the hospital.

Apart from his right hand, which he still couldn't freely use, only faint marks remained from his other wounds. However, he still had nightmares every night.

He dreamed that he was running in the dark while footsteps chased after him from behind, approaching closer and closer. He kept on calling the same number, but he could only hear busy beeps from the other end. Nobody ever picked up. Finally, a hand stretched out from the dark, wrapped around his ankle, and dragged him into an eternal abyss.

Scared awake by the dream, Shen Mo couldn't help but cry out, "Zhou Yang!"

The small rental apartment was so empty that he could even hear the echoes of his own voice. He and Zhou Yang had decorated it together. Traces of Zhou Yang lurked everywhere, but he knew the man would never come back again.

Shen Mo began to experience insomnia. Whenever he closed his eyes, he felt as if he had returned to the abandoned warehouse. He called Zhou Yang's name again and again, but no one ever came to save him.

Originally, he'd already found an art-related job, but now that his right hand was useless, the job was gone as well. Fortunately, he could still survive on the bread and instant noodles that he still had left at home. Every day, he stayed up until he could no longer stand the fatigue, and when he woke up the next day, he stared blankly out the window. Sunrises and sunsets were meaningless to him. He didn't even know how long had passed.

It had only been a few days; it seemed as though it'd been a lifetime.

On that day, it had just rained, and the air after the rain felt quite refreshing. Shen Mo opened a packet of bread. Just as he was about to eat, the doorbell rang. He hadn't been in contact with anyone in a long time, which made his mind grow a little sluggish. It took him some time to open the door.

Outside the door stood a tall, slender man. Against the light, his face looked blurry, almost somewhat unreal.

But Shen Mo's heart, which had been numb for too long, suddenly sprang to life—it almost leaped out of his throat. He put his right hand behind his back, as though he was afraid it would scare the man. In the softest voice, he called, "Zhou Yang."

The man was somewhat surprised. He said, "I'm not Zhou Yang."

Shen Mo blinked once and examined the man as he asked, "Who else could you be?"

Speaking, he pulled the man inside.

Since the place hadn't been cleaned in a few days, it was dirty and messy. Shen Mo took quite a while to clear up space for them to sit. He then said, "You said you were going out for just a couple of days. Why did it take you so long?"

But where had Zhou Yang been? How long had passed before he returned? Shen Mo could remember nothing.

The man didn't sit down. With folded arms, he only looked Shen Mo up and down before repeating, "I'm not Zhou Yang."

The man took a watch out of his pocket and said, "Someone found this in the old warehouse. I thought it might be yours, so I came to return it to you since I was passing by."

Shen Mo recognized it—it was a present from Zhou Yang. In a hurry, he accepted it and put it back on. Yet he still couldn't remember when he'd lost the watch. As he thought about this, his right hand ached.

He didn't dare think about it any further. On the table was the bread that he had just unpacked. Noticing it, he brought it over and asked, "You didn't eat yet, did you? Let's have something together."

The man's expression changed the moment he saw the bread. He grabbed Shen Mo's hand and said, "You've been eating spoiled food?"

The man's grip made Shen Mo's wrist throb, and he couldn't help but flinch. Zhou Yang didn't like eating these things, he recalled. "I think there might still be some food in the fridge. I'll make some noodles for you."

As he spoke, Shen Mo struggled out of the man's hold. But just as he took a few steps toward the kitchen, he felt his head spin. His legs gave out, and he almost fell to the ground. Luckily, the man saw and caught his arm in time.

Shen Mo felt somewhat embarrassed. "Maybe I stayed up too late yesterday."

He whispered again, "Zhou Yang..."

The man didn't correct Shen Mo this time. He only said, "If I didn't come today, you'd probably starve to death in this place and hit the headlines a few days later."

But Shen Mo still had some bread left, didn't he?

That was what Shen Mo thought, but before he had time to refute the man, the latter had already dragged him out of the apartment. The man was so strong that Shen Mo couldn't break his hold no matter what. He could only follow him.

The man led Shen Mo to a car. Someone who seemed to be his assistant went out and brought back a bowl of steaming congee. Under supervision, Shen Mo had to finish it up.

Shen Mo felt a little strange. It was such a bright day, but everyone's face looked blurry for some reason. Of course, Zhou Yang was an exception. Even amid a crowd, he could recognize Zhou Yang with a single glance.

Zhou Yang was the man he loved with all his heart.

Thinking about this, Shen Mo felt impossibly tender.

After he finished the congee, the man took him to the hospital. The doctor, who also had a blurry face, asked him some questions—some were extremely easy to answer, while others puzzled him. Once he answered all of the questions, he was brought somewhere to take some examinations. The man discussed his condition with the doctor before finally bringing him home, along with lots of medication.

Shen Mo fiddled with the bottles as he said, "I'm not sick."

The man looked at Shen Mo and calmly said two words: "Take them."

For some reason, Shen Mo didn't dare go against what the man had said. He got himself some water and took the medicine. The man never ended up taking a seat inside. Right after Shen Mo finished taking the pills, the man opened the door and got ready to leave.

Shen Mo caught up to him and asked, "Zhou Yang, where are you going?"

The man stopped, looked back at Shen Mo, and said, "I just happened to pass by today. I won't come here again."

Shen Mo was confused.

The man seemed to hesitate momentarily before he slowly lifted his palm to Shen Mo's cheek. However, he didn't touch Shen Mo's face. Word by word, he stated, "Of course, Zhou Yang won't come either. Whether to keep running away from reality or to face the truth, it's up to you."

Once he finished, the man withdrew his hand and left.

Shen Mo went downstairs and chased after him, watching him get in the car. In the end, Shen Mo wasn't able to catch up to the man. He didn't understand what had happened. Why had Zhou Yang left? They were so close.

His right hand ached again.

Shen Mo hurried to hold it with his other hand.

The sun only shone in the afternoon; it rained again in the evening. Shen Mo didn't go back to his rental. Empty-hearted, he stood in the passage downstairs. Even he didn't know what he was thinking about.

Although the rain wasn't heavy, it quickly dampened Shen Mo's clothes. Huddling into his shoulders, Shen Mo still refused to leave.

He stayed awake all night. Only when dawn almost arrived did he sit down against the wall. People who got up early for work walked past him one after another, all looking at him like he was mad.

Shen Mo couldn't help considering it either. Had he really gone mad?

Today was still grim and gloomy. The rain was not heavy but rather lingering and ceaseless. Shen Mo's hair was drenched as well, and water kept on dripping down. He didn't even know what he was waiting for, but he waited with all his heart.

In the afternoon, a car drove by and stopped at the other side of the passage. Shen Mo looked up before he lowered his head again.

When it was almost dusk, the rain grew heavier instead. The sliver of roof above Shen Mo's head couldn't keep out the rain at all now. Shen Mo still stayed in the same place, motionless. He didn't even think about standing up.

Like him, the car was also still stopped at the other side, unmoving.

When the sky completely darkened, the door of the car suddenly opened.

A man got out of the car.

As Shen Mo watched the man walk closer and closer to him, holding an umbrella, he could almost hear his own heartbeats.

The man finally stopped in front of Shen Mo, silently gazing at him.

Shen Mo stood up and hugged the man, crying out, "Zhou Yang!"

The man's body stiffened somewhat. After a long, long time, the man sighed and gently returned the hug.

Shen Mo had been out in the rain for the whole day. Unsurprisingly, his temperature rose in the evening. He fell unconscious from the fever—he was only vaguely aware that a doctor came over and gave him an injection to bring down his temperature. In his dreams, he kept calling out for Zhou Yang. He remembered that once he'd also called Zhou Yang's name in such a way, but Zhou Yang had never showed up.

This time, though, someone sat by his bed, holding his hand firmly.

Shen Mo had a weak constitution; he took several days to recover. By the time he could get out of bed, the place looked brand new to him. The living room had been cleaned up, the fridge had been filled with fresh produce, and some old furniture had been replaced as well. His Zhou Yang was sitting on the sofa for once, ordering the housekeeper to make him some congee.

Shen Mo walked over. "Zhou Yang."

The man gave an ambiguous answer. He took a few bottles of medicine from the table and handed them to Shen Mo, telling him, "Take these two after you eat. Two tablets each time, twice per day. Take this one before bed. Just one tablet is enough. And this one is..."

The man instructed Shen Mo on how to take each bottle of medicine. Then, he said, "Take everything on time every day. I'll come over in three days and take you to the hospital for a return visit."

Shen Mo only processed the last sentence. He asked, "Are you leaving now?"

"That's right."

"Won't you stay?"

The man was quiet for a while before he replied, "I have work to do."

"But before..."

The man's phone rang before Shen Mo could finish speaking. The man answered the phone, listened for a few moments, and replied in a cool voice, "I understand. I'll head back to the office right now."

After the man hung up, he turned back to Shen Mo and added, "Remember to take the pills."

Shen Mo's lips moved. He still had so much to say, but in the end, he didn't say anything and only watched the man leave. After making some congee, the housekeeper left as well. Shen Mo ate the congee alone and took the pills. He had nothing to do, so he continued to stare out the window.

He didn't understand why Zhou Yang had to leave.

But it didn't matter. Zhou Yang had said he'd come over in three days, didn't he?

In the next few days, the housekeeper visited according to schedule to cook for Shen Mo. On the third day, the man arrived as he'd promised. Shen Mo had close to no idea of how he'd passed his time. Only when he caught sight of the man did a hint of vitality show on his face.

The man was as cold as ever. He asked Shen Mo if Shen Mo had taken the medicine before driving Shen Mo to the hospital. This time, Shen Mo didn't do a bunch of tests. He only had a casual chat with the doctor, and the return visit was over. Before he left, he heard the doctor say to the man, "It's a form of post-traumatic stress disorder. He'll have to go through long-term treatment."

Shen Mo found it strange. He clearly wasn't sick.

On their way home, Shen Mo tried to start conversations on a few different subjects. To each, the man only answered perfunctorily. Shen

Mo didn't know why Zhou Yang had changed so much. When they'd first begun their relationship...

Shen Mo felt a little dizzy. His memory wasn't as good as before. There were many things from the past that he couldn't remember.

The night before, he had been unable to fall asleep again. Right now, the sun shone so brightly while the car drove quickly and steadily. He couldn't help but start to feel tired, although he didn't dare fall asleep. Forcing himself to keep his eyes open, he looked at the man over and over again. In the end, he fell asleep unwittingly.

He dreamed of boundless darkness.

Countless hands reached out from the earth, seized him, and pinned him on the ground. Little by little, they crushed his bones, devouring every drop of his blood, every piece of his flesh.

"Ahh—"

The nightmare scared him awake. He found that the sky had already darkened, and the car was stopped at an unknown crossing. While the man, whose face hovered close to his, stared at him intently.

Shen Mo was drenched in a cold sweat.

Everything from the dream felt so real to him, almost as though he'd really been torn to pieces.

The man reached out. With cold fingers, he wiped the sweat from Shen Mo's temple.

Shen Mo flinched and said, "I'm sorry. I accidentally fell asleep."

The man asked, "Did you have a nightmare?"

"Yeah."

"Do you often have nightmares?"

"...Only once in a while."

Shen Mo probably wasn't too good at lying. The man immediately exposed him, "Is it because you're too afraid to sleep at night that you look so pale?"

Shen Mo denied it in vain, "That's not true..."

The man said nothing else as he started the car.

Noticing that the man wasn't driving on the correct route, Shen Mo grew nervous again. "Zhou Yang, you're driving in the wrong direction."

"It's not wrong."

"Where are we going?"

"We're going to my place. You shouldn't be living alone in that apartment."

Shen Mo had always been gentle; everyone said he had a good temper. But this time, he cried out, "Don't!"

The man asked, "Why not?"

Shen Mo said, "I can't. I have to stay home and wait for..."

Who was he waiting for? Zhou Yang? But Zhou Yang was right beside him already.

Shen Mo's head was in a mess—the only thing he knew was that he had to wait there. Forgetting how dangerous a moving vehicle was, he almost lunged for the steering wheel.

The man had to stop the car. Then, he turned around and looked at Shen Mo.

Shen Mo returned the look, refusing to give in.

The man had no choice but to compromise. "All right. We'll go home."

After so long, they finally returned to the small rental. They'd rented it after their graduation, and Zhou Yang had decorated it with him. He didn't understand why all of a sudden, Zhou Yang didn't like it anymore.

They ordered delivery for dinner. After the meal, the man didn't leave and instead grabbed a blanket to sleep on the sofa.

Shen Mo grew even more confused. "Why aren't you sleeping with me?"

The man ignored Shen Mo, only waving his hand and saying, "Come and take your medicine."

Shen Mo did as he was told and took it.

Before getting into bed, Shen Mo left the bedroom door open. The door faced the sofa so that he could see Zhou Yang at a glance. After he said goodnight, he turned off the light, hiding in his blanket to gaze at the man quietly.

The sofa was way too small. Tall and long-legged, the man seemed as if he'd fall off anytime. As the man tossed and turned on the sofa, Shen Mo's eyes moved back and forth along with him.

The man noticed Shen Mo's gaze and looked inside the room.

Shen Mo immediately closed his eyes, pretending to be asleep. A while later, he heard the man ask, as if to himself, "Does everyone look like Zhou Yang in your eyes? Or am I the only one you mistake for him?"

Shen Mo found it amusing. Why was Zhou Yang saying such nonsense? Shen Mo then opened his eyes and declared, "Only you're special, of course."

The corners of the man's lips lifted. He seemed to smile within the darkness, although no laughter could be heard.

Shen Mo felt an inexplicable flicker of panic. He called, "Zhou Yang?"

Quite some time passed before the man answered, his voice gentler than ever, "You can sleep. I'm right here."

Indeed, Shen Mo slept through the night.

When he woke up the next day, the man was still asleep on the sofa, resting one foot on the sofa and the other on the ground. The blanket only covered up to his waist, and his shirt looked crumpled too. Only now did Shen Mo notice that the man had slept all night without changing into pajamas.

Afraid of waking up the man, Shen Mo carefully walked into the kitchen. The injury on his right hand hadn't healed completely. He couldn't yet use it as he pleased, but it was enough for him to make two bowls of noodles. When Shen Mo brought the noodles to the table, the man had already gotten himself cleaned and called someone for a change of clothes.

Shen Mo waited at the table. After the man hung up, he also sat down to eat the noodles.

He asked the man as they ate, "Is it good?"

Expressionless, the man looked up and said, "Not too bad."

But he finished the noodles in minutes.

Shen Mo was pleased beyond words.

The man was really busy with work. After finishing the noodles, he changed his clothes and went to work. But whenever it was time for one of Shen Mo's return visits, he always showed up punctually. At first, he only slept over on nights of the return visits. When he later found out that Shen Mo experienced nightmares almost every night, he gradually started spending more time with him.

The small sofa in the living room was soon upgraded to a larger one. The man sometimes sat there to deal with his business matters. Two assistants worked for him, and they called him Mr. Ji. Shen Mo couldn't figure out why they used such a title. He couldn't distinguish either assistant from the other, either. But it didn't matter. Only his Zhou Yang was special.

Shen Mo often sat quietly beside the man and watched him work. Even gazing at his handsome face from the side made Shen Mo feel at ease.

On the issue of not sleeping together, Shen Mo also protested many times. But each time, the man rejected him with a different excuse, such as "You're still unwell," "I'm too busy at work," and so on. Later, the man grew so annoyed that he snapped, "I'm impotent, okay?"

Shen Mo had to give up.

Accompanied by the man every night, Shen Mo no longer had nightmares. With a good appetite and decent sleep every day, he even put on some weight. The injury on his right hand gradually healed as well.

Shen Mo then thought about going out and working. He had gotten a job at a company in an art-related industry, but he'd lost it because of his injured right hand.

Luckily, he could still paint.

Painting was the only thing he could still do.

Shen Mo's tools had been abandoned for too long, currently collecting dust in the cabinet. Today, after the man went to work, Shen Mo took them out. He sorted them and thought about what to paint.

He wanted to paint Zhou Yang. Yet, for some reason, Zhou Yang was always obscured by a sheet of mist in his mind, blurry and indistinct.

Never mind, Shen Mo thought, I'll have Zhou Yang model for me after he comes back.

After much consideration, Shen Mo decided to paint the sofa in the living room. He hummed as he got his tools out. All was calm and pleasant until he took hold of the paintbrush.

Even though the injury had already healed, his right hand still throbbed painfully. As he let go of his grip, the paintbrush fell to the ground.

In a hurry, Shen Mo bent down to pick it up, but he couldn't hold it no matter what. His fingers ached as if they were splintering into pieces. Shen Mo ground his teeth. Fragmented scenes flashed across his mind.

He was pressed down onto the ground. A man with a scarred face rested a foot on his hand and stepped down hard, laughing while saying something.

Then the scene changed to a hospital room. A man he didn't recognize said something similar to him and told him that his right hand had been seriously injured. The injury might leave behind long-term effects and impact his daily life.

Just what had happened?

How had he hurt his hand?

In confusion, Shen Mo fell to the ground and curled up from the pain in his right hand. He took a while to catch his breath. Again, he strived to pick up the paintbrush, but the moment he got hold of it, his fingers trembled uncontrollably.

It was so painful.

He had to let go of his grip and make another attempt. He tried over and over again before he finally gave up on doing something so meaningless.

He still couldn't remember anything, but he knew in his heart that he would no longer be able to paint.

Shen Mo lay on the ground for a long time. Only after the sun went down did he hear the sound of the door opening outside.

Zhou Yang was back.

Shen Mo finally recovered some strength, hastily getting up to tidy up his tools. He didn't want Zhou Yang to find out about this. But halfway through, the familiar man had already pushed open the door.

The man took a glance and asked, "What are you doing?"

"Nothing. I... I just did some cleaning."

Shen Mo held the paint tools in his arms and tried to shove them back into the cabinet all at once. However, he was in such a hurry that he bumped into a corner of the table. Everything in his arms fell to the ground.

It was such a mess.

Especially the paintbrushes, which rolled all over the floor.

Panicking, Shen Mo was afraid that Zhou Yang would find out. He bent over and picked them up one by one with his left hand, telling himself he'd never touch them again. The whole time he looked down, and gradually his motions grew slower and slower. When he reached for the last paintbrush, the man suddenly stepped on it.

Surprised, Shen Mo didn't know if he should still pick it up.

In the meantime, the man had already reached out and gently grasped Shen Mo's chin, forcing Shen Mo to tilt his head.

Their eyes met. The man's pupils quivered.

Shen Mo found it somewhat strange, asking, "What's wrong?"

The man said nothing, still gazing at Shen Mo.

Shen Mo seemed to notice something. He lifted his hand to his face and felt a cold wetness.

Embarrassed that he'd lost his composure, Shen Mo hurried to wipe his face with his hands, fibbing, "I think I slept too long in the afternoon..."

The man looked at Shen Mo deeply, his eyes dark enough to hide any emotion. A while later, he bent over to pick up the last paintbrush and put it in Shen Mo's hand.

Shen Mo's fingers bent somewhat unnaturally. Even though he managed to hold the paintbrush, his face paled from the pain. He cried out in a begging tone, "Zhou Yang..."

As soon as the man relaxed his hold, the paintbrush dropped to the ground again.

The man stared at Shen Mo and asked, "It hurts?"

Shen Mo drew in a breath, habitually hiding his right hand behind his back as he said, "It's probably because it hasn't completely healed yet. It'll be fine once it heals."

Shen Mo thought for a bit before he added, "It's fine even if it doesn't heal. If worse comes to worst, I'll just give up painting and do something else. I can do sales or insurance consulting. I might even earn more."

The man didn't say anything.

After Shen Mo finished talking to himself, he hurried into the kitchen and splashed his face with cold water. When he calmed down, he took some food out of the refrigerator and made several simple dishes.

At dinner, the atmosphere was rather gloomy.

Both of them had their own concerns, so neither talked much. After dinner, the man opened his laptop to send a few emails and later lay down on the sofa to sleep. Shen Mo slept in the bedroom and looked at the man on the sofa through the parted door. He saw that the man kept turning about as if he couldn't sleep well throughout the whole night.

Shen Mo also woke up several times. He wasn't too energetic when he got up the next day. But he had already made up his mind. He locked everything related to painting into the cabinet and went out to look for a job.

He hadn't recovered yet, so he still couldn't recognize other people's faces. He wouldn't be able to find a job like insurance consulting, but other jobs were easy. In just two days, he got a job as a grocery clerk. It was part-time, so he didn't have to sign a contract. He negotiated the pay with the boss, and he could begin immediately.

Shen Mo worked hard, and he was willing to endure hardship. His boss was quite satisfied with his trial day. For lunch, Shen Mo didn't go home either and instead had a working meal with his colleagues.

When Shen Mo was organizing products in front of the shelves in the afternoon, he suddenly heard someone call his name, "Shen Mo!"

The call was quick and anxious, as though it concealed an indescribable feeling.

Shen Mo recognized the voice and turned around. As expected, it was Zhou Yang.

"Zhou Yang? Why are you here?"

The man wasn't wearing a suit. The sleeves of his shirt were rolled up and his tie had been loosened as well. He looked quite different from his usual composed self. Not saying a word, he strode up to Shen Mo, reached out, and pulled Shen Mo into his arms.

Slamming into the man's chest, Shen Mo asked in surprise, "What's wrong?"

The man tightened his grip and called Shen Mo's name in a low voice, "Shen Mo?"

"Yes."

"Shen Mo..."

"Yes, it's me."

"Shen Mo..."

Shen Mo heard heartbeats. He didn't know whether they belonged to him or the man.

The man closed his eyes and quickly suppressed his emotions. Gradually, he relaxed his arms and looked down at Shen Mo's face, asking, "What are you doing here?"

"I got a job here. I'm working as a grocery clerk. It's my first day on the job."

The man seemed to be holding something back as he asked coldly, "You didn't even leave behind a note?"

"Oh." Shen Mo finally realized what had happened. "Did you think I'd gone missing?"

Shen Mo asked carefully, "Were... Were you been looking for me this whole time?"

The man didn't admit or deny anything. "You haven't recovered yet.

Don't run around."

Shen Mo noticed that the man's breaths were heavy, and there was some sweat on the man's forehead. Wondering how long it had taken the man to reach here, he said, "Okay," and asked, "You're always so busy. How come today...?"

The man glanced at Shen Mo's right hand and said, "I happened to be free, so I went home at noon."

Shen Mo guessed that the man must have been worried about him.

In reality, it wasn't that big of a deal. Painting was the only thing he couldn't do. Working at a supermarket was also okay, wasn't it?

Shen Mo's work was far from finished. The man didn't force him to go back home. Instead, he waited for him in his car outside the supermarket. Whenever Shen Mo finished his tasks and looked outside, he could always see the car parked opposite the supermarket.

Shen Mo got off work at three in the afternoon. When he left, he felt that the way his coworkers looked at him was somewhat different. Many people had seen Zhou Yang hug him. Shen Mo was a little annoyed. He didn't know if he could still come to work tomorrow.

They went back home. After dinner, the man slept on the sofa as usual.

Shen Mo had had a busy day and fell asleep quickly. The man still tossed and turned on the sofa. In the end, he decided to get up altogether. Step by step, he walked to the bedroom.

Drowsy, Shen Mo patted the empty space next to him, generously inviting the man to sleep beside him.

The man only sat down on the edge of the bed and reached for Shen Mo's temple. He paused for a while, gently stroking Shen Mo's hair. His voice sounded unusually hoarse in the night, "I've seen your paintings. They're quite good."

Shen Mo replied with a grin, "Of course."

The man said, "Quit your job at the supermarket."

Shen Mo was a little reluctant. "Why?"

The man searched for Shen Mo's right hand in the dark, but he only held the very tip of it, whispering, "Let's treat your hand, and you can keep on painting."

The man kept his word. He quickly got in touch with the best hospitals and the top experts. Shen Mo quit his job at the supermarket and began to frequent the hospital. After much consultation, the conclusion was that his hand needed another operation.

Shen Mo wasn't afraid. Medicine was so advanced nowadays. There was nothing to worry about. Zhou Yang, on the other hand, was much more nervous than he was.

Of course, the man didn't reveal his anxiety on the surface. He always wore the same cold expression on his face. But the night before the operation, the man circled Shen Mo's hospital bed again and again.

Dizzied by all the circling, Shen Mo reached over to hold the man's hand, only to find that the muscles on his hand were extremely tense. But the man still comforted Shen Mo, "Don't be afraid."

"I'm not afraid." Seeing the man act this way, Shen Mo thought it was funny. "It's just a small operation. It'll be great if it succeeds, but there's no harm even if it doesn't."

The man squeezed Shen Mo's hand. Sitting down on the edge of the bed, he gazed at Shen Mo and said, "Sometimes, I don't quite understand you."

"What?"

"You have a good temper, almost as if anyone can take advantage of you, but once you get stubborn, you refuse to give up no matter what."

Shen Mo pretended to be angry. "Is that supposed to be good or bad?"

The man chuckled and drew closer to him, saying, "What do you think?"

The man's voice was always low and pleasant. Right now, it sounded so close that it seemed to brush against Shen Mo's ear. Shen Mo felt an itch in his heart. It was a pity that he had an operation tomorrow— he couldn't mess around, even if he wanted to. He held onto the man's hand. Noticing that the muscles there were still somewhat tense, he said tenderly, "Don't be so nervous. The operation will be over by this time tomorrow."

"It's fine. I just don't really like hospitals. My mother..."

"What?"

The man averted his gaze. He didn't continue the subject and only said, "We can talk about it later. You should rest well today."

"Okay."

Shen Mo was in a relaxed mood. He slept well tonight as well.

The next day, the operation turned out to be a great success.

This was only the first step of the treatment, though. Again, the man suggested moving out of the apartment, but Shen Mo was unusually stubborn when it came to this, refusing to give in. And so, the man let go of the matter.

Shen Mo had to go to the hospital every once in a while for rehabilitation. On top of that, he had to take quite a lot of medicine every day, especially traditional Chinese medicine, which tasted disgusting and was difficult to swallow. If it weren't for the man's company, Shen Mo didn't even know if he could get through all this.

The days were getting cold. A thick blanket had already replaced the thin one on the sofa.

Shen Mo was rather sensitive to the cold. In winter, his hands froze easily. Knowing this, the man used medicinal liquor to massage his hands every day after dinner, starting from his fingertips and then kneading his fingers one by one. The work was quite tedious and often took a long time, but the man was never impatient.

Sometimes, Shen Mo would feel confused as well. Had Zhou Yang always been like this?

The man seemed to be made of stone on the surface, hard and cold. Only when someone knocked open his shell and looked into him would they see just how soft he was on the inside.

But if he tried to recall how Zhou Yang had used to be, he really remembered nothing. Oh, well—as long as Zhou Yang was right at his side, what else was there to worry about?

Shen Mo laughed at himself for overthinking. Watching the man massage his fingers with such diligence, he couldn't help but say, "Zhou Yang."

The man did not reply.

The man often acted like this. Shen Mo had long since gotten used to it. He asked, "Do you think my right hand can really get better?"

"Of course." The man didn't even look up. "As long as you keep going, you'll definitely be rewarded."

Shen Mo smiled.

The man often said Shen Mo was stubborn. But, in truth, the man was just the same.

"Zhou Yang," Shen Mo looked down at the man's handsome face and gently called the man's name. "When my right hand heals and I start painting again, you'll be the first one I paint, okay?"

The man stopped for a moment before he continued massaging. He kneaded Shen Mo's fingers one by one, then rubbed them together in his palm.

Even Shen Mo's fingertips felt nice and warm.

The man lowered his eyes. Refusing to give Shen Mo a single glance, he gazed intently at Shen Mo's hand before he finally replied, "...Okay."

Now that his hands were warm, Shen Mo grew somewhat tired. Somehow, he fell asleep on the sofa. It wasn't a deep sleep; he was still vaguely conscious. He felt the man drape a blanket over him and circle him twice.

This was how the man acted when he was nervous.

Finding this strange, Shen Mo noticed the man bend over, his breaths drawing closer and closer. Then, almost imperceptibly, his warm lips brushed against Shen Mo's temple.

CHAP.07

Quite some time passed before Shen Mo awoke from his dreams. The moment he opened his eyes, he scrambled to search for the man, only to find that he himself was lying on the bed in his bedroom already.

The living room was quiet. The light had been turned off long ago. In the dim moonlight, Shen Mo could see the man's silhouette atop the sofa. The man breathed steadily and seemed to be asleep.

Shen Mo still felt somewhat stunned as he raised his hand to touch his temple. There remained almost a faint warmth, so he couldn't tell if the kiss had been real or no more than a dream.

If real, why did Zhou Yang have to kiss him so secretly?

If no more than a dream...

It was only natural. For so long, Shen Mo had been able to only look at the man, unable to do anything with him. Of course Shen Mo would dream about such a thing.

Recalling the strange excuses the man had come up with to evade sleeping with him, Shen Mo let out a helpless sigh. He wrapped himself in his blanket and fell asleep again.

The temperature dropped as the end of the year approached. Apart from Shen Mo, who had nothing to do, everyone was busy. The man was especially preoccupied with work; he had been sleeping out for several nights. But he was still quite concerned about Shen Mo's right hand, making time to go to rehabilitation with Shen Mo no matter what.

The man told Shen Mo ahead of time that he'd be spending New Year's with his family, so he could only spend Christmas together with Shen Mo.

Shen Mo was fine with that. He didn't really care for these so-called holidays, so it didn't matter to him whether or not he celebrated them. Now that the man had mentioned it, though, he began to consider it.

After all, Shen Mo had only injured his right hand, not anywhere else. He'd already knocked open the man's outer shell. It was time to taste the inside as well, wasn't it?

So on Christmas Eve, Shen Mo deliberately cooked a few of his best dishes and got a bottle of wine. He remembered that Zhou Yang's alcohol tolerance was... Fine, he couldn't quite remember. But Zhou Yang wasn't a heavyweight, was he?

Of course, the man also got off work early. When he came back and saw the table full of dishes, he revealed no emotion on the surface. At an unhurried pace, he sat down and began to dine, almost as though he intended to finish every single one of the dishes.

Shen Mo took the initiative and poured some wine for the man, asking, "When are you leaving?"

The man had said he'd go abroad to spend time with his family.

"A few days later. After I finish the work at hand." The man's chopsticks never stopped moving as he glanced at Shen Mo and said, "You'll be home alone..."

"It's okay." Shen Mo replied after some thought, "I also want to pay a visit home."

The man nodded. "Yes. You should."

The man then added, "I'll have my assistant book the tickets for you."

"Don't worry about it. It's in a neighboring city."

As he spoke, Shen Mo poured some more wine for the man. He was planning to get the man drunk, but the events didn't unfold as he wished. Even after the entire bottle of red wine was emptied, the man didn't blush in the slightest, whereas Shen Mo had already begun to feel tipsy. Moreover, the mealtime atmosphere was rather unromantic this time—the man was too determined to finish all of the dishes Shen Mo had cooked, so he spent the whole time eating. Shen Mo regretted not having prepared some digestive medication.

After, the man went to the kitchen unprompted to do the dishes.

As the effects of the alcohol took place, Shen Mo walked dizzily into the kitchen. Leaning against the door, he gazed at the man. The man had rolled up his shirt sleeves. While he washed the dishes, water sloshed loudly in the sink and splashed onto his arms. He had a tall, broad figure, and the contours of his waist was especially beautiful.

Not quite aware of what he was doing, Shen Mo walked inside. Under the influence of alcohol, he wrapped his arms around the man's waist from behind.

The man paused for a second before turning his head around. He said, "Don't mess around."

Shen Mo only hugged the man, pressing his face against the man's back as he whispered, "I miss you."

The man seemed as though his movements had been paused.

Shen Mo circled to the side and lifted his chin to kiss the man. Somewhat deliriously, he murmured, "Zhou Yang..."

The man froze before suddenly turning his head away.

And so Shen Mo's kiss didn't land on the man's lips but instead on the man's neck. His lips touched the man's quivering Adam's apple. The man drew back but couldn't retreat any further. His breaths were scattered.

Shen Mo planted a kiss on the man's throat.

The man let out a hoarse, restrained voice. "Shen Mo!"

Shen Mo felt his heart throb madly. Little by little, he kissed upward, from the neck to the chin, and finally to the man's lips.

His lips tasted much more delicious than Shen Mo had imagined.

Shen Mo didn't go further, although a smugness hung at the corners of his eyes. He drew back a little and said, "Zhou..."

The man's eyes darkened. Before Shen Mo could pronounce the second syllable, he grabbed Shen Mo's arm and pushed Shen Mo onto the kitchen counter behind them. Bending over, he kissed Shen Mo aggressively.

The kiss took away Shen Mo's breath. With his back against the cold counter, he wrapped his arms around the man's shoulders, feeling the heat of the body beneath the thin shirt. Their lips and teeth meshed as Shen Mo's body burned.

Shen Mo couldn't even remember his own name right now, let alone the man's name.

Only when all of the air within Shen Mo's lungs was used up did Shen Mo attempt to pull back a little. The man immediately caught up to him. But this time, the man slowed down, kissing Shen Mo's lips gently.

Not only did the heat inside Shen Mo refuse to fade, it intensified. Shen Mo lifted the tip of his foot and hooked it around the man's foot, calling, "Zhou Yang..."

The man's breathing hitched. He said, "I'm not Zhou Yang."

He hadn't said this in a long time.

Surprised, Shen Mo examined the man's face. Those handsome features certainly belonged to the person he'd always lived with.

How could he mistake such an important person for anyone else?

With relief, Shen Mo threw himself toward the man again.

But the man caught his shoulders and stopped him.

Shen Mo gazed at the man eagerly.

The man smiled and said, "You haven't recovered yet."

"But I'm not sick."

The man stopped for a moment. His eyes landed on Shen Mo's face. Unable to hold himself back, he raised his hand and touched the corner of Shen Mo's eye. His thumb slowly skimmed across Shen Mo's eyelid.

Shen Mo almost thought the man was going to kiss him again. He couldn't help but close his eyes, only to hear the man sigh. "Let's wait until you recover."

With these words, the man he let go and went back to washing the dishes. It was as if he found the bowls more attractive than Shen Mo.

Shen Mo had only messed around with the man due to the alcohol, but now he didn't dare go any further. The man wasn't interested. He couldn't force himself upon him, could he?

He watched the man wash the dishes, massage his right hand as usual, and then also... sleep on the sofa as usual.

At night, Shen Mo felt rather warm and had many strange dreams. He seemed to dream of the man coming into the bedroom, but after he opened his eyes, he saw no one here. When he woke up the next morning, the man had already gone to work.

The man only made time to enjoy a few meals with Shen Mo before he flew abroad in a hurry. But in the end, he still seemed worried about Shen Mo. He had his assistant come over to check on Shen Mo several times and book train tickets for Shen Mo.

Shen Mo thanked the man's assistant, but he locked the ticket inside a drawer right after the latter left.

He didn't go home. He stayed in the rental until the end of the year.

On New Year's Eve, he got up early and cleaned the place thoroughly. Only when he finished in the afternoon did he make a phone call.

The phone only rang twice before it was answered. A familiar voice came from the other end. Shen Mo couldn't help but call out, "Dad..."

The other end was quiet for a few seconds. Then, the phone call was hung up with a clack.

Blankly holding his phone, Shen Mo listened to the beeps of the busy signal. A while later, he called again, but no one answered this time.

A redness emerged in Shen Mo's eyes. He hung up in silence.

Right after he'd started dating Zhou Yang, he had come out to his family. At that time, the situation had escalated so far that he'd ended up getting beaten up quite badly. After that, he'd been kicked out by his parents. He hadn't been able to go back home since then.

But he wasn't alone. At least he still had Zhou Yang by his side,

didn't he?

Shen Mo tried to regain his composure. He picked up the piece of cloth and wiped the spotless floor once more.

Soon came the night. Shen Mo didn't want to cook too many dishes, so he made some noodles and watched television as he ate. Later, he waited for midnight on the sofa.

A while before midnight, bursts of firecrackers exploded one after another. Shen Mo's phone rang as well. He rushed to get the phone—he didn't recognize the number, but the voice he heard was reassuring.

"Are you asleep?"

"Not yet. I'm waiting for the new year. You?"

"I'm still having dinner."

"Oh." Shen Mo recalled that they were in different time zones. He asked, "Is it fun spending New Year's abroad?"

The man replied in the same indifferent tone, "Not really."

The two casually chatted about a few things. The man suddenly asked, "Shen Mo, where are you now?"

Shen Mo replied without thinking, "I'm home."

The man asked again, "Alone?"

Shen Mo's eyelid twitched. Seeing the empty apartment and the half-finished noodles on the table, he tried to make his voice sound cheerful. "I'm in my hometown. Mom and Dad are both here."

Shen Mo wasn't a good liar. He was afraid he'd expose himself. Just then, the firecrackers began to grow louder, so he said in a hurry, "My parents are calling for me. They want me to go set off some firecrackers with them. I'll hang up for now."

The man didn't reply. He only called in a peculiar tone, "Shen Mo."

Shen Mo thought the man was about to say something, so he held his breath waiting.

A long time passed; the man's voice came through right as the clock struck twelve. However, he only said, "Happy New Year."

Shen Mo returned, "Happy New Year."

He felt a sadness, but also an indescribable sweetness.

Shen Mo hung up and went to sleep. He slept on the sofa, where the man usually slept. The man appeared in his dreams again and again. He had stayed up late, so the next day he also woke up late. It was a knock at the door that awakened him.

Startled, Shen Mo had no idea who would knock on his door at such a time. He got up and went to the door.

And the door opened.

Feeling as if he was still dreaming, Shen Mo saw the man he'd been longing for standing right outside the door.

In astonishment, Shen Mo stood still and said nothing.

The man didn't say a word either. He looked Shen Mo up and down almost as though he was seeing Shen Mo for the first time. In the end, his gaze returned to Shen Mo's face and he asked, "Did you spend New Year's alone?"

Shen Mo had really dug his own grave, this time. He'd lied once and now had to patch things up with even more lies.

Shen Mo knew there was no way to explain this. He could only say, "Yeah, my parents... decided to go on a trip last minute, so I came back early."

Whether the man believed his terrible lie or simply had no interest in pointing it out, Shen Mo saw the man nod. The man then walked inside, glancing at the bowl of noodles that hadn't yet been put away, and asked, "Was this all you had for dinner last night?"

Shen Mo regretted being lazy last night. If only he'd cooked a few more dishes, he wouldn't seem so pitiful now. He uttered a vague reply as he hastened to clear the table. The man sat down on the sofa and watched him quietly. Wherever he went, the pair of eyes followed him.

Shen Mo felt that the man was quite different from usual.

Right after Shen Mo finished putting away the bowl and chopsticks, he heard the man call, "Shen Mo, come here."

Shen Mo had always obeyed the man. He walked over meekly. Just as he was about to reach the sofa, the man suddenly extended his leg and tripped him. Caught off guard, Shen Mo stumbled a few steps forward, and the man took him into a tight embrace.

It was then that Shen Mo realized the man had done it on purpose.

He stayed in the man's arms, somewhat afraid to move now.

The man caressed Shen Mo's back. As he had done during the phone call last night, he said in a very restrained tone, "Shen Mo."

"Yes," Shen Mo responded.

The man lowered his head and kissed Shen Mo's eye—his movements were extremely careful. His warm, soft lips brushed past Shen Mo's eyelashes.

The kiss almost seemed to fall on the tip of Shen Mo's heart. Shen Mo trembled slightly.

But the man suddenly stopped. Panting, he rested his chin on Shen Mo's shoulder. He held Shen Mo even tighter.

Worried that the man would find yet another excuse along the lines of how Shen Mo hadn't recovered, Shen Mo strove to ask first, "Didn't you say you'd be staying overseas for a few more days? Why did you come back so early?"

"Something urgent came up. I changed my schedule at the last moment."

"What was it?"

The man finally couldn't bear it any longer. He kissed Shen Mo's eye again and said, "Don't ask if you already know."

A sweetness rose from the bottom of Shen Mo's heart. "How did you know that I didn't go home and stayed here alone for New Year's instead? Oh, you had your assistant book the ticket for me. Was he the one who told you?"

"I didn't know until I called you last night. I found out a little too late."

"It wasn't late at all." Shen Mo knew that the man must have flown back as soon as he could. "How did you manage to book the plane ticket in such a short time?"

The man smiled and said, "Money can solve many problems."

Seeing the man's expression, Shen Mo felt as though the man was hinting at something else. He couldn't help but ask, "Is there anything money can't solve?"

"Yes." The man gazed into Shen Mo's eyes, his voice almost inaudible.

"Like... make someone begin to like me."

Shen Mo parted his lips to nip at the man's chin. "I like you—isn't that enough? Does anyone else need to like with you?"

He held Shen Mo's waist and said in a husky voice, "Say that again."

Shen Mo knew what the man wanted to hear. He repeated beside the man's ear, "I like you, I like you, I like you..."

Just as Shen Mo was about to utter the man's name, the man turned around and sealed Shen Mo's lips with a kiss.

"Shh," he gazed at Shen Mo with eyes glinting like water, whispering, "be quiet."

Shen Mo didn't make a sound. He only kissed the man back harder.

The two embraced each other on the sofa. Shen Mo's legs felt so weak that he almost fell off onto the ground. The man reached out to support his back and pinned him down on the sofa.

It'd be torture if they stopped now. Just in case, Shen Mo hooked his legs tightly around the man's waist. The man chuckled, his hand sliding down the collar of Shen Mo's pajamas. As his cold fingers brushed against Shen Mo's chest, Shen Mo couldn't help but tense up his body.

On purpose, the man thumbed Shen Mo's nipple, rubbing and pinching slightly.

"Ahh..." Shen Mo let out a trembling moan.

The man kissed the corner of Shen Mo's eye before quickly withdrawing his hand. He then lowered his head and licked Shen Mo's nipple over the pajama shirt. The thin fabric dampened immediately. Shen Mo thrust out his chest and writhed as though he could no longer endure the pleasure, crying, "Mm... Don't..."

Only now did the man undo Shen Mo's shirt, one button at a time. But he didn't tease Shen Mo's nipples any longer. Instead, his hands moved down and soon took hold of Shen Mo's member.

Shen Mo's back tingled, almost as though a fire burned inside of him.

And the man on top of him was his only antidote.

Shen Mo wrapped his arms around the man's neck and urged, "Hurry..."

As Shen Mo wished, the man wrapped his hand around Shen Mo's erection, aggressively kissing him as he slid his palm up and down the length. Dizzied by the stimulation, Shen Mo soon came in the man's hand.

Absently, Shen Mo tried to catch his breath.

The man's forehead was also sweating somewhat. With fingers covered in come, he moved farther down and soon reached Shen Mo's puckered entrance. Slowly, he pushed in one finger.

Shen Mo was too tight. Even with just one finger inside, Shen Mo's face already paled in pain.

The man curled his finger with difficulty, saying beside Shen Mo's ear, "I can't. It's too tight."

Shen Mo whimpered, clenching around the man's finger. He had already found the perfect weapon against the man. In a somewhat hoarse voice, he said, "Don't leave me. I like you so much..."

The man's expression changed. Biting Shen Mo's lip, he hissed, "You asked for it."

After he said this, he kissed Shen Mo fiercely, swallowing all of Shen Mo's voice.

Closing his eyes, Shen Mo felt the finger probe inside him and gradually enter a frighteningly deep place. He couldn't help but shudder in pain.

Only after a long while did Shen Mo start to relax, and the man withdrew his finger and replaced it with something hard and hot.

Shen Mo's legs trembled. Unable to even let out a sound, he only stared at the man with watery eyes. Yet, the man suddenly grew gentler. He pressed his own forehead against Shen Mo's and kept on kissing Shen Mo. Then, he parted Shen Mo's legs and, inch by inch, entered Shen Mo's body.

Shen Mo didn't know how to describe the agony. He felt as though he was being ripped apart. Even his soul was tearing into pieces. Something that didn't belong to him had embedded itself into his body by force.

The man separated from Shen Mo's mouth. He took Shen Mo's right hand and brought it to his lips as he kissed Shen Mo's fingers one after another, asking tenderly, "Does it hurt?"

Shen Mo didn't know if the man was asking about his hand or the place where they were connected to each other.

As the man thrust, sweat seeped from Shen Mo's back. Shen Mo couldn't even say a word. He only shook his head, letting out meaningless moans.

Holding down Shen Mo's limbs, the man sent his hips forward, grinding harder and harder. One of Shen Mo's legs was folded up, while the other hung at the edge of the sofa, swaying like a line of white seafoam caught by waves.

A moment later, the man bent over and rested all of his weight on Shen Mo. Shen Mo felt a warmth surge into his body. He couldn't move, stuck in the corner of the sofa. Only the tips of his toes tensed, almost as if his body was cramping.

Quite some time passed before his heartbeats could calm down.

The sofa was too small for the two of them. The man first had Shen Mo take a shower with him before they got into bed together. Shen Mo had gotten exactly what he'd wanted—he felt that this was the way things were supposed to be. Exhausted, he lay down in the man's arms and fell asleep again.

When Shen Mo woke up, the sky looked dim. He couldn't tell whether it was dusk or dawn. The man, who had woken up earlier than him, was playing with his hair. As Shen Mo looked up, his lips brushed against the man's chin. The new-grown stubble there tickled him.

The man asked him, "Hungry?"

Shen Mo did feel a little hungry, but he didn't want to move. He said, "I want to sleep a little longer."

The man also lay down beside Shen Mo, wrapping his arms around Shen Mo's body.

Shen Mo casually chatted with him, "Why didn't you open the door with your key when you came back?"

"I left in a hurry and forgot to bring it."

This was more like something Shen Mo would do. Shen Mo held

back his laughter and asked, "You came back so early. Won't your family have something to say?"

"It doesn't matter. My sister..."

Shen Mo found it strange. He asked, "Aren't you an only child?"

The man didn't reply. He only stroked Shen Mo's hair, messing it up.

Shen Mo felt that something was wrong, but before he could figure it out, he heard the man ask, "Why didn't you go home for New Year's?"

Clearly, the man didn't believe Shen Mo's lie.

While Shen Mo searched as hard as he could for another excuse, the man grabbed his shoulders and gazed at him. "Tell me the truth."

Shen Mo's lips moved. Only a while later did he say, "It's nothing. It was because... I got kicked out by my parents. You know. Over summer vacation that year, I went back home..."

Hastily, Shen Mo told the man what had happened, skimming over all of the anguish and heartbreak.

"I actually call home every few months. It's just that nobody picks up."

The man listened quietly. In the end, he wrapped Shen Mo in a tight embrace and said, "So you're all alone."

"Of course not. I still have you, don't I?" Shen Mo held the man's hand as he asked, "We won't break up, will we?"

The man's eyes were an unfathomable abyss.

For some reason, Shen Mo felt an anxiousness within him. He asked the man again.

The man finally smiled, covering Shen Mo's eyes with his palm. Shen Mo's field of view darkened. The world was pitch-black now, leaving behind only the man's voice. Shen Mo heard the man say slowly, "...Of course not."

Shen Mo's right hand gradually began to heal.

After several months of rehabilitation, the injury to his right hand no longer affected his daily life, although his hand still trembled slightly whenever he held a paintbrush. The doctor said that this was due to psychological factors; it'd recover sooner or later as long as he did his exercises properly. His ability to recognize people had also improved—he could already distinguish the man's two assistants. However, the man still made him go to the hospital for regular rehabilitation.

The man hadn't slept on the sofa since New Year's. As the days grew warmer, Shen Mo's heart blossomed as well. He felt that this was the happiest he'd ever been. He was in such high spirits that he almost couldn't recall most of what had happened in the past.

As Shen Mo practiced using his right hand, he also looked up recruitment information online. He was searching for positions related to painting, hoping he could get a job after his hand recovered. After all, they'd already graduated college and entered society. Now that they were beginning to age, they had to face reality sooner or later. Zhou Yang's family probably wouldn't let them stay together. If the man also got kicked out by his family, then he would at least be able to live off Shen Mo.

When Shen Mo mentioned this plan at the dinner table later, the man couldn't help but laugh.

Shen Mo glared at him, somewhat angered.

Seeing this, the man quickly changed his attitude and said, "Okay, okay. I'll live off you."

Only then was Shen Mo satisfied.

Shen Mo reckoned that at this rate, it was just a matter of time before his right hand fully recovered, and he'd soon be able to paint again. He had made up his mind long ago that Zhou Yang would be his first subject. After all, the man looked handsome from every angle.

Often, as the man read documents on the sofa, Shen Mo eyed him quietly from the side, considering the composition of the painting. The glow of the sunset splashed onto the man's face, drawing a faint light over his features. Shen Mo thought that the side of the man's face was particularly charming.

As Shen Mo mused, the man seemed to notice Shen Mo's gaze. He looked up and smiled at Shen Mo.

Shen Mo was somewhat surprised.

The man had already stood up. He strode toward Shen Mo, bent down, and kissed Shen Mo on the lips. Then, he straightened up and went back to reading the documents as if nothing had happened.

Meanwhile, Shen Mo blushed, then slipped into the kitchen to cook.

A few days later, the sky cleared up. Spring could be felt everywhere.

Shen Mo washed all of their winter clothes and blankets before drying them in the sun. Remembering how his tools were still locked in the cabinet, he fished them out and put them in order. When the man found out that Shen Mo was going to paint again, he even suggested buying him a new set. But Shen Mo turned down the offer, since he was more familiar with his old supplies.

After sorting out the art supplies, Shen Mo tidied up the cabinet as well. The rental was quite small; the cabinet was filled with miscellanea from fever medicine to bug spray. Shen Mo threw away everything he deemed useless. As he rummaged through the cabinet, he happened to find an album.

His previous photos had all been left in his hometown. This album only contained some photos from high school and college. The moment Shen Mo opened it, a graduation photo fell out.

It was a high school graduation photo. Now that Shen Mo thought about it, it'd been several years since then already. Right at first glance, he recognized himself in the photo, wearing his school uniform and really short bangs. Because he wasn't too tall, he had stood in one of the front rows. He looked for Zhou Yang next. Yet, even after searching around, he wasn't able to find the familiar face.

Strange. Hadn't Zhou Yang taken part in the graduation photoshoot?

Shen Mo could remember that he and Zhou Yang had been high school classmates. He had fallen in love with Zhou Yang, and he had been the one to ask Zhou Yang out. However, there were many details that he was unable to recall. As one would expect, he couldn't recall if Zhou Yang had taken part in the graduation photoshoot either.

Shen Mo knew it was because he was sick. But it didn't matter. He'd taken many casual photos with Zhou Yang as well. He'd printed out all of them and put them inside the album.

Shen Mo had nothing else to do, so he sat down and flipped through the album.

He didn't take photos often. Most of the photos had been taken at school, although a few had been taken on vacation. Some were single photos while others were group photos, but most were of him and one other person.

As Shen Mo went through the photos one after another, his heart seemed to sink into a cold lake, sending chills all across his body.

He was smiling so happily in the photos, especially when it came to shots of him and that other person. The affection seeping from his eyes was impossible to hide.

But that person wasn't Zhou Yang.

Or, not the man he had been living with and sleeping beside.

Shen Mo's palms sweat uncontrollably.

Who was this man?

Shen Mo pulled himself together before picking up the high school graduation photo and comparing it with the rest of the photos. This time, he looked at it carefully, scrutinizing one face after another. Finally, he found a set of similar features—on the person standing two rows behind him. This was his high school classmate indeed.

If this person wasn't Zhou Yang, why did they associate with each other so often?

But if this person was really Zhou Yang...

Without a doubt, it'd be even more terrifying.

Shen Mo sat on the chair, absent-minded. The beautiful springtime rays shone on him, but he couldn't feel a single hint of warmth. He tried his best to remember, but as though a veil was hanging before him, everything seemed hazy and unreal.

Shen Mo could remember that he and Zhou Yang had been high school classmates, that they had fallen in love with each other, and that... No matter what, he couldn't remember Zhou Yang's face. It seemed that something had happened in the middle, and he and Zhou

Yang were forced apart. Then, his right hand was injured, and he began to live alone in the rental. Every night, the same nightmare repeated itself over and over again. He was too afraid to fall asleep.

Until that day – he was about to open a pack of moldy bread when he heard the doorbell ring. In a trance he walked over to open the door and saw the man standing outside the door.

That had been his Zhou Yang, of course.

Shen Mo pressed his palm against his chest. Even now, he could recall that throb in his heart. Who could have rescued him, if not Zhou Yang?

As for why he couldn't see the man's face too clearly back then, it had only been because of his illness. Now that he was getting better, he knew that the man looked handsome, or at least much better than the nobodies in the photo.

In reality, it was easy to confirm the matter. All he had to do was to ask a high school classmate. But Shen Mo still sat there, unmoving. He felt somewhat afraid. He hoped that it was just some kind of misunderstanding. But if...

He didn't even dare think about it.

The afternoon passed quickly. As the sun went down, there came the familiar sound of the opening door. Shen Mo jumped up from his chair. He had used to look forward to this sound so much, but now he was scared for no reason. He hurried to shove the photos back inside the cabinet.

The man pushed open the door and entered the room. He wore a dark suit, his features the same as Shen Mo remembered. Seeing Shen Mo standing beside the cabinet, the man smiled and asked, "Tidying things up again?"

Shen Mo exclaimed, "Ah." He only stared at the man's face.

"What's wrong?" The man walked toward Shen Mo and took Shen Mo's hand, frowning. "Why is your hand so cold?"

Even the man's touch made Shen Mo nervous. Panicking, he didn't know how to respond.

The man asked, "Are you tired?"

And so Shen Mo replied, "Yeah, a little."

"I know you want to start painting again, but don't push yourself too hard. Just let nature take its course."

"I know."

Shen Mo's right hand had long since gotten better, but the man still rubbed it between his palms out of habit. He asked, "Where's dinner?"

Only then did Shen Mo realize, "Oh, I forgot to make it."

"You lose track of time whenever you think about painting, don't you?" The man smiled and said, "Let's get delivery."

In the evening, the two ate together. Shen Mo tried to act naturally, but his limbs were still somewhat stiff. He wondered if the man had noticed.

Shen Mo took a shower after dinner. When he came out, he saw that, quite naturally, the man had already gotten into bed. Neither of them had slept alone since New Year's, but it was different now. If the man wasn't Zhou Yang...

Feeling his throat tense, Shen Mo was reluctant to get in bed. Only after the man urged him several times did he finally lie down.

The man turned off the light and reached out to wrap his arms around Shen Mo, calling in the dark, "Shen Mo."

"Yeah?"

Shen Mo replied cautiously. He thought that the man had noticed something, but instead he heard him say, "Your birthday is in a few days. What do you want as a present?"

Birthday?

Oh, right. His birthday was this month.

Shen Mo had almost forgotten about this. He thought for a while before he replied, "I never go out of my way to celebrate my birthday. There's no need to bother."

The man seemed to have known what Shen Mo would say. A grin could be heard in his voice, "I'll do as I see fit, then."

The man wasn't aware of anything. All he cared about was celebrating Shen Mo's birthday.

Shen Mo's heart throbbed, almost as though it was sizzling atop a fire.

His eyes stayed open, and he didn't sleep. Only when the man next to him fell asleep, breathing steadily, did he carefully move his arm away. He turned around to sleep on the edge of the bed.

The man reached out for him in vain, murmuring in his sleep, "Shen Mo."

Shen Mo gritted his teeth and didn't respond.

The man even knew when his birthday was. How could he be anyone but Zhou Yang?

But if, if the man was really a complete stranger…

Why did he pretend to be Zhou Yang?

Why did he treat him so tenderly?

Shen Mo couldn't help but tremble. As the long night approached, he wrapped himself in the blanket and hugged himself tightly.

But he still felt cold.

The next day, Shen Mo woke up in warm arms. However, he'd fallen asleep last night, he'd ended up rolling into the man's arms again.

The man had woken up earlier than Shen Mo. Lowering his head, he kissed the top of Shen Mo's head and said, "I'll be working overtime these few days. I can take a day off during the weekend and spend some time outside with you."

The weekend was Shen Mo's birthday.

Shen Mo felt a thud in his heart. He kept silent in the man's arms.

The man added, "Do you remember that painting of yours from before? It was a vision of your dream home."

Absently, Shen Mo said, "Really? I don't remember."

A painting with such a definite subject had probably been an assignment from university. Even he himself didn't remember it—how could somebody else know?

But the man embraced him gently and stated, "Yes. There *was* such a painting."

The man pressed his chest against Shen Mo's back. Their heartbeats almost seemed to overlap.

Shen Mo almost yielded to the warmth of this affection. However, after the man got up and went to work, Shen Mo still cleaned himself up and visited the hospital. He met with his usual doctor. The examination showed that his illness was well under control, although he still had to take medicine.

Shen Mo asked carefully, "With this illness... is it possible for me to mistake someone for someone else?"

The doctor answered with much reservation, "Those with serious PTSD may choose to avoid reality and forget certain things or people. As for whether or not it's possible for them to mistake one person for another, it depends on the specific circumstances."

Hearing this, Shen Mo already had a guess as to what had happened.

He had indeed lost some of his memories. Just what in the world had happened for him to have forgotten even Zhou Yang's face? Even to, even to have mistaken a stranger for Zhou Yang?

The most straightforward solution was to ask the man about it. But the man had to work overtime for the next few days, leaving early and returning late every day. Shen Mo didn't even have the chance to meet him face-to-face.

It wasn't until Friday evening that the man came home early. The moment he saw Shen Mo, he asked, "Should we order cake for tomorrow?"

He was still thinking about Shen Mo's birthday.

Shen Mo shook his head and said, "No. I'll just cook a few more dishes tomorrow."

Glancing at the man's face, Shen Mo asked deliberately, "What do you like to eat?"

Oblivious, the man casually mentioned a few dishes.

Shen Mo made the comparison in his mind—those weren't dishes that Zhou Yang liked. The truth was already so close, and yet he began to hesitate, reluctant to expose the man right there.

To make time for the special day, the man had compressed his work to the several days before. Even now, he hadn't finished working yet. He took out his laptop to write emails.

Shen Mo sat at the side and watched the man quietly. For many nights, he had gazed at the side of the man's face like this, planning the composition of his painting.

But he hadn't even had time to finish the painting yet.

Shen Mo felt a soreness in his chest. Finally, he called, "Zhou Yang!"

The man paused, lifting his head slowly. He didn't respond and only gave Shen Mo one glance. His eyes were dark. His gaze was as cold as a snowy winter night as it collided with Shen Mo's heart.

Shen Mo felt as though a cold hand had clenched around his heart. Pain seeped from the cracks of his bones. He heard himself say in a hoarse voice, "You're not Zhou Yang."

The man didn't say anything.

The living room was quiet apart from the ticking of the wall clock. Shen Mo had never known that time could pass so slowly. Moments later, the man shut his laptop and loosened his tie, declaring, "That's right. Of course not."

Shen Mo had prepared himself for it, but after he heard this, his ears still buzzed. He took quite some time to regain his composure.

The man stood up from the sofa and walked toward him, calling, "Shen Mo?"

The man reached out to touch his face.

Startled, Shen Mo couldn't help but dodge to the side.

The man's hand stopped in the air. A while later, he drew it back.

Shen Mo looked up and asked him, "If you're not Zhou Yang, why did you pretend to be him?"

"I pretended to be Zhou Yang?" The man uttered something between a snort and a laugh. He said, "You were the one who mistook me for him first, weren't you?"

Shen Mo was speechless. According to his own memory, he was indeed the one who had mistaken the man for Zhou Yang first. He could vaguely recall that the man had even denied it several times. But he had been ill back then—how could he have acted rationally?

"You could have left me alone and let me look after myself. Or, if you were kinder, you could have just taken me to the hospital. Why did you pretend to be Zhou Yang?"

The man took Shen Mo's hand. Shen Mo's right hand had been injured. Even though it'd healed, some scars still remained. The man stroked the scars tenderly and said, "At first, I was afraid that you might starve to death alone in this place, so I visited you from time to time. But later, I realized how stubborn your temper is. I couldn't leave you alone. And after that..."

Shen Mo asked, "And after that?"

The man put Shen Mo's hand to his lips, almost as though it was a kiss. He gazed at Shen Mo and asked, "Do you really not know? Why I stayed by your side?"

As if realizing something, Shen Mo whispered, "Don't say it..."

But the man had already bent over to kiss Shen Mo's lips. "Because I like you, Shen Mo."

Shen Mo gasped, scrambling to escape the kiss. He stepped back again and again until his back was against the wall. The man reached forward and trapped Shen Mo in his arms.

Running his fingers through Shen Mo's hair, the man said, "Dr. Tang called me two days ago. I'd already guessed that you'd recover soon."

The surname of Shen Mo's doctor was Tang. It was then that Shen Mo realized the man knew everything but had only pretended that nothing was wrong.

"It's good that you've woken up to it, really. It's not as if you could have lived in your memories for the rest of your life, anyway." The man added in a gentler tone, "Shen Mo. Pack up your things. Let's go."

Shen Mo was confused. "Go? Go where?"

The man smiled. Little by little, the tip of his nose came up to Shen Mo's face. Amid an indescribable softness, he said, "You'll see when we arrive."

Before, Shen Mo had liked it when the man smiled like this.

No, no, no—at that time, he'd thought that the man was Zhou Yang. But now, the man was no more than a nameless stranger.

Shen Mo closed his eyes for a moment and said, "No. I can't leave."

"Why not?"

"I have to stay here and wait for Zhou Yang."

Shen Mo let out those words without thinking. When he finished, he saw the smile in the man's eyes turn cold.

"Zhou Yang went abroad. You broke up a long time ago."

Shen Mo didn't possess this piece of memory, but he unconsciously shook his head. "No. Zhou Yang and I are only apart for the time being."

The man kept quiet for a moment before he suddenly asked, "What about me, Shen Mo?"

Shen Mo's heart quivered as though it were immersed in seawater, half cold and half warm, floating and unable to touch the shore. Yet, he continued, "I thought you were Zhou Yang... The one I love has always been Zhou Yang..."

Before Shen Mo could finish speaking, the man silenced him with a kiss.

Unlike the gentle peck from before, the man was anxious and aggressive this time. He quickly took Shen Mo's mouth by force, as though he wanted to rob Shen Mo of all air, leaving no room for Shen Mo to breathe.

Shen Mo almost thought he'd die like this. He couldn't help but struggle, biting down hard on the man's lip.

As their tongues entangled, a metallic taste spread throughout their mouths. The man only let out a muffled groan. He didn't move at all, still gripping Shen Mo's shoulders as he kissed him.

Shen Mo managed to back off a little, calling vaguely, "Zhou Yang—"

The man suddenly stopped.

His lips were still against Shen Mo's. He seemed to tremble slightly. Only a few moments later did he slowly draw away. A scarlet trace of blood had been left by Shen Mo's bite, making his face seem even paler.

Shen Mo had never seen the man like this before.

But the man quickly concealed his emotions. He let go of Shen Mo, regaining his usual composure. Even his voice sounded calm and restrained. "Yes. The one you love is Zhou Yang."

The man casually wiped the blood from his lips and straightened up.

"It's unsuitable for me to stay the night, isn't it?"

Shen Mo didn't know what to say in reply. He'd just been living his days, and the person sleeping next to him suddenly became someone else. Who in the world would know what to do? His thoughts were a mess.

But the man had already nodded, saying to himself, "Of course you won't come with me. I'm the one who should go."

The man looked so composed, displaying no anger at all on the surface. As calm as usual, he took his laptop from the table and walked out the door.

Shen Mo's legs moved on their own; he followed the man for a few steps. He didn't stop until he reached the door.

He didn't even know who the man was. Why had he tried to follow the man just like that? At least he had to retrieve his memories and figure out what had happened between Zhou Yang and him.

Shen Mo sat back down on the sofa.

It started raining outside. The raindrops rustled. He and Zhou Yang had furnished this place together, but now the shadows of another man lurked in every corner.

Shen Mo didn't know how long had passed when he heard the doorbell ring again. He rushed to open the door. Outside stood the man who'd returned once again.

For a moment, Shen Mo was stunned.

The man should have driven here, but he'd been rained upon for some reason. His clothes were drenched. Water dripped from the ends of his hair. Even his eyes seemed to have been dipped in rain as they gazed at Shen Mo deeply.

Shen Mo opened his mouth, but he didn't let out a sound.

The man didn't enter the apartment. He only took Shen Mo's hand and stuffed a delicate box in its grasp. "I prepared this present a long time ago. I was going to show it to you in person..."

The rain was loud. Like a veil hung between them, his voice sounded somewhat unreal.

"You can go take a look on your own, or..."

Surrounded by watery mist, the man approached Shen Mo.

Shen Mo didn't avoid the man this time.

The man was so impossibly close to Shen Mo, almost as if he would kiss Shen Mo the next second. But in the end, he didn't do anything but whisper, "Or you can pretend that you never received it. That way, I'll know how you feel."

Shen Mo found the box in his hand to be warm and dry. It was raining so heavily. He didn't know where the man had hidden the box.

He clasped this early birthday present, as if he was clasping a person's whole heart.

Shen Mo only had a bowl of noodles on his birthday. He boiled the noodles in nothing but water and added no ingredients. Along with some soy sauce, sesame oil, and chopped green onions, he ate the noodles alone in the small rental.

If he hadn't exposed the man's identity yesterday, the current scene would definitely be different.

Shen Mo looked at the present box on the table as he ate.

It was a common present box, well-packaged and adorned with a beautiful bow on its lid. Imagining how earnest the straight-faced man must have looked while choosing this packaging, Shen Mo was somewhat amused.

Shen Mo had already opened the box last night. Inside it was a key and a note. The handwriting on the note, one he wasn't familiar with, must belong to the man. An address was written plainly on the note—the address was located in Jinxiu Villa, a famous residential area in the city, known for being well-located and tremendously expensive. Shen Mo had heard of it long ago, but he had never been there before.

Shen Mo knew how much effort the man must have spent on preparing the present. These feelings shouldn't be treated disrespectfully. So he closed the box again and put it away, planning to make his decision once he figured out what had happened between him and Zhou Yang.

The sky still looked gloomy today. It seemed as if it would rain soon. Shen Mo looked out the window. The man must be waiting for him in Jinxiu Villa.

For how long would the man wait?

A week? A month? Or even longer?

Shen Mo shook his head and stopped himself from thinking further. After he finished the noodles, he looked up Zhou Yang's number on his phone and made a call.

Zhou Yang's number remained powered off.

Shen Mo dialed the number over and over again. He felt that this had happened before, but he couldn't remember anything about it. He could only give up. Instead, he contacted several high school classmates and asked them about Zhou Yang.

"Zhou Yang? I haven't been in touch with him since we graduated."

"I don't know."

"I don't know. You were closer to Zhou Yang, weren't you? I used to see you two together all the time."

Only one classmate said, "I heard he went abroad."

The man had also said that Zhou Yang had gone abroad.

If it was true, Shen Mo had no idea what to do next. He didn't even know where Zhou Yang had gone. And, he couldn't go abroad chasing after Zhou Yang, could he? Although he had Zhou Yang's family address in his address book, he couldn't go straight to Zhou Yang's family. He'd probably be kicked out the moment he reached the gates.

Did he and Zhou Yang have to end just like this, with no explanation or whatsoever?

Shen Mo glanced at the box on the table before he made a few more calls, unwilling to give up. Of course, he didn't hear any more news about Zhou Yang. It had been so many years since they'd graduated from high school. Most of his classmates came from ordinary families.

They lived in a completely different world than Zhou Yang did.

In reality, Shen Mo was the same.

He knew that their relationship had been precarious. Every day, he felt as though he was walking a tightrope. If he weren't truly in love with Zhou Yang, he could never have persevered until now.

At this point, Shen Mo suddenly remembered someone—a person who had helped him and Zhou Yang handle the procedures when they rented this place. Zhou Yang had said it was more convenient this way, and they wouldn't be found out. Shen Mo recalled that the person, surnamed Fang, had been a middle-aged man wearing gold-rimmed glasses and a polite expression. Zhou Yang had called him Fang-*shu*[1] and had told Shen Mo that he'd worked at the Zhou family's enterprise.

The person had used to have quite a good relationship with Zhou Yang. He must know where Zhou Yang had gone.

With a goal in mind, Shen Mo could finally calm down. He went to bed early in the evening. Before he fell asleep, he glanced out the window. He seemed to catch sight of the familiar car, but the car disappeared again in an instant.

It was probably no more than an illusion.

Shen Mo got up early the next day. He cleaned himself up and headed out. The Zhou family's company building was in the city center, so Shen Mo went there by bus. Once he walked through the splendid glass doors, receptionists welcomed him with sweet smiles at the front desk.

Shen Mo walked over calmly, pretending that he had come for business. Indirectly, he inquired about Fang-shu.

"You mean Secretary Fang, don't you? His office is on the sixth floor."

"Thank you."

After expressing his thanks, Shen Mo turned around and pressed the elevator button. While he waited, someone else came through the doors. It was a woman with elegant features, wearing a befitting outfit and a set of pearl jewelry. She wasn't young, but there was a sophisti-

[1] An honorific suffix or title that, while literally meaning "uncle," is used regardless of familial relation for any man who's at least one nominal generation older than the speaker, or of the same nominal generation as the speaker's parent(s).

cated air to her.

The receptionists all put on respectful expressions the moment they saw her.

The elevator rang as its doors opened. Only after Shen Mo stepped into the elevator did he realize who the lady was. She was Zhou Yang's mother—Mrs. Zhou who had been born to a wealthy family and had always gone to great lengths to get what she wanted. Shen Mo had once seen her photo on Zhou Yang's phone.

As Shen Mo walked into the elevator, Mrs. Zhou gave him one glance.

Shen Mo met her eyes. His chest suddenly tightened.

In the nightmares that repeated themselves over and over again, a scar-faced man had also looked at him in the same way, stepping on his hand with a grim smile as he said something besides his ear. He couldn't hear any sound in his dreams. Only now did he remember what the sentence was.

"We're just teaching you a lesson this time. Don't ever think of seeing Zhou Yang again. He's out of your league."

No—it wasn't just a nightmare!

It had really happened. He had been abducted and beaten up, his fingers had been crushed... And the Zhou family had been behind everything!

The elevator stopped again. Not knowing which floor he was on, Shen Mo bolted the moment the doors opened. His head throbbed in pain. Many memories surged up, tangling up his thoughts.

As though countless voices talked right beside his ears.

"Get away from Zhou Yang!"

"Or your family will be in trouble next."

"Mr. Zhou went abroad with Miss Ji..."

Yes. And there had been a Miss Ji.

Pressing one hand against the wall, Shen Mo took a few steps forward. He saw an emergency exit, so he went back down using the stairs.

He remembered many fragments: he had been walking alone on

his way home, and a car came up to him from behind... the abandoned warehouse, the endless torture... and in the hospital, he broke up with Zhou Yang on the phone...

As well as...

As well as the man who visited him in the hospital. The man had a handsome face and a pair of eyes as cold as the night. The man said that his surname was Ji, and that he was Miss Ji's older brother.

No, no, no... That wasn't the first time they met!

Even before what had happened at the hospital, he'd seen that face before.

Only a few more steps remained on the staircase. Shen Mo was so absent-minded that he accidentally slipped and fell hard. The moment he crashed to the ground, a scene flashed across his eyes—

In the abandoned warehouse, he was curled up on the ground. His right hand was badly hurt. Just as he thought he was going to die, the door that had been tightly shut suddenly opened. A ray of light shone through. The man outside the door stood against the light with blurry features. Shen Mo saw the man walking toward him. Little by little, the man's face grew clearer.

The man who had rescued him.

Shen Mo's head ached even more, but he finally remembered the man's name.

—Ji Mingxuan.

***

Shen Mo woke up from his dreams.

The sun was almost down. The remaining sunset shone warmly on his body. He had taken a nap on the grass in the park, and pieces of grass were now stuck to his hair and clothes. He looked quite funny; passersby who saw him all smiled kindly at him. Shen Mo didn't mind it, though, smiling back at them. He stood up and picked up the drawing board on the ground.

He had begun to paint again several years ago, trying to paint with his left hand. He practiced slowly. Even though he hadn't yet caught up to the expertise of his past self, he was satisfied with himself anyway.

He had come out to sketch today, but the sunshine felt so good that he couldn't help but fall asleep. He had never expected to dream of something that had happened so long ago.

After he packed away all of his tools, Shen Mo put on his backpack and strode out of the park. He had a studio at Yongning Road. When he'd broken up with Ji Mingxuan that year, Ji Mingxuan had given him the property. Later, he simply renovated it and opened a small studio. The business was neither good nor bad, but it was enough for him to get by.

Due to the rush hour, traffic was heavy on his way back. When Shen Mo reached the studio, the sky had already darkened completely. He'd hired a young girl to help him with the studio. When Yang Yue saw Shen Mo come back so late, a slightly irked expression showed on her face. "Boss, you were out lazing around again!"

Mild-tempered, Shen Mo put away his things as he said, "Sorry for coming back so late. Did I keep you from your date with your boyfriend? You can get off work now."

Yang Yue had gotten this job after graduating college. Having worked here for a few years now, she was now quite familiar with Shen Mo. She hurriedly reapplied her makeup as she asked, "What are you eating tonight, boss? Takeout again?"

"That's right."

"Curry rice again?"

"Yeah," Shen Mo replied, adding, "I like curry."

"No matter how much you like it, you can't have it every day." Yang Yue put down her pressed powder. As though she had gone through it all, she advised, "You're already thirty, boss. Isn't it time for you to get yourself a girlfriend?"

Shen Mo was surprised for a moment. "I'm not even twenty-nine yet."

But to spry young girls, what was the difference between twenty-nine and thirty?

"Twenty-nine makes you an old man already." Yang Yue picked up her eyebrow pencil and filled in her brows. "The older you are, the less popular you'll be when it comes to dating."

Shen Mo replied, "I haven't met the right person."

"Should I introduce someone to you? One of my old classmates from college..."

Shen Mo hurriedly turned her down. "I'm okay."

"I've been here for almost three years, and I haven't ever seen you with a girlfriend." Yang Yue suddenly leaned over, staring at Shen Mo as she asked, "Boss, don't tell me there's already someone in your heart?"

She had just penciled in her eyebrows. Her two arched brows looked as dark as ink.

For a moment, Shen Mo's mind was elsewhere. He couldn't answer.

Yang Yue was the kind of young girl who loved to gossip. At once, her interest was piqued. She guessed, "Your first love? Or your crush? Or a goddess you've been chasing after for years?"

As Shen Mo recalled that dream from not long ago, his heart started beating faster. But he'd already learned how to regulate his emotions. He still looked calm on the surface.

"No," worried that Yang Yue wouldn't believe it—or perhaps that he himself wouldn't believe it—he reiterated, "there's no such person."

Yang Yue couldn't be fooled so easily, but just as she was about to dig deeper, she heard a honk from outside the door.

"Oh, my boyfriend's here to pick me up. I'll be off, then. Bye-bye, boss!"

Now that her boyfriend had come, Yang Yue immediately waved her hand. She left "old man" Shen Mo and dashed out with her handbag.

Shen Mo watched her leave before turning away to order delivery. He actually wasn't terrible at cooking, but he was too lazy to cook now that he was living alone—delivery was more convenient. The curry rice soon arrived. After he ate dinner, he had to deal with some chores. There were almost no customers around this time, so he closed the studio, set up his drawing board, and continued working on his unfinished painting.

During his afternoon at the park, he had already completed most of it. Amid the silence of the night, it was also particularly easy to concentrate. He soon finished coloring the painting. Putting down his paintbrush, Shen Mo stepped back to look at it. He felt quite satisfied with how it had turned out.

But he still hadn't signed it.

Shen Mo hesitated for a while before he picked up his paintbrush again. He changed it from his right hand to his left hand, and then from his left back to his right. His right hand still trembled slightly as he held the paintbrush, but he tried his best to control his grip. One stroke after another, he wrote the two characters "*Shen Mo.*" The signature was a little different from what it had used to be, but the style remained the same.

Looking at these two characters, Shen Mo almost couldn't stop himself from remembering that day a few years ago. He had opened the door of the study at Jinxiu Villa only to find a room filled with his paintings.

Some were work from university, some were commissioned portraits, and some were no more than doodles. He didn't know how much time and money the man had spent on collecting these pieces.

... So that was the secret of Jinxiu Villa.

At that moment, Shen Mo knew he must have lost some parts of his past.

After breaking up with Zhou Yang back then, Shen Mo had spent over half of the year in a trance. He wanted to ask Ji Mingxuan about what had happened, but when he finally got in touch with Ji Mingxuan, Ji Mingxuan refused to see him. In the end, he could only pay a visit to the hospital. Only with the help of a therapist was he able to remember the past.

He had once held the man's heart, but he let go of it.

Back when he'd fallen from the stairs, Shen Mo had been taken to the hospital by the building's security guard. Fortunately, he wasn't seriously injured. Apart from some minor external injuries, he only suffered a slight concussion. He was dizzy for a few days, during which his memory was a mess. Although he remembered having been abducted, he'd lost all memory of what had happened in the few months after it.

And Ji Mingxuan... had truly become a stranger to him.

Later, when his rent expired and he almost had to live on the street, Ji Mingxuan had given him a contract. Only then did the two of them cross paths again.

Once Shen Mo had recovered his memories, he had been eager to see Ji Mingxuan. He hadn't known how to contact Ji Mingxuan since Ji Mingxuan had been abroad, so he'd ended up turning to Mr. Chen. Mr. Chen had been quite kind—after some difficulties and communication, Shen Mo had finally gotten in touch with Ji Mingxuan again.

But Ji Mingxuan hadn't wanted to see him.

Only after Shen Mo had contacted Ji Mingxuan a few more times did Ji Mingxuan send a reply to him through Mr. Chen: "Don't trouble yourself."

Mr. Chen had also said euphemistically, "Miss Ji's condition isn't too good."

Shen Mo had felt a coldness in his chest. He had known then that everything had already come to an end.

No matter his lost memories or Ji Mingxuan's secret love, Shen Mo didn't need to pursue anything further. Ji An'an would always come between him and Ji Mingxuan. From then on, he and Ji Mingxuan would be in two different worlds. They did not need to see each other again.

On the afternoon of that day, Shen Mo had calmly thanked Mr. Chen and moved out of Ji Mingxuan's house. As for the things that Ji Mingxuan had given him, he'd only made use of the shop on Yongning Road. In the next few years, he'd opened up a studio and started painting again. Time had passed by so quietly, almost as if he had never known Ji Mingxuan in the first place.

It was just that he still dreamed of these things, once in a while.

Shen Mo laughed at himself. Seeing how late it was already, he felt it was time to go home and rest. After hastily packing up his things, just as he was about to leave, he caught a glimpse of the calendar on the wall. It was already late January. A few days later would be the Lunar New Year, and after that would be the start of spring.

Shen Mo stared at the date for a while before he slowly drew back his gaze.

He was a little absent-minded on his way home. Once he got back, he took a shower and opened up his laptop as usual, surfing the web. When he realized it, he had already booked a plane ticket.

It was a ticket to a small overseas island on the fourth of February.

When Shen Mo told Yang Yue about this the next day, Yang Yue's cheeks puffed up again. "You're going abroad for a trip? You're too lazy, Boss. You go out to have fun around this time every single year."

Shen Mo could only say, "You can go on your annual leave when I come back."

Only then did Yang Yue brighten up a little, asking, "Where are you going this time, boss?"

"The same place."

"S Island again?" Yang Yue was somewhat surprised. "But it's a honeymoon resort. Only couples go there. You're single, so why do you still go there every year? Are you waiting for a love affair or trying to steal somebody else's girlfriend?"

Shen Mo had a convincing reason. "I'm having an art block. I'm going to get some inspiration."

As expected, Yang Yue had nothing else to say. She only asked, "When are you leaving?"

"The flight is on the fourth of February."

Going through the calendar, Yang Yue said, "It'll be the start of spring that day."

She then exclaimed, "Huh," and asked, "If I remember correctly, you always head out around the start of spring, boss. Is there some special meaning to it?"

As though she had picked up on something, she turned back to Shen Mo.

Shen Mo's heart skipped a beat, but he was still wearing a smile on his face. "Of course there is. Spring is the beginning of the year. Everything comes to life in spring. All kinds of flowers bloom. It's a great time to go on a trip."

Hearing this, Yang Yue didn't ask any further. Shen Mo used this opportunity to tell her to make a cup of coffee.

Not before long, Yang Yue brought the coffee over. Shen Mo hadn't slept well last night; taking in the coffee's aroma, he still felt somewhat sleepy. As noon approached, the shadow of the coffee cup stretched long beneath the sunlight. With half-closed eyes, Shen Mo gazed out the window—this was the most at ease he'd ever felt.

But amid the serenity, Shen Mo still felt that something was missing. No matter how happy he was, there was no contentment. Perhaps, just as Yang Yue had said, a certain name had rooted in his heart. It had sprouted and grown over the years, springing up whenever he wasn't paying attention and sprawling across his chest.

He had never missed a person so much.

Even if Shen Mo reached inside himself and pressed hard, so much so that his heart began to bleed, he would still be unable to suppress his feelings.

Shen Mo celebrated New Year's quite simply. He gave Yang Yue a break, cooked a few dishes at home, and had dinner with a bottle of red wine. Since he was eating alone, no matter how exquisite the food was, it tasted just as bland and lonely as ordinary take-out did. He went to bed before the clock struck twelve. Wrapping himself in a thick blanket, he fell asleep amid the sound of firecrackers outside the window.

Right after New Year's, it would be the start of spring.

Shen Mo had been to S Island a couple of times, so he didn't make an itinerary. He only changed some foreign cash and packed his suitcase. He had his hair cut the day before his departure. He had always looked young, and now that his bangs were short enough to reveal his eyes, he looked a bit younger than his real age.

Just like... four years ago.

This time four years ago, Shen Mo had longed to go to S island together with Ji Mingxuan. But who could have known how much things had changed? In the end, he could only go alone.

Early morning, on the fourth of February, Shen Mo left home with his suitcase. It was a connecting flight; it took over ten hours for him to reach his destination. S Island was a famous honeymoon destination best known for its beaches—a beautiful white sand and blue seawater scene.

The hotel where Shen Mo would stay was situated on a cliff in the south of S Island. All of its suites and villas had been built along the terrain. Inside each room, one could hear ocean waves drum against the coast, and beyond the window, the entire ocean was within one's view—the scenery was spectacular. The room's interior design was unique as well. It not only incorporated modern elements but also retained the naturalness of its surroundings. The hotel had been built not long ago; its investor seemed to be Chinese as well. Even though it was costly to stay here, Shen Mo didn't care too much about it, as he was on vacation anyway.

It was already nighttime when Shen Mo arrived at the hotel. He first went to bed to get over his jet lag. Only the next morning did he get up and begin to enjoy the seascape at his leisure. He had chosen to come to S Island with some small and unspeakable hopes in his mind indeed, but the outward reason was still to get inspiration. So, after lunch, he brought a drawing board with him and toured the island.

Shen Mo biked around the small island village, lay on the beach to watch the sunset, and tried some local cuisine. He was having quite a good time these couple of days. Of course, he completed several paintings as well, a few of which were especially eye-catching.

Shen Mo had planned to rent a yacht and go out to sea, but he was truly exhausted. In the next few days, he only rested in the hotel room and focused on painting. The hotel faced the cliff on one side and had a swimming pool on the other. At times, when he felt tired after painting, he would go take a walk by the swimming pool.

It was rather sunny today. Shen Mo had nothing to do in the afternoon, so he went to the swimming pool after lunch, bathing in the sunlight as he thought about how to compose his next piece. As time passed, more people gradually came to swim. Shen Mo ordered a cup of coffee. As he sipped it, he suddenly heard someone call in Mandarin, "Mingxuan..."

It was a sweet female voice, lingering with coquetry.

Shen Mo's hearing went deaf for a moment, as if all sound had disappeared except for the two stark syllables. The tip of his nose sweat a little. He couldn't help but stand up, looking toward where the sound had come from.

What Shen Mo saw was an attractive woman in a swimsuit. She had fair legs and a shapely figure; her long, black hair was especially beautiful. Her hand clung to a man's arm—the man was Chinese as well and seemed to be in his forties. He'd already lost most of his hair, while his belly was as round as a ripe watermelon.

Oh. It wasn't Ji Mingxuan.

Shen Mo relaxed completely. He laughed at himself for being so suspicious. The name "Ji Mingxuan" was pretty common—who knew how many people had the same name? How could he think that the man was Ji Mingxuan, just by hearing that name?

Watching the other man named Mingxuan walk away so intimately alongside the swimsuit-clad beauty, Shen Mo couldn't help but ponder—what was Ji Mingxuan like now? Would Ji Mingxuan have gained so much weight as well? Shen Mo immediately shook his head, reminding himself that they'd never see each other again.

With a mirthless smile, Shen Mo was about to sit back down. And yet, as soon as he turned around, the smile froze on his face.

He saw Ji Mingxuan standing several feet away.

Ji Mingxuan, tall and well-dressed, only looked better than Shen Mo remembered, gazing straight at Shen Mo. His features still looked so handsome, almost as if he stood beyond the bounds of time.

Shen Mo stared at him, unable to let out a single sound.

Crowds clamored around them; it was still the same exotic hubbub. A few blond-haired, blue-eyed children were playing around at the side. One of them, running from his friends and screaming, dashed straight toward Shen Mo. Still absent-minded, Shen Mo didn't have time to dodge to the side, and the boy slammed into him.

The scene unfolded like a serial car crash. Shen Mo staggered a few steps back from the collision before knocking over the beach umbrella behind him. A waiter who happened to be passing by spilled the drink he was holding, and steaming hot milk poured right onto Shen Mo's hand.

Everything happened in but a few seconds, although Shen Mo felt as if someone had pressed the slow-motion button. His mind felt dull. Underneath the scorching sunlight, everyone's movement slowed and every detail stretched on. Amid the chaos, he saw Ji Mingxuan reveal a slight expression of surprise before striding toward him.

Only when Ji Mingxuan grasped his hand did Shen Mo recover himself, perceiving the burning pain on his scalded hand. He finally called out, "Mr. Ji..."

Ji Mingxuan didn't answer, only looking down at Shen Mo's hand. Seeing the redness on the back of it, he couldn't help but frown. Right away, he dragged Shen Mo away from the swimming pool and into the hotel.

They came across all kinds of people on their way, but Shen Mo didn't think about anything. All he did was follow Ji Mingxuan.

Ji Mingxuan pulled Shen Mo into the bathroom and turned on the faucet to rinse Shen Mo's hand. The cold water ran across the back of Shen Mo's hand, splashing loudly. Shen Mo looked up at Ji Mingxuan's reflection in the mirror, calling again, "Mr. Ji."

It was then that Ji Mingxuan finally spoke to Shen Mo. In a gentle and soft voice, he only said, "Yes."

The mere syllable was able to calm Shen Mo's restless heart.

Ji Mingxuan had his head turned down, examining Shen Mo's hand. The reddish skin had faded a little under the cold water. Shen Mo said, "Mr. Ji. It's enough."

Ji Mingxuan was still gripping Shen Mo's wrist. "Rinse it a little longer."

While he spoke, Ji Mingxuan looked up and glanced at Shen Mo before quickly turning away. He said, "You haven't changed much."

With no qualms at all, Shen Mo looked at Ji Mingxuan through the mirror, drawing along the side of Ji Mingxuan's face with his gaze. "You haven't changed much either, Mr. Ji."

Ji Mingxuan suddenly let go of Shen Mo, taking out his phone to make a call. "Yes, it's me... It's probably a burn. Bring the first aid kit..."

Halfway through the call, Ji Mingxuan paused and ordered, "Keep going."

Shen Mo could only keep rinsing the back of his hand with cold water.

A few minutes later, the hotel's manager hurried over with a first aid kit, respectfully calling, "Mr. Ji."

Ji Mingxuan gave a small nod. He said a few words to the manager before he found burn ointment in the kit.

Observing the scene, Shen Mo immediately realized that Ji Mingxuan must have been the one to invest in the hotel.

After sending away the manager, Ji Mingxuan turned back to Shen Mo and said, "It's too dark here. Let's go outside to apply the ointment."

So Shen Mo followed Ji Mingxuan again and went back out. They took a seat on a sofa by a window in the lobby. Soon after they sat down, a waiter brought them some coffee.

Ji Mingxuan ignored the coffee. He only took Shen Mo's hand and slowly applied the ointment on the burn, kneading as he asked, "Are you here on vacation?"

His tone was lukewarm, as if he was talking to a friend he'd known for years.

Shen Mo replied, "I started painting again. I came here to get inspiration."

Ji Mingxuan nodded and said, "S Island is very scenic..."

Ji Mingxuan started chatting about the local scenes and culture, and Shen Mo was quite cooperative as well, adding his two cents about the sunset on the beach and the seascape by the cliff. Both of the two were a little preoccupied, and yet they somehow had quite a proper conversation.

Later, Ji Mingxuan stopped for a moment before he asked, "Did you come alone?"

"Yeah. I'm the only one with so much free time."

"When did you get here?"

"Just a few days ago..." Shen Mo stopped, leaving his words unfinished.

What should he say? That he had deliberately come to S Island on Ji Mingxuan's birthday?

Shen Mo felt his ears burn. He picked up his cup of coffee to conceal it.

The two were silent again. Shen Mo didn't dare ask about Ji An'an. He'd heard about her back in China and found out that, three years ago, she had already... Ji An'an had been Ji Mingxuan's only family—how wretched must Ji Mingxuan have been? Even Shen Mo had been dispirited for quite a few days. After that, Shen Mo hired the newly graduated Yang Yue because her lively personality was somewhat similar to Ji An'an's.

Ji Mingxuan applied the ointment delicately. But, no matter how slow he was, he'd finish applying it sooner or later. When he finished, he scrutinized Shen Mo's hand before saying, "It's done."

Shen Mo replied blankly, "Okay."

Should he thank Ji Mingxuan or say goodbye?

Ji Mingxuan didn't let go of Shen Mo's hand yet. He had an unfathomable expression on his face.

Right then, there came the sound of footsteps.

Shen Mo saw a boy about three or four years old running toward them. He had black hair and fair skin with big, round eyes. Wearing a fitted suit, he looked far prettier than the Caucasian children at the swimming pool.

The boy wasn't accompanied by any adult, but he ran straight toward Ji Mingxuan and flew into his arms. Looking up, he called, in English, *"Daddy!"*

Ji Mingxuan squeezed the boy's cheek and said, "Use Mandarin."

The boy blinked. He seemed a little aggrieved, but he still said, not very fluently, *"Ba. Ba."*

Shen Mo felt as though somebody had slapped him. Half of his face numbed as he realized how ridiculous his thoughts had been. How could he not have expected this? Ji Mingxuan would never lack company.

At this point, a well-dressed, middle-aged woman who seemed to be a nanny hurried over. Ji Mingxuan motioned for her to leave before picking up the boy and placing him on his lap. Pointing at Shen Mo, he said, "Say hello to Uncle."

The boy was quite obedient. He eyed Shen Mo before he said, "Hello, Uncle."

The boy's features were still those of a child, although it was already clear that he had inherited the Ji family's beauty. Wearing the little suit, he looked like quite the young gentleman.

No matter how Shen Mo felt deep down, he couldn't help but smile back at the boy.

"Hello." Shen Mo reached out to stroke the boy's soft, black hair, asking, "What's your name?"

"Ning." The boy wasn't too fluent in Mandarin, but his pronunciation was rather accurate. "Ji Ning."

"How old are you, xiao-Ning?"

Ji Ning had dark eyes. He extended three fingers slowly and somewhat proudly, as if it was quite an accomplishment that he'd grown to this age.

Shen Mo imagined that Ji Mingxuan must have been as proud as this boy during his youth. Shen Mo took a liking to this boy for almost no reason.

"Are you hungry, xiao-Ning? Do you want any snacks?"

Ji Ning glanced at Ji Mingxuan and said, "Dad says that I shouldn't just randomly eat things."

Not at all shy, Ji Ning grabbed Shen Mo's hand. "Uncle, come play with me."

Before Shen Mo could reply, he heard Ji Mingxuan say, "Uncle's hand is hurt. He can play with you some other day."

As Ji Mingxuan spoke, he looked at the middle-aged lady, who understood at once. Walking over, she picked up Ji Ning and took him away. Ji Ning seemed to like Shen Mo, leaning out to wave at Shen Mo.

"Bye-bye, Uncle!"

Shen Mo followed Ji Ning with his eyes for a while before turning back to Ji Mingxuan. "Xiao-Ning is adorable."

"He's impossible at home. He only behaves himself when he's outside."

"Are you here on vacation as well, Mr. Ji?"

"I came for business. There's no one at home to look after Ji Ning, so I brought him along."

Shen Mo's face was still a little warm, but his heart had already calmed down. He said, "I didn't know you're married already, Mr. Ji. Congratulations."

Ji Mingxuan studied Shen Mo for a moment before revealing a smile. Unconsciously, he used his right hand to touch his left. Shen Mo noticed that he wasn't wearing a wedding ring. Only a thin, white mark remained on his left ring finger, a result of constantly wearing a ring.

Shen Mo's hand had a similar mark as well.

Ji Mingxuan held up his coffee and took a sip, asking, "What about you? Are you still with Zhou Yang?"

Zhou Yang?

Shen Mo almost forgot who Zhou Yang was. In truth, he could definitely tell a small lie. After all, Ji Mingxuan was living abroad—there was no way for Ji Mingxuan to investigate his love life. But he still told the truth, "I haven't seen Zhou Yang in a few years."

In fact, Shen Mo hadn't contacted Zhou Yang ever since Ji An'an's accident. He only occasionally heard some news. He knew that Zhou Yang had entered another arranged marriage with the daughter of some magnate.

"Oh—" Ji Mingxuan said meaningfully, "I thought you..."

Ji Mingxuan didn't finish his words, but they both understood.

Shen Mo felt that Ji Mingxuan really didn't know him well. After what had happened to Ji An'an, how could he have been so heartless as to stay together with Zhou Yang? And besides... Jinxiu Villa...

Shen Mo took a deep breath before he said, "I've been to the property in Jinxiu Villa. Mr. Ji, I remembered some of the things that happened..."

Before he could finish, Shen Mo's voice was drowned out by Ji Ning's yelling.

Ji Ning was playing with the other children; they had started a game of tag. Ji Ning ran and shouted, alternating between Mandarin and English, "Dad! *Baba!*"

The shout distracted Ji Mingxuan, who turned around to nod at Ji Ning. Ji Mingxuan was already a father, so naturally he'd put his child before anything else.

Shen Mo suddenly realized that things were different now. What was the point in mentioning what had happened so long ago? Was he waiting for Ji Mingxuan to introduce Mrs. Ji to him?

Shen Mo felt as if he had downed a glass of cold water on a winter day. The heat on his face receded completely.

Ji Mingxuan didn't turn around again until he finished interacting with Ji Ning. He said, "Sorry. What did you just say?"

"Nothing." Shen Mo smiled. "I said it's getting late. I should head back soon."

"Back to your room?"

"Yeah."

"We'll have dinner together." It was phrased as a statement, not a request, said in the same way that Ji Mingxuan had always spoken. Whether it was pretending to date or breaking up, it had always been Ji Mingxuan's words that counted.

But Shen Mo didn't listen to Ji Mingxuan this time. "I'll be painting in my room tonight. You know, it feels awful to be interrupted when inspiration comes."

Ji Mingxuan understood. "Tomorrow, then."

Shen Mo replied, "All right. We'll talk tomorrow."

Shen Mo stood up and extended his arm to shake Ji Mingxuan's hand. Momentarily surprised, Ji Mingxuan held Shen Mo's hand gently.

Shen Mo whispered, "Thank you."

Even he himself didn't know why he was thanking him.

And then Shen Mo fled. He didn't paint when he got back to his room; he only opened the window and gazed at the sea. Time flew by. As dusk came, the sea bathed in brilliance. The sunset looked breathtaking by the cliff.

Ji Mingxuan didn't come to interrupt Shen Mo. He only had a waiter bring Shen Mo dinner and some burn ointment. Shen Mo saw a note by the ointment that explained the number of times the ointment should be applied each day. The handwriting belonged to Ji Mingxuan.

The last time Shen Mo had seen Ji Mingxuan's handwriting had been back when he'd found Ji Mingxuan's present for him. A key and a note were inside the box. Later, following the address on the note, he found Jinxiu Villa and saw the study full of paintings.

If he had gone to Jinxiu Villa all those years ago and seen the paintings in that study, would everything be different now?

Shen Mo let out a long breath, relaxing his clenched fist. Perhaps this was fate that he always fell in love with that man at the wrong time.

The night was silent. S Island was as passionate and beautiful as always. According to Shen Mo's planned itinerary, there were still a few days left, but Shen Mo knew that this vacation would have to come to an early end.

The next morning, Shen Mo got up early to book a return ticket. While he was checking the available flights, someone knocked on his room door. He was still wearing his pajamas, so he hurried to change his clothes before dashing to the door.

Standing right outside the door was Ji Mingxuan.

It was still so early, and yet Ji Mingxuan was already dressed properly. The moment he saw Shen Mo, he asked, "How is your hand?"

Shen Mo was surprised for a moment. When he realized it, he had already extended his hand.

Ji Mingxuan took Shen Mo's hand and examined it from every angle. Only after he made sure that there was only a small patch of red on the back of Shen Mo's hand did he finally stop worrying. He said, "It's mostly recovered. Remember to apply the ointment two more times today."

Shen Mo could only agree to it.

Ji Mingxuan asked, "What are your plans for today?"

Shen Mo thought Ji Mingxuan was going to invite him to dinner again, so he tried to find an excuse. "I'll be painting in my room in the morning. I'm planning to take a walk by the beach in the afternoon."

"So you're free." Ji Mingxuan nodded and said, "Do me a favor."

As he spoke, he reached behind his back and pulled out a little boy with black hair and dark eyes. He dragged the boy toward Shen Mo.

Today, Ji Ning was wearing a baseball shirt, a pair of athletic shorts, and a red baseball cap. Lively and endearing, he smiled sweetly when he saw Shen Mo. "Hello, Uncle."

Shen Mo's heart almost melted. He greeted the boy at once and asked, "How come you got up so early?"

Ji Ning lifted his head, glancing at his father with pitiful eyes.

Ji Mingxuan raised his wrist to look at his watch, saying, "I'm meeting with a client today. I have to leave in ten minutes."

Ji Mingxuan paused. Looking at Shen Mo, he continued, "Help me look after Ji Ning."

"What?" Still surprised, Shen Mo didn't reply until a few moments later, "But I don't know how to take care of children..."

Of course, Mr. Ji never let anyone turn him down. He immediately said, "The nanny will be there. You just need to watch him from the side."

As Ji Mingxuan spoke, he stroked Ji Ning's head.

And Ji Ning came over and took Shen Mo's hand, blinking his wide eyes while saying softly, "Uncle, play with me."

Beyond adorable, really.

How could Shen Mo shake off Ji Ning's hand? As Shen Mo hesitated, Ji Mingxuan already took Ji Ning's other hand. Leading Ji Ning outside, he said, "Go to my room. I have everything ready there. If you need anything else, you can ask the nanny. I need to go out to sea during the day and I'll probably return in the evening, just in time for us to have dinner together."

Although Ji Mingxuan wasn't walking too fast, he still walked at the speed of an adult. Worried that Ji Ning would trip and fall, Shen Mo could only shut the door and hurry to catch up to them.

Holding one person in each hand, Ji Ning marched between the two. He looked rather enthusiastic.

Ji Mingxuan turned around to take a look at Shen Mo. The corners of his mouth lifted a little, and he slowed his pace. "Call me if there's anything urgent. Ji Ning knows my number. Don't you, Ji Ning?"

Ji Ning replied loudly in English.

So Ji Mingxuan said, "You have to talk to Uncle in Mandarin."

Ji Ning eyed Shen Mo before puffing out his chest and answering in a drawn-out tone of voice, "Yes."

Hearing the childish voice, Shen Mo couldn't help but chuckle. He thought he might as well look after the boy for a day.

Ji Mingxuan's accommodations were at the other end of the hotel. It was a three-bedroom suite with a spacious living room and a terrace. The furnishing wasn't luxurious, but it was extremely exquisite—every detail seemed deliberate. As for the sea view, it was of course incomparably better than what was in Shen Mo's room.

Ji Ning's nanny was the middle-aged woman whom Shen Mo had already seen yesterday. She seemed meticulous and reliable, and she didn't talk much either, only nodding politely when she saw Shen Mo.

Ji Mingxuan was in a hurry to leave, so he only said a few words to her. Right before he left, he told Shen Mo, "Ji Ning is quite spoiled, so he may be a little willful at times. You don't need to indulge him."

Shen Mo could only promise not to.

As soon as Ji Mingxuan left, it was as though Ji Ning had been released from a cage. He immediately took off both shoes and threw himself onto the sofa with a scream. Only then did Shen Mo understand why Ji Mingxuan had said that everything was ready here—the sofa was filled with toys.

There were only some food and daily necessities in the suite. No trace of a woman could be found.

The nanny's surname was Chen, so Shen Mo called her Chen-*jie*[2],

---

[2] This is an honorific suffix or title that, while literally meaning "older sister," is used

then he asked, "Where is Mrs. Ji? Didn't she come along?"

Chen-jie's lips were sealed. She said, "Mr. Ji came here on business. He only brought the young master with him."

Of course, Shen Mo couldn't ask any further.

On the other hand, Ji Ning was lying on the sofa, waving the Transformer in his hand at Shen Mo. "Hurry up, Uncle."

Shen Mo couldn't help but smile and walked toward Ji Ning. He remembered that he had also liked playing with Transformers when he was young. Who could have known that, after so many years, children still have so much fun with them?

The morning soon passed by.

Ji Ning was quite obedient, and with Chen-jie watching from the side, Shen Mo didn't run into too many difficulties.

At noon, a waiter brought over lunch. Ji Ning was able to eat by himself, but he still didn't know how to use chopsticks, so he ate with a spoon. On the table there was a dish of steamed eggs, which Ji Ning seemed to be quite fond of. Ji Ning scooped up a big spoonful of it, but he didn't put it into his own bowl. Instead, he brought it toward Shen Mo's lips.

Shen Mo was somewhat surprised.

Ji Ning gazed at Shen Mo with dark eyes and said, "Eat, Uncle!"

Beyond flattered, Shen Mo swallowed it in one gulp. The boiled eggs were still hot. As it travelled down his throat, even his chest felt a little warm.

Satisfied, Ji Ning happily continued eating. Shen Mo, on the other hand, kept on getting him more food. In the end, Ji Ning finished all of his rice. His appetite was much better than usual.

Even Chen-jie said that Shen Mo and Ji Ning really seemed to hit it off.

Shen Mo only smiled.

Ji Ning had the habit of taking naps. In the afternoon, he started yawning after taking a short break. Shen Mo hadn't slept too well last

---

regardless of familial relation for any girl or woman of the same nominal generation as the speaker.

night; he was growing somewhat drowsy as well, so he picked up Ji Ning and took him to the bedroom for a nap.

Shen Mo slept well. It was already past three when he woke up. Chen-jie made some powdered milk for Ji Ning, the whole bottle of which Ji Ning guzzled. Turning around, Ji Ning waved the empty bottle at Shen Mo. Shen Mo was quick to stroke his head and praise him.

As Ji Ning familiarized himself with Shen Mo, he did begin to show parts of his willful temper, sitting on the bed and refusing to put on his shoes. Only after Shen Mo spent quite some time coaxing him did he climb onto Shen Mo's back, whispering beside Shen Mo's ear, "Uncle, I wanna play games."

Shen Mo grinned. "What do you want to play? Uncle can play with you."

Ji Ning beamed. He rolled right onto the bed and rummaged beneath the pillows. Shen Mo thought he was going to fish out another Transformer, but he brought out an old phone instead.

The phone was an outdated model. Shen Mo remembered that when it had first come out a few years ago, Ji Mingxuan had one of the same models as well. He immediately understood, asking, "Is this your dad's phone?"

"Yep." Ji Ning nodded and said, "Help me turn it on, Uncle."

Shen Mo didn't expect such a young child to like playing mobile games. He felt that it wasn't too appropriate, but seeing how expectantly Ji Ning looked at him, he didn't have it in him to turn the boy down either. He thought about it for a while before saying, "You can only use it for a bit... well, ten minutes."

Ji Ning only urged Shen Mo, "Hurry up, hurry up."

So Shen Mo helped him turn on the phone.

The phone was fully charged. Shen Mo found it somewhat strange—ordinary people like Shen Mo kept old phones as backups, but was it necessary for Ji Mingxuan to keep a phone from several years ago? Would Ji Mingxuan care about saving such a meager amount of money?

But now, afraid of invading Ji Mingxuan's privacy, Shen Mo didn't dare do anything else.

Ji Ning didn't mind it too much, though. He seized it and started swiping around. He seemed to play on it often, at once opening up several apps. As Shen Mo saw that much of the phone's contents were empty and realized that it had probably been cleared out already, he felt a little more relieved.

And then Ji Ning opened a game and started playing. Shen Mo glanced at it several times. In the game, a small figure seemed to be finding its way through a maze. Shen Mo didn't see what was so entertaining about it, but Ji Ning appeared to be having a great time.

When the ten minutes were up and Shen Mo confiscated the phone, Ji Ning still wasn't satisfied and started begging Shen Mo. Keeping Ji Mingxuan's words in mind, Shen Mo didn't indulge Ji Ning and closed every app inside the phone. When he came to the messages app, he glimpsed his own name in the outbox.

Shen Mo's heart skipped a beat. Without him realizing it, his finger had already tapped open the outbox. The messages in the phone had been sorted out as well. He saw his own name in rows.

In Shen Mo's memory, Ji Mingxuan had rarely texted him. Yet, in the outbox were dozens of messages for him. They had all been sent on a particular day four years ago, from morning to night.

As Shen Mo read the messages one after another, his eyes gradually blurred.

"Where are you, Shen Mo?"

"Did you go with Zhou Yang?"

"Come back."

"Shen Mo, don't go."

"Stay here."

"...Stay by my side."

CHAP.09

Four years ago, right after Zhou Yang had returned to China, Zhou Yang had called Shen Mo once, asking to meet Shen Mo at the usual place. He'd said he wanted to elope with Shen Mo.

Of course, Shen Mo hadn't gone.

But Shen Mo hadn't gone to work either. He'd even turned off his phone, locking himself at home as he spent the day cleaning.

That day, Ji Mingxuan had come home reeking of alcohol. Having first gotten drunk and then also having tripped on his way home, he had been quite an embarrassing mess. He almost hadn't recognized Shen Mo when he'd seen him, and even after he did, he'd still behaved rather unusually. He'd pinned Shen Mo down on the sofa and fucked him hard. When he'd bitten down on Shen Mo's neck, Shen Mo had felt almost as though he'd become prey to Ji Mingxuan.

The two of them had slept until noon the next day. Ji Mingxuan had helped Shen Mo ask for a day off using Shen Mo's phone. Right after the phone was turned on, a series of text notifications had sounded. Shen Mo had assumed that the messages had been sent by Zhou Yang, and Ji Mingxuan had smiled at him, deleting the text messages in front of his eyes.

In the afternoon, Shen Mo had taken Ji Mingxuan's car to buy medicine. He then heard from the driver that Ji Mingxuan had originally wanted to go to Jinxiu Villa that night.

Shen Mo hadn't known what Mr. Ji had been thinking about back then, but now he understood everything. Thinking that Shen Mo had gone with Zhou Yang, Ji Mingxuan had gotten dead drunk. He had texted Shen Mo, asking him to stay, and then deleted each message by his own hand.

Although Shen Mo's memories had long since been restored, memories were still no more than memories. At this moment, he understood clearer than ever that somebody had once loved him to the bone.

For so long, Ji Mingxuan had waited for him at Jinxiu Villa.

But he had never shown up.

"Uncle," at the side, Ji Ning shook Shen Mo's arm, quietly asking, "are you crying?"

"No." Shen Mo recovered himself. He wiped the tears from the phone screen and replied, "I'm not."

Ji Ning was young, but he wasn't so easily fooled. He pointed to the corner of Shen Mo's eye and said, "Your eyes are all red, Uncle."

He asked again, "Why are you crying?"

Shen Mo turned around to look at Ji Ning, asking, "Xiao-Ning, can I hug you for a bit?"

"Sure." Ji Ning stretched out his arms, grinning. "Hug me, Uncle."

And Shen Mo gently hugged Ji Ning in the fading light of the sunset.

A child's temperature was somewhat higher than that of an adult. Shen Mo felt especially warm holding the boy in his arms. He rubbed the top of Ji Ning's soft hair and couldn't help but think—this person shared Ji Mingxuan's blood.

Unconsciously, Shen Mo hugged Ji Ning even tighter. He asked, "Xiao-Ning, does your dad love you?"

Ji Ning didn't seem to understand what love meant. Only after thinking about it for a while did he answer in a loud voice, "Yes!"

Shen Mo smiled. A while later, he asked again, "Then... does Daddy love Mommy too?"

Ji Ning was confused for a moment before he answered in an even louder voice, "Of course!"

And Shen Mo said, "That's wonderful."

Really. It was wonderful.

Shen Mo took a deep breath before he let go of Ji Ning. Patting Ji Ning's shoulder, he said, "All right. Let's go play in the living room."

Shen Mo put the old phone back under the pillow and left the room with Ji Ning. Not long after they sat down in the living room, Ji Mingxuan returned.

After the busy day, Ji Mingxuan had taken off his suit jacket and hung it over his arm. He was only wearing a light-colored shirt, which accented the curvature of his waist.

Ji Ning forgot about Shen Mo the moment he saw Ji Mingxuan, pouncing on him as he called, "Dad!"

Ji Mingxuan extended his arms and picked up Ji Ning, asking, "Did you behave yourself today? Did you listen to Uncle?"

Ji Ning said proudly, "Of course."

He turned to Shen Mo for proof. "Isn't that right, Uncle?"

Only then did Ji Mingxuan's gaze land on Shen Mo.

Shen Mo said yes and quietly met Ji Mingxuan's eyes, as if they were parted by thousands of seas and mountains.

No, wrong—in reality, they were indeed so far apart.

They had dinner in the hotel's restaurant. With Ji Ning there, they didn't have wine and only ordered a few dishes. Ji Mingxuan deftly took care of Ji Ning and chatted with Shen Mo at the same time, acting the perfect host.

Shen Mo didn't talk much to begin with, but he was even quieter today. Only his eyes kept on following Ji Mingxuan.

Ji Mingxuan said, "I wanted to treat you to a restaurant outside, but with Ji Ning here, going anywhere would be inconvenient."

Shen Mo agreed, "That's what having a child is like, isn't it? Parents put children before everything else."

Ji Mingxuan smiled and wiped the corners of Ji Ning's mouth.

Shen Mo watched them gently, like watching a beautiful and peaceful dream.

While his soul had already flown elsewhere.

It returned to four years ago, or perhaps even earlier, to that rainy night seven years ago. Gripping the key, he had opened that door in Jinxiu Villa with no hesitation and walked into someone's heart...

At the next table, someone knocked over some cutlery, which fell with a *clink*. Shen Mo shuddered. As though somebody had shattered his dream, he stood up from the table.

Surprised, Ji Mingxuan looked at Shen Mo.

Shen Mo's palm was covered in sweat. He knew he'd lost his composure, so he slowly sat back down and picked up his cup to have some water.

Ji Mingxuan glanced at Shen Mo and said, "Tomorrow..."

Shen Mo interrupted him, "Mr. Ji."

No, no, no—Shen Mo couldn't wait until tomorrow. What if the world fell apart the next second?

Shen Mo hastened to ask, "Are you free tonight, Mr. Ji?"

Ji Mingxuan raised an eyebrow. "I'm free right now, no?"

"I mean after dinner."

"There's not much that I have to do. My most important task will be to get Ji Ning to sleep."

Shen Mo looked at Ji Ning, who was poking his bowl with a spoon and not listening to the two of them at all. So Shen Mo said, "After xiao-Ning falls asleep, Mr. Ji, could you give me an hour... no, only half an hour?"

"What is it?"

"I would like to paint something for you, Mr. Ji." Shen Mo looked into Ji Mingxuan's eyes. His voice was a little hoarse. "We made this promise a long time ago, didn't we?"

Ji Mingxuan's gaze changed slightly. For a few moments, he didn't utter a sound. He swallowed once before he finally said, "Right. There *was* such a promise."

"So that's a yes, Mr. Ji?"

"Of course."

Shen Mo breathed a sigh of relief. Even his back was wet with sweat. He had been most afraid that Ji Mingxuan would forget the promise, that Ji Mingxuan would tell him there was no need to bring up the past, sentencing him directly to death.

Now, he felt as if he'd narrowly escaped death, gaining just a bit more time to live.

Dinner took quite a while. Both Ji Mingxuan and Shen Mo had things on their minds, so they didn't talk much. Ji Ning, on the other hand, had long since filled his stomach. He looked around here and there in boredom, playing with his spoon on his own. Having had a little too much fun during the day, he grew drowsy soon. He yawned again and again, his head nodding as though he'd fall asleep any second.

Holding Ji Ning's small arm, Ji Mingxuan thought about how easy it would be to get him to sleep.

After dinner, the two parted ways at the restaurant door. They decided that Ji Mingxuan would go find Shen Mo once Ji Ning fell asleep.

Ji Mingxuan held Ji Ning with one arm and walked back to his suite. He walked at a normal pace at first, but he soon sped up, returning to his suite in just a few strides.

Chen-jie had already had dinner as well, and she was currently waiting in the living room. After Ji Mingxuan had her get Ji Ning ready for bed, he personally put on pajamas for Ji Ning and coaxed him into getting in bed.

Ji Ning had been feeling drowsy before, but now that he was actually in bed, he refused to go to sleep. He demanded that Ji Mingxuan tell him a bedtime story, even asking specifically for the story of the big bad wolf and the little white rabbit.

Ji Mingxuan had no choice but to sit by the bed and begin, "Once upon a time, there was a little white rabbit..."

Ji Mingxuan's low voice sounded particularly pleasant in the night.

"In the end, the big bad wolf and the little white rabbit became good friends and lived together forever."

Wrapped in the blanket, Ji Ning blinked and said, "I don't think that's how the story went last time..."

"Yes, it is." Ji Mingxuan's gaze deepened. He said gently, "The big bad wolf and the little white rabbit loved each other and lived happily ever after."

When Ji Mingxuan finished his words, he caressed Ji Ning's cheek and said, "Good boy. It's time to sleep."

Ji Ning had always been a little afraid of Ji Mingxuan. He could only close his eyes, his lips pouting slightly.

Ji Mingxuan tucked Ji Ning in and turned off the light before he walked out of the bedroom.

It was only eight in the evening.

So Ji Mingxuan went back to his own bedroom to change his clothes. He then found a pair of cufflinks from the drawer. Only after carefully putting them on did he go look for Shen Mo.

The door to Shen Mo's room was unlatched. Ji Mingxuan knocked twice before pushing the door open and walking inside. Shen Mo was busy packing his belongings. On the ground lay a big suitcase, stuffed full. Obviously, it was already well-packed.

Seeing this, Ji Mingxuan asked with no change of expression, "Are you leaving?"

"Yeah. I've been here for quite a few days already. I've had enough fun."

Shen Mo folded his last garment and turned around. He said, "Just take a seat for now, Mr. Ji."

There was no balcony in Shen Mo's room; instead, there was only a floor-to-ceiling window, through which he could see the sea outside. Two chairs were placed by the window. Ji Mingxuan chose one and sat down.

Shen Mo got Ji Mingxuan a cup of water and said, "I'm sorry. It might take you some time, Mr. Ji."

"That's fine." Ji Mingxuan folded his hands in his lap, asking, "Would half an hour be enough?"

Shen Mo replied immediately, "More than enough."

Shen Mo's easel stood at the center of the room. His paintbrushes and paint were in a messy pile as well. He rummaged for the paint he needed and squeezed out a few drops. Lowering his head, he carefully mixed the colors.

Ji Mingxuan glanced at him once before turning away to look out the window, asking, "When did your hand recover?"

"It hasn't recovered yet. I paint with my left hand now."

"It should have healed a long time ago."

"Yeah. The doctor said it was due to psychological reasons."

"You can only get over it on your own, then. Nobody else can help you."

Someone can, Shen Mo thought. One person can.

Once he finished mixing, he tried the colors on the paper and was quite satisfied. At first, he held the paintbrush with his left hand, but after some hesitation, he switched to his right hand instead.

Holding the paintbrush, Shen Mo's hand trembled slightly.

Shen Mo tried hard to suppress the discomfort. With the paintbrush in his hand, he walked toward Ji Mingxuan and sat down on the chair opposite the man.

Noticing that Shen Mo hadn't brought over the painting board, Ji Mingxuan asked in surprise, "Aren't you going to paint?"

Shen Mo suddenly smiled. "I am."

He reached out and grabbed Ji Mingxuan's left hand.

Ji Mingxuan's hands looked beautiful, his fingers slender and fair. Only his ring finger showed the mark of having worn a ring. The tip of Shen Mo's paintbrush quivered—its first stroke landed right there.

For a moment, Ji Mingxuan was stunned. He couldn't help but shift his finger.

With a surprising strength, Shen Mo firmly pinned down Ji Mingxuan's hand and said, "Mr. Ji, don't move."

"Shen Mo..."

"The paint can be washed off overnight. I've already booked my return ticket. I'll leave tomorrow and I promise I won't disturb your life.

Just tonight, just this once..." His voice was impossibly low. As though begging, he continued, "Let me finish this painting."

Ji Mingxuan quieted immediately.

So Shen Mo continued to paint.

He was so nervous that sweat seeped from the tip of his nose, but he didn't care about it at all. His attention was dedicated solely to painting on Ji Mingxuan's ring finger.

Shen Mo's brushstrokes were delicate. Ji Mingxuan, upon examining the shape, realized that it resembled a ring.

As he painted, Shen Mo said, "I heard that the wedding ring is worn on the left hand because it's the place closest to the heart."

Shen Mo switched to a purest shade of red and gently marked the center of the ring. The paint spread slowly, almost into the shape of a heart.

Still holding Ji Mingxuan's hand, Shen Mo tilted his head and looked into the man's eyes.

"Mr. Ji, my heart is right here." This was probably the only chance he had in his life to say these words. As such, he spoke word by word, "It has been here since seven years ago."

When Shen Mo finished these words, he let go of Ji Mingxuan's hand slowly, as if he had already exerted all of the strength he had in this life.

On that rainy night seven years ago, Ji Mingxuan had given his heart to Shen Mo but never received a response. Everything was different now. Shen Mo only wanted Mr. Ji to take a look at his heart as well.

But it was time for the monologue to come to an end.

Shen Mo looked at the time and said with regret, "So it didn't even take half an hour."

Showing no expression on his face, Ji Mingxuan only gazed at Shen Mo.

Shen Mo avoided Ji Mingxuan's eyes and looked at the ring on Ji Mingxuan's left hand once more. It wasn't the best one he had painted, but it was definitely the most heartfelt.

And now, he was going to erase this heart with his own hand.

Shen Mo stood up and said, "Let me wash off the paint on your hand, Mr. Ji."

Ji Mingxuan, however, sat still and didn't move. Under the light, he studied the paint on his left hand and asked, "This is it? You won't be painting a portrait as well?"

Shen Mo stayed quiet for a few moments before he answered, "That wouldn't be necessary."

He was already in his heart. No paint stroke in this world would be able to recreate him. How would another painting be necessary, then?

Ji Mingxuan nodded and stood up. "I can wash it off by myself."

Shen Mo opened the bathroom door and filled the sink with water. Afraid that the paint wouldn't be washed off, he made a point of getting a piece of soap as well.

Ji Mingxuan followed Shen Mo inside, rolling up his left sleeve in front of him.

Shen Mo, catching a glimpse of the cufflinks Ji Mingxuan was wearing, suddenly remembered something, and felt his eyes grow warm. He hurried to turn his head away.

Water splashed inside the bathroom.

Shen Mo closed his eyes, feeling as though his insides were being stirred alongside the noise.

As Ji Mingxuan washed his hands, he asked Shen Mo, "What are your plans after you go back?"

"I'll still be painting, of course. I hold the paintbrush with my left hand now. My right hand..." Remembering the promise, Shen Mo paused before he continued once again, "I won't paint with my right hand anymore."

"Don't you plan on getting married?"

"I'll wait and see. I don't know if I'll be able to meet the right person."

"What kind of person do you think is the right person?"

Shen Mo was speechless for a moment, not knowing how to respond. When Ji Mingxuan repeated the question again, Shen Mo had to muster up the courage to say, "I don't have any specific requirements. As long as we have similar interests."

Just as he was running out of excuses, he heard Ji Mingxuan ask, "What do you think about me?"

Astonished, Shen Mo turned around. "Mr. Ji..."

Ji Mingxuan had already reached out to hold Shen Mo's chin.

Using his left hand.

Ji Mingxuan's left hand wasn't wet. The painted ring on his ring finger looked as vivid as before.

Ji Mingxuan lifted Shen Mo's chin and forced Shen Mo to look into his eyes. He gently stroked Shen Mo's lips with his finger as he asked in a low voice, "If this is your heart, why were you going to wash it off?"

Shen Mo felt his chest tighten. His lips moved, but in the end he said nothing. He had missed his chance—that was the truth. He was already lucky enough to have been able to steal half an hour. In the future, there was no need for him to see Ji Mingxuan again.

Shen Mo pushed Ji Mingxuan's hand away. Turning around, he walked out of the bathroom and said, "I'm flying back tomorrow. I have to go finish packing my things. You should also head back and have some rest, Mr. Ji. It's best that you wash off the paint on your hand. Mrs. Ji isn't here, but..."

Ji Mingxuan interrupted him, "Who said I was married?"

Shen Mo thought he had misheard. Blankly, he stood where he was. He couldn't find his voice until a while later, as he carefully tried to confirm this fact, "You're not?"

Ji Mingxuan waved his left hand and said, "If I were married already, how could there be nothing here?"

"But, Ji Ning..."

Ji Mingxuan calmly walked toward Shen Mo, taking one step at a time. "Can't the father of a three-year-old boy still be single?"

Of course, that was a possibility. Maybe he'd had a child out of wedlock, or maybe he had already gone through a divorce, or maybe... Shen Mo couldn't figure out which one it was.

Ji Mingxuan had already walked toward Shen Mo.

Shen Mo recoiled out of reflex. With his back against the floor-to-ceiling window, he had no way of retreat.

Ji Mingxuan reached out and trapped Shen Mo in his arms.

Ji Mingxuan's expression reminded Shen Mo of that night four years ago, except Ji Mingxuan had been drunk back then. But Ji Mingxuan was sober now, his eyes glowing. His breaths brushed faintly against Shen Mo's ear as he called, "Shen Mo."

Shen Mo was so close to Ji Mingxuan that even his voice began to tremble. He answered, "Yes, it's me."

Shen Mo only responded once before Ji Mingxuan immediately kissed him. The kiss was so light that it was as though Ji Mingxuan was afraid of scaring Shen Mo away. He only pressed his lips against Shen Mo's, the tip of his tongue sweeping across Shen Mo's teeth.

Shen Mo's body felt hot all over, but he still had some sense in him. Struggling, he dodged slightly to the side and said, "Mrs. Ji..."

"There was never any Mrs. Ji," Ji Mingxuan said. "Even if there were, it would have been the person in front of me right now."

Shen Mo's voice was stuck in his throat. He didn't ask until a few moments later, "Why?"

Ji Mingxuan didn't reply. He gazed at Shen Mo deeply before raising his left hand and touching his lips to the painted ring on his ring finger.

Shen Mo couldn't help but hold his breath, as if Ji Mingxuan had kissed him on the tip of his heart.

At once, he knew what the answer was.

In this world, only one thing was impossible to hide. When one person loved another, even if they didn't say a word, a single expression—a single look—was more than enough to give them away.

How oblivious had Shen Mo been that he'd never noticed anything? But at this moment, all of the misunderstandings, the pretenses, and the uncertainties disappeared. The fact that he loved him was beyond all doubt.

Shen Mo shifted forward a little. Just as he lifted his head, he was able to kiss the corner of Ji Mingxuan's lips. At first, he only tested the waters, leaving after but a gentle peck.

Ji Mingxuan didn't move. He was still looking at Shen Mo like before.

So Shen Mo said, "Mr. Ji." Trembling, he kissed Ji Mingxuan once more. Ji Mingxuan finally couldn't stand it any longer. He pinned Shen Mo against the floor-to-ceiling window and took the initiative in kissing him. Chasing Shen Mo's tongue, he kissed fervently and aggressively, stirring their breaths together.

Not until Shen Mo was almost struggling to breathe did Ji Mingxuan back off a little, although he still lingered on Shen Mo's lips. He kissed Shen Mo over and over, calling, "Shen Mo."

"Yes?"

Ji Mingxuan whispered a few words in Shen Mo's ear.

The fire within Shen Mo seemed to be ignited at once. Shen Mo gasped and reached forward to unbutton Ji Mingxuan's shirt. Perhaps the buttons were too difficult to undo, or perhaps his hands weren't steady enough; either way, even after a while passed, he was still only able to undo two buttons.

Ji Mingxuan caught Shen Mo's hands. "Too slow."

As Ji Mingxuan spoke, he lifted the hem of Shen Mo's shirt, one of his hands sliding inside.

His hand was a little cold. Shen Mo let out an exclamation, his body subconsciously tensing. But the heat inside him didn't fade—it burned stronger instead.

Stroking Shen Mo's chest, Ji Mingxuan leaned over and pressed his erection against Shen Mo's thigh.

Through the fabric, Shen Mo could feel Ji Mingxuan's passion. His own situation wasn't any better: he hadn't even been touched in the front, but he was already bulging hard.

Ji Mingxuan kissed Shen Mo as he ground his hips against Shen Mo's body in a rhythm that simulated intercourse, as if, again and again, he was aiming Shen Mo's weakest point.

Unable to withstand the thrusting, Shen Mo called in a begging tone, "Mr. Ji..."

But Ji Mingxuan didn't let go of Shen Mo.

Shen Mo had to change his phrasing. "Mingxuan..."

Ji Mingxuan shuddered. Panting harder, he kissed Shen Mo even more deeply and reached into Shen Mo's pants.

All of Shen Mo was inside Ji Mingxuan's hand now.

Shen Mo hadn't touched himself in a long time, so his body was particularly sensitive. After only a short while of Ji Mingxuan's fondling, he was already about to reach his limit. But Ji Mingxuan stopped at this point. With moist eyes, Shen Mo stared at Ji Mingxuan blankly.

Ji Mingxuan kissed the corner of Shen Mo's eye and said, "Wait a little longer."

There was lube in the hotel room. Ji Mingxuan found a tube in the drawer and squeezed some into his right hand. Then, he let Shen Mo turn over and got on top of him again.

It wasn't until Shen Mo was pushed against the cold glass window that he realized what Ji Mingxuan wanted to do. He blurted, "No... Not here..."

Ji Mingxuan stripped away Shen Mo's clothes. On purpose, he held Shen Mo down firmly as he said, "Don't worry. No one can see."

Shen Mo's nipples were also pressed against the glass. Feeling both discomfort and stimulation, Shen Mo couldn't help but exclaim out loud. Even the tone of his voice changed.

Ji Mingxuan held Shen Mo's hands in place with one hand. His other slid down Shen Mo's cleft, slowly circling at the entrance.

Even Shen Mo's back felt numb.

But Ji Mingxuan still asked Shen Mo calmly, "Do you want it?"

Of course, Shen Mo couldn't turn down the offer.

Ji Mingxuan asked again, "On the bed? Or right here?"

Shen Mo knew the answer that Ji Mingxuan wanted, but he couldn't say it out loud. He only urged, "Mr. Ji, hurry up..."

Only then did Ji Mingxuan push one finger inside.

Shen Mo hadn't done it for too long; he was especially tight. Patiently, Ji Mingxuan massaged Shen Mo until he could feel him relaxing.

Shen Mo couldn't wait any longer, crying out, "Mm... It's okay now..."

Ji Mingxuan was also getting impatient. Turning Shen Mo's face around, he planted a gentle kiss on Shen Mo's lips. Yet, at the same time, his movements were the exact opposite of gentle. Pressing against the soft entrance, he plunged into Shen Mo's body.

"Ah..."

Although there was lubrication, Shen Mo still trembled from the pain, tightening around the foreign object that had just intruded into his body. Ji Mingxuan didn't have it easy either. Only after pausing inside of Shen Mo for a while did he start to move, holding Shen Mo's waist.

As Ji Mingxuan thrust, Shen Mo collided with the glass again and again.

Outside the window was a vast expanse of night.

Shen Mo knew that no one could see the obscene scene unfolding inside, as the window faced the cliff. Yet his face was still burning hot; he felt an indescribable sense of embarrassment. The pleasure intensified too. He grew fully erect, leaving wet marks on the window.

In the beginning, Ji Mingxuan was still able to restrain himself, but he later thrust faster and faster, making Shen Mo's legs go limp. Shen Mo was dripping wet in the front as well.

Shen Mo couldn't help but moan, "I can't... I'm gonna to break..."

Ji Mingxuan laughed in a low voice, his fingers reaching for where their bodies connected. He asked, "Where? Here?"

As he spoke, he felt around and forced a finger inside.

Startled, Shen Mo could only squeeze Ji Mingxuan tighter.

So Ji Mingxuan withdrew his hand and pushed the finger, wet with their fluids, into Shen Mo's mouth. He licked Shen Mo's earlobe as he said, "If this window broke, we'd fall down together and drown in the sea."

Shen Mo couldn't help but tremble. He felt as though they had really plummeted into the sea—they rose and fell by the impact of the seawater before they climaxed together. The sea swiftly engulfed their bodies, and they died together just like this, never to part again.

The fantasy excited Shen Mo even more. Calling Ji Mingxuan's name, he came.

But Ji Mingxuan was still far from finished. Gripping Shen Mo's back, he thrust a few times and then brushed Shen Mo's hair to the side, kissing Shen Mo's nape over and over.

The kisses softened Shen Mo's body. Almost senselessly, Shen Mo called, "Mr. Ji," and, "Mingxuan."

As Ji Mingxuan kissed Shen Mo, he suddenly bit down. It was quite a hard bite, almost as if he wanted to mark Shen Mo's body. He whispered, "Shen Mo, you are mine now."

Turning around with difficulty, Shen Mo gazed at Ji Mingxuan and said, "I have always been yours."

Ji Mingxuan took a deep breath and immediately embraced Shen Mo tighter. After several thrusts, he released inside of Shen Mo.

Shen Mo shuddered, his body growing more sensitive after the orgasm. His legs were so limp that he couldn't even stand—he slowly slid downwards against the glass window.

Ji Mingxuan reached to wrap his arms around Shen Mo's waist, helping him get up before bringing him to the bathroom. The sex had taken the two too much energy. Once they showered, they fell onto the bed in each other's' arms.

Shen Mo fell asleep the moment he closed his eyes. He was soundly asleep until halfway through the night when he felt a hand on his waist. The hand moved skillfully, stroking his waist in a vague way that aroused a familiar lust in him. Shen Mo murmured, "Mm." Eyes half closed, he said, "Mr. Ji?"

"It's nothing." Ji Mingxuan hugged Shen Mo from behind and said in Shen Mo's ear, "You can keep sleeping."

But the hand continued to move, gradually sliding downward.

Shen Mo hurried to grab Ji Mingxuan's hand. "Mr. Ji, I'm out of strength..."

Ji Mingxuan kissed Shen Mo's temple and coaxed him, "You don't need any more strength."

As Ji Mingxuan spoke, he took off Shen Mo's pants, searching for the spot where he had taken Shen Mo's body. Reaching inside, he stirred with two fingers. With their previous lovemaking, Shen Mo had long since been softened, soon getting used to Ji Mingxuan.

So Ji Mingxuan withdrew his fingers. He pressed his body close against Shen Mo's and entered from the side.

"Ah..."

Shen Mo let out a short cry. He no longer felt like sleeping.

Ji Mingxuan, holding Shen Mo in his arms, slowly moved his body. This time, he did it gently, but he also dragged it on until Shen Mo's voice grew hoarse. In the end, Shen Mo couldn't help but beg.

Ji Mingxuan kissed Shen Mo's nape, asking, "Do you like it?"

"I do..." Unable to withstand Ji Mingxuan's teasing, Shen Mo stammered, "Mm... I like you, Mr. Ji..."

These words clearly pleased Ji Mingxuan. He held Shen Mo for a while longer and finally came. This time, the two were too lazy to shower. Drenched in sweat, they embraced each other, waiting for their breathing to calm down.

The sky outside the window still looked dim. It hadn't fully brightened yet.

Shen Mo was so exhausted that he no longer felt drowsy. Lying in Ji Mingxuan's arms, he asked, "You really aren't married, Mr. Ji?"

Ji Mingxuan chuckled. "You know who's in my heart."

Shen Mo smiled wryly. Had he not lost those memories, surely he would've understood Ji Mingxuan's heart. But fate had played a trick on him. He had been so close to losing Ji Mingxuan.

"If that's the case, Mr. Ji, why did you break up with me four years ago? I asked Mr. Chen to contact you. Why did you never give me a response?"

Ji Mingxuan went silent.

Little by little, the sky grew brighter. A long time passed before Shen Mo finally heard Ji Mingxuan utter, "An'an..."

Shen Mo's heart throbbed.

This was the last thing Shen Mo wanted to face. If it weren't for all those things between him and Zhou Yang, Ji An'an wouldn't have...

"After An'an woke up in the hospital that day, she listened to me tell her the truth behind everything, but she didn't shed a single tear. You don't know this, but she had always cried easily. Ever since she was young, she burst into tears at the smallest matters. But at the time, she was extremely calm. She only asked one thing of me."

"What was it?"

"Growing up, I tried my best to do whatever An'an wanted. I hated Zhou Yang so much, yet I still let him be my brother-in-law. It was the first time An'an had ever begged me so earnestly. How could I let her down?"

Shen Mo asked again, "What did Miss Ji ask of you?"

Ji Mingxuan closed his eyes before he said, "She asked me to set you free, and let you and Zhou Yang be together."

Shen Mo's eyelid twitched. He would never have expected Ji An'an to ask this of Ji Mingxuan.

After all, *she* was the one who had been deceived.

"An'an said that only two people who love each other should be together, and the person who's not loved... can only let go." Ji Mingxuan said, "She was much wiser than me, wasn't she? I was wrong right from the beginning. I thought that by binding two people together, feelings would occur sooner or later, but who could have known that the opposite would happen? I exposed your relationship with Zhou Yang, and I hurt you. I had An'an be engaged with Zhou Yang, and I..."

Ji Mingxuan struggled to finish his words.

Shen Mo hurried to hold Ji Mingxuan's hand. "No. I know you never meant for any of it to happen..."

"But it was too late to make up for what had happened. So I promised An'an to break up with you, to never disturb you and Zhou Yang from then on."

"Zhou Yang and I have been over for a long time."

"I didn't know until that day you told me." Ji Mingxuan kissed Shen Mo and said, "I kept my promise with An'an, and I haven't gone back once. I never thought I'd meet you here. That day, at the swimming pool, you just stood there..."

Ji Mingxuan didn't finish his words, only kissing Shen Mo again and again.

Shen Mo wondered if Ji Mingxuan had really never thought that all this would happen. Why had he invested in this hotel on this island, then? Perhaps he held the slightest ray of hope as he waited for Shen Mo on this island.

Just like how he had waited for Shen Mo at Jinxiu Villa.

But Shen Mo didn't expose Ji Mingxuan.

Ji Mingxuan took Shen Mo's hand and pressed it against his chest. "Shen Mo, you fell in the trap all on your own."

Shen Mo admitted calmly, "I did."

It was only because at the other end of the trap was Mr. Ji that Shen Mo had ignored everything else and jumped right in.

Shen Mo knew Ji Mingxuan better now. He realized that there were things Ji Mingxuan would never admit to doing, so Shen Mo had to be the one to show more love.

The sky outside the window was growing paler.

Shen Mo asked, "Mr. Ji, will you be going back early to keep xiao-Ning company?"

Ji Mingxuan replied, "Yes." Still holding Shen Mo in his arms, he said, "Let's stay like this for a little longer."

"Mr. Ji, if you're not married, then xiao-Ning is..."

Ji Mingxuan suddenly hugged him even tighter.

"While you were in China, you must have heard some news about An'an as well."

"Yes. I heard about her from Mr. Chen."

"After An'an went abroad with me, for some time, her condition had been stable. But she didn't listen to me and insisted on giving birth to Ji Ning—just like my mother had."

Shocked, Shen Mo sat up from the bed and asked, "So xiao-Ning is Miss Ji's child?"

Ji Mingxuan didn't deny it.

Shen Mo counted the years in his head. Three years ago had been when Ji An'an... Ji Ning was three years old now; the times did correspond. But, as for the child's father...

Shen Mo hesitated for a moment, but in the end he still asked, "Is xiao-Ning's biological father... Zhou Yang?"

Eyes darkened, Ji Mingxuan drew Shen Mo back into his arms. His voice sounded somewhat hoarse. "No."

Ji Mingxuan didn't regain his composure until a while later. He then continued, "Ji Ning's surname is Ji. He has nothing to do with anyone else. An'an wanted things to be this way."

Shen Mo immediately understood. Ji Mingxuan took Ji Ning into the Ji family to avoid further involvement with the Zhou family. Shen Mo couldn't help but say, "Miss Ji must have truly loved xiao-Ning."

Ji An'an had known that her life could be in danger, but she still decided to give birth to the child. After everything, did she still love Zhou Yang? Shen Mo didn't dare think about it.

Ji Mingxuan said, "But she was so cruel to me."

Shen Mo knew that Ji Mingxuan's parents had long since passed away, leaving Ji An'an as Ji Mingxuan's only family. For this matter, Ji Mingxuan must have blamed himself so much. All that Ji Mingxuan had ever wanted was to give his sister the entire world, but he used the wrong methods and lost her instead.

The sky had brightened completely. Lying in Ji Mingxuan's arms, Shen Mo wanted to look up at Ji Mingxuan's face, but Ji Mingxuan covered Shen Mo's eyes with his hand. He called, "Shen Mo."

Feeling a sadness in his heart, Shen Mo planted a hard kiss on Ji Mingxuan's chin and said, "Yes, I'm here."

Shen Mo regretted that he hadn't come to find Ji Mingxuan earlier. When Ji Mingxuan had lost Ji An'an, when Ji Mingxuan had been so dejected and so hurt, Shen Mo hadn't able to be by his side.

But in the future, that won't happen again, Shen Mo thought.

The two lay together quietly. Neither spoke again. Only when time was running out did Ji Mingxuan stroke Shen Mo's hair and sit up. He said, "I'll go check on Ji Ning."

Shen Mo also got up.

The clothes they had taken off last night were still scattered across the floor. Shen Mo pretended to be picking up the clothes so that Ji Mingxuan could use the bathroom first. Ji Mingxuan went in and washed up. When he came out, he recovered his usual impeccable self. Only his eyes were still a little red.

Shen Mo pretended that he didn't notice, handing Ji Mingxuan his clothes.

Ji Mingxuan didn't have a change of clothes, so he had to put on the shirt he'd worn yesterday. After he got dressed, he played with the pair of cufflinks for a while before he tossed them to Shen Mo.

For a moment, Shen Mo was surprised. He examined Ji Mingxuan's expression before he finally understood what Ji Mingxuan meant. Walking over, he put on the cufflinks for Ji Mingxuan.

Ji Mingxuan seemed to take it as a matter of course.

Ji Mingxuan's shirt, having lain on the floor throughout the night, was a little wrinkled. Shen Mo helped Ji Mingxuan fix his shirt collar, smoothing out the wrinkles.

Ji Mingxuan didn't say anything, but the corners of his mouth lifted a little. Obviously, he was rather satisfied. Before he went out, he turned around and glanced at Shen Mo once more, asking, "Will you still be going back today?"

He seemed to be afraid that Shen Mo would run away.

Shen Mo replied immediately, "I'll cancel the return ticket right now."

Ji Mingxuan nodded. "Stay here for a few more days. I'll show you around."

In truth, Shen Mo visited S Island for vacation every year and had been to most of the tourist attractions. But touring with Ji Mingxuan was different, of course. Even now, he was a little reluctant to part with

Ji Mingxuan. He asked, "How about I go see xiao-Ning too?"

"His temper is terrible in the morning. Don't bother. And you didn't rest much last night. Sleep for a little longer."

Shen Mo was tired indeed, so he didn't insist.

Ji Mingxuan then said, "Let's have lunch together."

Ji Mingxuan thought about it some more and added, "But before that, there's something you must do."

"What is it?"

Ji Mingxuan raised his left hand to show Shen Mo the ring—it hadn't faded yet. He then pointed at Shen Mo's hand and said, "Paint a matching one on your hand too. I'll inspect it at lunch."

Shen Mo said, "What I painted was my own heart. As for yours, Mr. Ji..."

"You'll paint it too, of course." Ji Mingxuan's gaze turned back toward him. "You know where my heart lies, don't you?"

Shen Mo certainly knew.

Feeling his face burn somewhat, he was too embarrassed to answer.

So Ji Mingxuan smiled. Waving his hand, he turned around and left.

Shen Mo stood at the door for a while and then lay back down in bed, wrapping himself in the blanket. He hadn't slept much last night, so he slept soundly this time and didn't even dream. When he woke up, the sun was already high in the sky.

Remembering Ji Mingxuan's words, Shen Mo found the paint he'd used last night and painted a matching ring on his own left hand. Although it was only to pass Ji Mingxuan's inspection, he still painted quite carefully. After he finished, he raised his left hand, looked at the ring in the sunlight, and gloated alone for a while.

Soon, Ji Mingxuan knocked on the door again. He'd already changed his outfit. By car, he took Shen Mo to an outside restaurant.

Looking around, Shen Mo couldn't find Ji Ning, so he asked, "Where is xiao-Ning?"

"The nanny is looking after Ji Ning." Ji Mingxuan said, "We never have the chance to eat alone, just the two of us."

As Ji Mingxuan spoke, he took Shen Mo's left hand and scrutinized it from every angle. Only when he confirmed that they were indeed wearing matching rings did he go forward, holding Shen Mo's hand.

"Mr. Ji." Shen Mo felt a little embarrassed. "We're in public."

Ji Mingxuan only gripped Shen Mo's hand more firmly. "What are you afraid of? No one knows who we are."

Ji Mingxuan behaved more than naturally. Holding Shen Mo's hand all the way, he walked out of the hotel and drove to a restaurant that captured the local culture quite well. The restaurant was built by the water. Decorative greenery could be seen everywhere, and a green pond was right beside the dining table. The environment was quiet and peaceful.

Ji Mingxuan ordered a few specialties and talked with Shen Mo while they ate. Neither of them was talkative, so they only chatted about how they'd been after they had parted.

Ji Mingxuan's life had been rather boring. Apart from business matters, most of his energy had been spent on Ji Ning. Shen Mo then realized how difficult it must be for a man to raise a child alone. The extent to which Ji Mingxuan loved Ji Ning was beyond doubt.

Shen Mo, on the other hand, had even less to talk about. He'd only opened a studio, living a leisurely life.

"You even hired someone?" Keenly, Ji Mingxuan captured this information and asked, "A man or a woman?"

Shen Mo answered honestly, "A woman."

So Ji Mingxuan uttered, "Hm," as if he was thinking about something.

Shen Mo added immediately, "She has a boyfriend. They're already talking about marriage."

Ji Mingxuan still replied, "Hm."

His expression brightened, however. He put some more meat into Shen Mo's bowl and commented, "You look thinner."

Shen Mo didn't feel like he'd lost weight, but because Mr. Ji thought so, he still ate more than usual. He felt quite full after lunch, so Ji Mingxuan dragged him to the beach for a walk.

Shen Mo had already gotten tired of seeing the scenery at the seaside. Paying it no attention, he followed Ji Mingxuan wholeheartedly. Once they got tired of walking, they found a random spot and rested there for a while. They had no destination.

The sea wind blew slowly. To Shen Mo, time like this felt short and yet long at the same time.

So short that the sky darkened in a blink of an eye.

So long that they might just spend their entire lives like this.

They watched the sunset at the beach before they went back. It was already late when they returned to the hotel, so they had dinner in the hotel's restaurant.

Shen Mo had been wondering why the paint on Ji Mingxuan's hand hadn't faded yet. Only later, after watching Ji Mingxuan wash his hands, did Shen Mo realize what was going on. Ji Mingxuan took great care in washing his hands, deliberately turning the faucet so that the water flow was as slow as possible, so that he could avoid the tiny area.

Shen Mo felt both touched and embarrassed. For once, he took charge and forced Ji Mingxuan to wash off the ring.

It displeased Mr. Ji quite a bit—his face was dark for the whole night.

However, Shen Mo didn't have time to indulge Ji Mingxuan, as Ji Ning kept asking him to tell a story.

Ji Ning didn't see the two until it was right before his bedtime. After a short while of excitement, he was told by Ji Mingxuan to go to sleep. Aggrieved, he lay in bed and demanded the story of the big bad wolf and the little white rabbit.

So Shen Mo sat by the bed and told Ji Ning the story.

After Ji Ning listened to it, he blinked and pouted. "It's different from how Dad told it to me last time."

"How did your dad tell it?"

"Dad said the big bad wolf and the little white rabbit lived together forever."

Shen Mo felt a little moved. He turned around to look at Ji Mingxuan. Only then did he notice that, while he had been telling Ji Ning the story, Ji Mingxuan had already fallen asleep by the bed.

Ji Ning pounced on Ji Mingxuan and called, "Dad!"

Shen Mo hurried to hold Ji Ning back, lowering his voice. "Shh, let your dad get a good night's sleep."

From last night to today, Ji Mingxuan must have been exhausted.

Shen Mo stuffed Ji Ning back in bed and coaxed Ji Ning to sleep. Then, he brought over a blanket from the next room and carefully draped it over Ji Mingxuan.

Ji Mingxuan was still sleeping soundly.

In the dim light, Shen Mo realized that Ji Mingxuan's eyelashes, especially long, cast faint shadows on his face.

Gazing at him, Shen Mo felt somewhat distracted.

Both Ji Mingxuan and Ji Ning were asleep. No one else was in the room. Shen Mo remembered that day many years ago. When he had been so tired that he fell asleep on the sofa, Ji Mingxuan had circled him many times.

Shen Mo's heart sped. He felt a little nervous. Placing his hands on the edge of the bed, he inched toward Ji Mingxuan and pressed his lips against Ji Mingxuan's face, gently kissing Ji Mingxuan on the cheek.

Just like what had happened all those years ago.

Shen Mo spent a few more days on the island. Only once he felt satisfied did he re-book the return ticket.

Ji Mingxuan had been developing his business abroad these years; the center of his business had moved overseas as well. He wouldn't be able to return to China on just a whim, so he didn't go back with Shen Mo this time and booked a ticket for a later date. On the day of Shen Mo's departure, he took Ji Ning to the airport to see Shen Mo.

Although they would part with each other soon, Ji Mingxuan didn't say any romantic words. He only told Shen Mo, "I'll go find you once I'm done with work."

Shen Mo smiled and said yes.

On the other hand, Ji Ning was reluctant to part with Shen Mo, ceaselessly asking questions like "Where are you going?" and "When are you coming back?" and "Why won't you be leaving with us?"

Patiently, Shen Mo answered each of Ji Ning's questions, "I'll be going home. I won't be coming back in a while, but you can come play at my place in the future, xiao-Ning."

"Really?" Ji Ning still didn't believe Shen Mo, insisting on a pinky promise.

So Shen Mo bent over and hooked his pinky around Ji Ning's. He said, "How about, if I lied, I would... get caught by the big bad wolf?"

Ji Ning finally believed Shen Mo. He said childishly, "Don't let the big bad wolf catch you, Uncle, or I won't be able to see you anymore. Dad has your photo, but I don't have one."

Shen Mo was surprised. "What photo?"

"The one he has in his wallet—"

Before Ji Ning could finish, Ji Mingxuan scooped him right up.

Pretending that he would spank Ji Ning, Ji Mingxuan said, "Uncle is boarding the plane soon. Let's stop bothering him and him rest for a bit, understood?"

Ji Ning replied unwillingly, "Okay."

Ji Mingxuan praised him, "Good boy."

Shen Mo couldn't help but call out, "Mr. Ji."

Ji Mingxuan looked into Shen Mo's eyes as though nothing had happened, giving him no explanation.

Speechless, Shen Mo thought for a while and said, "I'm thirsty. I want to go buy a bottle of water. Could you lend me your wallet, Mr. Ji?"

Ji Mingxuan's dark eyes narrowed. He said, "I'll buy it for you."

When Ji Mingxuan finished, he picked up Ji Ning and went to buy water.

Standing at the same spot, Shen Mo watched the two figures from afar.

No wonder Ji Ning had been so friendly toward him, even upon their very first meeting. So it seemed there had been a reason, after all. But... just which photo did Ji Mingxuan keep in his wallet?

Shen Mo did not like taking photos. He had no memory of taking photos with Ji Mingxuan either. The photos he'd taken before were all left in that rental apartment of his. Where could Ji Mingxuan have gotten such a photo?

Shen Mo was beyond curious. When Ji Mingxuan came back with the water, Shen Mo tried to beat around the bush. Ji Mingxuan, however, kept up his defense—despite Shen Mo's persistence, he revealed not a single word.

It was almost time to board the plane. Shen Mo's only option left was to ask Ji Ning, "Is it a good photo?"

Before Ji Ning could reply, Ji Mingxuan had already pulled Ji Ning into his arms. Then, he came over and kissed Shen Mo on the lips. He whispered, "It's beautiful."

Startled, Shen Mo pressed a finger to his own lips. "That's not what I was asking..."

Ji Mingxuan just smiled. He let go of Ji Ning and said, "It's time for security."

Seeing that his time was indeed almost up, Shen Mo said goodbye to Ji Mingxuan and Ji Ning and then walked over to check-in.

Shen Mo went to S Island every year, but only this time was his mood so different. Sitting in the plane, he looked back on what had happened in the past few days, feeling like he'd been dreaming.

Because of the layover, the return trip took quite some time as well. It was almost midnight when Shen Mo got back home. He texted Ji Mingxuan to report that he'd safely arrived before he crashed out from fatigue.

He didn't get up until noon the next day. After casually making himself some noodles, he drove to the studio in the afternoon. Of course, there were still no clients. Yang Yue was so bored that she even started swatting flies. Upon seeing Shen Mo, she was naturally pleased.

"You're finally back, boss! Why were you gone for so long this time?"

"Yeah. I couldn't help staying a little longer."

"Did you bring me any good food?"

"Of course." Shen Mo took out the local specialties he had bought. "I bring you food every year, don't I?"

Grinning, Yang Yue accepted them. "You're the best, Boss. Did you meet someone special this time?"

Someone special?

Did meeting Ji Mingxuan... count?

Shen Mo paused. For a moment, he couldn't answer.

Yang Yue immediately picked up the scent of gossip. "Really? Did you really? What's she like? Exotic beauty with long legs?"

Shen Mo shook his head. "You think too much. Go do your work."

"There isn't any business at all—what work is there to do?"

"There's no business now, but it'll come later." Shen Mo tidied up the place as he said, "School starts in just a few days. Many students will probably be interested in painting. Let's print out some ads—we should be able to get some business soon."

He glanced at Yang Yue and added, "If you think there's too much work, I'll hire someone else to come help."

Yang Yue's eyes widened in surprise. "What happened to you, boss? Didn't you use to be as lazy as a person could be? Why are you suddenly so diligent now?"

Shen Mo was a little offended. "I was never *that* lazy, was I?"

Then, he sighed. "But things are different now."

"Why?"

"Because..." As Shen Mo thought of the two who were still overseas, a faint smile spread to his eyes. "I have to support my family."

Yang Yue's expression was one of indescribable astonishment. She walked a few steps closer and stared at Shen Mo. "Boss, if I remember correctly—you're single, aren't you?"

Shen Mo's answer was subtle. "I was."

Just those two words were enough to arouse the young woman's vivid imagination.

"Ahh! Are you getting married, boss? Or are you already married? Love at first sight while you were traveling? A romantic encounter by the sea? Like what you see in movies?"

Shen Mo did not reply. Pointing to the cobweb in a corner, he said, "You haven't cleaned the place in a long time, right? Since we're free today, let's do some cleaning."

"Don't change the subject, boss!" Yang Yue caught up to him and asked, "Is the Missus a foreigner? Oh no, my English is terrible—how will I communicate with her?"

Shen Mo chuckled in his heart. He found "Missus" a befitting term in every way and almost wanted to praise Yang Yue for it. His relationship with Ji Mingxuan wasn't set in stone yet, but he was quite confident. He'd introduce Ji Mingxuan to Yang Yue sooner or later, so he revealed to her, "Don't worry. Mandarin is fine."

"Oh, good." Yang Yue sighed in relief. She then asked, "What does she look like? Does she have a good temper?"

Shen Mo took up the broom and swept the floor, throughout which a smile lingered at his lips. "A few years older than me. Really good-looking. As for temper... just a little too proud."

The image of a cold, seductive beauty immediately emerged in Yang Yue's mind. She didn't think her boss could handle this type of person, but seeing Shen Mo's determination in making money to support his family, she knew he must have fallen in deep.

"She spends a lot of money, doesn't she?"

"Probably."

Judging from the brands that Ji Mingxuan wore, Shen Mo knew that Ji Mingxuan's clothes were definitely expensive. He didn't need to buy a car or a house yet, but he liked to make long-term considerations.

"And the child's education expenses..."

"The child?" Yang Yue looked Shen Mo up and down. "Boss, you're really a man of action!"

Shen Mo knew that she had misunderstood. He didn't know what sort of expression to put on. "He's already three years old."

"This is her second marriage?"

"No. It's a little complicated."

Yang Yue nodded. "I understand, I understand."

Premarital pregnancy, right? The woman had been working hard, raising the child alone, when she finally met the love of her life—namely, Yang Yue's boss.

Yang Yue gave Shen Mo a thumbs-up. "You're a good guy, boss."

Shen Mo sensed that Yang Yue had misunderstood even more. He knew he wouldn't be able to explain everything in just one sitting; she'd understand after she met Ji Mingxuan, anyway. Thus, Shen Mo didn't talk about it any further and focused on cleaning.

All on her own, Yang Yue imagined an arduous yet beautiful love story, which somewhat satisfied her curiosity.

The afternoon passed quickly.

Yang Yue got off work in the evening. When Shen Mo was about to order delivery, he received a call from Ji Mingxuan. Of course, there was nothing important to talk about, and they only had a casual chat. Even so, they were on the line for quite some time. In the end, it wasn't until Shen Mo's phone started overheating that he finally hung up.

Ji Mingxuan still had much to deal with, and probably wouldn't be back for another month. So Shen Mo used this month to busy himself. After he sketched the pair of rings on paper, he worked on other things as well. He was out and about all day, and even on the rare occasion when he came back to the studio, he immersed himself in painting.

Yang Yue tried to sneak a look at what Shen Mo was painting, but Shen Mo refused to show her.

A month, compared to the days they had spent on the island, felt far too long. Finally, Ji Mingxuan came back. Shen Mo drove to the airport ahead of time to pick him up.

Carrying not much luggage, Ji Mingxuan strode out of the exit with confidence. Ji Ning wasn't with him.

Shen Mo walked up to him and asked, "Where's xiao-Ning?"

"Ji Ning is still too young. It wouldn't be easy for him to adjust to a new place, so I'll bring him over after we settle down here."

Shen Mo asked, "Where will you be living, Mr. Ji? Your house from before?"

For a moment, Ji Mingxuan was quiet.

Shen Mo knew the house was where Ji Mingxuan and Ji An'an had grown up. Living there now would inevitably remind Ji Mingxuan of the haunting memories. So he said, "How about my place?"

Hearing this, Ji Mingxuan didn't even respond. He only took Shen Mo's hand and said, "Let's go."

Like so many times before, Shen Mo followed Ji Mingxuan with all his heart.

But when they got into the car, Shen Mo was still the one driving. Ji Mingxuan asked him, "Where do you live now?"

Shen Mo smiled and said, "You'll see when we get there."

Shen Mo drove all the way downtown.

Ji Mingxuan had been abroad for a few years now. At first, he only noticed how H city had changed over the years. But, later, he gradually realized that he found the street somewhat familiar. Without turning to the side to look at Shen Mo, he faced straight ahead as he asked, "Shen Mo, where are you going?"

Shen Mo reached out to hold Ji Mingxuan's hand. What he said was still the same: "We'll get there soon."

At the prime location of the city center was a residential area, quiet amid its noisy surroundings. A boulevard separated it from the downtown hustle.

It was where Shen Mo was headed right now.

Ji Mingxuan's eyelid twitched, his palm growing slightly sweaty against Shen Mo's. The car stopped slowly. He already recognized this place—Jinxiu Villa.

Shen Mo parked the car and pulled the door open. "Mr. Ji, please come out."

Ji Mingxuan sat still. With eyes deep and dark, he looked at Shen Mo. "Why did we come here?"

"Did you forget, Mr. Ji? You asked Mr. Chen to take back the property here in Jinxiu Villa, but I never agreed to it, so I still have the key."

Ji Mingxuan's expression changed. "Yes. You kept the key."

This time, Ji Mingxuan opened the door and got out of the car before Shen Mo had to press him.

Jinxiu Villa hadn't changed much over the years. Only the security guards at the gate were different. These days, Shen Mo had been frequenting this place, so all the security guards knew him. When they saw him, he was quickly granted access.

Shen Mo's place was on the seventh floor. One would normally take the elevator, but he told Ji Mingxuan, "Mr. Ji, how about we walk up the stairs? I have something to tell you."

Ji Mingxuan didn't object.

The two slowly walked up the stairs, floor by floor.

People rarely passed through the stairwell, so it was naturally quiet inside. As Shen Mo walked, he recounted what had happened all those years ago.

"...I was sent to the hospital after I fell down the stairs. My injuries weren't serious, but I couldn't remember what happened in those six months."

When Shen Mo finished his words, he halted and gazed at Ji Mingxuan. "If not for this, I would have come to Jinxiu Villa a long time ago."

And... he would have also walked into Ji Mingxuan's heart a long time ago.

Ji Mingxuan listened quietly. He showed no emotion on his face, as though he was completely indifferent to the story, but he looked so calm that perhaps a storm was on its way.

Shen Mo felt nervous. A long while passed before he heard Ji Mingxuan ask, "Did it hurt?"

"What?"

"You fell down the stairs, didn't you?" In the end, the myriad emotions hidden within Ji Mingxuan's eyes only melted into a watery gaze, falling on Shen Mo. "Did it hurt?"

For an instant, Shen Mo felt that there was nothing in the world but his own heartbeat.

When he was ill, he had mistaken the man for Zhou Yang; when he recovered, he forgot about the man completely. But now that he remembered everything, the man mentioned not a single word about the past, and only asked him if he had been hurt.

"Ji Mingxuan..."

Somewhat losing his composure, Shen Mo squeezed his eyes shut to force his tears back inside.

Ji Mingxuan reached out and pulled Shen Mo into his arms. Smiling, he touched Shen Mo's cheek. "Looks like it really did hurt."

Shen Mo clung to Ji Mingxuan's collar. He didn't even say "Mr. Ji." Instead, he used his full name, calling it out again and again.

Ji Mingxuan answered several times and said, "There are three more floors. Let me carry you up."

Only then did Shen Mo look up, his eyes still red. "I'm just a bit sad. It's not as if I can't walk anymore."

In all seriousness, Ji Mingxuan said, "When you can no longer walk, I'll carry you this way too."

Hearing this, Shen Mo couldn't turn Ji Mingxuan down again.

Ji Mingxuan bent down and let Shen Mo onto his back. He took Shen Mo's weight onto him, and then carried him up the stairs.

Leaning against Ji Mingxuan's back, Shen Mo finally felt a little more settled. He asked, "Mr. Ji, you didn't know I lost my memory, and all those years... you thought I was ignoring you on purpose?"

Ji Mingxuan mocked himself, "I was no more than a stranger, wasn't I?"

Shen Mo mumbled, "No..."

Thinking about how Ji Mingxuan had been back then, Shen Mo felt heavy-hearted again. A while later, he asked, "Did you visit Jinxiu Villa very often, Mr. Ji?"

Ji Mingxuan replied immediately, "Only once in a while."

Shen Mo knew that he had to interpret the answer in the opposite way, so he asked again, "What were you doing here, all alone?"

Ji Mingxuan only ignored Shen Mo now.

No matter how many times Shen Mo asked, Ji Mingxuan refused to reply, carrying Shen Mo steadily on his back. He soon walked up the three floors. On the seventh floor, when Shen Mo got off Ji Mingxuan's back, he heard Ji Mingxuan whisper a few words. Ji Mingxuan's voice was so low that Shen Mo would have missed it if he weren't so close.

Ji Mingxuan said, "I was thinking about you."

Shen Mo froze where he stood.

Ji Mingxuan quickly walked to the door and waved at Shen Mo.

"Where's the key?"

Regaining his composure, Shen Mo fumbled for the door key. His hand trembled slightly. Holding the key, he wasn't able to slide it into the keyhole even after a few tries.

It was Ji Mingxuan who held Shen Mo's hand and helped Shen Mo insert the key.

Click. The door finally opened. Shen Mo and Ji Mingxuan met each other's eyes. An indescribable feeling arose in their hearts.

The place had been cleaned beforehand. The furniture and decor were the same as Ji Mingxuan remembered. Only a few places had changed: corner guards on the walls, safety covers on the outlets, and childproof locks on some appliances... These were what Shen Mo had achieved in the busy month.

Ji Mingxuan opened the bedroom door. He found that the master bedroom was essentially the same as before, while the second bedroom was now a child's room.

Shen Mo explained, "The furniture is all new, and there hasn't been any painting done, so xiao-Ning can move in right away."

Ji Mingxuan nodded. Only the study was left now, but Ji Mingxuan's footsteps were somewhat hesitant. After a while of pacing back and forth in front of its entrance, he slowly pushed the door open.

The study was still the same as how he had personally arranged it back then. The room's lighting was particularly good. The floor was covered in various painting supplies, and on the walls hung all kinds of paintings.

But the paintings were different from before.

The subject of all the paintings was the same person. Ji Mingxuan recognized himself upon first sight—smiling, frowning, and expressionless too. Every painting seemed to come alive.

The signature at the bottom was composed of two characters with which he was beyond familiar.

Shen Mo.

Ji Mingxuan turned around, looking for Shen Mo.

Standing right behind Ji Mingxuan, Shen Mo asked, "How do they look?"

Somewhat nervous, Shen Mo added, "It was too much of a rush to get them finished in just one month, and I used my right hand, so I couldn't paint in too much detail."

Ji Mingxuan, having already met Shen Mo's eyes, quickly averted his gaze. He said calmly, "Not bad."

Perhaps he was imagining things, but Shen Mo noticed that a small patch of skin behind Ji Mingxuan's ear was slightly flushed. Holding back the impulse to kiss Ji Mingxuan, he took what he had prepared out of his pocket and then reached out to hold Ji Mingxuan's left hand.

Ji Mingxuan asked, "Shen Mo?"

Shen Mo didn't say anything. Instead, squeezing Ji Mingxuan's fingertip, he slowly slid the ring in his palm onto Ji Mingxuan's ring finger. He didn't even dare to let out a single breath—it was as if he was adding the finishing touch to a masterpiece.

Shen Mo had designed the ring and had it custom made accordingly. It looked quite similar to the one Shen Mo had painted on the island.

Ji Mingxuan looked down at it, stunned. "What does this mean?"

"It's a proposal." Shen Mo swiftly put on his own ring and clasped Ji Mingxuan's hand. The two rings were exactly the same. "I want to spend my life with you, Mr. Ji."

Ji Mingxuan had already done too much. This time, it was Shen Mo's turn to take the initiative. Shen Mo had no idea why Ji Mingxuan had fallen in love with him, but now that they were together, he would be worthy of Ji Mingxuan's love only by becoming a better person.

"I'll work hard to make money and support the family. Mr. Ji, what do you think?"

For a long time, Ji Mingxuan didn't say anything.

Ji Mingxuan studied the ring over and over again. He then gazed at Shen Mo and, all of a sudden, pushed Shen Mo onto the wall.

On the wall also hung the portraits of Ji Mingxuan.

Ji Mingxuan's expression was more beautiful than what could be found in any painting. With the hand that wore the ring, he lifted Shen Mo's chin. "This is my answer."

Shen Mo was entranced for a moment. The whole room was filled with the man's handsome features, but the real Ji Mingxuan, standing right in front of him, leaned down and kissed him with infinite tenderness.

FIN.

Memories

It was an ID photo.

The person in the photo still seemed to be a student. Lips slightly pursed, he stared at the camera intently. He looked very serious, even though he was only taking a photo. His features weren't eye-catching, but the pair of eyes under his short bangs were so dark that even the red background behind him seemed dull in comparison.

The photo was glued to the investigation files that Ji Mingxuan had just received. Ji Mingxuan went through the files quickly. He found out that the person in the photo was named Shen Mo, that he was an art student at T University, having graduated just this year, and that he was still looking for a job.

Once, Ji Mingxuan had been invited to T University to give a lecture, during which he'd seen Shen Mo sitting in the first row. Shen Mo had sported a lost expression on his face, obviously confused by the lecture, but he had still taken notes attentively.

At that time, Ji Mingxuan had only found Shen Mo to be an interesting person. He didn't at all expect Shen Mo to be the person Zhou Yang was dating.

At the end of the files were several other photos taken secretly when Shen Mo and Zhou Yang had been together. Both were men, but one could tell with just one glance at their expressions that they shared an intimate relationship.

Ji Mingxuan raised his hand to press the center of his brows.

His younger sister, Ji An'an, was childhood friends with Zhou Yang. She'd had feelings for Zhou Yang since her youth. The Zhou family and the Ji family would love to see the two married, but now it seemed that the plan would fail.

At present, the car came to a gradual stop. The driver turned around and said, "Mr. Ji, we have arrived at the Zhou family's house."

Ji Mingxuan nodded and put the files back into the filing envelope. He thought for a while and didn't bring the envelope out with him, only tossing it inside before he got out of the car.

Knowing Ji Mingxuan was coming over today, the Zhou parents were already waiting in the living room. A servant gingerly brought over some tea and left without making a sound.

Ji Mingxuan picked up the teacup and took a sip. It was Iron Goddess oolong, a tea that he liked.

After exchanging greetings, Mrs. Zhou went straight to the subject. "Mingxuan, we agreed a long time ago that An'an and Zhou Yang are going to study abroad together, didn't we? Why are you saying that you'd like to think about it some more, now?"

With deliberation, Ji Mingxuan replied, "I don't think it's the best idea."

"We arranged this marriage between your family and ours so long ago—what's not good about it?"

"You know, An'an's illness..."

Mr. Zhou and Mrs. Zhou exchanged a look. Mrs. Zhou was still the one who spoke up, "We're not strangers, your family and ours. My husband and I have long been aware of An'an's physical condition. But it's nothing to worry about. Back then, your father and your mother married this way as well, didn't they?"

Ji Mingxuan hesitated somewhat.

Ji Mingxuan's parents had always loved each other—theirs was a well-known love story of the city. Even though they were also in an arranged marriage, his father loved his sickly mother for his whole life, taking care of her in every possible way. Even after she passed away from her illness, he never remarried.

Mrs. Zhou had also clawed her way through the business world, so she was most adept at observing people's expressions. She seized this opportunity. "In fact, with An'an's situation, it'd be best if she could marry Zhou Yang. At least our families know each other well. You'd be able to rest assured too, right?"

Besides, the two families shared the same interests. Such a bond was far firmer than so-called love.

Mrs. Zhou didn't say it out loud, but all three who were present understood.

Ji Mingxuan was wavering indeed, but she didn't convince him yet. He only said, "Even if An'an is fine with it, Zhou Yang might not be willing."

"Mingxuan, what do you mean by this?"

"From what I know, Zhou Yang is already involved in a relationship with someone."

Mrs. Zhou's expression changed slightly.

Mr. Zhou laughed instead. "Men, huh? Normally, they date a few girls before they marry. Those relationships are nothing serious."

Mrs. Zhou had an unpleasant expression on her face, but she also agreed, "Zhou Yang dated a girl or two in high school, but they broke up long ago. I haven't heard anything about the one now."

Zhou Yang is dating a man for a change—of course he wouldn't dare let his parents know.

Sensibly, Ji Mingxuan did not say it out loud.

Mrs. Zhou stared at Ji Mingxuan as she said, "So it seems, Mingxuan, that you've already had someone investigate Zhou Yang."

"I put my sister's happiness first, of course." Ji Mingxuan smiled. "In any case, on the matter of studying abroad, perhaps it's best that you ask Zhou Yang for his opinion before making the decision."

And then Ji Mingxuan changed the subject. He chatted with them for a while longer, showing them adequate courtesy before he left.

Ji Mingxuan didn't let Ji An'an know about this conversation. He only wanted his dearest sister to dress beautifully and remain the princess inside the castle. As for the storms outside, there was no need for her to worry about them.

Ji Mingxuan didn't expect that, a few days later, Ji An'an would bring up the matter of studying abroad on her own.

Concealing his surprise, Ji Mingxuan smiled and asked, "Who brought it up to you?"

"Zhou Yang did. Brother, he said his parents have already discussed it with you. Is that not the case?"

Ji Mingxuan's eyes darkened. He asked, "Zhou Yang has also agreed to study abroad?"

"Of course. Why else would he mention it?" Ji An'an shook Ji Mingxuan's arm, her voice saccharine. "Brother, are you going to let me go or not?"

Ji Mingxuan didn't reply. His mind worked rapidly, but he revealed nothing on the surface, only patting Ji An'an's hand. "Do you really love Zhou Yang so much, An'an?"

"Brother!" Ji An'an stamped her feet, her face blushing slightly. "I've loved him since I was young. It's not like you don't know."

"Why do you love him?"

"He... He's been my childhood dream."

Just like how Snow White looked forward to meeting Prince Charming, perhaps every girl had such a dream.

Ji Mingxuan gazed at his sister gently, asking, "What if Zhou Yang doesn't love you back?"

Ji An'an smiled sweetly. Not at all offended by the presumption, she only said, "Then I'll still love him. I always will."

She had inherited her mother's illness, but she was more like her father in character, particularly persistent when it came to affection. After the siblings' mother had died, their father had missed their mother so much that he'd fallen ill and passed away soon after.

This problem seemed to run in the Ji family.

Of course, Ji Mingxuan wouldn't act on emotions alone. Weighing the pros and cons, he thought that if Zhou Yang really hadn't been serious about those past relationships and would treat An'an well in the future, with the Ji family's financial resources as backing, the marriage was not completely out of the question.

"Brother," Ji An'an was still asking, "are you going to let me go or not?"

"Don't worry." Seeing the anticipation on her face, Ji Mingxuan smiled. "Your dream will come true."

All he had was this sister of his. Whatever Ji An'an wanted, he would certainly present it to her.

The procedures for studying abroad were soon completed. Half a month later, Ji Mingxuan saw Ji An'an off at the airport. Of course, Zhou Yang left together with her. Ji Mingxuan wasn't too fond of Zhou Yang, so he only nodded as a greeting.

Ji Mingxuan drove back alone. On the radio, someone was singing an old love song in a hoarse voice. Ji Mingxuan felt somewhat melancholy. As he waited at a red light, for some reason, he remembered a pair of dark eyes.

Those eyes looked clear and dark. No matter what they gazed at—a person or a camera—they held an earnestness within.

What was his name again?

Right, Shen Mo.

Ji Mingxuan thought that the name suited him well. Now that Zhou Yang was going abroad with An'an, Zhou Yang might have already broken up with Shen Mo. Before the red light turned green, Ji Mingxuan took the files from the back seat and looked over them once more.

When he saw the photo of the student-like young man again, Ji

Mingxuan suddenly felt a flicker of something. He pulled out his phone and made a call.

"It's me. Yes, keep an eye on the person I told you to investigate last month... It's nothing serious. Just keep it up for a few days..."

After hanging up, Ji Mingxuan drove home.

By the time he got a call back, he was already in his study. He received unexpected news—Shen Mo was missing.

"When did it happen? That's right—what else are we going to do? Look for him, of course." Ji Mingxuan decided at once. "Send some people to look for him."

He hung up and circled his study twice. He already had a guess in his mind.

Zhou Yang had just gone abroad with Ji An'an, and right after that, Shen Mo went missing. Who else could have done it? Ji Mingxuan hadn't expected Mrs. Zhou to be so ruthless outside of business matters, that she would act this way when dealing with her son's past affairs.

But all this had nothing to do with Ji Mingxuan. All that he had done was mention the existence of such a person to the Zhou family. Zhou Yang should have been the one to decide whether or not to break up with Shen Mo.

But if he hadn't hired someone to investigate Shen Mo...

Ji Mingxuan sat down slowly and read the files in his hands over and over. Finally, he reached out and peeled off the photo.

He didn't hear about Shen Mo until the next day.

Ji Mingxuan made time for this matter and traveled to quite a remote location by car. The car jolted violently on the way, while barrenness filled the landscape outside. After a long while, an old, abandoned warehouse came into his view.

He got out of the car, walking inexplicably faster than everyone else. As he was about to open the warehouse door, somebody stopped him. "Mr. Ji, things might not be too good inside."

Ji Mingxuan felt a sudden pulse at his temple. He said calmly, "That's fine."

Then, he pulled the door open.

A musty smell rushed into his nose. It was quite dark in the warehouse, and only with light from outside could he see a person curled up on the ground. He was covered in wounds—his right hand was especially heavily injured, battered and bloody. A jarring redness pooled beneath his palm.

Ji Mingxuan almost thought that he was dead. One step at a time, he walked over. The person on the ground moved a little, peeling his eyes open to look at Ji Mingxuan.

Ji Mingxuan walked closer and closer, and little by little, his reflection appeared in the pair of dark and quiet eyes.

Ji Mingxuan had always hated hospitals.

His sickly mother had passed away soon after giving birth to his sister. Moreover, his only sister Ji An'an inherited his mother's heart disease; she had spent most of her time in the hospital ever since she was a child. Ji Mingxuan was so used to going in and out of hospitals that he felt disgusted whenever he smelled the familiar scent of disinfectant.

But now he was sitting in a hospital room, waiting for someone to wake up.

Ji Mingxuan had still gotten there too late. When he'd arrived at the abandoned warehouse, Shen Mo had already been in bad shape. Shen Mo's whole body, especially his right hand, had been covered in wounds. His life was not in danger, but the doctor had said that there might be lasting damage. Ji Mingxuan remembered that Shen Mo had studied art and that even the jobs he was looking for were all related to painting. But his hand... might not be able to hold a paintbrush ever again.

Ji Mingxuan let out a light sigh.

He had only met Shen Mo once, and Shen Mo's abduction didn't have anything to do with him either. After he'd heard the news, he immediately rushed over to rescue Shen Mo. He even brought Shen Mo to the hospital afterwards—he had done more than enough. There was no need for him to stay here and waste his time.

But...

Ji Mingxuan remembered how, when he had walked into the old warehouse, those dark, earnest eyes had reflected his figure. He kneaded his brow, thinking he might as well wait until Shen Mo woke up.

Sometime later, the person on the bed let out a murmur. His long eyelashes trembled slightly.

Ji Mingxuan's heart also wavered. Right at this moment, his phone rang, and he had to go out and answer the phone. When he entered the room again, he found that Shen Mo was already awake.

"You're awake." Ji Mingxuan gazed at Shen Mo for a while. With no delicacy, he went straight to the point. "The doctor said you're no longer in danger, but the injury on your right hand is the most serious. There might be long-term effects."

Shen Mo's face looked even paler than it had looked while he was unconscious. His lips moved a little, but what he cared about was not his own hand. Instead, he uttered two syllables, "Zhou Yang..."

Ji Mingxuan had known that Shen Mo would ask about Zhou Yang. He replied coldly, "Zhou Yang is abroad. He's with my sister."

Ji Mingxuan paused before he added, "My sister is Ji An'an."

Sure enough, Shen Mo had heard of the name before. He looked up at Ji Mingxuan, his eyes dark yet lacking in vitality, almost as though nothing could be seen reflected inside.

Ji Mingxuan suddenly regretted staying here. He reached up to fix his tie, and only then did he introduce himself, "My name is Ji Mingxuan."

After that, Ji Mingxuan went to the hospital one more time to see Shen Mo. Shen Mo borrowed Ji Mingxuan's phone and, right in front of Ji Mingxuan, called Zhou Yang to break up with him. When Shen Mo had been beaten up and tortured, Shen Mo had kept his mouth shut, but now that he was out of danger, he instead chose to break up with Zhou Yang. He said he couldn't have his family be in danger.

Of course, none of this had anything to do with Ji Mingxuan. Later, Ji Mingxuan sent his assistant to visit Shen Mo several times, but he himself never went to the hospital again. A month later, Shen Mo recovered and left the hospital. Ji Mingxuan was so busy with work every day that he almost forgot about Shen Mo. However, after being passed around by many people, a watch reached Ji Mingxuan's hands. His subordinates had found it in the old warehouse. He knew it probably belonged to Shen Mo.

It was easy to return the watch to its owner. Ji Mingxuan had Shen Mo's address on file, so he could just ask his assistant to pay a visit there. It had just rained that day. Once the sky cleared, the weather was especially pleasant. Some sunlight seeped through the window and fell on Ji Mingxuan's slender fingers. Sitting in the back seat of the car, he watched the driver weave through the city's bustling streets before finally arriving at an old neighborhood. The apartment buildings there were more than a decade old, their walls overspread with ivy. Ji Mingxuan's gaze swept across the windows as he wondered where Shen Mo lived.

The car stopped. Just as his assistant was getting out of the car, Ji Mingxuan said, "Wait."

"Mr. Ji?"

Ji Mingxuan slowly drew back his gaze. Tapping his finger against his knee, he said, "Actually, I'll go."

Ji Mingxuan opened the car door and took the watch from his assistant's hand. He walked up the stairs to the third floor, then knocked on one of the doors.

Only after Ji Mingxuan waited for a few moments did someone come to open the door.

A damp smell poured out from within. Shen Mo was wearing a baggy shirt, and his face was bloodless—he looked worse than when he'd been hospitalized. But the moment he saw Ji Mingxuan, he smiled.

The smile was brighter than even the radiant sunlight outside.

Shen Mo opened his mouth. "Zhou Yang."

Ji Mingxuan was surprised. "I'm not Zhou Yang."

Shen Mo blinked once. He examined Ji Mingxuan and asked, "Who else could you be?"

As Shen Mo spoke, he pulled Ji Mingxuan inside.

The place was dirty and messy; obviously, it hadn't been cleaned in many days. Ji Mingxuan only said a few words to Shen Mo before he realized that something was wrong with Shen Mo—Shen Mo seemed to have mistaken him for Zhou Yang.

Ji Mingxuan didn't think he had anything in common with Zhou Yang. But this didn't have anything to do with him either. He returned the watch to Shen Mo. He was about to leave when Shen Mo asked him to eat together.

Ji Mingxuan saw the bread on the table, and his expression suddenly changed. He grabbed Shen Mo's hand. "You've been eating spoiled food?"

Shen Mo looked innocent, as if he didn't notice that the bread was already moldy. He didn't answer the question. "I think there might still be some food in the fridge. I'll make some noodles for you."

Shen Mo had walked only two steps when he lurched to the side and almost fell to the ground.

Ji Mingxuan helped Shen Mo steady himself, only to find that Shen Mo was incredibly thin. He tightened his grip around Shen Mo's arm. "If I didn't come today, you'd probably starve to death in this place and hit the headlines a few days later."

Shen Mo still looked blank, as if he didn't understand what Ji Mingxuan had said or didn't care that Ji Mingxuan was angry at him. He just whispered, "Zhou Yang..."

Ji Mingxuan didn't correct Shen Mo again. He only led Shen Mo outside.

His driver and his assistant were still waiting downstairs.

Ji Mingxuan got Shen Mo into the car and had his assistant buy some hot porridge nearby and bring it over. Eating the porridge, Shen Mo said nothing. From time to time, he looked up at Ji Mingxuan with eyes full of trust.

Ji Mingxuan knew it was because Shen Mo had mistaken him for someone else.

Sitting in the car, Ji Mingxuan thought for a moment before he told the driver, "To the hospital."

For the sake of this person named Shen Mo, Ji Mingxuan went to the hospital again. He found a doctor he knew well and had Shen Mo be examined. The results came out soon: it was post-traumatic stress disorder.

Watching Shen Mo squeeze his right hand unconsciously, Ji Mingxuan was well aware of what had caused the illness. Fortunately, Shen Mo's condition wasn't serious—as long as he took his medicine on time and regularly visited the hospital for therapy, he would gradually recover. Since Ji Mingxuan was the one who had involved himself in this matter, he could only help Shen Mo again, getting Shen Mo's medicine and, after driving Shen Mo back, watching Shen Mo take his medicine.

When Shen Mo finished, Ji Mingxuan knew it was time that he left.

He had already wasted too much time on such an irrelevant person. It made no sense to stay here any longer.

But right after Ji Mingxuan opened the door, Shen Mo caught up to him and asked, "Zhou Yang, where are you going?"

"Zhou Yang" again.

Ji Mingxuan sighed silently. Turning around, he looked at Shen Mo. "I just happened to pass by today. I won't come here again."

Shen Mo looked confused again.

Ji Mingxuan couldn't help but lift his palm toward Shen Mo's cheek. However, he didn't touch Shen Mo's face. Word by word, he stated, "Of course, Zhou Yang won't come either. Whether to keep running away from reality or to face the truth, it's up to you."

Once he finished, he withdrew his hand, turned around, and left.

Ji Mingxuan heard the footsteps of Shen Mo following him, but he didn't turn around. He had already spent most of his day around Shen Mo, which meant a lot of business matters had been delayed. After he got back to his office, he inevitably had to work all night. The next day, he was as busy as usual. Only once in a while, when he was taking a break, did the thought of Shen Mo pop up in his mind.

If Shen Mo was left alone, he would probably starve to death.

Of course, that might just be one more headline in tomorrow's newspaper. It had nothing to do with Ji Mingxuan.

Ji Mingxuan breathed a sigh of relief. He laughed at himself. He had been taking care of Ji An'an for so long that upon seeing someone who was sick, he couldn't help but worry about them. He had worked quite efficiently today and finished processing all of the documents in the afternoon. He'd just worked overtime yesterday, so he didn't stay in the office for too long. After tidying up his things, he drove back by himself. It began to rain as he was leaving his office. The rain wasn't heavy—it drizzled down and created a tender atmosphere.

Ji Mingxuan allowed his thoughts to wander for a while.

When his attention returned, he had already driven to the old neighborhood.

Ji Mingxuan was somewhat surprised. He had only been here twice, yet he'd somehow memorized the route so well. He quickly returned to his senses. Of course, he didn't intend to get out of the car, but with just one glance, he saw a familiar figure.

Shen Mo was sitting against the wall, still wearing the thin shirt from yesterday. The drizzle had long since wet his clothes. One could only wonder for how long he'd been sitting here, huddled up from the cold.

He would probably freeze to death before he starved to death.

Ji Mingxuan parked slowly. Myriad thoughts surfaced in his mind but, like the fluttering raindrops, escaped his grasp.

Ji Mingxuan gazed at Shen Mo through the hazy screen of rain.

Shen Mo knew nothing. He was only waiting there persistently.

He was waiting for Zhou Yang. He didn't know that Zhou Yang was a thousand miles away, that Zhou Yang would come for him neither today nor anytime in the future.

Ji Mingxuan drew back his gaze just a few moments later, but he still didn't start his car. His hands rested on the steering wheel, as if he was fighting his own mind. Only the rustling of rain was left in this world.

At dusk, the rain suddenly grew heavier. The sliver of roof above Shen Mo's head couldn't keep out the rain at all. Shen Mo was even more drenched than before, but he still remained motionless.

Ji Mingxuan felt a throb in his heart.

He knew he had lost.

There was a spare umbrella in his car. Ji Mingxuan opened the door, got out of the car, and went to Shen Mo with the umbrella. Seeing Ji Mingxuan, Shen Mo's eyes brightened at once, almost as if he saw light amid a boundless darkness. He stood up and hugged Ji Mingxuan, calling, "Zhou Yang!"

Ji Mingxuan froze. A long time passed before he sighed and embraced Shen Mo gently.

Having been rained on for an entire day, Shen Mo came down with a high fever in the evening, so Ji Mingxuan could only call a doctor to come and give him an injection. Even during his sleep, Shen Mo called Zhou Yang's name, waving his arm around as though he was looking for something. Ji Mingxuan wanted to put Shen Mo's hand back inside the blanket, but Shen Mo caught Ji Mingxuan and gripped him so firmly that he couldn't break free.

But after that, Shen Mo calmed down. Only his lips moved slightly, as if to say, "Zhou."

Ji Mingxuan couldn't help but wonder—just how charming must Zhou Yang be to have captivated Shen Mo like this? Ji Mingxuan's family had known the Zhou family for decades, so Ji Mingxuan was also familiar with Zhou Yang. If Ji Mingxuan was asked to comment on Zhou Yang... well, Zhou Yang was okay, but nothing more than that.

Ji Mingxuan took care of Shen Mo throughout the night. The next day, he called a housekeeper to come clean the house and watched Shen Mo take the pills before he left. Afterward, he had the housekeeper visit and take care of Shen Mo every day, while he himself also came to check on Shen Mo every few days.

Many times, Ji Mingxuan also tried to explain to Shen Mo that he'd mistaken him for the wrong person. But Shen Mo either told Ji Mingxuan that he didn't understand or asked rhetorically, a smile on his face, "Who else could you be?"

Ji Mingxuan was quite experienced in taking care of patients; he knew that ones like Shen Mo were the most difficult to deal with. Shen Mo was immersed in his own world—others could do nothing to help him.

Ji Mingxuan was sometimes puzzled as to whether Shen Mo mistook everyone for Zhou Yang or if it was only him. He once, on purpose, had his assistant walk around Shen Mo, but Shen Mo ignored his assistant completely.

Ji Mingxuan felt quite defeated.

He knew that he had been spending too much time on Shen Mo. He had tried to leave Shen Mo alone too, but in the end, he still found a reason with which to convince himself: he was long since used to taking care of a patient anyway, so what he was doing now was no more than a small favor.

After staying like this for almost a month, Ji Mingxuan noticed that Shen Mo experienced nightmares every night. They tormented him so much that he was too afraid to even fall asleep. No wonder he had lost so much weight, even though he was being fed such good meals every day.

As for what the nightmares were about, Ji Mingxuan knew without thinking.

Ji Mingxuan had just taken Shen Mo to the hospital for a checkup. Knowing Shen Mo's condition was no longer well enough for him to live alone, Ji Mingxuan immediately turned around and decided to take Shen Mo to his house instead. However, Shen Mo was unwilling— he even fought with him for control of the steering wheel, an act that almost caused quite a tragic car accident.

Shen Mo insisted that he stay in the rental and wait for somebody.

They both knew for whom Shen Mo was waiting.

Ji Mingxuan stopped the car and turned around to look at Shen Mo.

Shen Mo stared back, refusing to give in.

In the end, Ji Mingxuan was still the one to surrender. He drove Shen Mo back to the rental. He couldn't leave Shen Mo alone, though.

After much consideration, he grabbed a blanket and slept on the sofa. The rental was small, its bedroom door facing its living room. At night, Shen Mo didn't close the door. Once the lights were off, Ji Mingxuan could see how Shen Mo curled up under the blanket under the moonlight.

Ji Mingxuan was tall and long-legged, so it was natural that he felt uncomfortable sleeping on the sofa, tossing and turning, unable to fall asleep. Shen Mo didn't sleep either. His eyes were resting on Ji Mingxuan.

Ji Mingxuan decided that he wasn't going to get any sleep tonight. Turning around, he gazed at Shen Mo for a while before he asked, amid the silence, "Does everyone look like Zhou Yang in your eyes? Or am I the only one you mistake for him?"

Shen Mo seemed to smile at Ji Mingxuan. He declared, "Only you're special, of course."

For a moment, Ji Mingxuan's mind drifted.

Then he heard Shen Mo say, "Zhou Yang?"

The name immediately pulled him back to reality.

He was quiet for a while. In the dark, his voice sounded especially low as he said, gently, "You can sleep. I'm right here."

From then on, Ji Mingxuan lived in the small rental. With Ji Mingxuan around, unsurprisingly, Shen Mo no longer had nightmares. The two of them spent quite a calm, peaceful time with each other.

The first time Ji Mingxuan realized that things had gotten out of control was when Shen Mo suddenly disappeared one afternoon.

Because of his illness, Shen Mo was always in a bit of a daze. He had even lost some memories, having completely forgotten that he'd been kidnapped. But for some unknown reason, on that day, he dug out a paintbrush, something he hadn't used in a long time, and discovered that his right hand was injured and that he could no longer paint. He didn't say anything at the time and, hastily wiping away his tears, went into the kitchen to cook. Ji Mingxuan noticed Shen Mo's bad mood, so he deliberately paid a visit home at noon the next day. Yet, Shen Mo had disappeared.

Staring at the empty apartment, Ji Mingxuan stayed calm. Immediately, he asked his driver and his assistant to help him look for Shen Mo. He searched through the entire neighborhood, and finally found Shen Mo in a supermarket.

Wearing a supermarket employee's uniform, Shen Mo was intently organizing products in front of a shelf.

Something in Ji Mingxuan's heart finally landed. Only then did he realize that his palms were covered in sweat.

He felt as if he had lost something and found it again.

Shen Mo, as oblivious as usual, seemed to be unaware of the situation. He even asked, "Zhou Yang? Why are you here?"

Ji Mingxuan automatically blocked out the name that Shen Mo had said. Walking over, he hugged Shen Mo and called his name in a low voice, "Shen Mo."

Ji Mingxuan repeated the name many times. Obediently, Shen Mo stayed in Ji Mingxuan's arms.

Later, when it came to explaining what had happened, Shen Mo still spoke as if he'd done nothing wrong. He said that because he couldn't paint anymore, of course he had to find another job to make a living.

Ji Mingxuan didn't agree to it.

Ji Mingxuan had seen Shen Mo's paintings. Talent aside, he could at least tell that Shen Mo really loved painting. As such, he got in touch with the top experts and the best hospitals, determined to treat Shen Mo's hand.

In reality, it was a little too late to begin treatment. After much consultation, the conclusion was that Shen Mo's hand needed another operation.

Ji Mingxuan soon had everything arranged. Theoretically, this was no more than a small operation, but the night before the operation, as Ji Mingxuan waited beside Shen Mo in the hospital ward, he felt nervous for some reason.

The last time Ji Mingxuan was this nervous had been many years ago, when Ji An'an had entered the operating room. His parents had already passed away then, and Ji An'an had become the only family he had left.

At the time, Ji An'an had been the whole world to him. But now, another person had squeezed into his heart.

No matter how nervous Ji Mingxuan was right now, he didn't show it on the surface. He only circled Shen Mo's hospital bed again and again, his hand slightly tense as he patted Shen Mo's. "Don't be afraid."

"I'm not afraid." Shen Mo smiled and comforted Ji Mingxuan instead. "It's just a small operation. It'll be great if it succeeds, but there's no harm even if it doesn't."

Sometimes, Ji Mingxuan didn't quite understand Shen Mo. Shen Mo obviously had a good temper, almost as if anyone could take advantage of him, but when he got stubborn, he refused to give up no matter what.

And so, when it came to Shen Mo, Ji Mingxuan could only give in no matter how much he resisted.

Shen Mo's operation turned out to be a great success.

But this was only the first step of the treatment; he still had a whole series of rehabilitation to go through later. The doctor also prescribed a lot of traditional Chinese medicine, which tasted awful and was difficult to swallow. Fortunately, Shen Mo never threw a tantrum. No matter what he was fed, he always downed it in one gulp.

The days were getting cold. Shen Mo's physique wasn't good—his body was rather sensitive to the cold in the winter, and his hands were always frozen stiff, so Ji Mingxuan used medicinal liquor to massage his hands. Ji Mingxuan started from his fingertips, and then kneaded his fingers one by one.

This was definitely far beyond a small favor. But Ji Mingxuan enjoyed it, so he didn't need to find another excuse with which to convince himself.

On that day, as Ji Mingxuan massaged Shen Mo's fingers, Shen Mo chatted casually with Ji Mingxuan, bringing up the fact that he might not be able to paint again.

Of course, Ji Mingxuan firmly believed that he would be rewarded as long as he kept going.

Shen Mo smiled and called, "Zhou Yang."

He said, "When my right hand heals and I start painting again, you'll be the first one I paint, okay?"

Ji Mingxuan stopped for a moment.

The person Shen Mo wanted to paint was Zhou Yang.

Ji Mingxuan felt as if his heart had been pricked by something. It wasn't painful, but he felt strange and uncomfortable. With his head lowered, he folded Shen Mo's hands in his own. He gazed at the pair of hands for a while before he replied, "...Okay."

He knew he had fallen in too deep.

He had also tried to distance himself from Shen Mo, pretending to be busy at work and ignoring Shen Mo unless it was necessary. But Shen Mo understood nothing and clung to him as usual. Once, Shen Mo even sneaked up on him while he was washing the dishes.

Ji Mingxuan was so close to letting Shen Mo succeed. In the end, only by claiming that he was impotent was he able to make Shen Mo give up. But it'd be too dangerous for him to keep staying in the same room as Shen Mo.

Luckily, New Year's approached. Ji Mingxuan flew abroad to see Ji An'an. It was also an opportunity for him to keep himself away from Shen Mo. He still made some arrangements before he left, though: Shen Mo said that he was going to pay a visit home, so Ji Mingxuan told his assistant to book the train tickets in advance.

Even so, while he was overseas, Ji Mingxuan was still concerned about Shen Mo. Even Ji An'an couldn't help but complain, "You're always spacing out these days, Brother."

Ji Mingxuan could only force a smile.

But Ji An'an was constantly talking about Zhou Yang, which reminded Ji Mingxuan of the person he left behind in China. Perhaps Zhou Yang had been an archenemy of his in a past life—the two people he cared about the most both had nothing but Zhou Yang on their minds.

So on New Year's Eve, Ji Mingxuan was determined to refuse to invite Zhou Yang for dinner. Ji An'an had to give up, and instead enjoyed a wonderful meal with Ji Mingxuan alone. Ji Mingxuan, as usual, gave her a New Year's present. With a cheer, Ji An'an forgot all about not having Zhou Yang beside her. Hugging Ji Mingxuan, she gave him a hard kiss.

Ji Mingxuan glared at her with a straight face, but he felt quite pleased in secret. Estimating that it was almost midnight in China, he took out his phone and called Shen Mo.

Of course, Shen Mo hadn't slept yet. The two chatted about a few things: Shen Mo asked him if it was fun overseas, while he asked Shen Mo what Shen Mo had eaten on New Year's Eve. Shen Mo spouted a long list of dish names, but as Ji Mingxuan listened, Ji Mingxuan felt that something was wrong.

It was too quiet on the other end of the line. Hadn't Shen Mo gone home for New Year's? How could it be so quiet?

Gripping the phone, Ji Mingxuan asked out of the blue, "Shen Mo, where are you now?"

Shen Mo answered without a pause, "I'm home."

Ji Mingxuan asked again, "Alone?"

Shen Mo hesitated for a moment before he replied in a cheerful tone, "I'm in my hometown. Mom and Dad are both here."

After he finished, he added hurriedly, "My parents are calling for me. They want me to go set off some firecrackers with them. I'll hang up for now."

Shen Mo wasn't a good liar. Ji Mingxuan immediately knew what was going on, but he didn't expose him. Shen Mo's name spiraled in his heart before he uttered it in a strange tone, "Shen Mo."

Shen Mo didn't say anything.

The clock struck twelve amid the rumbling of firecrackers. Ji Mingxuan had many things to say, but across the phone line, across the tens of thousands of miles, he only said, "Happy New Year."

Shen Mo returned, "Happy New Year."

It was still early after Ji Mingxuan hung up. He finished the meal hastily and called his assistant to look into Shen Mo's matter. His assistant was quite efficient—he soon found out that Shen Mo hadn't returned to his hometown after all and had spent the New Year in that small rental.

Upon further investigation, Ji Mingxuan discovered that Shen Mo had long since come out to his family. Because of this, he had been kicked out by his family and definitely couldn't go back. So he was staying in that rental alone—perhaps he had even started having nightmares again...

Ji Mingxuan deeply regretted having been so negligent.

Although New Year's was not over yet, Ji Mingxuan's heart had already flown back to China. Ji An'an had always been a sensible person. Seeing how absent-minded Ji Mingxuan was after he made the phone call, she said generously, "Brother, if something happened at work, you can go back first. You've already spent New Year's with me anyway."

Ji Mingxuan stroked her hair and apologized.

After some difficulties, he was eventually able to get a return ticket to China. A dozen or so hours later, he was already standing outside the familiar rental.

Ji Mingxuan knew that Shen Mo was inside. But, just as he was about to reach up and knock on the door, he began to hesitate. He had decided to avoid Shen Mo, but now that he'd hurried back, wasn't everything back to square one?

What was worse was that Shen Mo might not even remember his name. In Shen Mo's eyes, he had always been the man named Zhou Yang.

Ji Mingxuan lifted his hand, drew it back, and lifted it again. A long while passed before he knocked on the door in front of him.

Shen Mo soon opened the door. He had clearly just woken up—his hair was disheveled, his pajamas were wrinkled, and he had on a blank expression. But the moment he saw Ji Mingxuan, he couldn't help but reveal a smile.

Ji Mingxuan felt a softness in his heart. Upon the sight of Shen Mo, all of his hesitations disappeared.

Ji Mingxuan looked Shen Mo up and down. Making sure that Shen Mo hadn't lost too much weight during the time they'd spent apart, he finally walked inside and sat down on the sofa. Waving at Shen Mo, he said, "Come here."

Shen Mo walked over obediently. Just as he was about to reach the sofa, Ji Mingxuan extended a leg to trip him. Caught off guard, Shen Mo stumbled a few steps forward, and Ji Mingxuan reached out to wrap him in a tight embrace.

Shen Mo looked up, gazing at Ji Mingxuan with eyes of pure dark as if he wanted to call the man's name.

Ji Mingxuan knew which two words Shen Mo was going to say, so he took the lead and lowered his head to kiss Shen Mo.

Shen Mo's right hand healed quite well. According to the doctor, he'd soon be able to hold a paintbrush again. And, after New Year's, Ji Mingxuan had begun to sleep on the bed too.

In the end, he still let Shen Mo succeed.

Rationality repeatedly reminded him that Shen Mo had mistaken him for someone else and that it'd be dangerous for him to continue indulging in it, but the indulgence just felt too good.

Like an addict who'd had a taste of opium, he found it far too difficult to stop.

Ji Mingxuan had investigated Shen Mo before, so he knew it was almost Shen Mo's birthday. Up until now, he had only given presents to Ji An'an before—he had no idea what he should give Shen Mo. He'd also asked Shen Mo tentatively, but Shen Mo wasn't really interested in the matter, so he decided on his own.

He had a property in Jinxiu Villa, located in a premium area, quiet amid the bustle of the city. But as he usually lived in his own place, the apartment had remained empty all this time. He remembered that he'd seen one of Shen Mo's paintings before, one that depicted Shen Mo's dream home, so he had someone redecorate the place based on the painting.

Most notably, what had once been the study was the room with the best lighting, and Ji Mingxuan went out of his way to turn it into a studio. He bought all kinds of painting supplies as well, although the walls still looked empty.

After thinking for a while, Ji Mingxuan decided to simply hang all of Shen Mo's paintings. Of the paintings, some were landscape while others were figures; some were official work while others were scribbled drafts. Only the signatures at the bottom were the same.

It had taken Ji Mingxuan quite some time to collect those paintings. But no matter how troublesome, it was something that money could solve.

The most difficult things were what money couldn't solve.

How to make one person fall in love with another, for example.

Having hung the paintings, Ji Mingxuan felt quite satisfied with himself. However, although he'd prepared the gift, he couldn't present it so bluntly. With his past experience in giving presents to Ji An'an, he knew what to do—he went to a gift shop and bought a box, inside of which he could put the key.

The sales assistant recommended a pretty box to him. Hearing it was a birthday present, the sales assistant even decorated it carefully and stuck a bowtie to it.

Today was Friday, and tomorrow was Saturday, which was Shen Mo's birthday. Ji Mingxuan finished some of his work ahead of schedule. As long as he dealt with a few more documents in the evening, he'd have the entirety of tomorrow to spend with Shen Mo.

After getting off work, he went to a cake shop to order a cake and drove back to the old neighborhood. When he parked the car, he didn't get out in a hurry, but instead clutched the present box holding the key and examined it from every angle. He put it inside the car for a while, and then he took it back into his grasp—as though it felt too hot to the touch, he didn't know where to place it.

Pulling himself back together, he looked up at the building in front of him.

If Shen Mo accepted the present, they'd move out of here soon. Having lived in the small rental for such a long time, Ji Mingxuan somehow felt a little reluctant to leave.

He took a deep breath and finally opened the door. Like the first time he'd visited here, he stepped up the stairs. He knew that the lights were on in one of the homes in this building.

Someone was waiting for him.

Ji Mingxuan's attention returned from his memories. He gazed at the pair of silver-white rings before him. Both rings were no more than two plain circles—he'd gone out of his way to have them custom made, and his assistant had just brought them back.

That birthday present... In the end, he'd indeed given it to Shen Mo, but Shen Mo hadn't accepted it.

The night right before Shen Mo's birthday, Shen Mo had recalled everything that had happened and realized that Ji Mingxuan wasn't "Zhou Yang," despite what he'd believed.

The doctor had actually also said that Shen Mo's illness was getting better and that one day he'd see the truth. But Ji Mingxuan hadn't expected the day to come so quickly, so suddenly. Shen Mo felt as if he'd been deceived, and even asked Ji Mingxuan why Ji Mingxuan had pretended to be Zhou Yang and lied to him.

Ji Mingxuan didn't know what to say to him.

Of course, Ji Mingxuan had also tried to explain it many times, but how could he argue with someone who was ill? Now that Shen Mo had recovered, all that Ji Mingxuan had done in the past became unforgivable.

But it was good to let Shen Mo know the truth. Shen Mo couldn't live in his own dreams for his whole life.

It was somewhat different from Ji Mingxuan's original plan, but Ji Mingxuan still gave the present to Shen Mo. He stuffed it into Shen Mo's hands by force. Shen Mo was quite cautious, refusing to go with him, so he could only let Shen Mo take a look at Jinxiu Villa on his own, or...

"Or you can pretend that you never received it."

It rained heavily that night. Ji Mingxuan went to Jinxiu Villa alone and waited there for three days.

Shen Mo never came.

This was probably the answer. But, whenever it came to matters related to Shen Mo, Ji Mingxuan could never control himself. A week later, he went to the rental again.

He parked his car and waited downstairs. When Shen Mo came down to take out the trash, they met each other's eyes. In an instant, Shen Mo averted his gaze.

As if Ji Mingxuan was no more than a stranger.

Once Ji Mingxuan knew how Shen Mo felt, he'd never bothered Shen Mo again. It wasn't until two months ago, when he'd heard about Shen Mo having been forced out due to overdue rent, that he had found Shen Mo, already almost living on the streets.

Shen Mo looked much worse than before—the weight that Ji Mingxuan had helped him put on had disappeared again, and he looked confused and dazed. Luckily, he was still mentally sane. He remembered having been kidnapped and having already broken up with Zhou Yang.

Ji Mingxuan originally wanted to take Shen Mo home and take care of him, but Shen Mo turned down the offer. Shen Mo said that they were just strangers, unwilling to accept Ji Mingxuan's kindness.

Ji Mingxuan knew how stubborn Shen Mo was. After considering it over and over again, he drafted a contract and gave it to Shen Mo. It was quite an absurd agreement: to ensure the happiness of his own sister, Ji An'an, Shen Mo had to pretend to be his lover.

In reality, Ji An'an was far away overseas, so how could Shen Mo stand in her way? It was all just an excuse.

But Shen Mo really believed it, and he also remembered that Ji Mingxuan had saved his life. To repay the deed, he readily signed the contract and moved in with Ji Mingxuan.

It was just that the two could never treat each other as they had before.

Shen Mo pretended that he didn't know Ji Mingxuan, so Ji Mingxuan could only try his best to cooperate. But, in the name of putting up an act, he was able to do many things, including having the pair of rings custom made.

The rings were of the most common style. Of the two, one had neither diamonds nor engravings, while the other had the same design but looked slightly different—there was something engraved on the inner side of the ring.

Ji Mingxuan looked at the two rings again and again and, in the end, gave the one without the engraving to his secretary. "Take it to Mr. Shen."

The secretary knew that Ji Mingxuan had spent quite some time on the rings, so he asked, "Should I put it in a box?"

"Don't bother."

"Then... should I tell Mr. Shen that you went out of your way to have it custom made, Mr. Ji?"

Ji Mingxuan didn't reply, only giving him a slight glance.

The secretary immediately knew he'd misunderstood. He changed his words, "Should I just say you bought it at a store?"

Ji Mingxuan paused for a few seconds before he spoke, "Say that I didn't have time and that you bought it at some random place."

The secretary's expression twisted for a moment; it looked rather amusing. But he still answered in acknowledgement and left with the ring.

Sitting alone in the office, Ji Mingxuan picked up the other ring and slowly brushed his fingertip across the letters engraved on it. And then he smiled, his gaze growing tender as he slid the ring onto his left ring finger.

Secrets

There was an ID photo in the wallet.

The person in the photo still seemed to be a student. His bangs were extremely short, revealing his smooth forehead and bright eyes. With his lips slightly pursed, he looked somewhat serious.

Shen Mo recalled that the photo had been taken when he was in college so that he could stick it onto his resume. He didn't know how Ji Mingxuan had gotten hold of it, but Ji Mingxuan kept it in his wallet every day. No matter how Shen Mo looked at it, he felt that it wasn't a good photo, but just as he was about to take it out of the wallet, he heard a sound from the bed.

He hurriedly stuffed the wallet into Ji Mingxuan's coat again and slipped back into bed.

Ji Mingxuan flipped over and wrapped an arm around Shen Mo's waist. His eyes still closed, Ji Mingxuan only rubbed his chin against Shen Mo's neck, asking, "Where did you go?"

The rubbing tickled Shen Mo, so he dodged a bit to the side. "The bathroom."

And I took a look at your wallet on my way.

Of course, Shen Mo didn't say the second part out loud.

Holding Shen Mo in his arms, Ji Mingxuan said, "I'm taking the day off today. Let's sleep a little longer."

Shen Mo had realized that Ji Mingxuan especially enjoyed hugging him in bed like this, refusing to get up even when they were awake. But those who had become fathers no longer had holidays. Shen Mo reminded him, "Xiao-Ning will be getting up soon."

Ji Mingxuan let out a muffled response and immediately opened his eyes. He looked at Shen Mo for a few moments before he took Shen Mo's chin and kissed him hard. Only once he'd had enough did he let go of Shen Mo and get up to dress himself.

Shen Mo was somewhat out of breath from the kiss. He lay in bed for a while longer before he heard Ji Ning knocking outside the door.

Ji Ning first called, "Dad!"

And then called, "Uncle!"

He rapped loudly on the door, as if he wouldn't stop until the door opened.

Now that Ji Mingxuan had finished washing, he already looked quite refreshed. He walked over to open the door and picked Ji Ning up. "Come, let's have breakfast."

Ji Ning waved his little arms, asking, "What about Uncle?"

Shen Mo heard Ji Mingxuan answer, "Uncle was very tired last night. Be a good boy and don't bother him."

Why did you do it so many times if you knew I was tired?

Wrapped in the blanket, Shen Mo didn't know whether to laugh or cry. He was the kind of person who couldn't stand leisure—he didn't like lying around, even on his days off. So he soon got up, thinking about taking advantage of the sunny day to clean the windows and whatnot.

But right after lunch, Ji Mingxuan gave Shen Mo a task: to go buy a pair of cufflinks with him.

Shen Mo was actually the one who brought up the matter first. Mr. Ji loved the pair of cufflinks he'd picked, but it wasn't a good idea to wear the same cufflinks all the time. Ji Mingxuan happily accepted the suggestion, immediately saying that he'd like to choose another pair, so long as Shen Mo went together with him.

They happened to be free today anyway, so of course Shen Mo didn't turn down the offer. After he coaxed Ji Ning to sleep in the afternoon, he went out with Ji Mingxuan.

Ever since Ji Ning had returned from overseas, Shen Mo and Ji Mingxuan had been constantly busy with him. They hadn't spent any time alone in a long while. On their way, Ji Mingxuan said, "We'll eat out tonight."

Shen Mo said, "But xiao-Ning..."

"Chen-jie is there to look after Ji Ning. It'll be fine. You don't have to spoil him like this."

"He's only just moved to a new environment after all. He's not used to it yet."

Ji Mingxuan gave Shen Mo one glance and let out a snort. "You've been spending a little too much time on him, haven't you?"

Was he getting jealous of even a kid?

Shen Mo chuckled. "Xiao-Ning resembles you a lot, Mr. Ji."

Ji Mingxuan snorted again and didn't say anything else. Sneaking a look at his face, Shen Mo figured that he was in quite a pleasant mood.

They hadn't chosen anywhere specific to shop, so they just strolled around the mall downtown. Shen Mo actually didn't know how to choose cufflinks—he looked here and there and still had no idea, so he could only ask Ji Mingxuan which styles he liked.

Right away, Ji Mingxuan flaunted the ring on his left ring finger. "Just pick a pair that matches this."

As he spoke, he turned the ring deliberately, almost as if to dazzle everyone around him.

Shen Mo felt quite embarrassed, but he still chose a pair of cufflinks accordingly. However, he hadn't expected to come across someone he knew. Really, it was quite a coincidence—the last time he'd finished buying cufflinks, he also met Zhao Yi, who'd had dinner with them once.

Shen Mo remembered that Zhao Yi had been popular for some time, but then gradually disappeared from the screen, perhaps because he'd retired. Shen Mo wouldn't have recognized him if he didn't stand out so much—one of his cheeks was swollen, obviously from having been injured; his left shoe was also missing, and he walked around limping.

Even in such a sorry state, Zhao Yi still acted calmly. Ignoring others' surprised looks, he went directly to a shop assistant, asking her to get him a pair of shoes.

Then, he sat down to try on the shoes. His motions were, elegant as if he was sitting right in front of a camera. When the shop assistants peeked at him, he even looked up and smiled, making the young girls blush.

Shen Mo wanted to take a closer look, but Ji Mingxuan turned Shen Mo's head around and said, "Mind your own business."

Ji Mingxuan and Zhao Yi's relationship was something Shen Mo had never figured out. Besides, it had been so many years already—it'd be embarrassing to mention it right now. So he didn't ask anything and conscientiously continued choosing cufflinks. In the end, he chose a wine-colored pair that matched Ji Mingxuan's ring rather well.

Ji Mingxuan looked at it and nodded in satisfaction.

So Shen Mo went to the checkout with his wallet.

By now, Zhao Yi had already changed his shoes. He came over and greeted Ji Mingxuan.

Looking at his face, Ji Mingxuan said, "Seems like you haven't been doing so well."

Zhao Yi let out a laugh and raised his chin. "I was the one who chose this."

He didn't seem to regret it at all.

As such, Ji Mingxuan didn't say anything else.

Zhao Yi glanced at Shen Mo, who was swiping his credit card, and asked, "How come Mr. Shen is the one paying?"

"Of course he is." Ji Mingxuan seemed quite proud. "I'm living off him now."

Taken by surprise, Zhao Yi had on a somewhat indescribable expression. After a while, he sighed. "I shouldn't have changed my target so soon back then. If I'd continued to go after you, Mr. Ji, maybe I'd be the one standing there right now."

Ji Mingxuan smiled. He was gazing at only Shen Mo. "You wouldn't have succeeded."

Zhao Yi let out another sigh. "I knew it."

He still seemed somewhat disheartened.

Ji Mingxuan didn't say anything in reply. After Shen Mo finished paying, he came back and, upon seeing Zhao Yi standing on the side, didn't know whether or not he should say hello.

On the other hand, Zhao Yi greeted him naturally, "Long time no see, Mr. Shen."

So Shen Mo chatted with Zhao Yi for a while.

They'd only exchanged a few words when Ji Mingxuan's eyes swept over. Shen Mo understood at once—he hurriedly took out the cufflinks he had just bought and put them on for Ji Mingxuan.

Zhao Yi couldn't watch this any longer. He said goodbye to the two and left with a wave of his hand.

Ji Mingxuan put his cufflink near the ring and compared the two, the corners of his mouth lifting slightly. Obviously, he felt much more pleased than before.

It was already late, so they went to a nearby restaurant for dinner. Shen Mo had figured out Ji Mingxuan's taste by now, so all he ordered were Ji Mingxuan's favorite dishes.

As they were eating, Ji Mingxuan suddenly spoke up, "Aren't you going to ask about my relationship with Zhao Yi?"

"Oh," Shen Mo asked, "what was your relationship?"

Ji Mingxuan replied, "I only had a few meals with him due to business matters."

Shen Mo still said, "Oh."

Even if something had really happened between the two, it'd been years already—why would Shen Mo be jealous about it? But Mr. Ji was clearly dissatisfied by Shen Mo's reaction, pulling a long face for the rest of their meal.

Shen Mo felt that Ji Mingxuan was becoming more and more temperamental, almost turning into Ji Ning at this point.

Just as they were about to finish their meal, Chen-jie called and said that Ji Ning was refusing to eat, so the two hurried back home.

Ji Ning hadn't seen them in a whole afternoon; he was a little sour indeed. Not only did he refuse to eat, he even started wailing, his tears rolling all the way down his cheeks. Shen Mo felt really bad, so he tried to coax Ji Ning by any means. In the end, only by taking out his phone and letting Ji Ning play games for a while did he get Ji Ning to start smiling again.

Chen-jie reheated the cold dishes, and Ji Ning obediently finished most of his rice. After dinner, he lay on the sofa and played on the phone with Shen Mo.

Ji Mingxuan rubbed them, "Take care of your eyes," and went to his study to read documents. Having taken the day off, he still had quite a lot of work to catch up on. But soon afterward, he heard Ji Ning calling him in the living room, "Dad, Dad! Come here! Come here!"

Ji Mingxuan kneaded his eyebrows, put the documents aside, and walked out.

Ji Ning and Shen Mo were laughing together at the phone, as if they'd seen something interesting. Ji Ning waved his arms and called, "Dad, come take a look!"

So Ji Mingxuan strode over and went to their side to take a look. Only then did he notice that the phone's front camera was on and that their three faces were reflected on the screen. Seizing the chance, Shen Mo quickly pressed the shutter icon.

Click.

The picture was captured right after the flash.

Ji Ning and Shen Mo were smiling happily in the photo, whereas Ji Mingxuan was frowning slightly instead. The three of them were closer than ever to one another.

Looking at the phone, Shen Mo said, "You're too serious, Mr. Ji."

Ji Ning shouted, "Let me see! Let me see!"

And the two began to discuss.

"It's quite a nice shot. I'll print it out later and put it in my wallet."

"I want one too!"

"But you don't have a wallet, xiao-Ning. Where will you put it?"

"Hmm..." Ji Ning thought about it intently before he said, "I'll just put it together with my New Year's money."

"Okay."

Ji Ning cheered happily. When he turned around and saw that Ji Mingxuan was still standing at the side, he waved his hand. "You can go, Dad."

Shen Mo also said, "You can go back to work, Mr. Ji."

As if they were throwing him away now that they'd finished using him.

Speechless, Ji Mingxuan stood there quietly for a while before he returned to his room.

That night, Ji Mingxuan naturally had his way with Shen Mo again—Shen Mo didn't even want to get up the next day. In the afternoon, however, he still paid a visit to the studio, both to supervise the work and to have Yang Yue print out the photo for him.

Yang Yue had already met Ji Mingxuan. When she first learned that Ji Mingxuan was the future "Missus," her expression revealed more shock than a magnitude ten earthquake. But Yang Yue quickly accepted this fact and even praised Shen Mo for his good taste, commenting on how super handsome Mr. Ji was. After that, she referred to Ji Mingxuan as "Mr. Ji" like Shen Mo did—she never called Ji Mingxuan the "Missus" again.

Shen Mo felt somewhat disappointed.

Fortunately, Yang Yue was quite an efficient worker—just a few days passed before she had the photo printed out. Shen Mo was quite satisfied with it. He not only put one in his wallet but also used another to replace the old ID photo in Ji Mingxuan's wallet.

Ji Mingxuan disagreed at first, but his weak resistance was quickly overpowered by Shen Mo. He still managed to save that old, yellowed photo, although Shen Mo didn't know where he kept it.

The last photo was for Ji Ning. The little guy had long since lost all interest in it, though. After taking a casual glance and making sure both Dad and Uncle were in the photo, he hurried away to play with his new toys.

Shen Mo still remembered the promise they'd made, so he stored the photo together with Ji Ning's New Year's money. Ji Ning was young, but he'd already saved plenty of money. His passbook was stored right in the drawer of the master bedroom's nightstand.

Shen Mo entered the bedroom. While he was opening the drawer, he pulled a little too hard, and the entire drawer came out of the nightstand. Just as he was about to put it back in, he found a small box hidden under the drawer.

The box was square and had a velvet surface—it looked quite familiar, just like the ones that often appeared at the end of certain romance dramas.

Shen Mo's heart skipped a beat. He couldn't help but reach out and pick up the box. Opening it, he indeed found a pair of rings inside.

They looked exactly the same as the one he'd painted on Ji Mingxuan's left hand, but they were finer than the one he was wearing now. Each with a diamond on top, they glowed and sparkled in the sun.

So it turned out that Mr. Ji had also prepared rings, but Shen Mo had ended up being a step ahead of him.

This was the confession that Ji Mingxuan had never said out loud.

Shen Mo felt moved, almost tearing up.

With his finger, he gently stroked the pair of rings. He didn't know how long had passed when he heard Ji Ning calling him outside, "Uncle, come out and play with me!"

Only then did Shen Mo's attention return. He put the pair of rings back in the corner and, as if he'd found out about nothing, carefully fixed the drawer back in place.

In the living room, Ji Ning was playing with his new toys enthusiastically. Ji Mingxuan, on the other hand, was reading documents at the side, and when he saw Shen Mo come out, he gave Shen Mo a casual glance.

He often said that it was Shen Mo who had pursued him first.

Yes, Shen Mo thought, *that's right.*

As for Mr. Ji's little secret, he might as well let it be a secret forever.

Happy New Year

There was a ring on the table.

It was a silver-white ring of the most common style, with neither diamonds nor engravings on it. Ji Mingxuan had told his secretary to buy one for the time being and bring it over.

Shen Mo was debating whether or not he should put it on.

He'd performed terribly in bed last night, so nervous that he had almost seemed like a dead fish. After they finished, Mr. Ji left the room without saying a word, probably quite dissatisfied with him. Well, it wasn't *his* fault—he'd dated Zhou Yang before, but Zhou Yang, who had only had girlfriends before him, hadn't had much experience with men, and it had probably been difficult for him to overcome the hurdle. Shen Mo hadn't wanted to force it either, so he'd thought he might as well let things happen naturally. Yet, in the end...

In the end, Shen Mo had broken up with Zhou Yang and spent over half of the year in a trance. He'd been almost living on the streets when

Ji Mingxuan had found him and brought him back.

Perhaps the breakup had been too much of a shock, but Shen Mo's memory of these past six months was rather vague. However, he could remember that Ji Mingxuan had saved him when he had been abducted, and Mr. Ji had even paid for his medical bills later on. Ji Mingxuan wanted to ensure his sister's happiness by pretending to be together with him, so of course he was willing to cooperate.

But Shen Mo hadn't expected to be stumped by the matter of having sex, before anything else. He'd signed the contract after all, so he thought he should be a bit more dedicated. Did he need to watch some gay porn and learn from it?

As Shen Mo's thoughts wandered, Ji Mingxuan came back from work. Seeing Shen Mo in a daze, he asked, "What are you thinking about?"

Of course, Shen Mo couldn't say that he was wondering where to download porn, so he could only say, "It's nothing..."

Ji Mingxuan glanced at the ring on the table. "Why aren't you wearing it?"

Shen Mo asked blankly, "I'm really supposed to wear it?"

Ji Mingxuan didn't reply and only reached out to grab Shen Mo's left hand. Shen Mo finally noticed now that Ji Mingxuan was already wearing a ring on his left ring finger. The ring was silver-white as well and looked the same as Shen Mo's—these were couples' rings. With his slender fingers, Ji Mingxuan held the ring and moved it toward Shen Mo's finger.

Out of reflex, Shen Mo tried to retract his hand.

Ji Mingxuan held Shen Mo's hand firmly. His gaze brushed casually over Shen Mo's face as he slid the silver-white band onto Shen Mo's finger.

Shen Mo felt somewhat surprised. *It's just an act—do we need to be so serious?*

As if he knew what Shen Mo was thinking, Ji Mingxuan looked down at their connected hands. "We should put on the full act."

For three whole years after this, the two wore the same rings, never taking them off once.

"What are you thinking about?"

Ji Mingxuan's voice suddenly sounded beside Shen Mo's ear.

Startled, Shen Mo returned from his memories. All those things had happened so many years ago. A while back, he'd proposed to Ji Mingxuan in the studio and succeeded. This time, Shen Mo was the one who had put a ring on Ji Mingxuan's hand.

The man belonged to him now.

Shen Mo felt infinite tenderness in his heart. Gazing at Ji Mingxuan, he said, "I was thinking about you, Mr. Ji."

Quite satisfied with the answer, Ji Mingxuan kissed the corner of Shen Mo's lips. "Wait a little longer. I'll be done soon."

Shen Mo could only manage a smile. He was currently in quite a dangerous situation—it was the same studio, but his hands were bound by a tie and his shirt was wide open while a paintbrush, dipped in syrup, swept across his chest.

Shen Mo had wondered why all of a sudden, Ji Mingxuan had suggested painting him something as a New Year's present. Only after he walked into the studio did he realize that the canvas... was *him*.

"Mm..."

As the soft tip of the paintbrush brushed his skin, Shen Mo whimpered, unable to bear it. But because his hands were tied behind his back, he had no way to escape, and could only beg, "Mr. Ji... I can't take it anymore..."

Although Ji Mingxuan had said he'd be done soon, he still painted slowly on Shen Mo's body. The tip of the paintbrush skimmed around as if in play.

While the sensitive spots on Shen Mo's chest were being teased, pleasure accumulated little by little, but it couldn't peak. The rising lust made him blush and gasp.

A long while later, Ji Mingxuan finally said, "It's done."

Shen Mo breathed a sigh of relief. He heard Ji Mingxuan say in his ear, "How do you like it?"

Shen Mo looked down and saw that Ji Mingxuan had painted a flower on his chest. The petals were a bright scarlet, whereas the stamens were his nipples, already somewhat erect. It was quite an erotic scene.

With just one glance, Shen Mo turned his head to the side—he was even starting to grow hard down below. But Ji Mingxuan grasped his chin and forced him to turn back around. "It doesn't look good. Should I paint another one?"

Of course Shen Mo didn't want that. He hurried to say, "I-It does look good."

Ji Mingxuan let out a low laugh. "Then let me have a taste."

As he spoke, he bent down and licked Shen Mo's areola, dyed reddish by the syrup. Then, he held the delicate nipple between his teeth and flicked his tongue against it.

Shen Mo's neck arched back, his body trembling all over.

Ji Mingxuan lifted his eyes to look at Shen Mo. "It's *sweet*."

Shen Mo felt his body burn. He called in a low voice, "Mr. Ji…"

Ji Mingxuan licked him again. Only after Ji Mingxuan ate up most of the petals he'd just painted did he look up at Shen Mo, asking, "Do you want to have a taste?"

His lips were tinged red, which made his handsome features look even more alluring. Shen Mo, unable to bear the temptation, leaned over on his own and kissed Ji Mingxuan's beautifully shaped lips.

The syrup almost seemed to glue their lips together.

Shen Mo thought as he kissed, *It does taste very sweet.*

He was originally sitting on the sofa, but now his whole body had sunken into it. Ji Mingxuan got on top of him, also erect. He took both erections into his hand and stroked them together.

Shen Mo, pinned down by Ji Mingxuan, found the stimulation to be unbearable. He tensed his legs, almost reaching his peak, but Ji Mingxuan stopped right then.

Left hanging, Shen Mo felt so tortured that his voice grew hoarse. He cried, "Mr. Ji… Give it to me…"

He didn't even know what he wanted.

Ji Mingxuan smiled. He switched to another paintbrush and squeezed some lubricant on it.

Shen Mo's mind was a complete mess. Only when he saw Ji Mingxuan reach downward, holding the paintbrush, did he finally realize what was happening. He kicked his legs. "No!"

"Don't worry." Ji Mingxuan parted Shen Mo's legs with his knee. "It'll feel good."

As Ji Mingxuan spoke, the paintbrush had already reached Shen Mo's lower half, sweeping back and forth at his entrance. Soon, the region between his thighs grew all wet and sticky.

In both pleasure and fear, Shen Mo kept calling, "Mr. Ji."

Ji Mingxuan lowered his head to kiss Shen Mo, but his hands didn't stop. The spot became moist and soft. With just a bit of strength, the tip of the paintbrush went in.

It was strange to hold a foreign object within one's body. Unable to tell if it was pleasure or discomfort, Shen Mo was almost crying. "Mr. Ji, I don't want this..."

Ji Mingxuan moved his wrist back and forth, asking, "What do you want, then?"

Shen Mo, while his insides were being stirred this way, almost came right there. In a crying voice, he said, "I want yours, Mr. Ji... Mnn..."

Right after Shen Mo finished his words, Ji Mingxuan pulled out the paintbrush, replaced it with his own erection, and plunged straight in. Shen Mo was already more than slick inside—Ji Mingxuan reached the deepest point in just one thrust.

Shen Mo drew in a shaky breath, feeling as if his heart would jump out of his chest.

Ji Mingxuan rammed into Shen Mo quite a few times before he slowed down, varying his thrusts between deep and shallow. He then found Shen Mo's most sensitive spot and pressed right against it, rubbing and grinding. Shen Mo couldn't stand the teasing—it didn't take long for him to come.

The white fluid splattered against their abdomens. Ji Mingxuan took some in his hand and smeared it on Shen Mo's lips. Engrossed,

Shen Mo licked it and lifted his head to kiss Ji Mingxuan.

Ji Mingxuan ground his hips and fucked Shen Mo for a while longer before he undid the tie that bound Shen Mo's hands. Pulling Shen Mo up from the sofa, he pressed Shen Mo against the wall of the studio, raised one of his legs, and entered his body again.

Shen Mo's legs had long since gone limp. He could only stand on tiptoes, trying his best to hang onto Ji Mingxuan's neck.

Ji Mingxuan drove deep inside, thrusting into Shen Mo's body again and again, and then brought Shen Mo's hand toward where the two were connected. Feeling how slippery it was, Shen Mo retracted his hand at once.

Ji Mingxuan laughed lightly and kissed the tip of Shen Mo's ear. "I've wanted to fuck you like this for a long time."

Hearing this, Shen Mo felt his abdomen burn, and he couldn't help but tighten around Ji Mingxuan. If he hadn't released just now, he would've come again right there.

As Shen Mo clenched up, Ji Mingxuan was also reaching his limit. After a few more thrusts, he climaxed inside of Shen Mo.

It was almost midnight. The sound of firecrackers came intermittently through the window.

The year was coming to an end.

Too many things had happened this year. Shen Mo had gone to S Island on vacation, but he just so happened to have run into Ji Mingxuan. And then, Ji Mingxuan had returned to China and accepted his proposal...

Shen Mo felt a sense of nostalgia.

Ji Mingxuan came out of Shen Mo, but he was still holding Shen Mo in his arms. Grabbing Shen Mo's hand, he planted a kiss on the ring and, amid the roar of firecrackers, whispered to him, "Shen Mo, happy New Year."

Present

On Valentine's Day, Shen Mo received a rose as a present.

It was a red rose, not yet fully in bloom, with morning dewdrops still on its petals—someone had quietly put it beside his pillow. Waking up in the morning, he saw the rose the moment he opened his eyes. He wasn't too interested in plants' reproductive organs, but he couldn't help but look over and over at the present he'd received on such a special day.

The sun outside the window was rising higher in the sky. It wasn't until Ji Ning called for him loudly from outside his door that Shen Mo got up to wash himself. It was the weekend, so he had gotten up a little later than usual. Ji Mingxuan and Ji Ning were already fully dressed, waiting for him at the breakfast table. After the three of them finished breakfast, Shen Mo found a vase and put the rose inside it, while Ji Mingxuan watched Ji Ning draw in the study. When Ji Ning had returned to China, he happened to be old enough to go to kindergarten here. Perhaps he had been affected by Shen Mo, but he was especially interested in art. Shen Mo was quite happy of course, and bought him a variety of art supplies.

There was no kindergarten today. Ji Ning had been making a fuss about wanting to draw since early in the morning. After finishing up other matters, Shen Mo went to the study as well, and saw that Ji Ning was drawing a giraffe—they had gone to the zoo last week and seen giraffes. It was quite a good drawing, in fact. Shen Mo gave Ji Ning some advice on the side, then took out his phone to take a photo.

Next, Shen Mo posted it directly to his WeChat Moments[1].

He'd never used these features in the past, but he'd recently hired a new girl for his studio. She was Yang Yue's age, and the two had hit it off immediately. They were always posting landscapes, food pictures, and couple photos to their Moments, and they'd even urged Shen Mo to join them.

At first, Shen Mo was only doing what they wanted, but as time went on, he gradually became addicted. Ji Ning was just too cute— like every silly parent, Shen Mo would show off his baby every day if he could.

Soon after Shen Mo posted the photo, Ji Mingxuan also took out his phone and looked at it. After that, he became somewhat distracted, looking down at his phone again and again.

Seeing this, Shen Mo said, "Are you busy with work, Mr. Ji? Don't worry, you can go to work. I can stay with xiao-Ning."

Ji Mingxuan replied with a grim face, "No."

His tone definitely sounded unpleasant.

Shen Mo was surprised, not knowing what had upset Ji Mingxuan. He'd been together with Ji Mingxuan for so long already, but he still couldn't figure Ji Mingxuan out. Was it because last night he'd said he was too tired and refused to do it a second time?

Shen Mo's face felt somewhat warm. Ji Ning was here though, so

---

[1]WeChat is a popular social media platform in China. Its main feature is direct communication with various contacts using only an internet connection, but it also has a Facebook-like function where one posts various things for one's contacts to see, its "Moments" section.

Shen Mo couldn't ask Ji Mingxuan directly. A while later, Ji Mingxuan finally lost his patience. He stood up and left the study.

Shen Mo thought that Ji Mingxuan had gone to work, but Ji Mingxuan returned quickly, holding in his hand the rose that Shen Mo had just put inside the vase.

Ji Ning looked up and exclaimed, "Flower!"

Ji Mingxuan placed the vase on the desk and petted Ji Ning's head, asking, "Do you want to draw this?"

"But I haven't finished my giraffe yet."

"You can draw this one after you finish the giraffe."

Ji Mingxuan was talking to Ji Ning, but he gave Shen Mo a deliberate glance.

Shen Mo suddenly came to understand what Mr. Ji was thinking—Shen Mo had shown off their kid, but he'd forgotten to show off their relationship with each other as well. Ji Mingxuan waited and waited. Not seeing what he wanted to see, he had to make it happen by himself.

Once Shen Mo figured this out, he didn't know whether to laugh or cry—he hurried to cooperate, taking out his phone to take photos of the rose. Ji Mingxuan was finally satisfied. He walked over and stood behind Shen Mo, watching him take the photos.

"That's not a good angle. Move a little to the left."

"Try turning on flash."

"No, adjust the lighting again."

Shen Mo took quite a few photos, but Ji Mingxuan wasn't satisfied with any. In the end, Ji Mingxuan even grabbed Shen Mo's phone and started taking photos on his own.

Ji Ning watched them from the side, asking curiously, "Uncle, is Dad also gonna draw?"

"No, he's just taking a few photos."

To Shen Mo's surprise, Ji Mingxuan spent a whole half hour taking photos.

Ji Ning had already finished drawing the giraffe. He'd even finished listening to a story from Shen Mo when Ji Mingxuan finally gave the phone back to Shen Mo, his expression calm. Opening the album, Shen

Mo saw that it was filled with photos of the rose, taken from every angle.

Which one should he post?

Shen Mo didn't dare decide on his own. He immediately asked Ji Mingxuan for his opinion.

With indifferent eyes, Mr. Ji casually picked one.

Shen Mo looked at it carefully—it was really the best photo. The instant after he posted it on his Moments, Ji Mingxuan liked his post.

Shen Mo thanked him.

The morning interlude passed just like this. After they had lunch, Ji Ning asked Shen Mo to take him to the amusement park. Ji Mingxuan happened to be free, so he volunteered to be the driver.

The three changed their clothes. Ji Mingxuan was in a full suit as usual, while Ji Ning was also in a small suit of the same color—the two, standing together, really looked like father and son. Ji Mingxuan led Ji Ning downstairs first. Shen Mo brought some fruit and snacks before he followed their way. When he reached the underground garage, he saw the two talking beside the car.

Somewhat confused, Shen Mo asked, "Why aren't you getting into the car?"

As he spoke, he reached out to open the car door.

But Ji Mingxuan grabbed his arm. "Let's drive another car today. This one... hm, it's time to take it to maintenance."

Shen Mo was a little surprised—he thought the car had been taken to maintenance just last month. However, they had many cars, and Ji Mingxuan always entrusted his assistant with maintenance, so Shen Mo wasn't sure if he was the one who had remembered wrong either. It wasn't a big deal to drive something else, though. He turned around and got into another car. Ji Mingxuan and Ji Ning walked behind him, even whispering some things to each other.

Ji Ning had a great time this afternoon. Shen Mo went on his favorite attraction, bumper cars, with him quite a few times. Because of the bright sunshine, both of their faces flushed red, and their foreheads were sweaty too.

In the evening, Ji Mingxuan booked a table at a restaurant for steak. It was almost eight when they got home after dinner. Ji Mingxuan still had a few emails to send, so Shen Mo had the nanny wash Ji Ning, then sat on the edge of the bed and told Ji Ning a bedtime story. Ji Ning had been too excited during the day—he didn't feel sleepy yet. Even after he listened to the story, he asked Shen Mo for paper and crayons and finished two drawings.

Both drawings were of cars. Shen Mo recognized that the first one was a bumper car, what they'd gone on in the afternoon, while the second one was their own car, the one Ji Mingxuan had said would be taken to maintenance. However, the car was covered in... flowers?

Shen Mo didn't quite understand. He asked Ji Ning, "Why did you draw so many flowers, xiao-Ning?"

"Because I saw them. The car was full of flowers." Ji Ning chose a red crayon to color the flowers. "But Dad told me not to tell you, Uncle."

Shen Mo felt his heart flutter. He asked, "Roses?"

Ji Ning blinked. Obviously, he didn't know what kind of flowers roses were.

So Shen Mo changed his question. "Did they look the same as the one in the vase this morning?"

Ji Ning nodded and replied immediately, "Yeah."

Shen Mo understood at once.

Ji Mingxuan had prepared a car filled with roses, but he only chose one of them and gave it to Shen Mo.

Shen Mo stroked Ji Ning's black hair. As he thought about it, he couldn't help but laugh.

Yes, it was exactly something Mr. Ji would do.

After Shen Mo got Ji Ning to fall asleep, he walked into the living room. For a long time, he stared at the rose blooming in the vase, and then finally returned to his bedroom to rest.

It wasn't until midnight that Ji Mingxuan finished his work and entered the bedroom. He didn't turn on the light. Quietly, he felt his way to the bed before he reached out and wrapped Shen Mo in his arms.

Shen Mo gently held Ji Mingxuan's hand.

Ji Mingxuan was somewhat surprised. "You haven't slept?"

"No." Clasping Ji Mingxuan's hand, Shen Mo said, "Mr. Ji ..."

"Yes?"

"Nothing."

Shen Mo thought for a while and, in the end, didn't mention the car of roses after all. He only turned around and kissed the edge of Ji Mingxuan's lips. "Thank you for the Valentine's Day present."

Ji Mingxuan let out a soft laugh. "You should sleep."

Shen Mo murmured a reply and fell asleep in the gentle embrace.

Birthday

Shen Mo was drunk.

It was the fourth of February: the beginning of Spring, as well as Ji Mingxuan's birthday. They had reunited with each other on S Island, so for Shen Mo's birthday this year, Ji Mingxuan had planned a vacation in advance and revisited the island with Shen Mo. This time, they lived in a villa with a sea view and a private swimming pool. Sunshine, the beach, the coast, and a candlelit dinner... Nothing could be more perfect. The only thing that surprised Ji Mingxuan was Shen Mo's alcohol tolerance—Shen Mo was drunk after just two glasses of red wine.

When Shen Mo got drunk, he never yelled or cried, but instead he talked ten times more than usual. Holding Ji Mingxuan's hand, he rambled on and on.

The beautiful night that Ji Mingxuan had imagined vanished right there. He didn't want to interrupt Shen Mo, though, so he could only be patient and listen to him. Shen Mo talked about everything—from fighting with his elementary school classmate to the math teacher he'd hated in high school. As he went on, he even asked Ji Mingxuan for his opinion: "Isn't that right?" "Don't you agree?" "Do I make sense?"

Ji Mingxuan could only nod again and again: "That's right." "I agree." "Everything you say makes sense."

Shen Mo seemed very satisfied with Ji Mingxuan's answers. With his eyes half-closed, he gazed at Ji Mingxuan.

Shen Mo seldom looked at someone so boldly. Under the gaze, Ji Mingxuan even felt his body grow warm. He grabbed Shen Mo's hand. "What are you looking at?"

Shen Mo didn't reply. Suddenly, he smiled and called, "Ji Mingxuan."

It was rare to hear Shen Mo call his name. Ji Mingxuan answered, "Yes, it's me."

"You..." In a drunken haze, Shen Mo asked, "You're hiding something from me, aren't you?"

Ji Mingxuan had nothing to feel guilty about. His face didn't blush and his heart didn't skip a single beat as he said, "No, I'm not."

"Liar!" Shen Mo, drunk as he was, slowly leaned on Ji Mingxuan's shoulder, murmuring, "I know about it... The pair of rings..."

Rings?

Had he found out about those?

Ji Mingxuan, remembering the rings he'd hidden somewhere in their house, felt his heart rate speed up. But he heard Shen Mo add, "And those flowers..."

Flowers?

He'd even found out about those?

Ji Mingxuan knew he must keep his cool, so he immediately calmed himself. Patiently, he tried to get an answer out of Shen Mo. "Where did you see the rings?"

Shen Mo frowned as if he was trying his best to recall the memory.

Afraid that Shen Mo wouldn't be able to remember it, Ji Mingxuan coaxed, "That's it. Think about it carefully."

But, even after thinking for a long time, Shen Mo only shouted, "I want to swim!"

Then, Shen Mo left Ji Mingxuan alone and went to the villa's private swimming pool.

Ji Mingxuan felt rather speechless. Drunkards were like this, after all, messing with other people's feelings with no knowledge of doing so. Seeing Shen Mo wobble as he walked, Ji Mingxuan worried that it might not be safe for Shen Mo to swim like this, so he hurried after him.

Without even taking off his clothes, Shen Mo jumped into the swimming pool. Ji Mingxuan could only get in the water like this as well, watching him fool around from the side. Shen Mo splashed about, but all of a sudden, he plunged into the water. Alarmed, Ji Mingxuan called for him and rushed over, reaching for him. But Shen Mo quickly floated back to the surface, splashing water onto Ji Mingxuan's body— he was almost as childish as Ji Ning was.

Ji Mingxuan really couldn't stand it any longer. With a swing of his arm, he pulled Shen Mo to his chest and seized him firmly. At first, Shen Mo still tried to struggle, but gradually he quieted.

The swimming pool was open-air. Right now, the moonlight shined on the two of them.

Shen Mo's gaze, like the hazy moonlight, brushed over Ji Mingxuan's face.

Gripping Shen Mo's wrists, Ji Mingxuan asked again, "What are you looking at?"

Shen Mo replied, "Ji Mingxuan."

Only then did Ji Mingxuan understand that this was the answer.

Ji Mingxuan couldn't help but draw closer to Shen Mo, asking in his ear, "What's there to look at?"

As if he felt tickled, Shen Mo dodged and giggled. "Every part of you looks good."

In case Ji Mingxuan didn't believe him, perhaps, he leaned right in and kissed Ji Mingxuan's eye. "Here."

And then Ji Mingxuan's nose. "Here."

The final kiss fell on Ji Mingxuan's lips. "And here... Mm."

Before Shen Mo could finish his words, Ji Mingxuan was already kissing him aggressively.

Both their clothes were wet. After the kiss, their bodies clung tight to each other's, inevitably rousing a certain heat. With Shen Mo in his arms, Ji Mingxuan swam to the side of the pool and pressed Shen Mo against the pool wall.

Shen Mo didn't resist at all. He only looked up at Ji Mingxuan, his eyes somewhat watery from the drunkenness, filled with bold affection.

Ji Mingxuan kissed Shen Mo again.

The kiss lingered this time. The water in the pool rippled slowly along with their movements, lapping against their bodies.

Shen Mo was soon turned on. He hung onto Ji Mingxuan's shoulders with his hands, refusing to let go.

The clothes stuck to their bodies were not easy to strip, so Ji Mingxuan only took off Shen Mo's pants. He brought one hand between Shen Mo's thighs and rubbed his entrance, reaching one finger inside.

"Mm..."

With the motion, cool water seeped into Shen Mo's body. He couldn't help but let out a moan.

Ji Mingxuan licked Shen Mo's neck. "Don't be afraid. It'll be all right soon."

As Ji Mingxuan spoke, he added another finger, spreading the entrance wider. With several stirs, Shen Mo gradually grew soft and slick inside.

Shen Mo called out again, unconsciously wrapping his legs around Ji Mingxuan's waist. Ji Mingxuan withdrew his fingers and pressed his own erection against Shen Mo.

But exerting strength underwater was difficult. Ji Mingxuan tried a few times but still couldn't enter him.

Ji Mingxuan wasn't impatient, but Shen Mo became restless, biting Ji Mingxuan's lips in dissatisfaction. Ji Mingxuan laughed. His lips felt a slight sting as he whispered in Shen Mo's ear, "Do you want me to come in?"

"Yes," Shen Mo admitted honestly.

Ji Mingxuan's voice sounded hoarse. "Then spread your legs and let me in, okay?"

If this were usual, Shen Mo definitely wouldn't do what he'd just been told, but now that he was drunk, he really thought about it for a while. He then let go of Ji Mingxuan's shoulders. Wrapping his arms around his legs, he parted them slightly to each side.

Ji Mingxuan ground his hips forward, deliberately rubbing the entrance, yet still refusing to go in. "Not enough. A little wider..."

With a whimper, Shen Mo simply turned his back to Ji Mingxuan and squeezed his buttocks, spreading them apart. Turning around, he said, "Ji Mingxuan... Hurry up..."

Shen Mo was wet all over. His upper half was covered by a shirt, but his legs were completely bare, revealing the entrance hidden in the crevice.

Ji Mingxuan felt himself grow even more erect. He reached out to hold Shen Mo's waist and drove straight in.

Shen Mo let out a sudden cry, his heart almost jumping out of his chest. Ji Mingxuan waited until Shen Mo got used to him, and then began thrusting hard.

Water splashed as his sack slapped against Shen Mo's buttocks.

Shen Mo swayed his hips in attempt to cooperate, moaning intermittently, "Ah... I can't, it's too fast... Oh..."

After several thrusts, Ji Mingxuan slowed down just as Shen Mo had wished. However, he found the sensitive spot inside of Shen Mo and slowly rubbed against it.

Shen Mo couldn't stand it anymore. In a crying voice, he could only beg Ji Mingxuan to move faster.

Shen Mo's whole body grew soft from the teasing—he couldn't do anything but beg. The way he begged was also quite interesting. He called out almost unconsciously, "Ji Mingxuan, help me..."

Amused, Ji Mingxuan wrapped an arm around Shen Mo's waist and kissed his nape. "Yes, I'm here."

Following Ji Mingxuan's voice, Shen Mo turned around. Even his eyes looked watery now.

Ji Mingxuan knew that he had teased Shen Mo a bit too much. Still buried inside Shen Mo, he flipped Shen Mo over and kissed Shen Mo's face. "Be good. Hold on a little longer. It'll be over soon."

From the stimulation, Shen Mo let out another delirious "mm," staring at Ji Mingxuan.

Ji Mingxuan breathed beside Shen Mo's ear, teasing him, "I really look that good?"

"Of course. Whenever I look at you, I just can't seem to move my eyes away." Shen Mo licked Ji Mingxuan's lips. "Ji Mingxuan, I love you..."

Ji Mingxuan suspected that Shen Mo had done it on purpose.

But immediately, Ji Mingxuan's body gave an honest reaction—he started fucking Shen Mo again. Shen Mo had been making so much noise that his voice had gone hoarse. Unable to stand up, he slid down the pool wall.

Ji Mingxuan lowered his head to kiss Shen Mo, sinking into the water with him.

It wasn't until Shen Mo thought he was going to drown in the water that Ji Mingxuan finally brought him back to the surface. Ji Mingxuan spoke beside his ear, "Shen Mo, say it again."

"Say what?"

"Tell me..." Ji Mingxuan pushed deep into his body. "Who do you love?"

"Ah..."

Shen Mo let out a low cry, feeling almost as if his soul would rise from his body. But he still uttered the name "Ji Mingxuan."

Only then did Ji Mingxuan let Shen Mo off. He clasped Shen Mo's hand, and their entwined bodies climaxed together.

Ambitions

The first time Liang Yunsheng met Zhao Yi was when Liang Yusheng was invited to attend a singing competition as a guest.

It had been three years since the devastating car accident. After rehabilitation, Liang Yunsheng was already able to walk on his right leg with the help of a cane. A friend of his had invested in the competition and wanted him to make an appearance. He owed this friend a favor, so he could only show up and go through the motions.

One of the contestants was Zhao Yi. The contestants were all young and lively, some with especially good looks and others with especially unique voices—Zhao Yi definitely didn't stand out. Despite his handsome looks, his singing was no more than mediocre. Liang Yunsheng only heard him sing once, but he knew Zhao Yi had no talent for singing.

And yet, Zhao Yi still made an impression on Liang Yunsheng.

All of the contestants were young adults who had just plunged into the industry; most of them still had innocence in their eyes. Zhao Yi was different. He was still so young, but he already seemed so experienced. He stood on stage generously, showing a certain ambition in his eyes.

Once, as Liang Yunsheng was walking out of the lounge backstage, he saw Zhao Yi standing right at the door. Smiling, Zhao Yi said, "Mr. Liang, I'm a fan of yours."

Liang Yunsheng nodded with courtesy.

He had heard these words too many times. Three years ago, when his name had been at its peak, thousands of people said the same words to him every day. But the car accident took everything away.

Zhao Yi added, "I love your songs, Mr. Liang."

Liang Yunsheng thanked him politely.

"Do you think I can win this competition, Mr. Liang?"

Liang Yunsheng couldn't help but smile. It was good to be young—so reckless, and even speaking so directly.

So Liang Yunsheng also gave him a direct reply, "You're not good at singing."

"I know." Zhao Yi's tone was brisk. He didn't seem upset at all. "But I want to sing one of your songs, Mr. Liang."

"That's a pity." Liang Yunsheng said, "I don't write songs anymore."

When he finished his words, he walked around Zhao Yi, his cane knocking dully on the ground, and left.

In the final round, Zhao Yi did sing a song by Liang Yunsheng. It was an old song from ten years ago, one that Liang Yunsheng had written when he was about Zhao Yi's age.

Zhao Yi didn't have a good voice, and his singing wasn't adequately emotional either. The results of the contest were just as Liang Yunsheng had predicted—Zhao Yi didn't even make the top five. The contest was broadcast live on TV, but there was fierce competition between similar programs. And so, despite the initial advertising, only the winner of the contest made a bit of a splash, whereas the others all faded into obscurity.

Two months after the contest, Liang Yunsheng's friend came to visit him, asking him to write a song for someone.

"He's new, but he has great potential."

Liang Yunsheng smiled. "You know I don't write songs anymore."

"Why not? It's been three years. Are you still thinking of..."

His friend stopped halfway through.

Liang Yunsheng was in the middle of making tea. Holding the teapot, his hand trembled, and he spilled a little.

The car accident from three years ago had not only injured his right leg but had also taken his beloved away. Whenever he closed his eyes, he'd remember the truck driving toward them that night. He'd turned the steering wheel immediately, yet it was still too late.

Liang Yunsheng gulped down the tea in his cup, turning down his friend's request.

His friend left in disappointment and, soon after, got someone else to write a single for the newcomer.

Liang Yunsheng heard the song on the radio in his car. It was the kind of old-fashioned love song that had been popular many years ago, and it imitated his own style from back then. The singer was Zhao Yi. His voice still sounded mediocre—even though he sang earnestly, there was no impressive quality to it.

After hearing it, Liang Yunsheng only smiled.

The song couldn't make any waves. After being broadcast on the radio a few times, it was gradually forgotten.

A year later, Liang Yunsheng saw Zhao Yi again on TV. Zhao Yi was playing a supporting role in a costume drama. Dressed in white and carrying a long sword, he looked as though he was made of pure jade.

Of course, the person backing him off-screen had already changed.

Liang Yunsheng's friend had ended his relationship with Zhao Yi peacefully. Upon mentioning Zhao Yi again, he only praised Zhao Yi, "He knows what the right thing to do is. He knows when he should laugh and when he should cry. Most importantly, he knows what he wants, and he'll do whatever it takes to achieve it."

But Liang Yunsheng couldn't tell whether this was praise or criticism.

As the two chatted about Zhao Yi, Zhao Yi's drama happened to be playing on TV. He was the third lead, a young, unfortunate hero whom the villain framed and the heroine misunderstood—quite a tough fate. In this episode, the heroine, thinking he was working with the villain, slapped him hard across his face. He didn't defend himself, and only turned his head slightly to the side. Two or three seconds later, a tear rolled down one of his cheeks.

This was much more touching than the love songs he sang.

Liang Yunsheng's friend gazed at the impeccable features on the TV screen. Suddenly, he asked, "Do you have any alcohol here?"

Liang Yunsheng had long since quit drinking. Luckily, he still had a bottle of wine at home, so he opened it for his friend to enjoy. He himself still drank tea, though.

Halfway, his friend asked out of the blue, "He's bound to become famous, isn't he?"

"Of course." Liang Yunsheng recalled Zhao Yi's eyes. "He's an ambitious person."

When Liang Yunsheng said those words, he didn't expect to meet Zhao Yi again in the future. Over the years, Liang Yunsheng had lived a simple life on his own, but some of his friends couldn't bear seeing him so gloomy and were intent on having him come to dinner. He couldn't turn down their kindness, so he had to go and socialize. Those who showed up were all old friends of his whom he hadn't seen in years. Everyone had their own achievements, but only he stood in the same place, as though time had stopped right before the accident.

After several toasts, their conversations became more casual. Some people encouraged him to cheer up, or restart his career, or begin a new relationship. Holding a teacup, Liang Yunsheng only thanked them distantly.

Right then, a sharp sound came from the next room, as if cups and plates had fallen on the ground. Arguing voices also came intermittently. Perhaps some people had gotten so drunk that they started fighting in the hotel.

Most of Liang Yunsheng's table felt that they'd had enough drinks anyway, and now that the clamor had spoiled their mood, they decided to end the meal right there.

Liang Yunsheng walked behind everyone. When he passed the room next door, he saw that the quarrelers had already left. The waiters were coming in and out to clean the shattered dishes. Through the half-opened door, he caught a glimpse of a familiar face.

Liang Yunsheng's footsteps paused.

The person inside saw Liang Yunsheng as well. He smiled and called, "Mr. Liang."

It was too late for Liang Yunsheng to pretend that he hadn't seen him.

Zhao Yi was a mess. His clothes were drenched—water dripped down even the tips of his hair, and his white shirt was also heavily stained. But he still had an elegance about him as he sat there with a smile on his face, as if he was attending a banquet in formal dress.

By now, Zhao Yi had already gone from playing supporting roles to main roles. His dramas aired on TV every day, and Liang Yunsheng had heard there'd be a movie soon. Some said Zhao Yi had good luck, but Liang Yunsheng knew how hard Zhao Yi must have worked.

Liang Yunsheng walked inside the room and asked out of politeness, "Would you like me to drive you home?"

Zhao Yi smiled and said no. Instead, he pointed to a glass of wine on the table. "Have a drink with me, Mr. Liang."

Liang Yunsheng replied, "I don't drink."

"Then have some tea."

As Zhao Yi spoke, he had the waiter bring over a pot of tea. Amber liquid poured into the wine glass. He toasted Liang Yunsheng and then gulped down all of the tea in the glass.

Zhao Yi had said only one drink, and this one glass was indeed all he drank. After, he gestured to Liang Yunsheng and said, "Sorry for taking your time, Mr. Liang."

Liang Yunsheng asked, "You're not leaving yet?"

"I'm waiting for my assistant to bring me clothes."

It was early spring, and the days were still somewhat cold. The wet shirt stuck to Zhao Yi's body, its fabric so thin that the skin underneath could be seen.

Liang Yunsheng thought for a while, then took off his jacket and handed it to Zhao Yi. "Wear this for now."

Zhao Yi was surprised for a moment. Next, a smile spilled from his eyes, and he put on the jacket without fanfare.

Liang Yunsheng thought, if this was acting, Zhao Yi's acting was excellent indeed. But he didn't say anything else and left with his cane.

A few days later, Liang Yunsheng received a call from an unknown number—it was Zhao Yi. Zhao Yi first thanked Liang Yunsheng for drinking with him that night and then said that he would like to return the suit jacket.

Liang Yunsheng didn't think Zhao Yi needed to go to such lengths for just a jacket, but he knew Zhao Yi must have had quite a difficult time asking around for his phone number. So, with much reluctance, he invited Zhao Yi to his house.

Zhao Yi came the next afternoon. When he entered the house, however, he paused for a second. "Your house is really clean, Mr. Liang."

Liang Yunsheng only smiled.

Everyone assumed Liang Yunsheng was living a decadent life, either drinking his days away or staying up every night. In reality, he had a regular routine. In his spare time, he made tea and grew flowers. His terrace was covered in all kinds of flowers and plants.

Zhao Yi smiled and said, "It's as if you're already living the retired life."

"There's nothing wrong with that."

"Your fans will be disappointed though, Mr. Liang." Zhao Yi took a sip of the tea made by Liang Yunsheng. "Don't you plan on making a comeback? Even if you don't write songs anymore, you can still sing them."

Liang Yunsheng didn't reply.

Zhao Yi continued, "I'll be doing a movie in two months. The theme song isn't decided yet. Would you be interested, Mr. Liang?"

Liang Yunsheng had heard that Zhao Yi had also invested in the movie—so it seemed this was true. But Liang Yunsheng wasn't interested at all, of course. As he was about to turn down the offer, Zhao Yi said, "You can take your time thinking, Mr. Liang. There's no need to give me an answer immediately."

When Zhao Yi finished, he took out his phone and made a call. Liang Yunsheng's mobile phone was right on the table, and soon, it began to ring.

Zhao Yi glanced at Liang Yunsheng's phone, grinning. "I knew you never saved my number."

Then, without waiting for Liang Yunsheng to reply, he took Liang Yunsheng's phone and saved his number on it.

It had already been many years since their first encounter with each other. Just like back then, Zhao Yi still smiled at Liang Yunsheng as he said, "I hope I'll get the chance to work with you, Mr. Liang."

The Past

"Shen Mo! Shen Mo!"

A-Wen, Shen Mo's roommate, stood beside the bunk bed and called Shen Mo's name again and again.

Shen Mo poked his head out of the blanket, glancing at the time on his phone. It was only half past nine.

"I don't have any classes today. Why are you waking me up so early?"

Below him, A-Wen laughed sheepishly. "I know you don't have class today. That's why I wanted to ask you a favor."

Shen Mo sat up, his short hair disheveled. He asked, "What is it?"

"Our department will be holding a lecture right this afternoon. Could you attend it for me?"

"Hey, you study economics and I study art. Do you think I can attend it for you?"

"Just show up and take some notes for me. It'll be really easy. Do you know who's invited for the lecture? A young entrepreneur, a successful man who has shown up many times on finance magazines—my idol."

"Then why aren't you going on your own?"

"I'd definitely go if I could, but I have a test, you see?" A-Wen put his hands together, pleading cheekily, "Shen Mo, please, please. I'll treat you to a big meal tonight."

Shen Mo was good-tempered, acknowledged by everyone as a nice guy. He'd always found it difficult to turn down others' requests, and this time was no different. He rubbed his hair and sighed. "Alright. Send me the time and place."

A-Wen cheered. After thanking Shen Mo, he hurried off to study for the test.

Now that Shen Mo had been woken up anyway, he didn't go back to sleep. He got out of bed and went to the bathroom. After he washed himself and came out, there were already two new messages on his phone. One was the time and place of the afternoon lecture; the other was from Zhou Yang, inviting him to have lunch together.

Zhou Yang had been Shen Mo's high school classmate. The two had the same interests and both loved painting. But whereas Shen Mo was studying art in university, Zhou Yang was studying financial management under the pressure of his family. Even so, they were still close friends who talked about just anything, and they'd agreed on going abroad to study art after they graduated.

Zhou Yang had gone home last week. They hadn't seen each other in several days by now, so the two of them went to a small restaurant off campus and ordered a few dishes.

Zhou Yang said as he ate, "You don't have class this afternoon, do you? Let's go watch a movie together?"

"I can't this afternoon. I promised A-Wen from our dorm to attend a lecture for him."

"Why does he always ask you to help him? You're too soft-hearted."

"We're roommates after all. We should help each other."

Zhou Yang could only shake his head.

Shen Mo asked, "What about you? Have you decided yet?"

"Decided what?"

"To study abroad with me, of course. You didn't forget about it, did you?"

"Oh, that..," Zhou Yang paused, still holding his chopsticks. He seemed somewhat hesitant. "I'll think about it some more."

Shen Mo knew Zhou Yang too well. Observing Zhou Yang, he guessed, "Are there any difficulties? Your parents disapprove?"

Zhou Yang's family ran quite a big business, and Zhou Yang was an only child too. His parents wanted him to take over the family business. They'd never approved of him studying art.

Zhou Yang frowned as if he had many things on his mind. "It's okay. I'll handle them."

Seeing how Zhou Yang refused to say anything, Shen Mo said somewhat impulsively, "I've already been in contact with a company for my internship. If you're not studying abroad, I'll just go get a job."

Zhou Yang waved his hand. "Yeah, yeah. I'll work something out. Let's eat first."

The atmosphere of the meal immediately dulled.

After the meal, the two parted ways in quite a bad mood. With this matter on his mind, Shen Mo strolled aimlessly around campus, and when his attention returned, it was already time for the lecture. He quickly collected himself and hurried over. When he arrived, the economics department's large classroom was already filled with people. Only the first row had a few seats left.

Shen Mo looked inside through the door, wondering if he should go in.

The guest invited by the college was already standing at the podium. Shen Mo took a glance—the man at the podium was young indeed. He also looked handsome and had a charming air about him, making an impression on anyone who caught sight of him.

For a moment, Shen Mo's mind wandered. He thought the man looked completely different from how he'd imagined a successful entrepreneur to look.

As he thought about it, he saw the man turn around and smile at him. "For how long are you planning to stand at the door?"

Right after the man spoke, Shen Mo became the room's center of attention.

"Sorry for being late..."

Shen Mo's face flushed as he gathered up his courage and walked in. There weren't many empty seats left in the classroom, though. Looking around, he could only take a seat in the first row.

As soon as Shen Mo sat down, the girl sitting next to him poked him in the shoulder with her pen.

"Yes?"

"This classroom has a back door." Holding back giggles, the girl whispered, "You could've come in through the back door."

Shen Mo gave an awkward smile, his cheeks burning even more as he cursed his roommate A-Wen in silence.

No other incidents happened afterward, but it was really a bit too hard for Shen Mo to attend an economics lecture. He listened for a long time and still felt confused, and he didn't know how to take notes either. He could only jot down a few points to fulfil his promise.

After the lecture, A-Wen's exam was also coming to an end. Keeping his word, he treated Shen Mo to a big meal. But when he saw Shen Mo's notes, he couldn't help but shake his head.

"Shen Mo, you really don't have a talent for this, huh."

"Of course not. I'm not an economics major."

"What a shame," A-Wen exclaimed, heartbroken. "I missed the chance to connect with my idol in person."

Remembering the man at the podium, Shen Mo couldn't help but ask, "Is he really successful?"

"Of course! He's what I strive to be."

Now that the subject had come to this, A-Wen started rambling on and on, praising the man non-stop, almost as if the man was an alien that nobody on Earth could compare to.

Shen Mo didn't want to upset A-Wen, but he still told the truth, "If he became so successful, he must've been born to a wealthy and influential family. You won't be able to catch up to him no matter how hard you work."

After a pause, A-Wen continued regardless, "I don't care. He's my idol anyway."

"Right, what's your idol's name again?"

"You attended the whole lecture, and you don't even remember his name?" A-Wen widened his eyes.

Shen Mo felt a little embarrassed. "I was late, okay? I missed the introduction in the beginning."

A-Wen tossed Shen Mo a brochure. "See for yourself."

Only then did Shen Mo find out what the man's name was.

His name was Ji Mingxuan.

Old Story

It was at the supermarket that Shen Mo received Zhou Yang's call. At the time, he was thinking about whether to make steak or pork rib soup for dinner. The moment the call came through, Zhou Yang said immediately, "I won't be back for dinner tonight."

"What happened? Didn't you say you weren't working overtime today?"

"Yeah..." Zhou Yang seemed somewhat hesitant. "Something came up at home. I have to go back."

"Go back? Are your parents not feeling well?"

"Something like that," Zhou Yang answered vaguely. "I'll probably have to stay there for a few days."

"Okay, I understand. Then take care of yourself too."

"Okay."

Hanging up, Shen Mo looked at the steak he had put in the shopping cart, and could only take it back out. He would be alone, so of course he wasn't be in the mood to cook a big meal. He could make do with some instant noodles.

After Shen Mo and Zhou Yang had graduated from university, their plans to study abroad were laid aside due to disapproval from Zhou Yang's family. But they didn't give up completely—they rented a house and lived together as they slowly saved up money.

Shen Mo recently found a job related to painting, with which he was quite satisfied. Their rental was close to the company too. It was a little small, but Shen Mo enjoyed cleaning, so he kept it quite tidy.

Shen Mo had nothing to do in the evening; he went to bed after watching TV for a while. Before he slept, he texted to Zhou Yang saying good night.

It was Saturday the next day, and Shen Mo stayed home. Seeing how good the weather was, he busied himself with some chores, spending all day doing the laundry and so on. In the evening, Shen Mo called Zhou Yang, but Zhou Yang didn't answer.

Shen Mo didn't take it to heart and went to the nearby supermarket as usual. When he finished and came out, the sky had already darkened, but the street lamps were not on yet. Everything around him was shrouded in the dim dusk of the night. As he turned a corner, he vaguely felt as if something was not quite right. He spun around—the alley was empty, except for a car that followed not far behind him.

Shen Mo ignored it and continued to walk forward. Yet, just a few steps later, the car caught up to him. With headlights bright as snow, it braked hard at his side. Next, someone leaped from the car and lunged for him.

Shen Mo had never been in such a situation before; he was frozen in shock. When his attention returned, his mouth was already covered by a pair of rough hands.

"Mmph... Mmmph..."

Shen Mo struggled to escape, his groceries scattering all over the ground. But another man jumped out of the car and quickly shoved him inside.

The car door slammed shut.

Shen Mo's hands were tied up behind his back. His head was spinning. A while later, a word finally emerged in his mind—*Abduction*.

But Shen Mo was just a poor student. What was the use of abducting *him*?

Did they take the wrong person?

Shen Mo's mouth had also been sealed with masking tape. Unable to make any noise, he could only stay lying down in the car trunk, jolting as the car sped on.

Shen Mo didn't know how long had passed, but he estimated that it had been more than half an hour. The car finally slowed, stopping in front of an abandoned warehouse. Only a single street lamp stood beside the warehouse. One could vaguely see the barrenness all around them.

The man who had seized Shen Mo opened the door and pulled Shen Mo out of the car.

The whole way here, Shen Mo had been thinking about what to do. Knowing this was his best chance to escape, he instantly bent down and slammed his head into the man's chest.

Shen Mo had been quite cooperative all the way. The sudden attack caught the man off guard—the hit landed.

The collision made a loud, dull sound. The man was knocked back a few steps, while Shen Mo felt a throbbing pain at his head as well. But he ignored it, and turned around and fled.

In the darkness, it was hard for Shen Mo to find his way. He didn't know in which direction to run either. All that he knew was that he must run as far as he could and avoid being caught. The wind roared in his ears. As he ran, his foot suddenly slipped, and he crashed onto the muddy ground.

He got up with difficulty, pain surging through his body. But thanks to the fall, the rope binding his hands had loosened. Shen Mo struggled out of the rope and tore off the masking tape on his mouth. Recalling that his phone was still in his pocket, he quickly called the police. He didn't know where he was, so he could only describe the scenery around him. After he hung up, he called Zhou Yang again, but Zhou

Yang still didn't answer.

As Shen Mo looked for a place to hide, he called Zhou Yang over and over again. In the night, his fingers trembled slightly. He had engraved that phone number in his heart. Whenever they chatted, he was always reluctant to hang up. This was such a critical situation, but he couldn't get through no matter what.

"Zhou Yang..."

"Zhou Yang..."

"Pick up..."

Shen Mo murmured amid the cold wind. All of a sudden, a flashlight struck his face with its light.

Shen Mo shuddered, blinded by the light. A while later, he realized that he'd already been caught.

The man in the front was the one who'd abducted Shen Mo. His eyes were chilly. With a distinct scar on his brow bone, he stared at Shen Mo coldly.

Shen Mo had no way of escape. He was soon brought back to the abandoned warehouse.

It was dark inside the warehouse. Shen Mo didn't know how long he'd stayed there. Perhaps it was no more than a dozen hours, but it seemed like a lifetime to him.

The scar-faced man stepped on Shen Mo's right hand, grinding over it with his leather shoe.

An excruciating pain shot up from Shen Mo's fingers. It hurt so much that he cried out—he couldn't help but call Zhou Yang's name.

Hearing this, the scar-faced man burst into laughter.

"You think Zhou Yang would come save you? What an idiot."

"Do you know where he is now? He's abroad. He went to study abroad with his childhood sweetheart."

"Get away from Zhou Yang."

"Don't ever think of seeing Zhou Yang again, or else..."

The scar-faced man stepped even harder. Shen Mo's right hand was a bloody mess—he could even hear his bones being crushed.

He lay on the ground, drenched in sweat, in too much pain to move.

Through the cobwebbed window, he saw a faint light emerge in the boundless darkness.

Even when Shen Mo was unconscious, he still called Zhou Yang's name again and again.

But Zhou Yang never came to save him.

Just as he thought he was going to die, the tightly shut door of the warehouse suddenly opened. A ray of light shone through.

Someone seemed to be standing outside the door. Against the light, their face looked blurred. Shen Mo watched them walk toward him, their features gradually growing clearer.

Shen Mo didn't know who the person was.

But he knew that they were his savior.

After the Rain

In those two weeks, it had always been raining.

The rain poured down from the sky, as if it would never end.

Ji Mingxuan came home from work. Just as he entered the house, he heard the sound of someone crying. Following it, he walked into the nursery to see the new nanny, Chen-jie, gently comforting the baby in her arms.

Chen-jie was a professional with over than ten years of experience taking care of children. But, facing the crying baby in her arms, she still seemed to be somewhat at a loss. Looking up, she said, "Mr. Ji..."

Ji Mingxuan stepped forward. Upon seeing the baby's face, flushed red from the crying, he took a step back before he asked, "What's wrong with him?"

"He just finished his milk. He's crying because he wants to sleep."

"Why is he crying so hard?"

"Children feel insecure easily. After all, his mother... uh..." Chen-jie uttered what was on her mind. Only after she spoke did she realize her words hadn't been the most appropriate. She revealed a remorseful expression.

Ji Mingxuan didn't take it to heart. He nodded and waved his hand. It was raining heavily outside. His gaze, swaying, drifted toward the window.

Half a month ago, Ji An'an, Ji Mingxuan's dearest sister, had left him.

She left him forever.

Ji An'an had a congenital heart defect. Ji Mingxuan had always known that he would lose her someday, but when the day really came, he still felt caught off guard. Ji An'an had been kind and gentle ever since her youth. Even as she'd lain on the hospital bed, her breath thin, she'd still tried to smile.

"Don't cry, Brother."

"I don't regret it at all."

"Take care of Ji Ning for me, Brother."

Ji Ning was the baby crying right now. Ji An'an had suffered unimaginably giving birth to him. She had named the child "ning" for "peace," hoping he could grow up safe and healthy.

Thinking this, Ji Mingxuan finally walked forward and told Chen-jie, "Let me hold him."

Chen-jie felt somewhat surprised. "Mr. Ji?"

Ji Mingxuan laughed at himself. "From now on, all we have is each other. I'll have to learn how to hold him, sooner or later."

So Chen-jie stuffed Ji Ning into Ji Mingxuan's arms.

Ji Mingxuan took Ji Ning over carefully—he found that the baby was incredibly soft. Afraid that he might hurt Ji Ning, he couldn't help but tense up his limbs, not knowing where to place them.

Chen-jie chuckled and helped Ji Mingxuan adjust his posture.

Only then was Ji Mingxuan able to steady his hold on Ji Ning's small body. Clumsily, he tried to get Ji Ning to fall asleep.

Of course, the baby showed Mr. Ji no respect as he continued to bawl.

"Don't cry." Ji Mingxuan lowered his head and kissed the small, crumpled face. "I know why you're crying. You know, I also miss her very much."

At this moment, the pain of losing Ji An'an finally filled Ji Mingxuan's heart.

It took Ji Mingxuan quite some time to get Ji Ning to fall asleep. He was covered in sweat, even though it was already early autumn.

But, in the end, the baby had still fallen asleep in his arms.

Ji Ning's small face was ruddy. He really resembled Ji An'an, now that he was sleeping soundly like this.

Ji Mingxuan stared at Ji Ning. He remembered that many years ago, when his sister had just been born, he was leaning against the hospital ward's window, watching Ji An'an sleep just like this.

Absent-minded, he suddenly heard someone exclaim outside the window, "It stopped raining!"

Ji Mingxuan looked up. The rain that had lingered for over half a month had really stopped. The sun hadn't set yet. In a corner of the clear, blue sky, a faint rainbow hung sideways.

The world had brightened.

The first time Ji Ning called Ji Mingxuan "Dad" was when he was ten months old. It happened as Ji Mingxuan was in the middle of a phone call with Mr. Chen, who was in China.

"...The other properties have all been processed. But the house in Jinxiu Villa—Mr. Shen wanted to keep it."

Ji Mingxuan paused for a while before he replied, "Let him have it, then."

He thought about it for a bit. In the end, he still couldn't help but ask, "How is Shen Mo doing now?"

"Mr. Shen opened a studio on Yongning Road. The business isn't excellent, but it isn't bad either. He can afford his daily expenses."

"A studio? He started painting again?"

"I believe so."

"Really? That's... very good."

Mr. Chen seemed to have hesitated for a moment before he said, "When I contacted Mr. Shen last time, he said that he hoped he could meet with you once more, Mr. Ji. What do you..."

Ji Mingxuan was surprised.

He remembered that before Ji An'an had passed away, she had requested one thing from him—she said, "Let Shen-ge be free. Let him, at least, live freely."

How could Ji Mingxuan turn down An'an's request?

So all this time, Ji Mingxuan had never gone back to China. He'd even tried his best not to ask for any news about Shen Mo. He didn't want to disturb Shen Mo's peaceful life any further. But now, Shen Mo was the one who had asked to see him...

"Mr. Ji?" Mr. Chen asked on the other end of the phone, "What do you think...?"

Ji Mingxuan didn't make the decision right away. Instead, he glanced at Ji Ning, who was playing with some toys in the crib opposite him. As if they could read each other's minds, Ji Ning also looked back at Ji Mingxuan with a pair of wide, blinking eyes. And then, he opened his mouth and articulated, "*Baba!*"

Ji Mingxuan was astounded.

Seeing no reaction from Ji Mingxuan, Ji Ning kept on calling, "*Babababababababa—*"

It was a sing-song tone, but to Ji Mingxuan's ears, it was definitely the most beautiful sound in this world.

Ji Mingxuan strode over and picked up Ji Ning. He hadn't hung up on the call yet. With Ji Ning in his arms, Ji Mingxuan said to Mr. Chen on the other end, "I won't meet with him."

"Oh? But Mr. Shen really wanted to meet with you."

"Tell Shen Mo something for me. Just say that..." Ji Mingxuan gazed at Ji Ning, whose little body was in his arms, and continued, "I'm doing well now, and tell him not to trouble himself."

Ji Mingxuan hung up. He touched Ji Ning's face with his forehead and said, "Say it again."

Ji Ning pouted his lips, but he still sang, "*Babababababababa—*"

Ji Ning had always been clever. By the time he was two years old, he had become a complete chatterbox, always pestering his dad, asking him this and that. Ji Mingxuan was busy with work, but he still put Ji Ning to bed every night, telling him stories and telling him about Ji An'an.

Every year, after New Year's, Ji Mingxuan would take Ji Ning traveling. He had invested in a hotel on S Island, so he always took Ji Ning to the island for vacation. All across the world, there were so many places worth visiting. Why did he choose S Island, where he and Shen Mo had once wanted to visit? Even Ji Mingxuan himself couldn't tell if he had some unspeakable hopes in his mind.

As usual, a great number of visitors came to S Island this year. After Ji Mingxuan spent his birthday on the island, he stayed there for a few more days with Ji Ning. Ji Ning was just three years old—quite a lively, playful age. He ran wild in the hotel whenever he had the chance; Ji Mingxuan had to look after him in person.

On that day, it was the same.

Ji Ning was playing by the pool with his new friends, and Ji Mingxuan watched him from not too far away. Suddenly, Ji Mingxuan heard someone call, "Mingxuan!"

Ji Mingxuan turned around to find an attractive woman in a fashionable swimsuit. Holding the arm of a middle-aged man, she walked past the pool.

Ji Mingxuan could only smile, thinking it must have been someone with the same name as him. But once the couple walked past him, he saw Shen Mo.

Shen Mo was gazing at him as well.

Their eyes met, and the world was silent.

The start of spring had just passed. The weather was especially good that day, with no clouds in the sky for miles. But Ji Mingxuan seemed to feel that only now did the rain that had lingered in his heart truly stop.

New Year's Eve

The busiest time of the year was always the period of time surrounding the Spring Festival, when everyone traveled to be with their families for the various festivities of Lunar New Year. During such a time, the family of three: Ji Mingxuan, Shen Mo, and Ji Ning, were currently sitting on a train.

Ji Ning had just started kindergarten—children this age were the most energetic. He usually traveled by plane or car, but this was his first time going on a train. Everything he saw seemed novel to him. Unable to sit still in his seat, he kept on trying to squeeze into the crowd, wanting to explore the other compartments.

Afraid of him getting lost, Shen Mo had to follow closely behind him. Even on the winter day, sweat formed over Shen Mo's body.

In the end, it was Ji Mingxuan who said, "Ji Ning, come back."

Ji Ning could only come back reluctantly.

Ji Mingxuan patted the seat next to him. "Sit here."

Ji Ning jumped onto the seat and obediently put his legs together, resting his hands on his knees.

Ji Mingxuan gave Ji Ning's head a rub. "Good boy. Take a look at the view out of the window."

Outside, scenes of Southern China's creek towns were flying past. Apart from the expansive paddy fields, one or two dainty Western-style houses could also be seen at times.

But Ji Ning couldn't sit still. After looking out for just a short while, he began to wriggle in his seat again. Turning around, he asked, "Dad, how much longer until we get there?"

Ji Mingxuan glanced at his watch and replied, "About half an hour."

"Yay!" Ji Ning cheered.

However, Shen Mo had a completely different expression. He mumbled, "So soon?"

Somewhat amused, Ji Mingxuan gazed at Shen Mo and asked, "What's wrong? Feeling a little nervous?"

"...No."

Despite what he said, Shen Mo unconsciously tapped his finger on the table.

The destination of their trip was Shen Mo's hometown—a scenic town in Southern China.

Back then, because of Zhou Yang, Shen Mo had fallen out with his family and hadn't gone home in years. Only after he began to raise Ji Ning together with Ji Mingxuan did he really come to understand the difficulties of raising a child, and he had been trying to mend his relationship with his parents. Unfortunately, though, he hadn't made much progress.

Once Ji Mingxuan found out about this, he bought train tickets to Shen Mo's hometown without telling Shen Mo. It wasn't until New Year's Eve that he dragged Shen Mo onto the train. Shen Mo hadn't prepared anything—even his luggage had been packed last minute—so of course he was nervous now.

"What are you worried about? That your parents might kick you out?"

"It's definitely possible."

"If worse comes to worst, we can book a hotel. No matter what, we won't be out on the street."

Shen Mo forced a smile.

Ji Mingxuan reassured him, "Don't worry. I made sure to bring the secret weapon this time."

"What secret weapon?"

Ji Mingxuan pointed at Ji Ning, sitting next to him.

With a pair of wide, innocent eyes, Ji Ning smiled sweetly.

Shen Mo asked, perplexed, "Xiao-Ning?"

Ji Mingxuan nodded and turned to Ji Ning. "Do you remember what Dad taught you?"

"Yes!"

"What do you call Uncle's parents?"

"Grandpa and Grandma."

"What else do you do?"

"Say 'happy New Year' and 'wishing you prosperity' and..." Ji Ning got stuck. Thinking hard, he managed after a few moments, "Give me red packets, please!"

Ji Mingxuan cleared his throat, reminding Ji Ning, "Not the last one."

"Okay." Ji Ning pouted, looking somewhat disappointed. "Fine, then."

The father-son duo was finally able to amuse Shen Mo. He didn't know whether the "secret weapon" would work, but he himself felt much more relaxed.

The half hour passed quickly, and the train arrived soon. Ji Ning's excitement surged again. Putting on his backpack, he skipped out of the station.

It was New Year's Eve already, so not many pedestrians were walking in the street. It took the three of them quite some time to get a taxi. They then headed toward Shen Mo's parents' house.

Shen Mo's parents lived in an old-style compound. The exterior walls of its residential buildings were already mottled. Shen Mo stepped into the corridor and climbed the narrow stairs. At last, he paused in front of a door on the third floor.

Looking at the place where he had grown up, Shen Mo couldn't take another step.

Ji Mingxuan walked to Shen Mo's side and asked "Why aren't you knocking?"

"What if... they refuse to open the door?"

"You won't know until you've knocked."

"That's right, Uncle." Ji Ning also came up. Holding Ji Mingxuan's hand in one hand, he grabbed Shen Mo's with his other. "Hurry up and knock."

Gazing at the two of them, Shen Mo finally smiled. He lifted his hand and knocked.

On New Year's Eve, Shen Mo and his mother were making dumplings in the kitchen.

"...This friend of yours, he's really considerate. For three whole months, he called lao-Shen every night. Your dad's such a stubborn person, and even he gave in and agreed to see him once."

"And then what happened? How did he persuade my dad?"

"Your dad doesn't have many hobbies. All he likes is to drink tea." Mrs. Shen pressed her lips together and smiled. "Your friend brought him some good tea."

Shen Mo couldn't help smiling either.

He knew it—when would Mr. Ji ever do something he wasn't confident in? It turned out that Ji Mingxuan had already bribed his parents. Shen Mo had been so anxious for their entire journey, afraid he might be kicked out, but when the door was opened, he found that his parents had already finished preparing the reunion dinner and were waiting for him.

Remembering how touched he had felt at that moment, Shen Mo felt a little teary-eyed even now.

Ji Mingxuan was with Mr. Shen in the living room, studying the tea set Ji Mingxuan had brought them. Ji Ning was watching TV, at times running over and popping into the kitchen to ask, "Are the dumplings ready yet?"

He seemed desperately eager.

Mrs. Shen grinned widely and answered, "Almost, almost. Just go outside and wait a little longer, xiao-Ning."

"Okay. Thank you, Grandma."

Ji Ning was quite a sweet kid. The second he had come in, he'd called the elders "Grandpa" and "Grandma," easily winning over their hearts. Eating dumplings wasn't actually a New Year's tradition in the South, but because Ji Ning had wanted to eat dumplings, Mrs. Shen immediately pulled Shen Mo into the kitchen and had him make dumplings with her. Even Shen Mo, her actual son, felt a little jealous.

Once they finished making the dumplings, everyone gathered in the living room to watch the Spring Festival Gala, while Shen Mo went to tidy up his bedroom. Shen Mo's house had only two bedrooms and one living room, so it was a bit cramped with the three additional people, especially when it came to sleeping. After much discussion, they could only let Ji Ning sleep in the bigger room with Mr. and Mrs. Shen while Ji Mingxuan would sleep with Shen Mo in the smaller room.

As Shen Mo was making his bed, Ji Mingxuan knocked on the door. He walked in and asked, "You're not finished yet?"

"No, the room is too small. It's a little messy."

"I'm fine as long as there's a place to sleep at night. Don't stress about it."

Shen Mo still felt embarrassed. "Maybe... you should take Ji Ning and go spend the night in a hotel."

"Ji Ning likes it here quite a lot." Ji Mingxuan looked at Shen Mo. "I do too."

"Mr. Ji..."

"Besides, I've always wanted to see the place where you grew up."

There were no chairs in the room, so Ji Mingxuan sat down on the edge of the bed, tilting his head as he watched Shen Mo make the bed.

Slowly folding the blanket, Shen Mo whispered, "Mr. Ji, thank you."

"For what?"

"You must've spent quite a lot of effort on my parents."

Ji Mingxuan only smiled. "Just a few phone calls."

He patted Shen Mo on the shoulder. "All right. Let's go watch some TV."

Shen Mo and Ji Mingxuan went back to the living room together. The whole family was huddled on the sofa, watching the Spring Festival Gala. Only when Ji Ning began to yawn did they retreat to their bedrooms to sleep.

Shen Mo's bed was really a bit too small. With two full-grown men lying on top of it, it creaked with the slightest movement.

Of course, Shen Mo couldn't fall asleep. Staring at the ceiling, he said, "I wonder if Ji Ning is sleeping well."

A while later, he said again, "Should I sleep on the floor instead?"

Hearing this, Ji Mingxuan couldn't help but laugh. "That's enough. Don't bother."

When he finished, he sat up from the bed.

This startled Shen Mo. "You're not sleeping anymore?"

"It's almost midnight. We should go set off some firecrackers."

"Oh... right."

Household fireworks and firecrackers had long since been banned in large cities—Shen Mo had almost forgotten about such a custom. Since Ji Mingxuan was heading out, Shen Mo got up too and put on some layers. The two didn't wake up Mr. and Mrs. Shen, who were sleeping next door, and felt their way downstairs in the dark.

Outside, many people were already setting off firecrackers. Bursts and crackles sounded one after another. These days, the weather was still cold. Shen Mo stomped his feet, suddenly remembering something. "We didn't buy firecrackers, did we?"

"Don't worry. I have it all ready."

With astonishing familiarity, Ji Mingxuan brought a box of fireworks out of Shen Mo's family's garage.

Shen Mo wanted to ask Ji Mingxuan when he'd prepared all this, but then he thought about it some more. Ji Mingxuan had already dealt with his dad behind his back, so what was there that Ji Mingxuan couldn't do? A box of fireworks would have been a piece of cake to Ji Mingxuan.

Ji Mingxuan glanced at his watch: only two minutes until midnight. He asked Shen Mo, "Do you remember that year, on New Year's Eve, when I called you while I was abroad? You said you were spending New Year's at your parents' house, but I knew you were lying the moment I heard you."

"Of course I remember." Shen Mo could also recall that later on, Ji Mingxuan had even flown back looking for him.

"At the time, I thought"—the street lamps lit up Ji Mingxuan's face, revealing the tinge of tenderness hidden deep within his eyes—"that one day, I was going to go back to your hometown with you on New Year's Eve, and set off fireworks with you."

Shen Mo felt his heart skip a beat.

Right then, the clock struck midnight. Ji Mingxuan tossed a lighter toward Shen Mo. "Let's light it up together."

Once the fuse was ignited, the blazing fire soon sprang up, bursting into brilliant colors in the night sky.

But the beautiful scene wasn't what Ji Mingxuan looked at. He turned around, toward Shen Mo, and like many years ago, uttered in a low voice, "Shen Mo, happy New Year."

EXTRA.11

Sunny Days

It was New Year's Day.

For once, Shen Mo woke up naturally.

The days before the Lunar New Year had been filled with rain, yet surprisingly, the sun showed its face right on the first day of the new year. At about nine in the morning, Shen Mo woke up from his sleep. Still dazed, he looked at the time. The first thing that came to his mind was to prepare breakfast for Ji Ning. But he immediately remembered that he was spending New Year's at his parents' house. With his parents here to take care of Ji Ning, Ji Ning definitely wouldn't starve.

The blanket was enveloped in the smell of sunlight.

Shen Mo rolled around under the blanket, and then lay in bed for a while longer before he got up to dress himself. Once he was done, he walked out of his room, although only to find that Ji Mingxuan was alone in the living room.

"Mr. Ji, where are my parents?"

Ji Mingxuan was reading the news, holding a cup of tea in his hand. Even as he sat in the small living room of Shen Mo's house, his elegance still didn't diminish at all. Lifting his chin, he said, "They took Ji Ning out to play."

"Huh? Where did they go?"

"Some amusement park, from what I heard."

"They went out that early? Then what are we going to do?"

"That's right." Ji Mingxuan put down his newspaper and revealed a faint smile. "So it seems we've been set aside."

Shen Mo didn't know what he meant.

Ji Mingxuan sighed. He could only ask, "Tell me. Where do you want to go?"

Shen Mo finally understood, although somewhat belatedly. Ji Mingxuan was always busy with work, and Shen Mo's work wasn't easy either. They rarely had any time for leisure, so they should really use this as a chance to relax properly.

Shen Mo thought for a while and said, "It's quite a small place. There probably aren't many things to do."

Ji Mingxuan seemed as if he'd known Shen Mo would say this. He suggested, "Let's go watch a movie, then."

"Sure. What should we watch?"

Ji Mingxuan handed Shen Mo a movie theater's brochure. "You can choose."

Shen Mo accepted it and took a look. A whole row of New Year's movies was printed on the brochure.

Why did he feel... that Mr. Ji had been planning this for a long time?

But Shen Mo didn't ask. He looked through the brochure carefully. Most New Year's movies were for families to watch together—they weren't too different from one another. In the end, Shen Mo chose a comedy film. "Let's watch this one."

Right after, Shen Mo remembered something and asked, "It's not that easy to buy tickets now, is it?"

"That's not a problem."

Ji Mingxuan glanced at the name of the film that Shen Mo had chosen. He then called his assistant. "Yes, it's me. Bring me the tickets."

In less than ten minutes, a young man wearing glasses came upstairs and gave Shen Mo two movie tickets.

Shen Mo looked at the seat numbers. The seats were quite good, but—

"This isn't the movie I chose."

"Hm? Oh, I'm sorry. I got the wrong ones."

The assistant apologized as he fished out a fistful of movie tickets from his pocket.

Shen Mo glanced at it. What a surprise—tickets for every single movie that was on during New Year's. Not knowing what expression to make, Shen Mo stole a glance at Ji Mingxuan.

Ji Mingxuan looked unruffled. As if nothing had happened, he explained, "He's a new assistant."

"Yes, I'm new."

The assistant rummaged for a long time. Once he found the movie tickets Shen Mo wanted, he was finally able to leave.

Ji Mingxuan pointed at the congee breakfast on the table and said to Shen Mo, "Have some breakfast. We'll go watch the movie after you finish."

Obedient, Shen Mo sat down for breakfast. But he couldn't help asking, "What about the other movie tickets?"

Ji Mingxuan said with a smile, "Don't worry. There will be people to watch those."

The town's movie theater wasn't too far away. After Shen Mo had breakfast, he went out with Ji Mingxuan, and the two walked there slowly. When they arrived, they found that the theater was filled with people.

Even Shen Mo was surprised, murmuring, "How come there are so many people? Is everyone here for movies? I wonder if it's crowded at the amusement park too."

Ji Mingxuan didn't reply. He bought a cup of popcorn, stuffed it into Shen Mo's arms, and said, "Let's go in."

So Shen Mo entered the theater, hugging the cup of popcorn.

It was a full house. Even the front-row seats were all filled. Fortunately, Ji Mingxuan had bought the tickets early, so they had good seats and were able to watch the movie comfortably.

The movie had nothing special in terms of its plot, but there were plenty of punch lines and the actors performed well, which made it quite a decent New Year's film. Shen Mo laughed easily; most of the time, he laughed when the audience laughed. On the other hand, Ji Mingxuan was much more reserved. Only when Shen Mo laughed so hard that he started tugging on the hem of Ji Mingxuan's clothes did Ji Mingxuan laugh along somewhat.

The end of the film was rather sentimental. It won over a few tears from Shen Mo.

When they finished the movie and walked out, it was already noon. Shen Mo and Ji Mingxuan found a nearby restaurant for lunch.

As they ate, Ji Mingxuan asked, "Do you have any plans for the afternoon?"

Shen Mo looked out the window and said, "It's rare for the weather to be so good. Maybe I should go paint in the park."

"You paint every day. You're not tired of it yet?"

"Of course not. I'll never get tired of it."

With what Shen Mo had said, Ji Mingxuan could only reply, "Let's go, then."

All of Shen Mo's paint tools were at home, so the two stopped by Shen Mo's family's house before they went to the park. The park was crowded too because of the good weather, and some people were even flying kites. Warm sunlight fell on Shen Mo's body. There was already a touch of spring.

Shen Mo chose a good place and sat down. He then set up the easel and started painting. At first, he chatted with Ji Mingxuan every so often, but he gradually sank into his own world, focused only on painting.

Time flew by. When Shen Mo finished the painting, the sun was already setting in the west.

Shen Mo stretched and turned around. "Mr. Ji…"

Shen Mo trailed off as it turned out that Ji Mingxuan, sitting under a tree, had already fallen asleep. Shen Mo didn't want to wake him up. He only took off his own jacket and gently draped it over Ji Mingxuan.

Even when asleep, Mr. Ji still looked so handsome.

Shen Mo turned around and gazed at his painting. He thought for a while, then picked up the paintbrush and added a stroke to the canvas. He hadn't painted a specific person—he'd only added a vague silhouette in the corner.

The irresistible spring breeze brushed past a corner of the man's clothes. It was beyond tender.

Villa

Kids always grew up quickly. When Ji Ning had first returned to China, he hadn't even begun kindergarten yet, but in the blink of an eye, he was already about to start elementary school. Living in the house in Jinxiu Villa was comfortable indeed, but considering the school district and transportation to and from school, Ji Mingxuan still decided to move back to the Ji family's house.

The house was where Ji Mingxuan and his sister Ji An'an had grown up. It was once a place of sorrow for him. Yet, as time passed, especially as he watched Ji Ning mature day by day, the wound in his heart gradually healed.

Since Ji Mingxuan had decided to move back, of course Shen Mo had no objections either. The house had been renovated just two years ago, but as it'd been left empty for a long time, there was still a sense of loneliness. Shen Mo planned to take some time to clean up the house before they moved in.

At first, Ji Mingxuan didn't agree to this. "Can't you leave those things to the cleaning service?"

"But xiao-Ning will be living here. I don't feel comfortable leaving the cleaning to someone else."

After living together for several years, Shen Mo thought of Ji Ning as his own child. He was more committed than even Ji Mingxuan, Ji Ning's father. Unable to persuade Shen Mo, Ji Mingxuan could only nod and give in.

Shen Mo's work schedule was quite flexible. He went out his way to take an entire day off to do the cleaning. After the renovation, people were hired to clean the house regularly, so there weren't many places that needed to be cleaned. Shen Mo busied himself for the morning, mopping the floor and wiping the windows until the house looked spotless. He was going to tidy up the rooms that they'd be sleeping in in the afternoon. He made do with some bread at lunch and then sat down on the sofa to rest for a while.

The pleasant springtime sunlight shone warmly through the window. As he sat on the sofa, without realizing it, he gradually fell asleep.

When Shen Mo woke up again, he discovered that dark clouds had gathered outside the window, almost as if there would be a heavy storm soon.

Strange—the weather report hadn't said that it'd rain today.

Shen Mo yawned and got up to close the window. Looking around, he felt that the living room's furnishing looked vaguely different.

When he'd been cleaning in the morning, the room didn't look like this... did it?

But it was impossible that the house had changed in the span of just a short nap, right?

Shen Mo suspected that he was still half asleep. He rubbed his eyes and was just about to continue his work when he heard a sound come from upstairs.

Apart from him, somebody else was also inside the house?

A thief had broken in?

Suddenly growing nervous, Shen Mo looked in the direction that the sound had come from. He only saw a boy slowly descending the stairs.

The boy had delicate features. He wore a white button-up, and his hair was slightly messy from just having woken up. Although his age was different, Shen Mo still recognized who he was by just a single glance.

M-Mr. Ji...?

No. How could Mr. Ji be so young...

Could this be an illegitimate son?

No way. He's too old to be Mr. Ji's child.

Shen Mo was completely stunned. He stood there, not knowing what to do. The boy looked quite calm, however, only frowning as he asked, "Who are you? Why are you in my house?"

That's exactly what I want to ask, Shen Mo thought.

Seeing that Shen Mo didn't answer, the boy glanced at Shen Mo's outfit and asked, "Are you the new cleaner?"

Remembering what he was wearing today, Shen Mo really couldn't deny it. He could only mumble, "Yes."

The boy didn't doubt him and nodded. "You can keep working."

As he said this, he was about to step on the last stair, but he slipped. He almost fell from the stairs.

Luckily, Shen Mo was quite close to him. He grabbed the boy's arm and immediately asked, "What happened? Are you okay?"

It was obvious that the boy wasn't used to body contact with others. He took off Shen Mo's hand right after he steadied himself.

Shen Mo felt a warmth in his palm. Studying the boy's complexion, he realized that, as expected, there was a faint redness on this face that looked strikingly similar to Ji Mingxuan's.

"You're sick?"

The boy replied coldly, "No."

Shen Mo felt the boy's forehead and confirmed, "You have a fever. I'll take you to the hospital."

Hearing this, the boy's expression changed at once. "I'm not going to the hospital."

"You're afraid of the hospital?"

"I'm not afraid. I just don't like it."

Shen Mo thought of Mr. Ji.

Ji Mingxuan also hated going to the hospital. Shen Mo hadn't found out why until much later. Thinking for a while, Shen Mo said, "You don't have to go to the hospital, but you can't even walk properly. You should at least eat something. Do you want me to make you some congee?"

The boy was probably really hungry. After glancing at Shen Mo, he agreed reluctantly.

Shen Mo helped the boy go back to his bedroom to have some more rest. He found that the room the boy was living in was Ji Mingxuan's.

On his way to the kitchen to make the congee, he checked the calendar inside the house—this was twenty years ago.

All right. So it seemed there was no doubt that the boy was Mr. Ji.

Shen Mo didn't understand why this sort of supernatural phenomenon would occur, but taking care of Mr. Ji while he was sick was the top priority. So Shen Mo made use of the ingredients in the kitchen and, with dedication, cooked a pot of chicken-and-greens congee. Only after he tasted it, making sure that it was neither too salty nor too bland, did he take it upstairs to Ji Mingxuan.

Young Ji Mingxuan wasn't asleep. Rather, he sat leaning against the bed's headboard, absorbed in a book.

Shen Mo was somewhat surprised. He asked, "Trying so hard, even when you're sick?"

"I have a younger sister. She's always been in poor health." Ji Mingxuan didn't even look up as he spoke, his voice low, "I want to become a reliable older brother as soon as I can so that I can protect her."

Ji Mingxuan was still so young, but he had declared something so mature.

Hearing those words, Shen Mo felt both amused and sad. "You will. I'm sure you will."

Ji Mingxuan glanced at Shen Mo, finding him a bit strange, and asked, "The congee is ready?"

"Oh, right. Hurry up and eat it while it's hot."

Shen Mo hastened to pass Ji Mingxuan the bowl of congee.

Ji Mingxuan tried a mouthful, and then glanced at Shen Mo again.

Somewhat nervous, Shen Mo asked, "What's wrong? You don't like it?"

Ji Mingxuan's expression was indifferent. "It's not terrible."

But in the end, he finished the entire bowl.

Shen Mo found it funny, thinking to himself that this was definitely the man he knew.

After Ji Mingxuan ate the congee, Shen Mo pulled the blanket over his body. "Stop reading. A sick person needs to rest up. I'll buy you some medicine later."

"You're just a cleaner. Why are you so nosy?"

Ji Mingxuan complained. But, despite his words, he still lay down under the blanket.

"Sleep well. You'll feel better when you wake up."

Shen Mo tucked Ji Mingxuan in and took away the book that Ji Mingxuan had left beside his bed. Watching Shen Mo's motions, Ji Mingxuan suddenly said, "You know. My name is written on the book."

Shen Mo was momentarily surprised. When he realized what Mr. Ji had meant, he smiled. "I know what your name is."

Ji Mingxuan made a sound under the blanket, satisfied with Shen Mo's answer.

But Shen Mo was curious now. "Aren't you going to ask me what my name is?"

Ji Mingxuan covered his head with the blanket. "Why do I need to know the name of a cleaner?"

In a while, a muffled voice came from the blanket. "Just tell me the next time you come."

Shen Mo gazed at Ji Mingxuan, who had curled up into a ball. He couldn't help but wonder—when would be the next time they met?

With no reply from Shen Mo, Ji Mingxuan lifted the blank and asked, "Hey, don't tell me you won't come here again."

Shen Mo didn't know what answer to give him.

Disappointment flashed across Ji Mingxuan's face, but he concealed it well. Soon, his expression was back to nonchalance. Waving his hand, he said, "Whatever. Don't come again, then.

"It's always been this way anyways. Mom left early after she gave birth to my sister. And even though my sister is really cute, the doctor said she could leave anytime. There won't be anyone who stays by my side."

No—that wasn't it!

Shen Mo opened his mouth. He wanted to comfort Ji Mingxuan, but suddenly, he could no longer make a sound.

"Shen Mo."

"Shen Mo."

Someone seemed to be calling his name in the distance. Shen Mo felt dizzy. When he opened his eyes again, he found that he was still lying on the sofa in the living room.

Looking down at Shen Mo, Ji Mingxuan asked, "How come you fell asleep on the sofa?"

Not the cold, proud boy, but instead the handsome, mature man.

Shen Mo felt as if he was in a bit of a daze.

Just now... was that a dream?

"Good thing I came to check on you. If you kept on sleeping here, you'd catch a cold." Ji Mingxuan dropped a blanket on Shen Mo's body. "If you want to sleep, you should go sleep in your room."

"Okay."

Shen Mo stood up slowly, still somewhat immersed in the dream.

He parted his lips. "Mr. Ji."

"Hm?"

"Someone will be there."

"What?"

"Someone who stays by your side." Gazing at Ji Mingxuan, Shen Mo stated, "They'll definitely be there."

Wishes

Ji Ning had only two birthday wishes.

The first was to own an adorable kitten. The second was for his dad to spend more time with him.

After he finished his cake, he fell deep asleep, hugging his little dinosaur. The next day, just after the sky brightened, he heard a loud noise from next door. It sounded as if something had fallen on the ground.

Ji Ning woke up, still drowsy, and called, "...Dad?"

No one replied.

Even Uncle Shen, who always spoiled him the most, was nowhere to be seen.

Ji Ning rubbed his eyes. He put on his small coat and ran out of the room, his slippers pattering. The next room was unlocked, so he pushed the door open and poked his head in to take a look. It was dim inside. The blanket on the bed was bunched up in a ball. Uncle Shen was the only one sitting on the messy bed.

Uncle Shen waved at him, so he ran over and asked, "Where's Dad?"

Somewhat guilty, Shen Mo glanced at the bunched-up blanket. "He... went to work."

"He has to go to work even though it's the weekend?"

"Yeah. There was something urgent."

Ji Ning revealed a disappointed expression. "But Dad promised to play with me today."

"I'm sorry. It's really a special situation this time. How about I play with you?" Shen Mo stroked Ji Ning's hair and said, "It's still early. Go back and get some more sleep, xiao-Ning."

Ji Ning had always been an obedient kid. He didn't throw a tantrum, only walking away dejectedly.

Shen Mo finally sighed in relief.

The bunched-up blanket on the bed wriggled slowly. Then, out came an odd-eyed white cat. Its fur was snowy and soft, while its fluffy tail swished left and right. Its different-colored eyes looked especially beautiful.

Shen Mo was so mesmerized by the big white cat's beauty that he didn't return to his senses until a while later. Staring eye-to-eye with the cat, he asked, "Mr. Ji, what should we do? Do you want to go to the hospital? Hm, or maybe an animal hospital?"

The big white cat ignored Shen Mo. He only raised his chin and gracefully leaped down the bed.

Shen Mo grabbed his phone and ran after the cat. Having experienced such a shock on the first day of the new year, he really wanted to post a Moment on WeChat, asking, *What should I do if I woke up and found out that a family member turned into a cat? Urgent! Waiting for answers!*

After all the trouble of stopping his hand from posting the Moment, Shen Mo followed the big white cat into the study. He saw the cat dexterously jump onto the desk, reach out its paw, and pat the computer on the desk.

Three seconds later, Shen Mo came to understand what he meant and immediately turned on the computer. He then watched as the big white cat, sitting on the keyboard, started to wave its squishy paws and type. It was quite a bizarre scene.

Shen Mo didn't say anything to disturb the cat. In silence, he decided that his second Moment would be: *What should I do if a family member's still a workaholic even after he turned into a cat? Still waiting for an answer!*

Right then, scurrying footsteps sounded outside the door. Ji Ning, who had already dressed himself, barged in and called, "Uncle, play with me..."

His voice paused before it instantly heightened, turning into an ecstatic cheer. "Kitty!"

Shouting, he rushed over and hugged the big white cat, who was still busy with work.

Shen Mo's eyelid twitched. He was sure that Mr. Ji... no, the big white cat's face had darkened.

Ji Ning, of course, was completely oblivious. He asked, "Did Dad buy this for me?"

"Um, you can say that."

Ji Ning fell in love with the big white cat at first sight. Now that he had seized the cat, he refused to let go no matter what. "Uncle, what should we name the kitty?"

"Oh? What do you think?"

"What about xiao-Bai[1]?"

"Uh..." Shen Mo sneaked a glance at the cat's expression. "I don't think he'd like it..."

But Ji Ning was already running to his bedroom, holding the big white cat in his arms. He said as he ran, "Xiao-Bai, let's play fetch."

Ji Ning had a pretty little ball that he really liked, given to him by Ji Mingxuan. Now, he took it out as if he was presenting a treasure and tossed it toward a corner, yelling, "Xiao-Bai, fetch!"

The big white cat crouched elegantly on the ground, wagging his tail lazily.

---

[1] This is a common name for pets. Literally, it means "little white."

"Oh." Ji Ning scratched his head. "I'll fetch, then."

As he said this, Ji Ning scampered over to pick up the ball.

Shen Mo found this quite funny, so he let them play. It wasn't until lunchtime that he called Ji Ning out of his room.

Hugging the big white cat, Ji Ning asked, "Uncle, what is xiao-Bai gonna eat for lunch?"

"Hmm..."

This was also what Shen Mo was thinking about. In the end, he made some noodles and put them into a small bowl for the cat to eat.

The big white cat had on an expression of distaste, as if he'd kick over the small bowl in front of him anytime. Eventually, however, he ate a few mouthfuls out of respect.

After lunch, the big white cat slipped into the study again. But just as he jumped onto the computer desk, Ji Ning came in with a picture book in his arms.

"Uncle gave this to me yesterday for my birthday. I wanted to read it together with Dad today, but..." Ji Ning waved at the big white cat and asked, "Xiao-Bai, can you read it with me?"

"Meow—"

The big white cat glanced at the computer on the table, and then at Ji Ning, who looked ever so pitiful. Finally, he jumped off the computer table and nimbly walked toward Ji Ning.

At once, Ji Ning was beaming. He sat down by the windowsill and opened the picture book that Shen Mo had given him. With an effortless leap, the big white cat got onto Ji Ning's lap and lay down.

Ji Ning didn't mind the cat's weight either. Holding him, he continued to turn the pages.

"Once upon a time, there was a shepherd boy..."

"Meow."

"Oh no, I forgot how to pronounce this word."

"Meow!"

"Okay. I'll write it down first and ask Dad when he comes back."

"Meow meow."

The two of them didn't speak the same language, but they still seemed to be communicating well.

Shen Mo saw this from outside the door. He didn't go in so that he wouldn't disturb them; he only closed the door gently.

The big white cat read the picture book with Ji Ning for the whole afternoon. They played hide-and-seek in the evening too. Only when Ji Ning started to yawn sleepily did Ji Ning reluctantly go to bed.

Shen Mo and the big white cat both stayed beside the bed, putting Ji Ning to sleep. Once Ji Ning was asleep, Shen Mo whispered, "You didn't work at all today, Mr. Ji. Is that okay?"

The big white cat didn't reply. He only bit a corner of the blanket and tried his best to pull it up, tucking Ji Ning in.

Shen Mo couldn't help but smile. He said, "I wonder if you can turn back tomorrow, Mr. Ji. What if you never turned back?"

"Meow—"

The big white cat gave Shen Mo a stern glare.

Shen Mo immediately said, "I'm sorry. You'll definitely turn back!"

Hmph.

The white cat flicked his tail and raised his head proudly. Then, he curled up into a ball and lay down beside Ji Ning.

He was probably going to sleep beside Ji Ning, then.

The corners of Shen Mo's lips lifted. He stroked the cat's soft fur and turned off the wall light.

Good night, Mr. Cat.

Make Up

Click.

Yang Yue sent Shen Mo the photo she had just taken, adding the caption: *Ran into the "Missus" while I was shopping. Looks like he's out shopping with quite a beautiful lady.*

In the photo was a luxury car; a slender woman was getting out of it. Only her back could be seen, but one could tell from just her stylish outfit that she must be beautiful.

Around five minutes later, Shen Mo finally replied: *I've told you so many times. There's no "Missus."*

Yang Yue took a sip of the milk tea in her hand. She couldn't help but feel amused.

Shen Mo was the owner of the studio where Yang Yue worked. He was good-tempered and good-looking, but his only shortcoming had been being single in his thirties. Even Yang Yue, his employee, had started worrying for him. Over the last Lunar New Year, Shen Mo spent his vacation travelling abroad, and when he came back, he said he wanted to work hard at his job so that he could provide for a child. It gave Yang Yue quite a shock.

Later, Yang Yue went out of her way to coax Shen Mo for the details. She managed to find out that Shen Mo had met a beautiful lady overseas, one who was divorced, single, and raising a child. Shen Mo fell in love with her at first sight and immediately started planning to make money and support the family as a stepdad.

A romantic plot that could only be seen in a movie!

Yang Yue, who loved watching romance shows, instantly dreamed up a cliché drama. She couldn't wait to see the future "Missus." However, when she eventually saw the real person, her jaw dropped in astonishment.

Yep, beautiful indeed, but a beautiful man instead of a woman. If Yang Yue didn't already have a boyfriend, she'd rush over toward him at once.

After Shen Mo's introduction, Yang Yue learned that Mr. Ji was taking care of a three-year-old alone. The child's mother had long since passed away. Shen Mo knew the mother too, and because of various complicated reasons, he had decided to raise the child together with Mr. Ji.

It wasn't as cliché as what Yang Yue had imagined, but having a handsome man to look at wasn't so bad either. From then on, Yang Yue called the man "Mr. Ji" as Shen Mo did. Only when she teased Shen Mo did she sometimes mention the word "Missus."

This time was the same. Yang Yue came across Mr. Ji while she was shopping, so she joked about it with Shen Mo. She didn't take it seriously and had a great time over the weekend, but she discovered that Shen Mo was already in the studio when she went to work on Monday.

"Boss? Why did you get here so early today? I thought you lived in Jinxiu Villa. The traffic should've been quite bad on your way over."

"Yeah." Shen Mo's complexion didn't look too good. It seemed as if he didn't sleep well. "I didn't go home last night."

"What? Why?"

Shen Mo replied vaguely, "There was a lot of work. I was worried I couldn't finish in time."

"You mean the painting Mr. Tang ordered last time? The timing is a little tight, but you didn't have to work overnight, did you?"

Giving no explanation, Shen Mo only waved his hand. "Get to work."

Yang Yue didn't say anything, but she felt quite surprised. Strange—her boss was the absolute model of a good man. Why was he suddenly not going home at night?

But even stranger was what happened next. During her lunch break, a familiar car stopped in front of the studio. A man got out of the car and walked straight in.

"Mr. Ji?"

Mr. Ji rarely came to the studio at such a time. Yang Yue hurried over to greet him. "Boss didn't sleep well last night. He's taking a break inside right now. I'll go get him"

"There's no need." Ji Mingxuan smiled at Yang Yue. "I came here for you."

"Me?"

"Do you happen to have time for a cup of coffee, Miss Yang?"

"Of course!"

At this moment, Yang Yue had completely forgotten about her boyfriend. She'd make time for the coffee even if she didn't have time.

There was a coffee shop right opposite the studio, so Ji Mingxuan invited Yang Yue to go over and sit down for a while. Each of them ordered a cup of coffee, and after some small talk, Ji Mingxuan cut to the chase and started asking about Shen Mo. In front of such an attractive face, Yang Yue naturally told him everything she knew.

"What he's been up to lately? Nothing in particular."

"He's in good health. I never saw him go to the hospital."

"Setbacks at work? Definitely not."

"The studio's business is great. There shouldn't be financial issues."

"Girlfriend? No way. He goes home right after work every day. He's got no time for a girlfriend."

Even after much discussion, Yang Yue and Ji Mingxuan still didn't find out why Shen Mo hadn't gone home last night. Yang Yue remembered the photo she'd sent Shen Mo over the weekend, so she mentioned it as well.

Hearing this, Ji Mingxuan paused. "What photo?"

Yang Yue found the photo on her phone and asked somewhat uneasily, "It was only a shot from behind. It doesn't count as infringement of privacy, does it?"

Ji Mingxuan's expression looked rather serious. He studied the photo for a while, as if he was thinking about something, and then returned the phone to Yang Yue. "Don't worry. I think I know what's going on."

Yang Yue asked, "What is it?"

Ji Mingxuan didn't answer her question. He only said, "I'm sorry for taking so much of your time, Miss Yang. I'll go back with you."

Beyond puzzled, Yang Yue still couldn't hold back her curiosity. "Mr. Ji, is that lady your girlfriend?"

"No." The corners of Ji Mingxuan's lips lifted slightly. "It was my car, but I lent my car to a friend that day."

"Oh. I made a mistake, then."

Ji Mingxuan responded with a soft hum of acknowledgement.

There shouldn't be any emotion in the sound, but for some reason, Yang Yue felt that Mr. Ji was in quite a good mood.

In the evening, when it was time to get off work, Ji Mingxuan came by again. This time, though, he brought his son, Ji Ning, with him as well. Shen Mo was still locking himself in the resting room, probably busy with work. Ji Mingxuan pushed Ji Ning forward and said, "Go knock."

Ji Ning turned around and stretched out three fingers. "Three toys."

"One."

"Then I'll take two."

"Okay, deal."

Ji Ning immediately revealed a smile. He knocked on the door and coaxed, "Uncle, it's me."

"Xiao-Ning?" Hearing Ji Ning's voice, Shen Mo opened the door, as expected. "Why are you here?"

Ignoring the question, Ji Ning threw himself into Shen Mo's arms, clinging onto Shen Mo's waist. Seizing the chance, Ji Mingxuan took a step forward and squeezed through the door as well.

"Mr. Ji..."

Shen Mo only had the time to call his name once before the door slammed shut.

A while later, the door opened a crack, and little Ji Ning was urged out of the room. Next, the sound of an easel falling to the ground came from within, and then there was silence.

Stunned by what she saw, Yang Yue asked Ji Ning, "What happened?"

"They were arguing with each other. They just had a fight."

"And then?"

Ji Ning blinked his large eyes at Yang Yue.

Yang Yue understood at once and gave him a piece of chocolate.

Ji Ning tossed the chocolate into his mouth. He spoke as if he'd already seen this too many times, "And then... they made up, of course."

Afterword

February 4th, Start of Spring

As spring returns to the land, all things are reborn.

I've always liked spring. It's a gentle season. Tender winds in spring are intoxicating. So I set Mr. Ji's birthday on the start of spring.

When I began to write this story, the character of Mr. Ji was actually quite vague to me. Such a beginning just suddenly came to my mind, so I wrote it down casually. I did not know what would happen in Chapter Two even when I had finished Chapter One. So at the very beginning, Mr. Ji was only a handsome figure. He's proud and indifferent; he had great control over the things around him. Shen Mo often felt him temperamental and unpredictable when getting along with him. In the chapter when Zhao Yi appeared on the scene, Mr. Ji put on the cuff-links Shen Mo chose and introduced Shen Mo as "the future Mrs. Ji". It was then that I suddenly realized that Mr. Ji loved Shen Mo all along!

The following plots also flowed reasonably, Mr. Ji began to reveal his heart. Dull as Shen Mo was, he inevitably indulged in such tenderness. But when Shen Mo walked into the Jinxiu Villa and saw the room filled with paintings for the first time, I hit the wall. It was too difficult to handle the flashbacks, I stopped serializing for more than half a year and once wanted to leave it unfinished. However, I finally decided to give the two an end.

When I began to write about the memories, it was not as difficult as I thought it would be. Things happened naturally when Shen Mo got along with Mr. Ji. Although Shen Mo lost his memories, his heart was always determined—who he loved was the one that saved him in danger. Later the two met again in the island; it was then that he finally plucked up the courage and drew his own heart on Mr. Ji's palm.

There were actually many regrets in the ending part. I thought I ended it too fast and was not able to write down much content. But this is only the end of the book; the story between Mr. Ji and Shen Mo is still happening.

I like many plots of the book, but what I like the most is always this one:

Mr. Ji introduced Shen Mo, slowly and casually, "This is the future Mrs. Ji."

—He had long known that the person was the one.

That's the end of the Afterword. I also added some extra fragments at the end.

Enjoy reading ^_^

Work Diary
By Yang Yue

January 28th, Sunny

So surprised that boss suddenly came back when I was slacking off.

Fortunately, boss's just going abroad for a trip as usual. He goes to the same place every year. It's so boring....

After all, he's an old man at his thirties. Perhaps I should set him up with someone to date.

February 3rd, Sunny
Slacking off.

February 4th, Sunny
Slacking off.

February 8th, Cloudy

Boss called back, saying that his travel plan changed and would stay overseas a week longer. Huh... That's not what boss would do. Did he meet someone overseas? He wouldn't come back with a Missus, would he?

February 10th, Sunny
Slacking off.

February 11th, Rainy
Slacking off.

February 15th, Sunny
Boss's back, looking quite radiant on his face!

Ahhh, that must be a Missus soon. Could I slack off casually later on?

Quite worried about my future days...

February 18th, Cloudy
I beat around the bush and knew more about the future Missus—a beauty in her thirties, divorced, single, and raising a child.

Boss was so deep in love with her. She seemed to be the type of person that was not easy to handle.

February 23rd, Rainy
Slacking off.

March 6th, Sunny
Slacking off.

March 14th, Sunny
The future Missus would come to inspect tomorrow. What should I do? Should I wear fancy makeup or not?

Oh, life is hard. It's too difficult for corporate slaves.

March 19th, Rainy
Ahhhhh!!!

March 20th, Rainy
I calmed down a little and finally could continue the diary.

How should I describe the future Missus?

At thirties? Not wrong.

Divorced, single and raising a child? Not wrong either.

Gorgeous? Not wrong either, of course.

But when all of these go together, that wasn't what I imagined at all! Breathe, breathe, take a deep breath. I need to calm down.

March 22nd, Sunny

Working here is quite nice.

March 24th, Sunny

Working here is really happy.

March 28th, Rainy

Missus came here with afternoon tea desserts and snacks to inspect .... no, to greet employees.

The strawberry cakes were yummy!

Missus's beauty was quite pleasing(erased) and he's such a feast to the eye(erased)...

Oh, Missus told me to keep an eye on boss's emotion and contact him at any time if anything happened? Although he did not say it directly, he had made it clear. He might be worried if boss had an affair, so he asked me to be his spy?

Huh...

March 29th, Cloudy

I finally made the decision after struggling for a whole night. Boss's such a nice guy, how could I betray him?

I would, of course, — stand by Missus's side and sneak on boss anytime and anywhere!

I had decided to end the Work Diary here and begin Boss Observing Diary next week. Please stay tuned!

END.

The Missing Piece

The Missing Piece

Copyright © 2022 by KUN YI WEI LOU

If you have any questions, please send e-mail to
info@vialactea.ca

Via Lactea
Publishing Co.